YVONNE KALMAN'S

GREENSTONE

AND NOW THE STUNNING SEQUEL TO GREENSTONE. . .

SILVERSHORES

YVONNE KALMAN

Other Avon Books by
Yvonne Kalman

GREENSTONE

SilverShores

YVONNE KALMAN

AVON
PUBLISHERS OF BARD, CAMELOT, DISCUS AND FLARE BOOKS

AVON BOOKS
A division of
The Hearst Corporation
1790 Broadway
New York, New York 10019

Copyright©1982 by Yvonne Kalman
Published by arrangement with Arbor House
Publishing Company
Library of Congress Catalog Card Number: 82-72069
ISBN: 0-380-68676-7

First Avon Printing, September, 1984

AVON TRADEMARK REG. U. S. PAT. OFF. AND IN
OTHER COUNTRIES, MARCA REGISTRADA, HECHO EN
U. S. A.

PRINTED IN THE U. S. A.
WFH 10 9 8 7 6 5 4 3 2 1

To my mother, Lou Flavell,
and to my dear friend Suse Hubscher

One

SAN FRANCISCO, 1870

When the hansom stopped outside the tall iron gates, Hal Bennington alighted, pressing some coins into the driver's gloved palm as he did so.

"There's no need to return for me. I'll make my own way back later," he said.

The driver glanced down, noted the meager tip, then stared at the imposing mansion at the crest of the driveway. "Not plannin' to step it, surely, sir? That's a fair march down to the harbor. Five an' a half miles at least an' all steep goin'." He shook the coins into his pouch and added with sarcasm, "I can come back, no trouble. The cost won't ruin you neither." All the same these officer types, he thought. Tight as barnacles' backsides, not like the common sailors who would tip you their last quarter, then borrow to buy you a drink. The driver was watching with dislike as suddenly a tug of wind whipped one side of Hal's cape loose, revealing a braided epaulet. A captain, hey? Not more than a lad, either, and handsome, too, despite the too-pale eyes and the fringe of whiskers that bordered his jawline like moss. Ugly fashion that. Made a fellow look as if he couldn't decide whether to be clean-shaven or bearded.

The rank, the wealthy house, and the slackness of trade forced the cabby into trying once more. "Just name the hour an' I'll be here, sir. There's thugs about these nights. A dollar's a small enough price to pay for safety."

Hal was intending to walk; he always enjoyed a brisk constitutional the evening before sailing, but the insinuation of cheapness stung him into replying, "My uncle, Captain Yardley, will place his carriage at my disposal."

So this was the Yardley mansion. All San Francisco knew of Captain Yardley, of course, who was not content with having his fist in the pie of the giant Richmond Shipping Line but had to be full owner of the smaller Mondrich Line as well. And this was Stephen Yardley's nephew. That should have guaranteed at least a five-dollar tip. What else were the wealthy here for but to distribute largess to those fortunate enough to give them service? Yet here he was with a miserable ten cents and a curt dismissal.

"An' a fine voyage to you, Cap'n," he called, tone belying his words. "Be sure to ask your uncle for a raise since you seem so short of the ready."

Whipping the horses up, he turned in the high seat. Gratified by Hal's flush of anger, he tossed out a parting remark. "Your uncle should give it gladly—tell him he can't take it with him where he's bound."

"What do you mean?"

But the cabdriver's coarse laughter was the only reply.

Hal frowned. He tried to shrug away his worry as he strode up the drive between the rows of grim stone lions. "Where he's bound"; was Uncle Stephen ill again? If so, Hal doubted that the Mondrich Line could continue strengthening its position. A shipping line needed an able leader. Just look at how the Richmond Line had drifted since the captain relinquished control after his last illness. Run as it was now by a group of squabbling geriatrics (how delighted Grandmaire would be to hear herself described thus), it was beginning to founder. Without Uncle Stephen's strength and vision . . . but no, he told himself firmly. If the captain were ill, the harbor would have been humming with the details.

As Hal reached the steps, a pandemonium of barking erupted from the watchdogs' kennel near the stables. They could announce his arrival, he decided, turning away from the door with its brass anchor door knocker and going toward the carriage house, greeting the dogs by name as he passed them.

Lucas, the stableboy, opened the side gate for him, and

while he fumbled with the latches, Hal pulled out his fob watch and clicked it open with his thumbnail; a Roman-lettered dial faced an enameled miniature of Queen Victoria. Almost five, and it was still damnably hot.

He was about to speak when a rippling skein of feminine laughter fluttered around him, the unselfconscious kind that is heard only when there are no men about.

Hal nodded toward the banks of pink azaleas. "Is Mrs. Yardley entertaining friends at croquet today?"

"No, Mr. Bennington, sir. She's playing with the babies, sir."

"And the others, where are they?"

"Master Daniel is roller skating with friends, and—"

"Roller skating?"

"Yes, sir. And Miss May is on the veranda, restin' like always, and the master is still at his club with—"

"Tell me, and tell me honestly: Is the captain well?"

"He's in perfect health, as much as can be expected, sir. Miss May, she had another turn last week, but the master is never better, sir." He glanced at Hal oddly. "Why do you ask?"

"A silly notion. Never take stray remarks seriously, Lucas." He cocked his head as another giddy trill of laughter reached them. "My aunt certainly dotes on those boys, doesn't she?"

Lucas beamed. "Indeed she do, sir."

Hal could understand that. The boys had been born after many barren years; Aunt Juliette had resigned herself to having only May from her first marriage and Daniel from Stephen's. Hal's mother, Abigail, declared it a scandal that her sister should be conceiving at her advanced age, but the only criticism Hal might make, though he would never voice it, was that Juliette focused far too much attention on the youngest children. Daniel was shunted off to play with friends, while May's life seemed spent in the endless solitude of recuperation.

The shade of the high-ceilinged veranda was as refreshing as a cool drink; hanging ferns screened the glare of the ocean far below. Hal approached the white wicker daybed, his boots silent on the rush matting.

May Yardley lay sullenly, her eyes screwed shut with

3

boredom, an open copy of *Morning Glories* beside her. From the French doors beside her came a faint rattling as Parker set plates and cups on the afternoon tea trolley.

Unnoticed, Hal gazed down at her with the feeling of surprise that she always inspired. For a girl of twelve her face was unusually mature; her delicate features and pale skin always made him think of lilies. The veins at her temples were a faint mauve, like striations on petals, and her lips were defined by a ridge of soft pink as if someone had drawn around them with a coloring crayon. But her most distinctive feature was that abundant hair, distinctively plum color, not brown, not auburn, but peculiarly *hers*—as Juliette swiftly pointed out to anybody tactless enough to comment on May's resemblance to Maire Yardley Peridot, her paternal grandmother. And Aunt Juliette was right, thought Hal. May was nothing like Grandmaire; she was elfin rather than handsome, and her eyes were soft brown, while Grandmaire's were as hard and cold as greenstone.

With a swift gesture, he slipped off his cloak, slapped the peaked captain's hat on his head, and cried, "At your service, Miss Yardley!"

May's eyes jolted open, and she squeaked in fright, then in the next instant was laughing weakly with pleasure. "Oh, but you are wicked to terrify me like that, Cousin Hal."

"Captain Bennington, please." A salute for emphasis.

"Of course." She studied the cap and braid. "You look so splendid, too. I'm so pleased that you came to see me."

"Are you?"

"Oh, yes." Her voice was shy and soft. "Father said that you were so busy this time that I must not expect to see you, but I was hoping—" She stopped, blushing. "I tried to read this book, but it is so tedious that I cannot get interested. I wish there were a new Dickens book to read. His stories are so thrilling, with such menacing atmosphere, don't you agree?"

"I never find time for reading," said Hal, who was such a poor reader that he abandoned any book after only a few pages.

May looked surprised. "How curious. Father often says that when he was at sea, he had all the time in the day he

4

wanted to spend with his books. He says that he did so much reading—"

"Oh?" said Hal, ill at ease, for he knew that once May fixed her mind on a subject she would pursue it tirelessly, and he did not welcome the topic of reading. Glancing around, he noticed Daniel's pony, Sioux, tethered in the shade of a maple tree. Leaving May in mid-sentence, he placed his hat and cape on the balustrade and strode across the lawn. Sioux looked up warily. A moment later with a wild "Yeeeeeyup!" Hal was cantering him around the lawn, sitting backward in the saddle.

"Yaaaaah-he!" shouted Hal, jumping to the ground, running alongside for a few paces, then leaping back again, this time the right way around. Then, with another exuberant shout, he was standing in the saddle, balancing first on one foot, then on the other while Sioux trotted out a circus orbit on the lawn.

By now May was up off her daybed and leaning over the rail, laughing feverishly and clapping her thin hands.

Parker heard the shouts and was there at once. "Miss May! You know what the doctor said. Look at your color!"

May's eyes were glowing with adoration. "Isn't he *clever*? Look at how nimbly he can jump from one side of the pony to the other. Oh, well done, Captain Hal!"

"You'll be well done, too, if your mother sees you. Get yourself back onto that bed right sharpish." As she expected, May ignored her, so Parker retreated inside. Ignorance would be the best defense if Mrs. Yardley discovered May's disobedience.

Hal tossed May an orange flower as he galloped past, then wheeled the pony about and reared him to an abrupt stop.

"I say, are you all right?"

Though May nodded, she was gasping rapidly and her face had darkened as though a shadow had settled over it.

Hal was alarmed. Having hitched Sioux to the banister knob, he hurried to the frail girl. He lifted her up—she weighed almost nothing—and placed her on her bed, cursing himself as he spread a shawl over her slippered feet.

"Thank you," she whispered. A dry scrape of sound.

Parker returned. "Just look at you! I'll fetch your

mother right away." She picked up the stick to beat the brass gong.

"No. Oh, please, Parker, please . . ."

"Are you sure?" said Hal when Parker paused. "Aunt Juliette will know if the doctor should be called."

"The worst is over, truly." And she tried to smile, just to prove it. "The pain has gone."

Parker tucked the shawl around her knees, smoothing the long skirts. "No more nonsense then," she said. "It's this hot weather, Captain. The least bit of excitement, and her breathing constricts. The doctor insists that she stay calm."

"You frightened me," said Hal when Parker had gone. "I had forgotten how recently you had to be carried everywhere."

"Everybody thought I would die," she agreed cheerfully. The gray was fading quickly. "Now all I have are these silly little turns."

"Parker didn't seem to think it was silly."

"That's only because of the bad turn I had last week, when I was playing with Daniel's roller skates. I had to stay in bed and was so afraid that I would still be there when you came and I would miss seeing you."

"What are these roller skates?"

"Boots with a wheeled device fastened underneath. They are such fun, and all the craze here now. Daniel was given some for his eleventh birthday. I begged and begged for some, too, but Mother forbade it."

"So you used Daniel's."

She nodded, eyes aglow again. "You should have seen me skim along the veranda. Quick as a thin whistle."

"You never cease to amaze me. When I look at you, I see a creature as fragile as porcelain, but you're a ruffian at heart, aren't you?"

She giggled. "It was fun—until I fell over and couldn't get up, and then the attack came on. I was struggling to pull the skates off and had just tugged them loose when Parker came out. She called Miss Von Sturmer and Mother, but they didn't find the skates. I'd pushed them under the plant table. You would have admired my initiative."

"I'm sure I would."

"You won't tell Mother, will you?" She plucked at his sleeve, appealing. "And don't say anything to her about this little turn."

"But it was my fault."

"Please, Cousin Hal. I'll be sent to bed early, and I would miss having dinner with you. You *are* staying to dinner, aren't you?"

"That's the arrangement." He paused. "These roller skates. Are they available anywhere?"

"In most of the big stores. Why?"

"I might send Lucas to buy me a couple of pairs. Young Kendrick would be over the moon if he had something like that. Nobody in New Zealand has heard of roller skates yet."

"Cousin Kendrick. Yes, he would like that." And with that sudden change of direction characteristic of kittens and small children she said, "I was thinking about Kendrick only last week. Then the letter came, the one with 'Bennington' written on it. Do you have relatives in California?"

"Not that I know of," he said, wondering how much skates would cost. Should he get two pairs or three?

"In Los Angeles?" she pursued. "Patrick Bennington was the name. I thought it must be Kendrick at first, but when I looked closely it was Patrick, so I realized it couldn't be—"

"What? *What* did you say?"

Obediently she said, "Patrick. Patrick Bennington. What is it, Cousin Hal? Is he someone you know?"

Hal was unable to answer immediately. Rage throttled him. Patrick bloody Teipa still had the gall to call himself Bennington and had overstepped the mark by a mile in pestering Uncle Stephen. That illegitimate Maori upstart! What was Father thinking of, planting him here in California? If he wanted to send his bastard away, why not to Borneo, or Hudson Bay, or Moscow? Why here, of all places?

"What is the matter, Hal?"

"Patrick Bennington? Are you sure that was the name you saw?"

7

Frightened by his transparent anger, May backed away from the subject. "I might have been mistaken. Yes, I probably was. The letter was on the hall stand. It's rather dark in there, and . . ." She paused, feeling her chest tighten again, and noticed with relief that a pale swirl of blue silk was coming into view. "Here comes Mother," she said as Juliette hurried across the lawn with both hands outstretched in greeting. Following were two nurses, each carrying a curly-haired infant.

"Hal!" cried Juliette. "How splendid to see you."

He choked back his feelings enough to smile and say, "You look well, Aunt Juliette," though he realized as he spoke that it was a belittling understatement. She was incredibly radiant for a woman of forty, bright-eyed and with a flush of joy under her skin, but when she took off the wide-brimmed straw hat and shook her head with a girlish gesture, Hal noticed that her chestnut hair was streaked with gray.

Patrick Teipa! he thought bitterly. It was all he could do to keep a smile on his face while Juliette settled herself on a wicker sofa with the boys on either side of her. As soon as they were buttressed by chintz cushions, she turned back to her nephew, smiling at him with a special warmth reserved for family. In her long exile from New Zealand Hal was the only relative with whom she had personal contact. It was a pity the distinction should have been reserved for Abby's son, but despite that formidable handicap, she had to admit that he was a pleasant lad. Stephen was enthusiastic about him; the children adored him. She was canny enough to realize that only he could convey authoritative information about her back to New Zealand, and because of this, she always treated him with gracious kindness.

After expressing delight that he could find time to join them after all, she said, "You must tell me how handsome my boys have grown since your last visit. They are your youngest cousins. Can you imagine yourself at their age? You were a handsome child too, you know. Look at Edward—he was only two months old when you last saw him, and now he has four teeth and is cutting more, poor lamb. I'm up most of the night with him. He does suffer so, and he needs his mother, don't you, my pet? And Albert is so fearfully *energetic.* You should have seen him toddle after the ball. . . ."

Hal tried to return his aunt's smile while his mind raced. Patrick Teipa! Why would he correspond with Uncle Stephen? May must have been mistaken surely. No, she was a sharp little thing. She had pulled back only when she noticed the depth of his anger. *Damn.* If only he could learn to keep cool, to smother his feelings the way his brother did. Nobody ever guessed what Jon was feeling; he called it his weapon and defense. Damn. If he could have imitated Jon's blandness, he might have encouraged May to tell him a great deal more. What *was* Patrick Teipa doing in California?

"—don't you agree?" said Juliette. "Why, Hal, I declare, you've been daydreaming. That's not like you."

"I was thinking how young you look," he said with uncharacteristically quick wit. It was true; whenever he looked at his aunt, he marveled that she and his mother were sisters. Abby was bloated and shrewish, with hair dyed such a brassy yellow that Hal was secretly ashamed to be seen with her.

Juliette brushed the compliment aside and returned to the more interesting topic of the boys. Hal accepted a butterfly cake from the stand Parker offered. As he glanced up, he caught May's eye. Her face was still distinctly gray, but when he began to speak, she shook her head in warning.

Juliette, cooing over Albert, did not notice.

Dinner was delayed that evening until Stephen and his nephew had finished conferring in the study. Though he was only twenty, Hal's intimate knowledge of the workings of shipping companies and his familiarity with the main Pacific ports made him sensitive to trends and market changes. On this particular evening there were more facts than rumors to be passed on, and almost all the information about the Richmond Line was disquieting.

Stephen came down to dinner so deep in worry that he had forgotten to change out of his smoking jacket and was still wearing the round velvet hat he wore in his study to protect his patriarchal white hair from tobacco fumes.

9

At the door the butler whispered to him.

Stephen touched his head. "Oh, thank you, Norris. Go on in, Hal. Tell them I shall be down directly."

"Excuse me, Captain Bennington," said Norris. "The package you sent for is on the hall table. Here is your change, sir."

Hal was about to take the wrapped coins when he suddenly recalled the sneer on the cabdriver's face. He waved the money aside.

Norris bowed from the neck. "Thank *you*, Captain."

Hal entered the parlor, feeling almost self-satisfied. With the roller skates he would again experience the triumph of introducing a novelty craze into Auckland society. Young Kendrick and his friends would be the first boys in New Zealand to have them.

Juliette poured him a glass of sherry. It was not like his home, where a butler served whiskey on a silver tray. His aunt preferred gentler customs.

Hal took the sherry, thinking as he did how much more agreeable Juliette was now that the boys had been put to bed. In their company she was never quite relaxed, watching them with half an eye, constantly referring to them or talking to them. Before they were born, Juliette had been the most charming and lovely person he had ever met, but since the births she had been transformed. Now she was not so much a person as the keeper of priceless treasures which she must guard on the pain of death.

He had commented as much to his mother on his last visit home. It was a mistake. Eyes glinting, Abby had pried at him for more details. Juliette had ruined her first boy, Leigh, the one who had been killed in the war. She had turned him into a wretched child by her indulgence. Was she doing the same to Stephen's sons, too?

Hal was dismayed. Knowing that his mother was incapable of mentioning her sister without a catty remark, and feeling he had betrayed Aunt Juliette, he shrugged and said uncomfortably, "Who can tell? They are only babies after all."

But she *was* spoiling them, thought Hal. Even he could see that there was something not quite right in the way she responded immediately to every shrill demand for attention. He wondered why Uncle Stephen permitted it, then realized at once that his uncle was so pressed with business worries that he paid little attention to what went on at home.

Juliette was saying, "Do tell me, Hal. How is your dear mother? It is sometime since I had news of her. She is quite well, I hope?"

Hal noted the unfailing courtesy, but May caught the acid undertone and nudged Daniel. Mother used that medicinal note only when discussing distasteful subjects—or Aunt Abigail or Grandmaire. This intrigued May, who was curious about these mysterious relatives.

Hal replied that she was well enough, then paused before adding a lie. "She sends her love and hopes that you will send her a photograph of the two babies."

"How refreshingly sweet of her," said Juliette, undeceived. "And you must beg her to pose at a studio so that I may have a photograph of her. It has been more than ten years since I saw my sister, and no doubt she is greatly altered."

"Perhaps a little."

"And your father?" asked Juliette, her tone again warm. "How is dear Jack?"

Hal stared into his glass, suddenly stiff-faced. Patrick Teipa still rankled like a fishbone in the throat.

"I do hope that he is not ill."

"No, of course not. That is, I imagine he is keeping good health. We seldom see him." Hal was scowling.

"I'm sorry to hear that." So, she thought, that unfortunate business with the half-caste Maori woman—Rosaleen Teipa, that was her name—was still going on. A pity. When Jack Bennington had asked Stephen's help in placing the boy in an American college, they assumed the relationship had ended.

Poor Abby, thought Juliette. How ghastly to be shamed so publicly and for so long. The illegitimate boy, Patrick, must be fifteen by now, and Jack and the woman were still associating. Most Maori women were smothered in lard by their mid-twenties, but this Rosaleen had obviously kept her allure. Juliette had seen her only once, in a carriage with Jack. She recalled vividly how beautifully the Maori

11

and European strains were mingled in her features. Juliette's brother, Samuel Peridot, had been with her that day at the races; he was besotted with her on sight and had caused a minor scandal by driving off with her later. Samuel had never married nor shown the slightest interest in anybody after that. A fatal attraction.

But a shame about Abby and more so about the children. Jack's conduct was so blatant that all Auckland sympathized with her, even though everybody liked the loud, vulgarly charming Jack. It was a predicament that tried everyone's loyalties.

Juliette said gently, "Your father is a kind and generous man. He tries to do his best, I'm sure, but nobody can even come close to perfection."

"Especially not him!" He flushed, aware that his aunt knew what was bothering him.

Juliette changed the subject. "Tell me, Hal. What do you think of the new laws which will allow the women in Utah and Wyoming to vote in the next elections?" But before he could reply, Stephen came in, so Juliette turned to him, explaining, "We were discussing the new suffrage. Hal was about to give us his views about the ladies' vote."

Hal hesitated; these were the first words he had heard on the subject.

Stephen noticed his confusion. "A lot of unnecessary nonsense if you ask me. How typical of women to clamor for something that is no use to them. All the good wives will vote as their husbands direct, and the rebellious ones will cancel out their husbands' votes—which will be no loss at all. Overindulgent husbands most likely vote Democrat in any case."

"You seem to have thought it all through."

"The entire subject is not worth a worry. There was a cartoon in the *Post* recently. One lady is saying to her friend, 'Have you decided how you are going to vote?' and her friend replies, 'Why yes, Ethel. I think my merino costume with the fox trimmings will be most suitable.' "

"Very amusing." Juliette smiled lightly. Hal realized that he had never heard her snap at one of Stephen's provocative remarks; his own parents were unable to conduct a civil conversation no matter how trite the topic.

12

"What about you two?" asked Hal of his cousins. "How would you vote if it was your privilege?"

"I d-don't know," said Daniel, a pleasant-looking, cream-and-butter-toned boy with a nervous manner.

"I do," put in May, tossing her head as if to butt her stepbrother aside. "I would vote for President Ulysses S. Grant because he ratified the Fifteenth Amendment. He tries to be fair to everybody."

"Well reasoned, May," said Stephen. "Now if *you* would read all those passages in the newspaper that are marked for your consideration, Daniel, you would be equally well informed."

The reprimand was harsh, but not surprising. Everyone knew what a disappointment the boy was proving to be. It was something of a joke that Captain Yardley's heir grew seasick in a dinghy, balked when hustled toward a gangplank, and, instead of clambering over rigging and annoying the sailors he would one day command, preferred the company of girls and boys younger than himself.

May said, "Please don't scold Daniel. Mr. Lancaster marks so many tedious passages in every edition that often I cannot manage them either."

Stephen glanced at the pertly upturned face. The rose-tinted lamps gave her skin a soft glow, and her eyes were so luminous that it seemed her soul shone out of them. Just like her mother at that age, he thought wistfully.

But he said, "Your tutor does that for a purpose. If Daniel cannot learn how to cull the trivial and focus on the important, how can he run a complex company one day?"

"But the trivial things are so much more diverting," whispered May as she tried to take Daniel's arm. They were following their parents into the dining room.

"L-leave me be."

Hal saw the rejection and with a bow offered his elbow instead, turning tiny defeat into considerable victory. As he held her chair for her, she looked up into his face with an expression of blissful ownership. Stephen noticed and smiled.

Standing and walking, Stephen Yardley looked older than his fifty years, bent and stiffened as he was by salt water, freezing winds, tropical storms, and doses of anti-

13

scorbutic lime juice. But seated at the head of the table, he assumed such an air of authority that all who dined with him immediately pictured him behind his desk. His patriarchal appearance strengthened the image, though once the impression of command had registered, what one noticed about the captain were his shrewd, warm eyes, his firm handshake, and his direct, kindly voice, all of which compensated for the fact that like most self-made men of fortune, he wasted little time on pleasantries. Even now, as soon as the first course had been served and grace obtained, he began to discuss Hal's new iron-plated ship.

May listened to her stepfather in dismay. If it were true that Hal would not be back in San Francisco for years, then why couldn't they have a more sociable, even festive dinner in farewell? As she spooned up her Brown Windsor soup, she glumly detested the *Mondrich Zephyr.* A great ugly thing, it was, with sails and funnels and decks surrounded by a hideous web of scaffolding. Built for safety, they had been told on the tour of inspection, though she had heard more than one sailor refer to it as a dirty stinkpot. Many sailors disliked engines, but even May could see the advantage of engine power. Guaranteed delivery dates were important for business, and if the winds were very strong or very weak, a clipper's time could vary by more than a month on a long voyage.

"I shall expect full written reports on the practicability of all our experimental innovations," Stephen was saying. "I doubt whether the interchangeable yards on the masts will be of much advantage to you this trip, but those lifting bridges should alter your day-to-day running of the vessel. And try your best to extend her."

"Sheridan's of the opinion we'll not get much speed out of her, sir. And he's worried about the lifting bridges. He thinks they are top-heavy."

"Could be, but they'll save lives if the sea whips up rough. They will slow you down, but no matter. She's built for dependability rather than dash." He laughed at Hal's expression. "Aye, son. You young lads are all alike. No doubt you'd like to try your hand at outdoing Bully Baines's records, but I'd sooner ply a safe trade and pocket the underwriters' fees. The *Mondrich Zephyr* will never

14

come close to the *Flying Cloud*'s three hundred seventy-four miles in one day, but she'll arrive in good shape and I hope with all hands still aboard. In the past twenty years more than thirty thousand ships have been lost at sea. To date the Mondrich Line has lost none, nor did the Richmond Line when I was running it. Look at our main opposition, the Dragon Line. Ten ships down in a year. All heavily insured, of course, but what they must skin out in underwriters' fees would ruin us in no time. No, son, reliability is our aim. Safe delivery of cargo and passengers, that's the image we want."

After clam fritters came the roast, a turkey glazed the color of toffee with golden yams tucked around it, a dish of mint-scented peas, and a basket of cockade-shaped popovers covered with a napkin. Fluted bowls on stands held bread sauce, corn relish, and berry preserves. Parker came in to serve dishes of acorn squash and wild rice.

"You do me proud, Aunt Juliette," said Hal.

She summoned Parker to help him to a second plateful. "I do enjoy the sight of a healthy appetite. Both Edward and Albert are big eaters. A portent of an excellent constitution, don't you agree?"

Hal winked at May, making her blush with pleasure.

With panic in his voice Daniel blurted, "L-look at my plate, Mother. I've finished all mine, too."

May's nose wrinkled. It had amused her to see how Daniel had been watching Hal greedily in order to copy everything he did, sprinkling salt by tapping on his knife blade, buttering his popover when Hal did, and even inclining his head attentively toward Stephen with the same respectful expression.

"So you have. Very good, dear," said Juliette, but as he looked hopefully at Parker, she shook her head and warned, "No more, dear. And remember, nothing to drink," she added as he reached for the water jug. Hal was sipping wine now. "You know the rules. You don't want to—to wake up in the night, do you?"

Daniel ducked a scarlet face. His stepmother smiled at him reassuringly, knowing his secret had not been given away. Though she was fond of Daniel, Juliette worried that the little boys might grow up with his weak personality. This reversion to baby habits was a problem: not only bed-wetting but this persistent stammer that hours of making him read aloud through clenched teeth did nothing to alleviate. Juliette blamed it onto the earthquake of almost two years before and never suspected that the introduction of young Albert and then young Edward into the household had been more of a shock than any earth tremor.

When Daniel looked at her, Juliette said, "You must save room for dessert, dear. Mrs. Terrill has made the almond pudding you like so much."

Food and ships, thought May. Ships and food! Hal is going away, and all we do is discuss boring things. She burned to ask him serious, vital questions. Did he have a lover? Was he planning to marry? (Oh, please God, no!) Did he ever think about her when the moon shone on the ocean? Did he remember how he had once told her she looked like a creature made from moonlight? Did he ever wonder if one day, when she was old enough, he and she might . . .

She sighed aloud for all the questions she would never have the courage to ask, questions she could only whisper to herself.

Hal heard the sigh, misunderstood the cause of her frustration, and tossed her another sly wink. What a lonely child she is, he thought. No one seems to notice her. He turned his head in response to a comment from his aunt.

"Yes, that is so," he told her. "The Richmond Line is wallowing, though how seriously I cannot say. Grandmaire has employed a Mr. Thomas Peake to manage the financial side of things. Someone practical. But what it really needs is for the captain here to take the helm again. He does have a major shareholding in it, and it seems a shocking waste—"

"Never," whispered Juliette. Her dark blue eyes were fixed on him in a tense expression, and she sounded cold and hot at the same time. "Never, do you hear me? Never! I don't care what happens to the Richmond Line, but we are *not* returning to New Zealand to save it."

"I say, Sweet Olivine," interrupted Stephen, using both his pet name for her and his kindest tones. "We may have to intervene. I couldn't let my father's company sink completely."

"She's doing it. Your mother . . ." She stood up, the rest of the sentence choked off by her quickened breathing. After turning swiftly, she hurried from the room.

"I'm sorry," said Hal to his uncle.

"You weren't to know. Odd how some hurts never quite heal. All the time in the world won't fix that. A favor, please, son. Not a word of this to Abigail. Nor—"

"Grandmaire. I understand."

May said, "I wish the thought of New Zealand didn't make Mother so unhappy. Daniel says it's because the Maoris killed my father and my brother."

"That was in the war. Lots of people are killed in wars."

"Just the same, I wish we could go back there."

Hal grinned. "I'd see you every time my ship returned to port."

"That would be lovely."

They would suit each other perfectly, Stephen thought. His favorite young man married to his favorite young woman. Perfect but impossible. He couldn't imagine Juliette permitting May to marry Abigail's son. These feuds were like cobwebs, draped in the corners of every family he knew. Sticky, hindering, and a god-damned nuisance.

"You can bring the port in now," he told Norris.

Two

SAN FRANCISCO, 1875

"The museum of Curiosities!" May sighed as she arranged herself in the carriage. "What a treat this will be. The last time the museum came to town I was permitted to see only two exhibits for fear I might overtire myself. I spent so much time trying to decide which to choose that I wasted almost the entire afternoon doing nothing."

"You're so much better now," said Juliette, noting with approval her daughter's graceful posture. There was an air of elegant confidence about her that Juliette was sure she hadn't had at that age. Seventeen, she thought. When I was seventeen, my life was a wretched ruin, whereas hers is ordered and bolstered. I almost envy her.

The boys clambered in noisily, managing to sound like half a dozen instead of only two. Juliette patted the seat beside her, smiling with love. "Here you are, then. Edward, sit here, and Albert on the other side. No, don't kick May's gown with those muddy shoes. Gracious, where have you been playing?"

"They were down by the front fence again, ma'am, giving lip to those people outside the gates," said Miss Von Sturmer, their governess, who was still panting from the chase to catch them.

"Conversing," corrected Juliette. "You must take better care of them. Once they are dressed to go out, they should sit quietly in the morning room or the nursery until it is time to leave."

"Yes, ma'am."

May moved to make room for Miss Von Sturmer. She

18

said, "It is such a luxury to be able to see everything I want to. Which exhibits should I see first, Daniel? What do you recommend?"

Daniel was hunched in the corner. Like many other sixteen-year-olds, he spent much of his time pretending not to exist. He answered reluctantly, saying, "I think you'll like the little d-dog that works the knitting machine."

"That's soppy!" cried seven-year-old Albert.

"Soppy!" echoed the six-year-old Edward.

Albert said, "The dog's not clever."

"Why not, dear?" asked Juliette.

"Because it only runs on a wheel, Mother. May should go see the anaconda first."

"Accaconda," said Edward.

"Anaconda, silly. It's enormous." His eyes grew enormous, too, and his voice swelled. Juliette placed a hand on his knee to lower the volume, but he was still shouting as he continued. "It wraps itself around and around its prey and then squashes it all to bits and swallows the mush. Then I'm going to see the arm of Tim Turkestan, the famous pirate."

"Pirate! Shake hands!" cried Edward.

"Shake hands with a severed arm?" May shuddered.

"That sounds gruesome, dear," murmured Juliette.

"There's lots more gruesome things than that."

"Never mind, Albert," snapped Miss Von Sturmer. He was clearly going to supply details. She intercepted a glance from her employer and changed tack. "We mustn't spoil this outing for May. Let's keep everything a surprise for her."

The carriage stopped so that Lucas could open the gates. Daniel said, "I wonder if those p-people will shout at us again today? Why do they hate us?"

"They don't hate us, dear," said Juliette.

"Father said that it's because of that nasty article in the newspapers," May said. "They blame us because hundreds of Chinese people keep coming on Father's ships. They think there are too many Chinese people here already."

"It is fear bred from unemployment," said Miss Von

Sturmer. "Chinese are willing to work for less money. They steal jobs from other people."

"Maybe we could get a Chinese governess," said Albert.

"Could we, please?" cried Edward.

"There now, boys," said Juliette. She glanced out the window with distaste. "It does not surprise me that these people cannot find work. I shudder at the coarse things they scream after us. Really, it is hardly *our* fault! Pull the curtains down, children. And do not let them alarm you. Your father says they are a symptom of the times we live in, but I prefer to regard them as a seven-day plague. Nobody bothered us last week, and by next week they will be tired of standing outside our house. I think the press is largely to blame for their presence anyway. That article was totally irresponsible. Don't encourage them, boys."

But instead of pulling the curtain down, Albert was kneeling on the seat. "I told them to go away, didn't I, Edward?"

"Me too! Go away!"

Yes, thought May. And threw stones at them and hurled insults worse than those shouted at us. But she was not interested in reporting her brothers' misdemeanors and watched with only mild displeasure as Albert pressed his face against the glass and cupped his hands around his cheeks so that the others in the carriage would not see the faces he was pulling at the crowd. As if we couldn't guess what he was up to, thought May.

Juliette was straightening Edward's pleated silk collar. She glanced up suddenly in alarm. "What was that?"

Miss Von Sturmer said, "Edward, did you kick against the seat?"

He twisted his mouth at her in reply, but this time the impudence was ignored even by the governess, for at that moment a drum roll of thumps shook the carriage.

Juliette's face drained. "An earthquake," she whispered under her breath. "Sweet Mary, I pray to you . . . not another earthquake . . ."

Nobody heard her. May was peering through the unscreened gap beside Albert. "Those people are throwing things at us! Mud and stones, I think. They're throwing things at the carriage. How strange! Why would they do that?"

She nudged the governess but received no reply. Miss Von Sturmer was also convinced they were poised on the brink of an earthquake and was doggedly counting her rosary beads.

The carriage stopped. A hail of rocks clattered around them.

"Albert, for goodness' sake, pull that curtain down!" Juliette said, rapping on the communication hatch. "What in the world is happening? I wonder why we've stopped moving." She glanced at Daniel, who was slipping the bolt into place. Her voice was shaking as she said, "Surely they'll not try to harm us? Not outside our own gate!"

May was more interested than frightened. She had lifted her curtain half an inch and reported, "We've stopped because people are grabbing at the harness." She raised her voice above a windsharp wave of shrieking. "Mr. Terrill is whipping the people to keep them away from the horses. Oh! One lady has tripped over in the mud, and people are trampling all over her. They are so *horrible*. . . . They're all shouting and trying to grab at the carriage." She glanced at her mother's white face. "Mr. Terrill is managing quite capably, Mother. Don't be afraid. I'm sure they mean only to frighten us."

"Then we must not be cowed by them." But her voice warmed with relief as she added, "We're moving again." As she fanned herself with her handkerchief, the bitter odor of lavender wafted through the dim interior of the carriage.

One arm was around Edward, who had snuggled silently against his mother's side, his thumb anchored in his mouth. Albert, however, was still kneeling on the seat, face pressed against the glass.

"Shoot them all, Terrill!" he shouted. "Shoot the dirty, ignorant swine!"

Juliette plucked the hem of his jacket. "Albert, dear, come away . . ." she began.

Too late.

They all heard the noise, loud and dull as the cracking of ice on a pond, but nobody realized at first what had caused it. It seemed to take long, spiraling seconds for the huge rock to smash through the glass right where Albert's grimacing face had been framed. They all saw it too late; nobody had time to whisk him out of the way. All were frozen in their seats.

Juliette's scream filled the carriage and hung there, sharp as the scent of her perfume. Albert toppled slowly backward into his mother's lap.

They stared at him in horrified disbelief. It seemed incredible that only moments ago he had been a bright-faced, laughing boy. Now his face was a pink pulp studded with shards of glass, a stretched, bellowing mouth in the center.

"They tried to kill him," said May, disbelieving. She was too stunned to cry, too frightened to move.

"It could easily have been a tragedy," said Stephen that evening. "It chills me to think how close you came to being hurt, Sweet Olivine."

"Albert was hurt."

"Yes, but only minor cuts. He could have—"

"Minor?" She stiffened, thinking that Stephen's lack of sympathy bordered on the insufferable. Oh, he had reacted with swift shock—had a doctor there within minutes and the culprit rounded up and arrested within the hour—but as soon as he had satisfied himself that Albert's injuries were not serious, his indignation had melted. Juliette, however, was still taut with her own repressed anger. She said, "His injuries are hardly *minor*, Stephen."

"I grant you that he looks a mess, but all that was needed was bathing and the application of a salve. He could have been disfigured or lost his sight, but the worst he'll have are superficial scars that will fade quickly. He must be aware that is was partly his own fault."

"His fault?" Tears sprang into her eyes. "How can you say that?"

He put his arms around her soothingly. "That sounded harsh, and I didn't mean to be harsh. I'm as worried as you are, but in a different way, I suppose." He paused, trying to read her face. "And I have had some serious worries lately, you realize."

"The Richmond Line? But you've been working on their problems for years!"

"And nothing seems to cure what ails it. These troubles have to be sorted out by someone on the spot." He felt her shoulders tighten under his fingers, but he pressed on. This had to be said. "This nasty incident has jolted me, Juliette. I think the time has come to rethink our whole situation. Please, Sweet Olivine, try to understand that some things are inevitable."

But she pulled away and stood with her back to him. They were standing on the widow's walk on the rooftop, she facing the wide gate of the harbor. The sun had just dipped its edge into the sea and was dissolving in a rosy stain along the horizon.

She said, "If you mean that we should go back to New Zealand, then no!" Whirling suddenly to face him, she added, "It's not inevitable. It can't be!"

His voice was sad. "Would it be so bad to leave here? Think about it frankly. The city has changed. This is not the glittering San Francisco your mother dreamed of. It's dirty and noisy, crammed with refugees, rotten with crime and disease. It's ugly, and today ugliness touched our own family."

"It was an isolated incident."

"Was it? Just like the filth smeared along our walls and the dead cats tied to the railings? I fear worse could come. You are right when you say that we must not be forced from our home, but events have piled up on us now, and we must acknowledge them. Since Mr. Peake died, the Richmond Line has been in total disarray, losing customers so rapidly that I fear it will soon sink completely, unless something is done."

"It's not your responsibility. Your mother—"

"Ah, but it is. And the reputation of the Richmond Line is bound up so closely with our Mondrich Line that I cannot allow the situation to deteriorate further. This is part of me, part of our lives. We must go."

She turned away, but he took her shoulders and made her face him. At first she would not look into his eyes, but then she shuddered, as though all her will to struggle were expiring. She gazed at her husband with pure desperation.

23

"Must we all go? Could you not go alone, sort out the problems, and then return?"

"That could take years. Besides, I couldn't leave you here when the situation is so volatile. And I would miss you. Be honest, dear. Are you never curious about New Zealand? Wouldn't you find a return journey interesting?"

"As long as I could remain on board ship, in the harbor," she returned with spirit.

He was sufficiently encouraged to laugh.

"But *you* are curious, aren't you?"

Stephen shrugged. "I admit it. I long to go back. As the years slip away, I find myself thinking about New Zealand more and more. I lie awake at night recalling past events, and the nostalgic longing is more painful than my worst rheumatic aches. I'm getting old, Sweet Olivine. I feel as though it were time to 'return to that place whence I came.'"

His tone alarmed her. She had always refused to look at Stephen as anything but the darkly handsome young man she had fallen in love with so long ago. "You're not old. You are young. Exactly the same age as the queen."

"And that fact surprises me these days. She seems a young widow, while I am a scarred and ancient warrior. It's frustration and uselessness, Juliette. There is so little for me to do here now and so much to be done there."

"But your clubs . . . your friends . . ."

He sighed, "Please try to understand. I had to make this decision sooner or later."

She was about to protest further, but the word *decision* stopped her. It was final. Suffocated by the fatigue and strain of the day, she began to weep.

Stephen was wretched. He stroked the side of his wife's face, where wisps of gray-streaked hair strayed from under her shawl. He was bitter about having to hurt her, especially like this, with broken promises and betrayal. They had been so close until the little boys had begun their magnetic pull on her affections, forcing her to drift away from him. She smelled more often of milk puddings and warming oil than she did of cologne, and her embrace was passive, not passionate. He feared what this blow might do to them both.

"You know how dearly I love you," he said, and waited for her to accuse him of making her unhappy, but she wept silently, locked in her own emotional snarl. He said, "Auckland will not be as bad as you fear. You need never see Abigail or Mama if you don't want to. The town is so large that we can make friends without having to break into their circles."

"I hear that your mother is at the center of everything, exactly as she always was."

"She's not Queen Victoria. People don't have to do her bidding. We will build a house well away from Fintona. Perhaps on that land the Maoris gave in memory of your father. Samuel can build it for us. He is the king of timber in New Zealand, I hear. It will be ready and waiting for us. You can hold your own court in the grandest house Auckland has ever seen."

"And people will come to stare at me and whisper behind their hands," she flung at him. "Stephen, have you really considered what it will be like for me to return to a place where I was ostracized?"

"Circumstances were different then. Three-quarters of the population will never have heard of you. You will be returning as my wife. Don't you think I will protect you from gossip?"

"I know that you will do everything you can."

"Then please trust me. And don't be afraid of Mama or Abigail. What they did to you was unforgivable, but they cannot hurt you now."

Her glance was incredulous. "Do you really believe that? Knowing what they are capable of, can you really believe that?"

"You are stronger than either of them," said Stephen.

I'll soon be seeing Hal again, thought May in delight. Skirts bunched, she hurried up the stairs after Daniel. It was a week after the riot, and Stephen had broken the news at dinner. May sang in time to her footsteps: "Hal, Hal, Hal, Hal!"

"Do you think it is odd that Hal has never married?" she asked Daniel as she followed him into his room. "He is twenty-five or twenty-six now at least."

25

"That's not old," said Daniel. "He'll be married as soon as he can find someone who will have him no doubt." He scrabbled in a bureau drawer until he found a box of stereoscopic pictures. "Ah, here they are. I didn't throw them out after all." After holding several up to the light, he fitted one in the bracket and stared into the eyepieces before passing the stereoscope to May.

She put down a portrait of a flaxen-haired woman—Daniel's mother, who had died shortly after he was born—and peered obediently through the lenses. "Ugh." She shuddered. "Your tattooed chiefs and maidens. I wonder if we will see any like this. Is one of these Te Kooti, the famous cannibal chief?"

"No. But Mr. Lancaster says that cannibalism is a r-religious rite. We need not be afraid of Maoris. He s-says that our Indians are f-far more ferocious."

"Our Indians are more sensible, too. I still cannot understand why they daub their faces with paint, for who would want to appear even uglier than God made them? But the Maori custom of scribbling *indelibly* over one's features is beyond my comprehension."

Daniel fitted another pair of pictures into the stereoscope. "Look at this one. G-go on!"

"It's the shrunken head, isn't it? I'll not look at that."

With awe in his voice he said, "This Maori sold his own head for the price of a hatchet. Imagine walking around knowing that your head belonged to someone else, and the minute you died they would hack it off for a curio."

"They probably use the same hatchet to do it, too," said May. She flipped through the pictures and selected one of a Maori maiden cooking a basket of food in a boiling spring. "You're really excited about going to New Zealand, aren't you?"

"Especially since we can't t-take our horses. I'm going to call Sioux Te Kooti from n-now on."

"Negus will remain plain Negus." She picked up the silver-framed portrait again. "I'm nervous about going. Everything I know is here in San Francisco, and I love living here. This house, our friends . . . Oh, the adventure excites me, and the prospect of seeing Hal again makes my skin go shivery, but if only we didn't have to give up every-thing first."

"We won't be giving up anything. J-just changing it."

"I suppose so. But it's scary." She studied the portrait, then her own face in the mirror. "Do you think Hal will find me pretty?"

"Only if he has excellent taste," said Daniel.

As their departure date approached, that question plagued May with increasing frequency. Within the space of a few months she swung from a total unconcern for her appearance to an attitude of intense vanity.

Juliette paused at her doorway one afternoon and was puzzled to see her daughter staring into the mirror with the expression of a subject in a hypnotic trance.

"What is the matter, dear?" she asked, standing at her shoulder.

"Everything!" The tone was pure tragedy. "My brow is too wide—I look like an owl—and I am so deathly pale. Pos-itively, repulsively pale."

"You've always been pale. You should be pleased. It's all the vogue to have white skin."

"But not this white! My forehead looks like a blank page. Do you think that if I cut bangs and frizzled them, like Lorna Martine's, I might look more sophisticated?"

"Nobody could look more sophisticated than Lorna Mar-tine. All right, I do know what you mean. Yes, bangs would soften your forehead. They'd become you. But why all this interest in your appearance? It is so unlike you."

May bit her lip. "It's Hal. I do so hope that he finds me attractive."

Juliette tried to laugh, though in her ears it dinned like a hen's squawk. Not Hal! Anybody but him. Not Abby's son, not for her May. If they married, she and Abby would share grandchildren, and she'd not be able to visit her own daughter without fear of bumping into her sister. It would be intolerable!

But she spoke lightly. "Does Hal matter so much? I'd not set my heart on him in advance, dear. He could be engaged or even married by now."

"But surely Uncle Samuel would have mentioned it

when he wrote to us about Hal's father drowning in that shipwreck. I sent Hal a letter of sympathy after that, but he didn't reply. I was wondering whether I should write again."

"We'll be seeing him soon enough. And dozens of other eligible young men, too. Now then. The tailor is measuring the boys up for riding costumes. Miss Von Sturmer wonders if you would like a new costume, too. Yours could be adapted for her with very little difficulty." She smiled at May's raised eyebrows. "Everybody rides in Auckland. You'll probably have to learn to drive your own dogcart, too. Auckland is not the cosmopolitan city that this is, you know."

May said, "You don't want to go either, do you, Mother? You want to stay here just as I do."

"There now," chided Juliette, who hated self-pity. "We must make the best of it. If I sound wistful, it is simply because I love San Francisco, and I've had the happiest part of my life here."

Very slowly May said, "Weren't you happy in New Zealand? Oh. But you were married to Father then, my real father."

Juliette's face clouded, as it always did when her first husband, Stephen's brother, was mentioned. She smoothed her skirts in a gesture that betrayed her anxiety.

As she turned to go, May said, "Please, Mother, won't you tell me about him? I know it pains you, and I'm sorry, but I desperately want to know."

"You always want everything desperately, dear. Even another helping of dessert."

"This is different, Mother."

"I know, dear. Very different." She patted May's outstretched hand. "One day I shall answer your questions. When you are older perhaps."

Alone, May scowled at herself in the mirror. It wasn't fair. Daniel knew all about his mother, but she had never seen even a photograph of Leigh Yardley. All she had been told was that he had died in the war against the Maoris. With him had died May's brother, who had apparently run off to be with his father. May could not remember young Leigh at all, only the stories her mother had told her. She

28

could not recall the games, the outings, the stories he used to read her. All she remembered was a little black and white dog that whined for days and days after Leigh disappeared. She had mentioned the dog to her mother once, and Juliette had burst into such a storm of tears that May was terrified.

"I shouldn't ask her about Father," May said aloud to her reflection. "Mention of the subject upsets her far more than suppression of it upsets me."

But as she smoothed her hair before going down to the tailor, a thought slid into her mind. Of course! Once they were settled in Auckland and surrounded by relatives, she would be able to find out every detail about her father. All she had to do was ask the right questions of the right people. Mother need never be troubled again.

"How perfectly simple," she said, shutting the door behind her.

Three

Because the weather was generously brisk and steady, the *Mondrich Arrow*'s voyage to Auckland took only forty-three days, but they were a long forty-three days for Captain Aulde. Not only did he have the tension of hosting his master, but he also had the dilemma of trying to keep the two young boys out of mischief before they caused real damage. If they were not tangling themselves in the rigging, they were prying in the sailors' deckhouse or fiddling with sensitive instruments on the bridge. In their father's presence they behaved impeccably, but most of the time Captain Yardley worked in his office, surrounded by thick files of Richmond Line business. And though Mrs. Yardley was a sweet, well-spoken lady, it was plain that she was ruining those two boys. Handsome little scamps they were, almost identical except for tiny scars on Albert's face, but so naughty that after the first few days he found himself watching for them with a feeling of increasing dread. What would be broken or thrown overboard today, and would it be in full, tolerant view of their mother? It was a long, long voyage for Captain Aulde.

And even more protracted for poor Daniel. He had begun to feel queasy as they stood on the wharf watching Albert and Edward clambering on the martingales, and by the time the clipper's jibboom had thrust through the Golden Gate and pointed out to the wide Pacific beyond, Daniel was green-faced and retching on his bunk.

As Miss Von Sturmer spent most of the first week also stricken with seasickness, May had to help her mother look after the boys. That meant mainly following them about and watching to make sure they did not put themselves into any danger. This task was, to say the least, embarrassing. Albert and Edward were so badly behaved and so impudent in their dealings with the crew that May often had to blush as she apologetically tried to coax her brothers away.

"We can do whatever we like!" protested eight-year-old Albert as she tried to make him desist from untying the foreshroud ropes. "Those sailors can't stop us. This ship belongs to Father."

Edward pinched her hand as she rescued his velvet jacket, which had been twisted like a rag in the rigging. When she leaned over to deal him a well-deserved slap, he dashed away, crowing with laughter, and sat beside Juliette.

"Do look at this, Mother," urged May in exasperation. "One of the sleeves is torn almost right off. Surely the boys can play without being destructive."

Juliette smiled. "It's natural high spirits, dear. When you have sons of your own, you will understand."

When I have sons of my own, I shall insist that they behave in a manner not offensive to other people, thought May grimly as she strode off to the cabins to see if she could do anything to hasten Miss Von Sturmer's recovery.

The *Mondrich Arrow* had been specially fitted out for its important passengers. Marble-topped sideboards railed around with brass, walnut tables and writing desks with fiddle slats for rough weather, and even a piano were installed in the best cabins while pastoral paintings and velvet portieres were hung to soften the square lines of the small rooms. May could see that the idea was to make life aboard ship as similar to life ashore as possible, an idea she thought unfortunate. How much more fun it would be to have everything as different as possible so that each day on board was an adventure. As at home, the Yardleys drank French wine from Waterford crystal glasses and took their meals on Wedgwood china—though Mrs. Terrill, while nosing in the galley, noticed that the food was not a patch on what they were used to. "They'll not complain, of course," she confided to her husband with satisfaction. "They're too genteel for that. But imagine how glad they'll

31

be when we reach Auckland and my meals are set before them again." It was a matter of considerable pride to her that apart from Miss Von Sturmer, only she, her husband, and six-year-old son, Bobby, were accompanying the Yardleys to New Zealand. And a matter of pride that her quiet Bobby was compared so frequently and so favorably with the master's boys. Day after day, while the "horrors" (as they were called in the deckhouse) careered about the ship, Bobby sat alone with a thin string fishing line strung tautly over the taffrail.

May often stopped to speak to the child on her frequent strolls around the deck. She loved this ship and found no fault with it. Like all ships in both the Mondrich and Richmond lines, it was white as foam, with a royal blue stripe along the hull and royal blue jibtopsails, spanker, and skysails. From the monkey gaff flapped the ensign, royal blue with a silver-and-black *M* for Mondrich enclosed in a circlet of fern leaves. With their distinctive coloring they could be recognized easily. On their fifth day out they sailed near to a Richmond Line five-masted down easter. Captain Aulde smiled at May's excitement and said he was sorry but they'd not be pulling up alongside, for there was no news to be exchanged.

"I suppose not," said May. "She's come from China or Japan, hasn't she?"

"And how would you be knowing that, Miss Yardley?"

"I can tell by the gun turrets. Oh, I know they're not really gun turrets. They're just painted on to discourage pirates. Tell me, Captain. Have pirates ever overrun one of the Mondrich Line ships?"

"I can't rightly say, Miss Yardley," he replied uneasily, knowing that to be not a fit subject to discuss with young ladies but not wishing to say so. What an odd creature she was—so delicate in appearance, and in health from all accounts, but as direct as a man in her questions. He'd heard it said that people of unusual appearance often had strange natures. Perhaps she was like her grandmother, a striking-looking woman, who was interested in commerce to a degree most unbecoming to a lady—and successful at it, which was worse. If she wasn't careful, this delightful lass with the mahogany hair would end up the same way.

It wasn't right that a girl could name all the sails, even the crossjack.

She smiled at him coaxingly, "You don't want to tell me, do you? It seems so puzzling to me that I can read an account in the newspapers of how Maoris killed a missionary, then cut his heart out and ate it, but I cannot hold a conversation with you about pirates."

"Your father would not thank me if I did, Miss Yardley."

"You are perfectly correct, and I'm sorry," she said at once. "My interest in life sometimes gets the better of me, I'm afraid, and I do love your ship so much that I feel such compulsion to ask questions. I am utterly captivated by everything—the smells of tar and rope, the snapping noises the sails make, and the sad creaking of the timbers. And the sea—I'm astonished that it can present such a different aspect so frequently. Sometimes it is gray, sometimes green or blue; sometimes smooth and oily and sometimes violently chopped."

"Ah, but you should see it in a storm. Right majestic it be then."

Her eyes shone. She had the clearest, most gentle-looking eyes Captain Aulde had ever seen. "It would be so exciting if we had a storm. Do you think there is any chance of it?"

"Not likely at this time of year, Miss Yardley. But don't look downcast. You'd not find it half so much fun as you imagine. All the furniture in the cabins would be tied down, and you'd have leeboards on the bunks to stop you from tumbling out. In a bad sea the waves come surging right through the ship, over the weatherboards in the doorways and washing around the decks. I've had some irate passengers in my time, trying to dry everything out afterward, and nothing's the same after it's had a soaking in brine, you know."

"But to see the huge waves and the sails all tied in—"

"Begging your pardon, miss, but storms are dangerous to life and limb."

Having said that, he suddenly recalled whom he was speaking to and broke off abruptly with a "Well, then!" and a gruff "Never mind." When she continued to stare at him with that tranquil, innocent expression he ventured, "Perhaps you'll marry a sea captain yourself one day, Miss Yardley, since you're so taken with the sea."

"Perhaps," she murmured softly, turning to gaze out over the feather-tipped waves. Tiny drops of water scattered like a peppering of gravel in each smooth trough. She wondered when she would see Hal again. Father had said that his ship would have left for a new voyage some days before their arrival in Auckland, unless—unless they were very much ahead of schedule. "Captain Aulde," she heard herself ask, "if you put on more sail—the royals and the skysails, for instance—would we be able to shorten the journey by many days?"

His leathery face settled into bemused rumples. "Why, Miss Yardley, I thought you would have wanted me to slow down, not go faster. What's brought about this change of heart then?"

In the first class section the only other passenger was a Professor Wood, a scientist who was traveling to the antipodes in order to study the life and customs of the Maori and aboriginal peoples, before, as he put it, there were no natives left and no customs to be studied.

As he cut his roast pork into small pieces and heaped it at the side of his plate, he confided, "I believe that your government is about to implement a policy of systematic extermination."

Juliette heard herself say, "I cannot believe that! Our policies are based on a friendly cooperation with the Maori people. Even the war has not altered that."

"But haven't they been herded into reservations? And isn't that a preliminary requisite to—"

"Not herded, sir," said Stephen in annoyance. "They are bound to stay behind a certain boundary in a place called the king Country—for the Maori king, you understand—but they are free to leave there as soon as they have sworn fealty to Queen Victoria. Both they and the settlers must have guarantees for their safety. Oh, the Maoris are being exploited in many ways—you will see that for yourself—but nobody is harming them."

"Extermination indeed!" said Juliette. I defended New Zealand! she thought.

"Then I must be confused. Is it in Tasmania or New South Wales where parties of settlers go out to hunt and slaughter natives? Where they leave poisoned food out for the poor wretches?" He glanced at May, who was not eating. "I do apologize, Miss Yardley, if my observations have blighted your appetite."

"They have not," said May, and begged to be excused. When the main course was served, she had understood to her dismay why Blossom had not been in her pen this morning, waiting for her breakfast muffin.

"But you've not touched your plate," said Juliette. "And this pork is excellent."

May fled.

"I fear my frankness upset you," said the professor the next day. He was an earnest, elderly fellow whose lumpy features and bristling shock of hair reminded May of a pineapple.

While she protested that he had not offended her, she watched him set up a tripod and unpack a large black camera from its carrying trunk.

"A Morrison stereoscopic twin-lens model," he explained as he shook out a black cape and disappeared underneath it to focus on the lifeboat nearby. "Part of my assignment is to capture a selection of stereoscopic images to be marketed under the title 'Strange Places and Interesting Phenomena.' Many people collect such pictures."

"Daniel does. He has more than five thousand sets in his collection."

"Really? Then he probably has some of mine. Is that the poor lad who is still below with *mal de mer?* Such a shame for a ship owner's son to be so afflicted. Now, Miss Yardley, if you would care to pose for me over there by the capstan?"

At his direction she stood very still, one hand on the pinrail to brace herself. He dashed away and returned with an object wrapped in black cloth. There was a strong odor of chloroform as he slid it into the camera back.

"Are you ready? Now keep your gaze fixed where I instructed and remember—don't blink."

As soon as he reached the count of thirty, she relaxed with a laugh. "Why should it be that as soon as you said that, all I wanted to do *was* blink? My eyes are burning with the effort of resisting. Professor Wood, why did you have that object wrapped in black? And what chemical do I smell?"

"It's the collodion which fixed your image onto the glass."

"And is the glass wet with that when you put it into the camera? Is that why it was wrapped up?"

"That is to keep light from getting to the chemical film." He could see that, childlike, she was brewing with more questions, so he said, "Would you like to try taking a picture yourself? One of me, with perhaps your nurse in the picture, too? You seem intrigued by the process, and it is a lot of fun."

So, with her head in the warm darkenss, May peered through the viewfinder at the tiny, bright scene.

"Don't smile," the professor warned Miss Von Sturmer as he stood beside her. "Ready to begin now," he told May.

She was still measuring the half minute when Juliette saw the group and came hurrying over, her bustled skirt held clear of the deck by a cane with a hook at the end. "What about the boys?" she asked. "Will you be so good as to take their picture, too, please, Professor?"

"That was fun," exclaimed May. "Everything looked so sharp and bright, as though the scene had been trapped in a tiny silver bottle or shrunk and glazed with sugar. When can we see the results?"

"Tomorrow, but don't expect too much. This fierce light is excellent for recording the details of the ship but will not be kind for portraiture."

"Come along, boys," said Juliette. "Come and pose nicely for Professor Wood."

The pictures were ready in the morning, and at breakfast the professor showed them to May. "See how the light has bleached out the contours of your cheeks?" he said, pointing. "Notice how dense the shadows are under your chin and hatbrim? It is too harsh to be flattering. Portraiture requires a soft, even light. Now here, in the picture of your brothers we have . . ."

May listened avidly. In her hands she held the double image of the professor and Miss Von Sturmer. It was a poor likeness, awkwardly posed and starkly contrasted, but for all its faults, the frames were full of marvelously crisp detail. Above the heads looped ropes as fibrous and twisted as in life. *More* clearly than in life.

That was it! The image was more intense than anything perceived by the eye. The deck was smoother, the canvas on the rail more gritty of texture, and the professor's silver watch chain heavier-looking than in life. Her photograph had not merely captured the scene but heightened it. And she had created this by looking through a viewfinder and pressing a button for the right length of time. It was incredible.

Moreover she could have done even better. If she had thought to ask Miss Von Sturmer to sit and had posed the professor slightly behind her, they would have made a more pleasing combination. Had she tilted Miss Von Sturmer's hatbrim, less of her face would have drowned in shadow. And if . . .

She said, "How long does it take to learn the mechanics of photography? Is it something I could accomplish?"

"It is a complex process, Miss Yardley, and I doubt if you would want—" He glanced at her sharply. "You are in perfect sincerity, aren't you?"

"Oh, yes! I don't think I have ever wanted anything quite so much. Do you think I could learn?"

"Perhaps you had better discuss this with your parents," he said, feeling uncomfortable. His tactlessness had caused a distinct coolness last night, and Mrs. Yardley would not be pleased with the blurred portrait of her sons. Still, he had warned her that unless they kept still, it was no use. "Yes," he said. "You must discuss this with them."

"I really don't think that photography is a suitable occupation for a young lady," said Juliette. "You are starting a new life in a new country and must observe the proprieties of correct behavior. Besides, you do not have the strength to carry a heavy trunkful of equipment. And your health is fragile. Breathing toxic gases would be dreadfully harmful. Remember what the doctor told you."

May's eyes watered with the intensity of her disappoint-

37

ment. "I must rest frequently and live a gentle, undemanding life. Oh, it sounds so dull—like having to eat only gruel or being permitted to wear no color but gray. Sometimes it seems that my life is like one long Sunday afternoon. I am permitted to do nothing interesting."

"You are exaggerating again, dear."

"But photography is so fascinating. The possibilities are endless, and already I am a fever of ideas I want to try. Please, Mother, consider—"

She was interrupted by a shriek from Miss Von Sturmer, who had discovered Albert holding Edward over the side of the ship. Juliette rushed to help in the rescue, and May, wasting no time in self-pity, sought out her stepfather.

Stephen listened with tolerant amusement. What a captivating creature she was; what a lively mind she had. Always some new interest to be devoured and absorbed. What a pity that photography had such unsavory connotations. Not that he knew much about it, nothing specific apart from the collection of smutty stereoscopic pictures that had turned up in Daniel's packing.

Daniel, he thought, noticing how some of the shine dulled at the mere thought of his son's name. Why couldn't he have been like May? She was pleading her cause with enthusiasm but was frank enough to relay Juliette's objections. Nothing sly about her. Direct, honest, and visionary. What a marvelous son she would have made.

He felt he was consoling them both when he said, "Life often seems unfair."

"You are saying I may not have a camera of my own?"

"Your mother was right, dear. Photography is not for you." He noticed that she was struggling manfully to hold back tears. "Try not to be too disappointed," he told her.

"Now I know what unrequited love feels like," May told Daniel as she leaned against his bunk. "I shall *die* if I cannot have a camera."

He smiled, thinking that her face was gloomier than the stifling atmosphere in here. "You are so dramatic. What is s-so special about a camera?"

"It's what I could achieve with it. If only I could find a way. I *must*. Daniel, do you think that you could develop an interest in the science of photography? If you had a camera, then I could use it as often as I wanted, and—"

"F-Father wouldn't agree. Never mind why. I know it, that's all."

"How can you be certain?"

"I'll n-not go into that. But I have faith in you, dear sister. You were never going to be permitted to ride a horse, but you h-had your way with that. I have supreme confidence that you *will* find a way, as you always do." He groaned. "Five more days. I d-doubt that I will survive that long."

"You will," she told him unsympathetically.

Late that afternoon she strolled on deck, unconsoled. When she saw young Bobby Terrill at his line, she showed him her picture and was soon explaining all the finer points she could remember.

"One day I shall have a camera of my very own, so that I can compose wonderful pictures that look below the surface of all things and reveal the substances of their inner cores."

He flashed her a gap-toothed grin. Although the technicalities were beyond him, *one day* he understood well.

"One day I shall have a carriage and pair and a fine house of *my* very own," he told her.

She looked at him blankly, caught up by the hopelessness of it all. I'm smitten all right, and badly, too, she thought.

Ruffling Bobby's hair she said, "We're dreamers, you and I. Nothing more than dreamers."

"If you say so, miss," he said.

Four

"I shan't forget," said Stephen with a wink. "The moment the harbormaster boards I shall ask whether the *Mondrich Zephyr* is still in port. You are anxious to see your dashing Captain Bennington, aren't you, lass?"

"Hush!" May poked at his arm with a gloved finger. "He's not *my* captain.

"Then you'd best try not to blush at every mention of his name," said Stephen teasingly. "Mind you, there is nothing I would like better than to see you two happily—but I'm being premature." He turned back toward the harbor, where two scows loaded with sawn timber slipped toward the open sea, their sails gray with dawn dampness. Closer to shore half a dozen Maori canoes moved in mechanical convoy, paddles dipping in unison. They looked like long red water beetles. Stephen grinned broadly at the sight, happy to be home.

He pointed to a promontory beyond the canoes, where a pale house faced them, quite alone on the crest of a cliff. "That's it. Our new home. See it? That building with the towers and long verandas."

"I can see it, but not clearly enough to do more than guess. So that's where we'll be living. It looks as though there are no other houses for miles."

"There are two cottages nearby. Fencible cottages, built to house retired soldiers, or fencibles, at the time of the Maori wars. The government built a whole string of them to encircle the outskirts of Auckland, the idea being that they would give the alarm if Maoris massed to attack the city. One cottage is dilapidated, I believe, but your uncle Samuel lives in the other whenever he condescends to return to civilization. Your mother will appreciate his company, I'm sure."

"Fencible cottages for soldiers, on that land? But that land belonged to the Maori tribe before they gave it to Mother's family. Why did the government build on it?"

"If I were cynical, I'd say because it had an idea of claiming the whole tract after the war. As it was, the Maoris were driven right around that point—where the lighthouse is, see it?—and as far as I know, they still live there. They're our closest neighbors, in fact."

Her eyes widened. "That will be exciting. Mr. Lancaster said they are a quick-tempered race who like nothing better than to provoke a quarrel."

"They crave drama and excitement, but at heart they are gentle. And these are family friends. Your maternal grandfather Thomas Peridot, traded with them for many years, just as your uncle Samuel does now. After the wars they were alarmed to see how, all over the country, millions of acres of tribal land were being seized in retaliation. Quite rightly they feared for this piece of land, so before it could be taken, they had gifted it to Thomas Peridot's children—your mother, Abigail, and Samuel."

"They must have thought very highly of him."

Stephen tugged at his long chin whiskers. "Thomas Peridot was one of the first settlers, and he appreciated and understood the native customs. I often think it was a blessing that he died before the worst of the fighting began. What it would have done to him to witness the tearing apart of his beloved people . . ."

"But the Maoris lost their land anyway if they gave it to us."

"Not really. They keep the use of it, and they trust us never to sell. It was clever of them really."

"What is it called? Whenua—I keep forgetting."

"Whenuahakari, a gift of land. *Whenua* means 'land,' and *hakari* means 'gift.' Try to remember that as a courtesy to the people who gave it to us."

"Whenuahakari," she repeated obediently. "We should have that name put up on the gates."

"It has been, but to no avail. Samuel reports that the

41

sightseers who come to gape at the house have dubbed it Mondrich House, and he suggests we do likewise."

"What is Uncle Samuel like? Mother says he is vastly wealthy but lives like a wandering trader."

"Which he is. He has some interesting viewpoints, but when you listen to him, bear in mind that like those of all strong men, his opinions have a definite slant. Ask him about the wars. He believes that the white people started them to steal tribal land systematically."

"You think that, too, don't you? But it's absolutely shocking."

"I neither believe nor disbelieve. Without the facts, how can one form an opinion? But ask him, and see what he has to say." He pointed. "Here comes the pilot boat. I wonder what the news of your captain will be?"

"Please, Father. If that becomes a habit, you may forget yourself and address him so to his face."

"I wonder if he would object?"

"I would expire of embarrassment, I promise you!"

An hour later, when they were safely under tow, Stephen found Juliette on deck, her arms around the boys' shoulders. She had dressed them in velvet coats—totally unsuitable for the colonies, he thought—and had taken pains to dress and groom herself faultlessly. Her hands had trembled as she fastened the pearl brooch at her throat; he had almost blurted out the joking remark that she looked as though she were going to her own execution but had stopped himself in time.

Tempering his jubilant mood so that it would not highlight her apprehension, he approached them, saying, "Don't you think Auckland has changed, Sweet Olivine? In the name of Jove, I declare it's more like Liverpool or Pittsburgh than the quiet backwater I remember. Steam power, soot, and smoke. There seems to be no escaping them anywhere these days."

Juliette did not reply, but the boys took advantage of the moment to wriggle free and dash away. Taking his wife's limp arm, Stephen continued conversationally, "Official Bay looks unchanged, don't you think? I recall most of those houses, and with a little effort I could probably tell

42

you who built them." A glance at Juliette's face confirmed his suspicions. She was staring coldly at an imposing Oriental-looking house on the ridge beyond. Fintona. His mother's house. It, too, had not altered: The trees had grown up and vines had a sturdier grip on the veranda but otherwise, it appeared exactly as it had that morning years ago when they had left, supposedly forever.

"Still the same old place," he said, struggling to sound disinterested. He was so elated to be home that it was impossible to disguise his joy. "There's Saint Paul's. And the Northern Club. I must renew my membership—if they'll have me back! And there's the windmill. Now what was it called? Partington's. That's it." He stopped. Juliette's arm was quivering.

Alarmed, he said, "Please, Sweet Olivine. It won't be so bad. When you were here before, you didn't have me by your side."

She shook her head. "You don't understand. I dreamed about Maire . . . dreamed about her funeral. When I woke up, I prayed it was an omen. I wished her dead, Stephen."

The flicker of shock was brief and swiftly smothered. "Dreams and wishes don't matter. What does matter is that Mama must not be able to see your tears. You do realize that she's probably in that hideous Turkish study of hers, peering at us right this instant through her spyglass." Putting an arm about her waist, he waved mockingly with his free hand. "Hello there, Mama."

"Don't," begged Juliette, but her spine stiffened, and she raised her chin with determination, putting on a creditable imitation of a smile.

Farther along the deck May was saying, "It would have been so much more fun to have had Hal here to introduce us to our other cousins. We missed him by only one week, and now we must wait at least six months before he returns."

Daniel was staring at the brown volcanic cones that served as a backdrop to the sprawling red, green, and white town. All the cones had blunt ridges that rose like steps up their sides. "P-Professor Wood told me that ancient Maori tribes cut the hills to that shape. They set pointed logs in rows above every ditch to make fortifications to repel enemy warriors. He says that they d-did all that using only stone tools and wooden spades. It's incredible."

"They look like a row of gigantic copper jelly molds. Don't you think they would make an intersting photograph?"

"Everything you see would m-make an interesting photograph, it seems." Idly he watched as dozens of women in servants' uniforms hurried from a ferryboat and along a spindle-legged jetty. The air was so clear that scraps of chatter and laughter reached the ship. Daniel said, "This is an ugly little place: all factory chimneys and garish signs."

"It's quaint. Quaint and picturesque." She read some signs. "Snow White Steam Laundry. Ritchie's Steam-Powered Hat Factory. Hugglesworth Steam Printing Works. Everything is run on steam. And by Maoris, I shouldn't wonder. Have you noticed that all the small vessels we've seen have Maori crews and most of them ornately tattooed?"

Daniel smiled at her expression. She, too, had seen the cutter manned by almost naked men with indigo whorls adorning thighs and buttocks. She'd not want to photograph *that.* He said, "Father told me that almost half the coastal shipping is owned by Maoris and that these c-canoes are bringing fruit and vegetables to sell in the Auckland markets."

"There was a whole flotilla of canoes outside the harbor riding the swells while the Maoris fished. I thought at the time that—"

"They would m-make a perfectly splendid photograph!"

"Am I so very tiresome?"

He shrugged and said, "I wonder who will be at the wharf to meet us?"

"Wouldn't it be marvelous if all our relatives were there? All those cousins we've heard so much about? Ellen and Lena and Kendrick, Jon and Dora, and—"

"And bouquets and a b-brass band. Didn't you know that Father asked to keep our arrival quiet on account of Mother's feelings? Do you know why she is so upset about coming back here?"

44

"Not really, but I intend to find out when I get a chance to talk to our cousins. There's no need to look shocked either. I'm not being sneaky. Just because Mother can't bring herself to talk about it doesn't mean that she would forbid us from finding out. Does it?"

At this early hour the port was quiet. A few Maoris with handcarts watched as the *Mondrich Arrow* was maneuvered into place alongside other ships at the wharf. Two Maori women with black coats and head scarves sat hunched in a doorway, silently smoking pipes. Outside the Mondrich Line Chandlery Shop were three waiting vehicles—a closed victoria, a large coach with a blue sign, Auckland Hire Stables, and a spring cart.

"We're here, we're here," said May, wishing that Hal were standing on the wharf. "I wonder if—" she broke off with a squeak of pain as Albert collided with her.

"Let me go!" He was brown after the voyage, the scars no more than tiny white ridges. He broke free and dashed away, with Edward shouting in pursuit.

May glanced after them in annoyance and then noticed that her mother was coming toward her, leaning on the arm of a white-haired man in a rumpled suit who walked with an odd dragging limp. When they were closer, she noticed that he had tobacco-colored skin, puckered like dry leaves.

"Uncle Samuel?"

His pale blue eyes regarded her gravely. "You couldn't possibly remember me. What a tiny little dot you were then."

"Mother has told me how kind you used to be and how I adored you. I have been looking forward to meeting you again."

"And I to meeting you." He had a thickly accented voice. "Hal told me that your portraits do not do you justice. He was right." She was hoping he would say more about Hal, but he turned to Juliette. "I suppose you are anxious to see the house? My wife and I had planned to have it all prepared—the luggage unpacked, the furniture arranged —all the things servants cannot do. But she took sick again, so—"

45

"Your wife? Your *wife?* Oh, Samuel!"

He looked pleased and bashful. May guessed that he had waited for the right moment to break the news.

"A wife after all these years? We had given up hope. . . ."

"I'm glad you're pleased. I fear it will not be a popular move with the others. Abby doesn't know yet, but when—"

"Never mind what she thinks!" Juliette kissed his cheek. "Who is your bride? Do I know of her?"

"Perhaps. I've married Rosaleen Teipa." He looked away. "When Jack Bennington died, she was alone and ill. I proposed, and she accepted me."

"You've loved her for years, haven't you? Ever since that day at the races—how long ago was that? Twenty years?"

"Not quite. I tried to get her to marry me then, but Jack was good to her—he was always good to her—and she'd not leave him on account of the boy. Jack doted on young Patrick. Tried to do right by him all his life, even adopted him legally and set him up in business before he died. I'd not tell Abby that if I were you, but if you like, you can break the news to her about the marriage. It will be easier if it comes from you."

"Highly unlikely. But I doubt whether our paths will cross."

"They will cross much sooner than you think." When he grinned, May noticed that he had bare gums. "Abby will be out to pay a visit the minute she senses you've arrived. She wants to sell the land around Whenuahakari, and she can, provided one of us agrees to her plan. She'll be visiting, and she'll be as sweet as nectar, trying to persuade you, for she's failed completely with me. Yes, she's even had poor old Mr. McLeay writing me stiff letters on the subject."

"The same old Mr. McLeay? Grandmaire's lawyer?"

"He's waiting in the victoria with letters for you and Stephen. Grandmaire is hopping about like a hen on a hot perch trying to prevent Stephen's takeover of the Richmond Line."

"So we didn't arrive in secret after all."

"They didn't know you'd be on this ship, but they are expecting you. Either Mr. McLeay or his assistant, Vincent

46

Opal, have been meeting every vessel from San Francisco for these past weeks. They'll be relieved to see you at last."

"I can hardly say it has been an uneventful arrival. Oh, Samuel. I'm delighted for you. And I'm so glad you'll be living close by."

"Stephen said that you dreaded coming back to Auckland."

"Seeing you has heartened me considerably. I remember what a true friend you were when I desperately needed someone to help me. I need you again now."

"Not as much as you may imagine. You have a lot of warm support here, you know. And even if Abby or Grandmaire proves awkward, it will be interesting."

Very interesting, thought May. She wondered what this Patrick was like, this paragon whom Jack Bennington had preferred to Hal or his other legitimate sons. To her, he sounded like a priggish and arrogant usurper. Recalling Hal's violent reaction to her unthinking mention of his name, May decided that she disliked the young man already.

Five

Everybody who saw Mondrich House found something to admire in it and also something to criticize, Samuel told them as the hired coach drove them along the inland route to their new home. If the Indian cupolas found favor, then the Maori patterns on the balustrades did not please. People who admired the gatehouse disliked the gazebo, and those who raved about the frosted glass in the conservatory inevitably found the emerald floor tiles too gaudy.

"But I have tried to please you all, and I've enjoyed the task. In truth, I was sorry to see the house finished. This is the longest I've lived in the city since I broke my leg under a rolling log."

May listened while she stared at the passing scene. The description *city* dismayed her, for this drab, rural place was nothing like beautiful San Francisco, and already she was beginning to appreciate her mother's reluctance to return. The main business area was disappointing—a wide, dusty street, and expanse across which a quaintly odd assortment of brick, stone, and unpainted wooden buildings faced each other, like armies squared off with shields raised. Then came a bleak suburb where rows of identical box-shaped houses stood shoulder to shoulder in squares of tan weeds. Only when they were beyond that did the scenery give way to a more "select" area, where individually designed houses were screened behind gardens and a feeling of graciousness prevailed. May watched silently, while beside her the young boys fidgeted, not daring to talk under their father's stern gaze. In the corner Daniel was hunched and silent. He had lost a lot of weight on the voyage.

"Auckland has changed in many ways," said Samuel. "Money sets the pace now that the government has moved to Wellington, and there's plenty of money thanks to the Thames gold fields. Gold was Jack Bennington's undoing, of course. He went down along with a hefty gold cargo he'd purchased. A gambler, he was. Nobody knows how much he lost in that last fatal speculation."

"I do hope that Abigail was left properly provided for," said Juliette. "It would be dreadful if she had to scrape to make do."

"Scrape? Lordy, no, she'd never scrape. As extravagant as ever, she is. Would make a dent in the queen's own fortune if she were given the chance to try. But you should be warned that she's always crying poor. I've never had one conversation when she's not suggested I give her some of my money instead of buying more land with it."

"Why *do* you need so much of it?" asked Stephen, amused.

"To stop it from being desecrated. When you go inland, you'll see what I mean. Or even here." They were traveling through farm country now, where wooden-railed pens marked off muddy enclosures for pigs and where Indian corn grew dark and lustrous. Maori children playing at the roadsides waved and pulled faces. Their dogs ran beside the coach, barking.

Samuel said, "This was fern country, but inland the beautiful forests are gone and the land is strewn with blackened logs."

"People have to farm, old boy," said Stephen. "The settlers have to earn their living somehow."

"But the country is overrun. When your family and mine lived in the Bay of Islands in the thirties, there were fewer than two thousand of us in the whole of New Zealand. I hear that now there are more than half a million, and hundreds more pouring off every ship. We outnumber the Maoris by a dozen to one, and I fear that in a few years the whole country will be an imitation England."

"Is that so bad?"

"It would be terrible. I loved the land when it was cloaked with bush and the air was thick with birdsong."

"You sound just the way Father used to," said Juliette. "Our Governor Grey said he was more Maori than pakeha."

"Which thrilled Grandmaire." May noticed that like Hal, he pronounced it Granmaree. "Fortunately Patrick shares my sympathy for the land. He's a fine lad, that. He's inherited the best of both Maori and pakeha blood and has a feeling for both cultures and one of the sharpest business minds in Auckland."

May's resentment built steadily. No wonder Hal exhibited rage at the sound of Patrick's name—she was irritated by it already, and she'd never met him. Nor would she want to. He was probably tatooed all over with white-tipped feathers skewering a frizzy topknot and the scantiest of loincloths for a garment. There, she had pictured him and now could dismiss him.

Stephen must have been sated with news of Patrick, too, for he said, "And how is my mother keeping?"

"Hale and hearty. Everyone calls her Grandmaire now, except the newspapers, which keep to Mrs. Yardley Peridot. She's gained weight, and in her widow's cap with the long streamers she looks uncannily like a well-known royal lady. Children point at her and shout, 'There's the queen!' "

Stephen laughed and slapped his knee, while Juliette changed the subject by saying, "Will your wife be meeting us at the house?"

"Unfortunately, no. Her health restricts her to a quiet life of reading, sewing, or sitting in the garden. Patrick tries to keep her company when he can, and she says he's better than any number of nurses. Dr. Forster comes every day, though little can be done for her. Consumption is an evil thing."

Consumption! Juliette drew back, her plans for socializing dropped instantly. Consumption was rumored to be fearfully contagious. The children must be forbidden to go near. May's weakness made her susceptible, and if anything happened to the boys, she would never forgive herself. Juliette felt like crying. They had been in New

Zealand less than an hour, and already problems were casting their shadows.

They were nearly there, rumbling across open country where expanses of crinkly brown fern dipped and rose to allow glimpses of the sea. Samuel leaned across to tell May that if she looked along the road as they rounded the next bend, she should be able to see their new home in the distance. Obediently she was staring across a gully of feathery tree ferns to where a hillock rose in a crumbly slope away from the road when a sharp movement snagged her attention. It must have been a mane tossing, for when she looked up, there was a young man on horseback. At first glance she thought of Hal, but that impression faded at once because this young man's face was lean and finely boned, not square and open like Hal's. There was a haughty precision in the way he paused with the reins gathered loosely into gloved hands, and May studied him with interest. Cashmere jacket, silk cravat, embroidered waistcoat—and was that a university cap? New Zealand *was* up with the latest styles then. As the coach turned the corner, she twisted her neck to keep him in view, thinking what a striking photograph he would make, posed like that, when to her horror he smiled and swept the cap from his head in a parody of a salute.

Why, I'm gaping like a shopgirl, she realized, and jerked her shoulder away from the window ledge. Aware that her uncle was watching her, she said, "A man on horseback was staring at us."

"What did he look like? Young and well dressed?"

She nodded.

"That will be Kendrick. He'll make haste back to Fintona and tell Grandmaire you're here. No doubt Abby will be there, too." To Juliette he said, "That Kendrick is spoiled hopelessly. Abby ruins him the way you ruined young Leigh. He's a charmer, just like young Leigh; but he's inherited his father's gambling streak, and he's not averse to spending time in the taverns. I hear that three public houses in Queen Street have silver tankards engraved with his name. He'd be the same age as Daniel here. I say, you still look seasick, lad. Nobody would believe that a genuine seadog like Stephen could have a

51

landlubber for a son. Never mind, lad. I'm scared of the sea meself, I don't mind admitting it. Never go out in a rowboat if I can help it."

Later May whispered to her father, "I do like Uncle Samuel. His mannerisms are rough, and he looks funny when he smiles; but he does have a warm heart."

"He's a decent fellow," was the reply, but then his voice cooled to the tone he used when disapproving of Daniel. "But he talks too much."

Despite predictions that Abby would be their first visitor, the morning brought, instead, Dr. Adrian Forster, Stephen's brother-in-law. With him came his eighteen-year-old daughter, Ellen, and Mrs. Rugmore, the doctor's elderly sister. Rose Yardley Forster did not come. Like other Victorian ladies who wished to escape from certain harsh aspects of life, Rose had taken to her couch after Ellen's birth and left it only for formal occasions.

When they arrived, Juliette was down at the beach with the young boys, Stephen in town on business and Daniel in the stables tending Te Kooti, who had enjoyed the voyage much more than his master. May abandoned her packing and hurried downstairs to find two women in the hall, a strikingly tall, slender young woman standing aloof from a contrastingly tiny person who was rummaging in a tea chest of knickknacks, loudly exclaiming over each treasure she brought to light.

"Do look at this plaque, Ellen! How like dear Pindleton—isn't it a charming scene? That church spire, those elms, that humpbacked bridge! Ah, for a glimpse of such beauty in this savage land."

"You are not going to cry again, are you, Aunt?" said Ellen in a bored tone. Instead of looking at the plaque, she gazed out into the driveway where their dogcart waited and fanned herself with a broad-brimmed hat as if anxious to get away.

"Do look at these English wild flowers, Ellen! Pressed under glass just as I used to preserve the blossoms I gathered from the fields around Pindleton. Why, my dear!" And quite unfazed at being caught snooping, she came forward, peering at May through her wire-rimmed glasses.

52

"They are actually Himalayan mountain flowers which Father himself collected," explained May. "Most of these things are souvenirs of his adventures."

"Uncle Stephen has been everywhere," said Ellen in the same bored tones. "He even witnessed Blondin's tightrope walk over Niagara, is that not so? I am Ellen Forster, and this is my aunt and chaperone, Mrs. Rugmore." With that she held out a thin silk-gloved hand for a limp handshake.

May, introducing herself, was thinking that her cousin's entire effect was one of blasé disinterest. She was like a sagging vine held up only by the tight black clothes she wore. Her eyes were narrow and green, limpid, like the rest of her, and her full, almost puffy lips seemed to hint at a sullen nature.

"Father is attending Mrs. Peridot, so we came on ahead."

"How splendid," said May, infusing as much warmth into her tones as she could. "I shall send for Mother. She will be eager to make your acquaintance, Mrs. Rugmore, and you can help me with my unpacking, Ellen. It is such a tedious chore that someone to talk to will be more than welcome."

Ellen followed languidly, but once in May's room, she settled herself on the bureau stool and examined the objects in front of her with just as much curiosity as Mrs. Rugmore had displayed. Every item was disguised as something else. Scent bottles masqueraded as vases, hairpin boxes looked like painted eggs, and upended porcelain parasols contained hatpins.

Putting down a silver hand that was, in fact, a ring tree, Ellen said, "You and I are nothing alike."

"Who said we were?"

"Uncle Samuel, when we called in with Father. He said we were almost identical, but I fancy that we have nothing in common at all. Except Yardley blood. You do know that Captain Yardley is not your real father?"

"Of course I know," said May, thinking: Already! Here, already, is someone who will tell me what I want to know. "My father was Leigh Yardley, wasn't he? I suppose you know all about him?"

"I suppose I do." She pursed her lips, looking at them in a small hand mirror.

"Will you tell me his story?"

"His story?"

"Oh, you must know what I mean! All about him, what he looked like, *was* like . . . how he met Mother . . . everything!"

A strange expression came into Ellen's eyes, and her face softened with the hint of a smile. "I never gossip."

"Why not?" cried May.

"Mama insists that I repeat only what I know to be accurate, and since I never pay full attention to anything, I am never certain which details I have heard and which I have imagined. Grandmaire knows all about it. She should. Both your father and Uncle Stephen are her sons."

"I should love to meet Grandmaire! I hope I can before too long. She has always seemed like a legend to me. Mysterious and intriguing."

"She is intriguing all right." Ellen's lips twitched. "Would you like to go to Fintona? We could go riding and just happen by. Tomorrow, would that suit you?"

"I'm not sure . . ."

"Don't you want to meet your cousins? Aunt Abigail's children are always there. Dora lives there with her, and the others are forever visiting. Grandmaire treats them like her own family, although they're not, of course. I am her only true grandchild, apart from your family."

Is she jealous? wondered May. She said, "I'd love to meet them. So will Daniel. I'll ask Mother's permission."

"No. Don't do that," drawled Ellen. "We'll just go riding. That will make it more interesting. I like intrigues, too."

Juliette said, "Ellen seems a pleasant young woman. Did you like her?"

"Yes, I did. And I hope we'll be friends." She added guiltily, "We are going riding together. Daniel, too."

"That will be nice," said Juliette with such an approving smile that May felt even guiltier. "If she brings her chaperone, then Mrs. Rugmore can stay and help me ar-

54

range a nursery-classroom for the boys. She appreciates a fresh audience for her reminiscences of Pindleton."

"Isn't she tiresome! At afternoon teatime I counted, and in the space of ten minutes she uttered the word *Pindleton* no less than fifty-seven times."

"I sympathize with her. The colonies are full of lonely old folk like Mrs. Rugmore who long to go home but have not the money or perhaps the courage to do so and whose minds are full of memories that interest nobody but themselves." She paused with a powder bowl half unwrapped in her hands and a sad expression on her face.

"You miss San Francisco, don't you?" asked May.

Juliette shook herself. "Yes, but I'm determined not to mope. It's curious, but I have the strongest feeling—an instinct, almost—that I shouldn't be here. That something terrible is going to happen. Don't look alarmed. It's probably simply a mixture of old age and dread."

"You're not old." May had always been proud of how young Juliette seemed, especially when compared with the other San Francisco matrons.

"Thank you, dear." She hugged her daughter.

May said, "I understand if you feel homesick. It's very interesting here, but every once in a while I stop short, seized by such a painful longing to be home again. The flavor of this place seems wrong, alien somehow. I don't belong here."

"You'll soon make friends."

"And so will you, Mother." She was going to add, And please don't worry about Grandmaire, but the feeling of guilty betrayal rose again, choking the words in her throat.

Juliette, polishing the powder bowl, noticed nothing amiss.

By midmorning May's excitement had curdled into nervousness at the prospect of meeting so many of her new relatives at once. Would they notice that her riding bonnet was crushed from being packed or that her jacket smelled faintly of mold? Would they be friendly or aloof and watchful like Ellen? Should she wear jewelry and risk being thought ostentatious or none and appear patronizing? As she rummaged in her trinket casket, she found an old

55

locket brooch containing a faded ambrotype portrait of Hal. She opened it; the picture had always been too small and blurred to be a satisfying memento, but she had worn it often over the years, telling herself it brought good luck. Impulsively she pinned it to her collar.

Stephen was greeting a party of top-hatted businessmen in the front hall as May, Ellen, and Daniel emerged from the morning room, ready for their ride. He called his son aside.

"Have you finished copying those confidential documents I left in your room?"

"N-Not yet, Father. I—"

"I shall need them for a meeting tomorrow. Perhaps you should stay—"

"Oh, please, Father. They are expecting me. Kendrick is—" He stopped, confused.

"This little ride is not going to happen by Fintona, is it, by any chance?" When Daniel blushed, hanging his head, Stephen laughed and clapped him on the shoulder. "Then be sure to tell my mother that I send her best wishes. We cannot give her the satisfaction of thinking you are there without my consent. Off you go then. And be sure not to forget."

Breaking his neck to meet Kendrick, thought Stephen, shaking his head. Though the lad sounded like trouble, in fairness it must be admitted that Samuel was extravagant with his exaggeration. And an adventurous young rogue might be what Daniel needed—he couldn't be worse than the milksops he had kept company with in San Francisco.

Daniel ran to the stables and found May already mounted on Negus; Bobby Terrill helped Ellen into the saddle of an elderly dappled mare.

May patted Negus's neck. "He's still very restive, though he should be used to long sea voyages by now," she said. "It's less than two years since he traveled all the way from Valparaiso. Father bought him at auction. It was so amusing. Mother asked for a quiet pony for the boys, and he came home with Negus instead. He and I fell in love, and they had to let me ride after that."

"Dolly was given to me eight years ago. She's plain, but I have no prospect of owning anything more spirited."

Hearing the sour tone, May could have kicked herself. She knew that Ellen was poor, that since Dr. Forster's retirement he accepted only "special favor" patients who brought in less income than his other string, phrenology readings. When the Richmond Line prospered, Aunt Rose's ten percent shareholding allowed some luxuries, but those once-lucrative shares were almost worthless.

Sensing pity, Ellen lifted her chin. Her face was tight behind her veil. "Father is going into trade soon on his own account, did you know that? He is speculating on wool, buying cargoes here for resale in Europe." But having said that, she seemed to regret the confidence, for she said, "Have you seen the fencible cottages yet?"

"Mother has put them out of bounds," said Daniel, coming up alongside.

"For goodness' sake, why? They are over there, behind that macrocarpa hedge. That smoke is from your uncle Samuel's chimney, and beyond is the disused cottage. It is filled with old junk. All manner of things. I sometimes wait there when Father is visiting Mrs. Peridot."

"What are they like?" asked May.

"They?"

"Mrs. Peridot and—"

"Patrick? She is a Maori, and he's an untouchable. He owns a *brewery*. All that expensive overseas education, and that's all he's fit for. Mind you, Hal says, 'Scrape a Maori, any Maori, and the savage shows underneath.' "

She sounds just like Hal, thought May, wondering why Ellen hated Patrick so much. She was about to ask when Ellen said, "I'd not mention Patrick to any of the Benningtons. He's a touchy subject with them, but never mind why. And don't mention Uncle Samuel's marriage. Grandmaire knows—she always knows everything—but your aunt Abigail must be kept in ignorance."

"If you say so." Auckland was seething with secrets, it seemed.

Ellen squinted up at the sky. "Grandmaire will be wondering what has happened to us. Let's take a shortcut along the beach."

Out of consideration to Ellen's mount May kept Negus reined in to a trot, but the coastline was so pretty that she was glad of the opportunity to admire it. Creamy sandstone cliffs were crowned by huge pohutukawa trees, which clung for support with twisted ancient roots. The scarlet-mottled branches were like Christmas colored parasols, while under them, on the sand, fallen petals made blood-colored shadows. At the edge of the sea, where hooves cut scallops into the sand, the water was edged with an antique embroidery of foam.

"There it is," said Ellen, urging Dolly toward a sloping path.

May and Daniel followed to where a wide-verandaed house sat in a spread apron of flower-edged lawn. A Maori girl in a white uniform was beating mats on a line near the stables. She stared at the three and jabbered to some Maori boys, who skipped over to help them dismount.

"All Grandmaire's servants are Maoris," explained Ellen, leading her cousins to the front door. "This is Tawa," she said as a stout woman with smudged indigo chin tattoos and a rustling violet dress opened the door. "Tawa is Grandmaire's housekeeper."

"For forty years, Miss Ellen. Since I was a wee *tama-hine,*" said Tawa in Uncle Samuel's thick accents. Her dull black hair was piled on top of her head and fastened with wide shell combs the same shiny yellow color as her teeth. She said, "Come this way. *Matua,* she been waiting for you." And she waddled ahead, along a dim corridor.

Ellen said, "Lena's and Kendrick's horses are outside. You'll meet three Benningtons today."

"That will leave only Jon. He's twenty-five, isn't he? I expect he's busy with business."

"Politics now, I think," said Ellen. "He's very ambitious."

"And Hal I know, of course," prattled May. "I do wish he could be here today. What a shame we missed him."

Ellen did not reply. May wondered if she imagined the cold glance her cousin gave her.

Fintona was one of Auckland's original grand homesteads. May knew that Grandfather Thomas Peridot, Grandmaire's second husband, had been an avid collector of Maori artifacts. Here both walls were lined with feather

58

cloaks, grotesquely carved panels, and paintings of richly tattooed chiefs, many in wing collars and frock coats.

Grandmaire was holding court in the morning room, where rattan furniture was arranged on fine flax mats. In contrast with the native atmosphere, the tea trolley was pure England, set with a silver teapot, rose-patterned cups, and crystal cake stands.

When they came in, Grandmaire held up her beringed hands in pretended surprise and cried, "Ellen, dear! You bring me guests. How delightful!"

May was first. "Grandmaire," she murmured, leaning to kiss a soft cheek that smelled of powder. When she stood back, the old woman was scrutinizing her, taking her measure, so May stared candidly back, noting the wealth of resemblances to her father and to Daniel (around the chin and mouth) and especially an overwhelming likeness to Ellen. Grandmaire was strikingly handsome, with an obvious vanity revealed in the dramatic hairstyle, with wings of white hair pulled back imperiously, and in the discreet makeup and extravagance of jet jewelry.

She's cold, thought May. And she doesn't like me at all. I can see that. I'm glad I don't look like her.

As if in answer to that thought, Grandmaire sucked in her chest and announced, "You look like Leigh. He took after Richmond, his dear father."

Then she turned to Daniel, and her face thawed.

While Grandmaire questioned him, fussing over him and patiently ignoring his stammering awkwardness, May sipped her tea and smiled nervously at her Bennington cousins, hoping that they would like her better than Grandmaire seemed to.

Dora, a woman of about thirty, was sitting beside Ellen. She had lived at Fintona as Grandmaire's companion since she was a child and was a drab, beaten-looking figure with a doughy face and ceaselessly working hands. From her waist hung a Singapore cricket cage in which a ball of green wool tumbled as she crocheted. When she glanced up, May smiled at her. Dora hesitated for a few seconds before smiling briefly in reply. I'll ask her about that mourning brooch she's wearing, thought May. Perhaps it's her —and Hal's—father.

In contrast with their sullen sister the younger Benningtons smiled almost constantly. Lena was almost nineteen—May knew that her birthday was within a week of her own—and she looked invitingly friendly. She had pale skin splashed with freckles and frizzy hair the color of powdered ginger.

Beside her sat sixteen-year-old Kendrick, a neckless youth with prominent eyes and dark hair slicked flat to his scalp. May thought he looked like a ventriloquist's dummy and was disappointed to discover that he was not, after all, her aristocratic horseman.

Grandmaire had had Daniel draw up a chair beside her own thronelike seat. She was patting his hands and leaning toward him, saying, "I recall your dear mother well. Such a charming, beautiful woman she was. It was a tragedy when she died. I have never seen Stephen so distraught. I feared that we could never comfort him. If she were alive today . . ."

May cut in loudly, "Then Father would not be married to Mother, would he?" The reason behind Grandmaire's rejection of her was so clear now that she wondered why she had not seen it immediately.

Daniel flushed in embarrassment. He was enjoying the attention, though the last remarks of Grandmaire's had made him uncomfortable. Juliette had been a loving and generous mother to him, so much so that he had never regretted not knowing his true mother.

Kendrick was hooting with laughter. "Bravo! Well spoken, Cousin May. Aunt Juliette is going to make things interesting for all of us, one way or another."

Grandmaire's age-hooded eyes studied May. "I was mistaken. You are very like your mother, dear."

"Why, thank you, Grandmaire."

"That was not a compliment."

"With your permission, I beg to differ."

The old woman sucked in the pouches on her cheeks, then unexpectedly laughed. "Leigh was weak in many unfortunate ways, but he was my most beloved child." She rapped a buffed nail against the locket brooch. "This secret that you carry above your heart, is it a picture of Leigh perhaps?"

"No."

"Of course it must be. Don't blush, child. Let me see." And she snapped her fingers.

"G-Give it to her," whispered Daniel.

"It has no significance," said May, unpinning it. "I wear it for good luck."

"Hal! Well, well, and this is interesting."

Conscious that everybody's gaze had switched toward her, May said, "It really has no significance . . . I've not seen Hal for years."

Kendrick exploded with laughter. "What a turnup! Our beautiful cousin is wearing Hal's picture. What a turnup!"

"Do be quiet, Kendrick," snapped Ellen. Her tanned skin had taken on a greenish hue, and she looked furious.

Grandmaire reached out toward Ellen. "There now. Don't upset yourself. If the picture has no significance, we must replace it with a better one. Dora, my album please. Ellen"—she prized out the oval portrait and thrust it toward her—"you take this for safekeeping. Now then, miss. You would like a photograph of Leigh, wouldn't you?"

"I'd love one. I don't even know what he looks like. . . ." She watched expectantly as Dora set a brass-bound album in front of Grandmaire, who then unlocked it with a key from her chatelaine. A treasury of family secrets, and soon she would be sharing them.

But instead of raising the cover, Grandmaire said, "Kendrick, take your cousin into the garden, and make friends with him. Firm friends and no mischief, is that clear?"

"Mischief, Grandmaire? But I am a perfect saint, especially on Sunday mornings when I accompany Mama to mass."

"Aye, and be making up for it the rest of the week."

"Not fair. All the bad hats in Auckland cannot be hung on me."

"Out, shoo. Lena, show May the roses. Ellen, stay here. Dora, my room, please."

As soon as they were clear of the veranda, Lena whispered, "Grandmaire often has to excuse herself. It's her bladder, you see. She cannot go more than a short time without—"

"Oh," said May, thinking that Ellen had not exaggerated when she said that Lena would gossip on any subject at all. She said, "Why did my picture of Hal cause a stir?"

"Stir? It caused a sensation!" When Lena talked, her features worked energetically. "Ellen would never have mentioned Hal, but you should know. She loves him."

"Does he love her?" whispered May.

"Oh, they have an understanding," said Lena, blithely unaware of the pain her words were causing. "It's mostly on Ellen's side. She won't go to any social occasion unless he is her escort."

"Then they are engaged?"

"Not at all. He's fond of her and gentlemanly in his attitude, but just between us, he was most disappointed, *most*, that he was not here to greet you when you arrived. I say, won't it be fun if Hal falls in love with you? Grandmaire would be beside herself."

"What has she to do with it?"

Lena looked astonished. "Everybody is mindful of Grandmaire's wishes, and Grandmaire tries to make sure that Ellen gets everything she wants. She cannot give her expensive gifts because Aunt Rose won't permit that, so she makes up to her in other ways. And Ellen wants Hal." She laughed, a tiny, infectious laugh that failed to lift May's spirits. "What fun this will be! Hal *will* fall in love with you—I don't see how he will be able to resist your beauty, though in all frankness I think *you* could do better. He has a bad temper, and he cares about nothing but ships; but sisters have a myopic view of their brothers, so don't mind my opinion. I say, it is fun to meet you. Ellen spent *hours* yesterday describing your home to Grandmaire. She's so envious of you."

"Is she? I'm sorry to hear that."

Lena patted her hand. She was wearing bright pink mittens that did not suit her freckled skin. "Ellen is envious of everybody. Kendrick says that she studies everyone she meets, searching for some trait or possession she can envy. And you are especially interesting to her because you are Aunt Juliette's daughter, and you know what *that* means!"

"Do tell me." She took Lena's arm and said earnestly,

"Will you tell me all about the family feuds, or troubles, or whatever they are? I'm especially anxious to find out all about my real father, and nobody—"

"There's the bell. We had best go in now. Grandmaire can't abide waiting. She will tell you about your father if you ask her." She laughed. "I'd tell you if I knew, but I'm only aware of who hates whom, not why."

However, not only did Grandmaire refuse to be led on the subject of Leigh, but she had also tired of their company and dismissed them as soon as the locket had been pinned back on. The atmosphere seemed strained, and it was even worse on the way home.

This is ridiculous, thought May, as Ellen rode, tight-faced and unfriendly, beside her. Ellen has no more claim on Hal than I do, and I shan't apologize for carrying his picture.

But her resolve melted when they arrived at Mondrich House. Without looking at May, Ellen took the oval ambrotype from her waist purse and said, "This is yours."

"Oh, Ellen, please . . ."

"Rich people think that the world revolves solely for their benefit," she said coldly. When May did not move, she let the picture flutter to the ground and strode off toward the house.

May stumbled after her. "You must understand. For years Hal was the only cousin I knew. Daniel and I both worshiped him."

Ellen lifted the veil from her face. "That was years ago. He was a youth then. Now he is a grown man, and I know him well. You are no more than a stranger."

May bit back a hot protest. Hal would never be a stranger to her.

"Everybody favors our match. Everybody."

"Then, when you do become engaged, I shall be pleased to offer my congratulations."

The corners of her mouth tightened. "You are my rival. Is that what you are saying?"

"I don't know what I'm saying, except that this is ludicrous. Please don't quarrel with me. I've been looking forward to being your friend for so long. Let's not spoil it by quarreling."

"Quarrels are demeaning. I never quarrel."

This time May did not try to follow.

Daniel cantered to the fence and swung down from the saddle. He was flushed and excited, his butter-colored hair damp from exertion. "That K-Kendrick is a card! He's been arrested twice already; but Grandmaire pays the fines, and he goes free. She's a grand old lady, isn't she?"

Stooping to retrieve the picture, May said, "I imagine she is unique." Glancing at her brother's glowing face, she thought: In one hour today he's received more praise and approval than in the last six months. With warmth she said, "I'm glad she likes you."

"Good. I was afraid you might be jealous."

Hal's picture was sharp and cold in her palm. "I hope I never know what jealousy feels like. It is the ugliest most destructive, strangling force. . . ."

"You sound morbid."

"I'm homesick for San Francisco, I think. I always knew how I would feel about everything there. Here, everything is mysterious and uncertain."

"You do d-dramatize! Is this because Grandmaire wouldn't tell you about your father?"

"Yes, I suppose so. And I wonder why she wouldn't give me back the locket until I promised not to tell about it. What reason could she possibly have?"

Daniel shrugged. "Perhaps she j-just enjoys scheming."

It was not until late that evening that May had an opportunity to examine the new picture. Holding the locket close to her lamp globe, she stared at the tiny image of a young man—an impossibly young man—in uniform. Could this be he, this *boy* whose youthfulness was paradoxically accentuated by a full beard that obscured the lower half of his face? "Father," she whispered, staring at the grave dark eyes. "Father, my own father." But though she concentrated fiercely, the image failed to stir any emotions. All she could see was a sad little portrait of an anonymous soldier who had died almost before his life had really begun.

May replaced Hal's picture in her locket and was pressing an affectionate kiss onto his cheek with the tip of her

64

little finger when Juliette tapped on the door and looked in. She seemed disturbed.

"Daniel tells me that you went to Fintona today."

May flushed with sudden guilt. "I'm sorry I didn't tell you, but we went on impulse, and it *was* very pleasant. Some of our cousins were there. I hope you don't mind—"

"I mind, but I accept the situation. You must feel free to go wherever you please. Is that the old locket with Hal's picture? Did you wear it?"

"And it caused an upset. It appears that Ellen plans to marry Hal. And with Grandmaire's full consent."

Juliette said, "Perhaps they suit each other." Her voice softened as she continued. "You are very young, dear. And you have an idealistic picture of Hal. An unreal picture."

May's fingers fastened over the locket. "I *care* about him."

"So you should. He is your cousin after all." Juliette's lips brushed her brow. May could smell the bittersweet rose perfume that she wore. "Perhaps it is time that you gave up wearing childish lockets."

Not now, thought May when her mother had gone. She lifted out Hal's picture and stared at Leigh once again, but still, she was disappointed. Not the slightest breath of emotion stirred within her. "Father," she said sadly. "Father, please. . . ."

Six

Daniel and May came out as soon as they heard the carriage, but though they leaned over the upstairs balcony and waved, Lena and Kendrick disappeared onto the porch without seeing them.

"Wait," said May, for Daniel was going to rush away to greet them. "There's somebody else."

The driver was helping a portly man from the coach. He had a florid complexion and a bristly, paintbrush beard, and he stood in the drive, his billycock hat tipped back while he stared at the house.

"Look . . . that must be Aunt Abigail. Gracious, isn't she enormous!" whispered May as a woman dressed in tight lilac satin swayed on the folding steps. Glossy ringlets bounced behind her shiny pillbox hat, and a pastel veil hovered like smoke around her face.

"Kendrick s-said her gowns always seem on the point of exploding."

"He is wicked to say that about his mother." But she had to smile at the accuracy of the observation. "And who is the gentleman? Aunt Abigail's lawyer, I suppose. Poor Father. He has had to receive so many lawyers from Grandmaire that he is heartily sick of them."

"That might be Mr. Kine. D-Derwent Kine. He once whipped a man to death, so Kendrick says."

"Whatever for?"

Daniel looked uneasy. "He didn't say."

"He must have told you why—" but Daniel had fled.

"It was probably in a duel," said Lena later as she postured before May's dress mirror, a hat clustered with poppies on her head. "Mr. Kine often fights duels. He wants to marry Mama, did you know? I don't like the man, but I should be grateful. He is helping Jon become elected to the central government as a provincial representative. Jon's already in local government, and we are terribly proud of him, but this would be a marvelous advancement to his career. He wants to be prime minister one day." She removed the hat and tried a navy blue one trimmed with gold ribbons. "Mr. Kine's daughters are such tedious company, and he brings them when he comes to call on Mama. They follow me about, copying what I say and do and giggling. Mind you, they're only ten and thirteen. Lucca and Verona, their names are. Can you imagine that? There was a boy called Rome, but he and his mother died in a carriage accident." She bit her lip. "This one suits me better. I should have been a nun like Aunt Sarah. Black and navy blue are the only colors that suit me, and Mama forbids us to wear anything drab. Let's go for a walk, shall we? I'll show you a beautiful glade . . . if you can walk far. Hal always described you as a pale angel lying on a chaise lounge all day. It sounded romantic as I pictured you. Were you terribly ill?"

May thought how different the cousins were. Lena chatted like a runaway carriage, while on her visits Ellen watched inscrutably. "I suffer a weakness of the lungs but am perfectly recovered. However, Mother and Father use the illness as an excuse to forbid me from doing anything they deem unsuitable." She laughed and added. "I regard that as a challenge, of course."

While Derwent Kine accompanied Stephen to the study, the sisters settled warily over tea in the parlor. Their artificial courtesy failed to mask their mutual distaste.

Of the two, Abby was more distressed, with strain cramping at her chest. It was not fair, she reflected bitterly. Now that Jack was thankfully dead, her life should be easier. No longer did she have the fear that one day he might leave her for that Maori slut. He had flaunted the woman so openly for so many years that Abby was terrified he would do what was being speculated—ask for a divorce. Abby had borne gossip and humiliation, but *that* would have been unendurable. In death Jack should have been hers at last, exclusively, and the rumors should have stopped.

But the shipwreck had not finished the chapter. Abby had no body to mourn over, a smaller estate than expected, and instead of retiring decently to the king country with the other Maori rabble, Rosaleen Teipa and her family were here, squatting on land which belonged in part to Abby herself! Surely Juliette would see the delicacy of her predicament—how at all costs these Maoris must be evicted, and the land sold to developers. Juliette must see how this woman's presence was spreading a taint over their whole family.

But Juliette was saying, "Samuel told me that we have no moral right to sell this land. It was given to us as a kind of trust so that the Maoris could stay here as long as—"

"Samuel is mistaken. Mr. Kine has examined the deed, and there is no clause anywhere to prevent us disposing of it as we wish. My dear, Whenuahakari is worth a fortune. Thousands of pounds! People will clamor to bid for a piece of it."

"But we cannot even consider—"

"I assure you that I know what I am talking about. Samuel refuses to see any but the Maori side in any question. Sometimes I think that he weighs the merits of an argument by scrutinizing the color of a person's skin. The darker it is, the more Samuel is convinced that person is correct."

Juliette sighed. "We are talking around in circles and arriving nowhere. Perhaps all of us should discuss this—"

"Samuel will discuss nothing! He is fixed against the idea and refuses to listen. Even Mr. Kine cannot make him see reason. But we do not need his approval. You and I can settle on a decision and force him to go along with it."

"But I couldn't do that."

Abby exhaled sharply in frustration. She said, "Samuel is a dreamer. He never had any use for money, and I suppose I cannot expect you to do anything but gloat over me now that I am a poor widow."

"Are you poor, Abby? I didn't realize—"

"I'll not have your pity either. But you must see that the land is of no use to me, while the money would be most appreciated. But don't you think this land should be used for settlers, rather than just lie idle?"

"It's not idle. If you followed the road, you would see the Maori farmland on the other side of the hill. They grow most of Auckland's vegetables there. But if you are in need of money, Samuel and Stephen will buy your share of Whenuahakari. You must have known they would offer to do that. Is that what you want?"

"Of course not, and Samuel knows it. Oh, don't raise your eyebrows at me in that superior way. Samuel knows what humiliation I suffer by having that woman and her son living here." To her horror she was losing control, unable to prevent her temper rising higher as her voice climbed. "But why should you care? It wouldn't matter to you that the illegitimate wretch has the impudence to call himself Bennington. Or that he mysteriously managed to acquire an education abroad and funds to set himself up in a brewing house. He and his wretched mother must have blackmailed my poor Jack, that's clear. Can you not appreciate why I must be rid of them?"

"I do appreciate your problem, but it is none of my concern. I cannot judge or condemn, nor can I do anything to help."

"You would say that, of course," flared Abby. "Having borne an illegitimate child yourself, *you* could hardly criticize. That would be hypocritical, wouldn't it?"

Juliette rose. Only her tightly corded hands betrayed her anger. "There is no point in continuing this conversation," she said. "However, if you wish to pursue the matter then we must do so with all interested parties present, and by that I mean Samuel, his wife, and, of course, an impartial lawyer to—"

"His wife?"

In one glance Juliette knew that Abby had heard about the marriage. Heard and refused to believe it. The admission was there in her beaten, bleached face. Juliette felt dreadful. She had never intended to tell her sister and had flung it out only in spiteful retaliation, but it was too late to retract it.

"Try to put it out of your mind," urged Juliette. "Samuel has loved her for years. You could not have prevented it."

"I could have killed her. I should have killed her."

"Would that have quelled the gossip? She is ill and not likely to recover. I advise you not to think about it." She rang a silver bell. "I shall order a brandy to calm your nerves."

Abby was slumping. Though winded, she was babbling furiously. "You cannot understand how much I hate her . . . and that detestable son of hers. . . . I hate being pitied . . . the whispers that start when I arrive anywhere. . . . Oh, I cannot endure—"

She was interrupted when Mary came in. This lass was a scatty, negligent type, about as much use, as Stephen remarked, as a half-broken horse. When Juliette gave her the order, she nodded and announced, "Mr. Patrick Bennington called to see you an' the captain, but when I says to him that Mrs. Abigail Bennington were here, he said he won't wait. Just called to thank you, he said. He'll come back, he said."

"Well," said Abby, choking, "no wonder I get precious little sympathy from you. Thank you for not laughing right into my face."

"Abby, please . . . you don't understand."

"I understand perfectly. Tell Mr. Kine I shall send the carriage back for him and the children. I cannot stay here a moment longer."

May and Lena were descending the hill behind the house, laughing over their difficulties as their tight, bustled skirts hobbled their progress. When they paused to rest, Lena said, "Papa brought us up here for a picnic once. He said the view was as pretty a sight as could be found anywhere in the world."

"Glorious," agreed May.

Far to their left sprawled the gray and red tangle of Auckland itself; in front of them lay North Head, indistinct in the glare off the brilliant sea; far to the right loomed the soft blue gulf islands and the rugged mysterious peninsula of Coromandel. It was there that Lena's father had drowned; on a day like this shipwrecks and storms seemed impossible.

Directly below, a clutter of unpainted huts with thatched roofs was strung carelessly along the shore. May was thinking how quaint the rickety jetty and row of beached canoes looked, when Lena said scornfully, "That's the *pa.*"

"The pa?"

"Maori village. Not that they'll be there for much longer."

May thought it best not to comment. The village was tranquil. Laundry hung on bushes. Capering children chased a tiny dog along the beach. Acres of vegetable gardens shimmered in the sunshine.

"Let's go back," said Lena.

They emerged onto the archery lawn just as a figure on horseback rode away from the house. May interrupted herself in mid-sentence to say, "Who is that? That young man with the university cap. Do you know him?"

"It could be anybody. Lots of young gentlemen wear such caps."

"Oh. I thought you knew everybody in town."

Lena giggled. "Dearest cousin! You must spend an hour someday perusing one of the shipping lists in the *Southern Cross.* Each occupies a full page and a good proportion of those names are 'sirs' or 'esquires' lately from Brighton, Chester, or wherever. That was probably someone delivering a message to your father."

"I shall ask him."

"Why the particular interest?" asked Lena as they entered the orchard where bitter-scented orange trees were still only waist-high. The Maori assistant gardener sat on a piece of sacking smoking a clay pipe. He was so old that his tattoos had merged with the wrinkles on his cheeks.

"*Kia ora,*" said May, and after they had moved by, she said, "I saw that young man when we first arrived. He looked interesting. Like a centaur, very arrogant and aristocratic."

"I know of a dozen young men who fit that description. Unfortunately the more aristocratic they are, the greater the arrogance they display." She glanced at May with

71

uncharacteristic shrewdness. "But I dislike this conversation. You are supposed to be thinking about Hal and nobody else. I am determined to have you for a sister."

"What would Grandmaire say if she could hear you?"

"It's strange." Lena paused near the bathhouse where wood was stacked in readiness for the boiler fire. "When I am with Grandmaire, I feel compelled to do anything she wants of me, but when I go home, her influence gradually weakens and my own desires assert themselves. We all feel like that. Even Dora, who grumbles quite sourly about her, still rushes to do her bidding."

"I feel it, too. Daniel even more so. He thinks Grandmaire is the most forceful person he has ever met." She refrained from adding that Daniel was impressionable, his loyalties easily won.

"Perhaps she casts a spell on everyone who enters her presence. Most people at least. Uncle Stephen certainly doesn't try to please her." She chuckled.

"Oh? What makes you say that?"

"Didn't I tell you? We were still there at Fintona when he called yesterday afternoon. Their voices carried right across the lawn; they were going at it hammer and tongs. He accused her of deceiving Aunt Rose and Uncle Adrian and of using the Richmond Line to finance new stores for the Peridot Emporiums chain. At first she scoffed at him and told him he couldn't possibly prove such charges, but then someone else—a lawyer Uncle Stephen brought with him, I think—talked quietly to her, and after that she grew so angry that we were quaking and hardly daring to move. Grandmaire kept ordering Uncle Stephen to leave, but he wouldn't go until he had finished telling her that all her power had gone and she had to pay back all the money she had 'borrowed' or forfeit some of her shares."

"Did you listen to everything?"

"Oh, don't be shocked. We were hardly eavesdropping. Grandmaire had set Dora and me out under the grape arbor to mend some of her Brussels lace cloths, and we simply couldn't avoid hearing the whole thing. Dora said none of the accusations surprised her, and Kendrick said that everybody in town knows that Grandmaire has been making hay while the sun shines, and he hopes she has a stout, waterproof umbrella now that Uncle Stephen has returned."

"Kendrick is quite a wit, isn't he?" May commented to Daniel as they waved good-bye to their cousins.

"He is. I l-like him enormously."

"Lena is fun, too. She's made me feel as though I knew everybody intimately. What did you two do today?"

"We explored the old f-fencible cottage."

"The one next to Uncle Samuel's place? Mother said we were on no account to go beyond the hedge."

"It's all right. Don't f-fuss. The boys were having riding lessons, and they couldn't have seen us. You know perfectly well that Mother is worried only about *them.*"

"But why did you want to go there anyway? Ellen says that the old cottage is filled with junk. That would scarcely interest you."

"K-Kendrick wanted to go there. He wanted to see if he could see—" He broke off, coloring.

"See what? Oh, I think I understand. He's interested in seeing Uncle Samuel's new wife."

"Did you know that she and Kendrick's father were lovers?"

"I did know." She frowned. "And I think it's quite wrong for Kendrick to be snooping around, trying to catch a glimpse of her. She's an ill woman. It's not right that he should be spying on her."

"Oh, is it?" he retorted. "And who are you to judge? It's no different from your wanting to know all about your real father. Besides, he wasn't trying to see her. K-Kendrick was trying to see Patrick." He stalked away and was halfway up the stairs when May caught up to him and plucked at the hem of his jacket.

"Did you see him?"

"No," he returned haughtily. "But we saw something else. S-Something that would really interest you."

"What was it? Oh, do tell. *Please,* Daniel." She followed him into his room and stopped suddenly.

Beside the window, propped on a battered tripod and covered with dust, was a camera. The wooden sides were scratched, the removable back was stained by chemicals,

73

and the concertina bellows were stiff with age and cracking at the folds; but it had a lens and a cover, and her first excited examination indicated that all the knobs and levers were there in place. It was, undeniably, a working camera.

May tried to speak. Daniel laughed. "You should see your face. I t-told Kendrick you'd be pleased."

"Pleased! I'm overjoyed, delighted, enraptured!" She hugged him. "You are sweet to find that for me. But whose is it? It cannot possibly be nobody's. We can't simply take it. Oh, it's *beautiful!* If only you knew how much I longed to have one . . ."

"Of course I know," he protested. "I have to listen to all your talk about photographs, don't I?"

The camera belonged to Samuel. He explained that it was a gift from one of the British soldiers who had used it during the Waikato wars.

"He made ambrotypes. I have a few there at the cottage. Yes, by all means you are welcome to it," he said. "I thought that one day I might find the time to learn how to use it, but if I haven't by now, I doubt I ever will." He turned to Stephen and Juliette. "As I explained, there is no danger from chemical fumes, and as long as May has somebody to carry the equipment for her, she cannot overexert herself."

"There. I told you so," said Daniel later. "N-No matter what it is you want, Mother and Father always give it to you in the end."

Impulsively she dropped the brush she had been using to clean the bellows and flung her arms around his neck. "I know you said so, and I think that I am the luckiest sister in the world. Why? Because no matter how stern Father is with you and how indulgent he is with me, you never seem to mind. You have a truly generous nature, Daniel. Did you know that?"

He backed away, grinning. "Uhh-uhh. No, thank you. I absolutely refuse."

"Refuse?"

"I refuse t-to be the lackey Uncle Samuel referred to.

The slave who is going to have to carry that thing every-where."

"I haven't asked you to do that!"

"No, but you were going to, weren't you?"

"Oh, Daniel, who will help me then?"

"Not me, and that's final. Kendrick and I have the re-mainder of the summer all arranged, and m-my plans do not include being a photographer's assistant. I know. Why not rope in young Bobby Terrill? He's just a sprat, but he's strong and wiry. What will you photograph first?"

"Everything! Absolutely everything!" Her eyes shone with enthusiasm. "I cannot wait to begin. It's going to seem an eternity until Mother takes me to a studio to pur-chase the plates and developing equipment, but in the meantime, I shall make a list of all the photographs I have planned already and draw little sketches. I'll concentrate on portraits first—Mother wants several studies of Albert and Edward, if I can make them keep still for long enough to take exposures, that is!—and if I practice carefully, by the time Hal returns I should be sufficiently expert to take a splendid portrait of him in his captain's regalia."

Daniel ran a finger along a bellows leaf. "Th-Then I hope that Ellen is endowed with a truly generous nature, too."

May said, "If by that you are referring to the story that they are all but engaged, *I* say let us wait and see what Hal thinks, shall we?"

"Poor Hal, because I d-don't envy his position at all. If I was in his situation, I should transfer to a transatlantic run and never return to this part of the world." He ducked, grinning, as she threw a hairbrush at him. "But s-seri-ously, May. I hear that Grandmaire has it all arranged."

May tossed a rope of hair over her shoulder. "I heard that Ellen is infatuated with Hal, and *his* affections are not engaged. And Lena says that Dora says Grandmaire would prefer Ellen to marry Jon because Jon always obeys Grandmaire. And I say I don't know why all the fuss and feathers."

"Tell me, May," said Daniel. "Do you really love Hal or just the idea of him?"

May flushed with determination and said, "I have

always loved him. Oh, Ellen does make it more of a challenge, and I enjoy a challenge; but I think that Hal reminds me of happy days in San Francisco." She raised her soft eyes and looked into Daniel's face. "I feel so terribly homesick at times. I think I want Hal to talk to me and make me feel that I am back there again. Do you understand?"

"Perhaps you should marry Hal and have Father b-base him there. He needs a good man in the San Francisco office."

"Perhaps I should," said May. She smiled impishly. "But in the meantime, I am going to set myself the task of learning how to use this."

Seven

Grandmaire and Dora sat on the veranda over-looking the harbor. Dora opened letters and read them aloud, while the old woman concentrated on a platter of sweet green grapes. The early sun made her look decep-tively frail, and without paint her cheeks showed a bur-nish of fine red veins.

Dora said, "Uncle Stephen accepts the invitation, but he sends Aunt Juliette's regrets."

Grandmaire used the grape scissors with unnecessary force. "What is her excuse this time?"

"Albert and Edward suffered sunstroke and have both been sleeping poorly. She is reluctant to leave them."

"Rubbish." She popped a grape into her mouth. "She is afraid of me. Six months, and she has not shown her face at a single social function."

Dora slit another envelope. "Mama did say that Aunt Juliette was never one to enjoy dinners and grand occa-sions."

"Hmph! She enjoyed parties when they gave her the op-portunity to throw herself at my sons. Make no mistake about that. I do pity poor Stephen, being tied to her. She's so self-centered and jealous that she's sending poor young Daniel away to England, just to get him out of her sight. Every time she looks at him it must remind her of dear Danielle."

"Daniel told me that his father is sending him to study maritime law at Oxford."

"Not that it will do him any good. As soon as those boys—*her* sons—are old enough, Daniel will be thrust aside." She waved the scissors at Dora. "I have known Ju-

77

liette since she was a small girl, and she was devious and underhanded then, too. She is sending Daniel away because she wants to be rid of him."

Normally Dora would not waste breath in refuting such allegations, but she knew that Grandmaire was repeating them to her friends, and unless checked, these views would soon be circulating as facts. Mildly she said, "I rather think that they wish to separate Daniel from Kendrick."

"What a ridiculous notion."

"It's not really, Grandmaire. The constabulary have been to Mondrich House twice recently, and last week both boys were escorted home in a state of intoxication."

"Boyish pranks, no more than high spirits. Kendrick is a fine young man, and it's only natural he and Daniel would get into small scrapes. Goodness, how dull the world would be if we all behaved like angels! Juliette is too blind and uncaring to see it, but Daniel needs someone with a strong character to befriend him." Irritated because Dora merely sat passively, not agreeing, she said, "Next letter, child. At this rate we will never finish our correspondence. Look . . . there, beyond Rangitoto. Unless I'm very much mistaken that will be the *Mondrich Zephyr.* Leave that, Dora. Fetch Tawa, and quickly. I shall send word to Ellen so that she can go out to meet Hal. She misses him so! I recall when Richmond Yardley and I were engaged and how long the last few days of his voyages always seemed to be. Poor Ellen positively *pines* for Hal."

At Mondrich House Stephen had identified the ship and had ordered the brougham to be brought around to the front door. Upstairs May was excitedly dressing, ready to go with him to the wharf. For weeks she had been planning what to wear to make her important "first impression," but now she was panicking.

"Please, Mother, try to remember, does Hal like blue?" she asked as she picked up one, then another gown from the bed. She turned as Albert put his head around the door. "What do you want? You're not to come in here without knocking."

He made an ugly face. "Father says it's time to go."

"I'm not ready. Oh, I'm so nervous I could shriek."

Juliette ruffled Albert's hair and shooed him out, saying, "There now, dear. May will be down soon." And to May she said, "This yellow one flatters you best."

"The buttercup silk? But it's so . . . extreme. Those puffed sleeves and that waterfall bustle."

"Don't forget that Hal sees all the latest styles in London. He'll not think it extreme."

Fifteen minutes later she was in the hall, her hair smoothed back into a chignon, her bangs fluffed over her brow, and her eyelashes brushed with a trace of macassar oil to make them glisten. She was biting her lips for color when the butler walked through with a tray of polished glasses.

"Why, no, Miss Yardley. Young Master Albert assured your father that you had changed your mind about going. He went in the brougham instead."

"Did he indeed? Did he?" She was momentarily dismayed by this turn of events, but the frown had hardly settled when she noticed young Bobby Terrill playing in the drive. After hurrying out onto the veranda, she issued urgent instructions.

"Very well, if the dogcart has a broken harness, then fetch the trap," she said over his protests. "I cannot ride Negus as I am, and there is no time to change." She jabbed her parasol in his direction. "But be quick. If my mother sees us, she will stop us, and I must catch up to Father."

But driving the trap was not as simple as managing the dogcart. The flat cliff road and first small gullies presented no problems, but as they neared town, the road swooped into a series of long downhill bends. Here the horse responded to the weight on the shafts by trotting faster, then faster still until finally it surged into a gallop that all of May's strength could not retard. The trap rocked ominously at each twist in the road.

"This is fun, miss!" shouted Bobby.

May was unafraid. The road was smooth, and the foot of the hill close around the next bend. Almost, almost, her brain sang as she braced hard for the fling of the trap into that final corner, but as her view widened, she gasped in horror.

Not fifty yards ahead of them was a carrier's wagon

loaded with ale barrels. One wheel was at a crazy angle, props were under the shafts, and the whole immovable heap was in the middle of the road. At the roadside, where a creek cut close, the driver stood talking to a man on horseback. May heard their belated warning shout as her horse veered and plunged toward the other side of the road, where a fern-covered bank overhung a shallow ditch. Bobby yelled and clung to May's frozen arm. She felt nothing—not his digging fingers nor the wrenching lurch or the slapping wet tongues of fern that raked over them. It was not until the vehicle had rolled to a stop far beyond that May realized they were safe. Shuddering, she rested her face in her welt-covered hands and cried with relief.

Bobby recovered immediately and scrambled down. "No damage, miss," he reported cheerfully. "There's mud and weeds caught underneath, but nothing broken."

May breathed deeply to calm herself. "Then get back in and we'll be on our way."

Bobby was staring at her with an odd expression. "Beg pardon, miss, but do you think we should?"

"Quickly now, we have no time to squander." He was still studying her oddly, so she said, "Climb in. Hurry. Father will be almost at the wharf by now." As she spoke, she reached up a hand to pat her hair and was puzzled when her fingers encountered a hard, bristly substance. Fern, A glance down at her dress showed her that her bodice was soaked and smeared with leaves, muddy water, and brown pollen, and more pats revealed that her tiny bonnet had been torn loose and her chignon pulled awry.

"Oh, no," she groaned. "I can't possibly go to meet Hal looking like this."

"Shall we go back then?"

"We shall have to."

Bobby grasped the harness and was starting to guide the horse around when he said, "That young gentleman is riding up."

"Oh, no!" The words *young gentleman* rang an alarm in her mind. This was hardly the time to be talking to any young gentleman, not while she was looking like this. Flapping the reins, she said, "Leave that and jump in, quickly. We'll go to Fintona, and I shall tidy myself there.

Hurry up. Open the parasol, and hold it behind me. There's a lap rug under the seat. As soon as we get up the road, I'll ask you to get it out to spread around me . . . hurry, horse! Gee-up! Gee-up!"

But the young man on the sleek black horse overtook them swiftly and, when she held the reins out of the way, stopped the trap easily by reaching across the harness and jerking at the straps.

May was furiously fighting back tears. "How dare you! Let us go at once. First your friend blocks our way and almost causes a nasty accident; then you have the insolence to accost me when it is clear that we are in a hurry. Let us by at—" She faltered, swallowed, and trailed to a miserable halt.

Leaning toward her, still grasping the harness strap, was the young man she had seen on her first morning in New Zealand. She recognized him with dismay, noting that he was handsomer than at first glimpse, with a decidedly Arabian cast to his narrow face, of dark eyes and full, curved lips. All arrogance had gone; his eyes were lit with condescending humor as he doffed his university cap and said, "I trust, Miss Yardley, that the rest of your person has suffered as little damage as your voice."

"How do you know who I am?"

His voice was rich as port and brushed with a faintly American drawl. "Everybody knows who you are. I have seen you and your camera bearer"—he nodded at Bobby—"many times on your excursions. Surely photography does not demand this urgency?"

"Not content with spying on me, you are now accosting me in order to offer insults?" she heard herself quaver. If only there were some way to disappear, to remove herself from this humiliation. It was a nightmare.

"I stopped you merely to see if you were in need of my assistance. Obviously you have little experience in driving, and—"

"That is most unfair," she flared. "If your friend had not left his wagon sprawling across the road, we would have come to no harm."

"It could not be your fault for driving at a reckless speed, of course."

81

"You would not be so impertinent if my father were here."

"The incident would not have occurred if Captain Yardley were here. Does he know where you are?"

"That is no concern of yours."

"Really?" An eyebrow arched in amusement. "You should take care, Miss Yardley. The bush hereabouts is full of fierce Maoris."

Tugging at the reins, she said, "I don't know who you are, sir, nor do I ever wish to be enlightened, but I consider you insufferably rude. On the morning of our arrival you stared at me, and now you delay me in order to harass and insult me. Please let me pass at once."

Instead of releasing the reins, he laughed with a genuine delight. "Now I've heard everything. Some Eastern kings and potentates are so filled with their own importance that they refuse to allow their subjects to gaze upon them, but I would never have imagined that a shipowner's daughter would insist on such a privilege."

"Please." Suddenly she was near to tears.

Her tone sobered him, and he dropped both smile and sarcasm. "Miss Yardley, I apologize. You are under strain, suffering from shock, and I have misinterpreted your antagonism. I did stop you only from concern, but if you will permit me to advise you, I urge you to go home rather than continue. You could find yourself disadvantaged—shall we say?—by your present appearance."

He means I look a terrible fright, she thought wretchedly, but because of her struggle against breaking down, she was unable to reply or to protest as he turned her horse around and led it along the bank back onto the road.

"There." He patted the horse's flank. "Go safely. Might I suggest that you allow the lad to drive next time? He's likely to make a much better fist of it."

She had been silently phrasing a few stiff words of thanks to acknowledge his conciliatory gesture, but when he said that, she bit them back at once. Though she averted her head, she sensed that he was grinning as they drove off.

"Who was that, miss?" asked Bobby when they were

safely out of sight. "I ain't never seen him before. What a fine gentleman."

"Most emphatically he was not."

"But those clothes and that grand horse. And the way he spoke—why I didn't understand more than half of it."

"You missed nothing by that," she said tightly. A few tears were cool on her cheeks, and she flapped the reins to hurry the horse, wanting to put as much distance as possible between her and that distasteful incident. Humiliation scorched her. Since early childhood she had been trained to cope with nasty remarks of the type made by poor people who envied her advantages, and the irony of this morning's encounter was that if the wagon driver had criticized her driving, had suggested the accident had been her fault, or had even made slighting remarks about shipowners, the comments would not have bothered her at all. This was different. Here she had been insulted by an attractive, well-educated, and obviously wealthy young man. He had mocked her, laughed at her, offered patronizing advice, then chased her off home as though she were a child.

"Who was that?" asked Bobby again.

"Nobody of any importance at all," she said firmly, at the same time suppressing the memory of the many times during the past six months that she had paused at some social event and wondered if her mysterious centaur would appear. She said, "You and I are going to forget all about this incident and never mention it again. Is that clear?" But even as she spoke, she pondered Bobby's question. Who was he? Presentable, well spoken and well-to-do, he would blend well in any society gathering. Why had she never seen him?

When Juliette had finished listening to an abbreviated version of the accident, she shook her head and said, "Perhaps it's just as well that you wait here for Hal to come to you. It might be best not to appear overeager. Now up you go change out of that mess. Try the ice blue. It is a calm, cool color."

She was anything but calm when Hal finally arrived. For the previous hour she had been pacing the morning room, lifting her head to catch any sound which might have been the clattering of hooves on the drive. Edward, who was annoyed at having been left behind, came in frequently to report that the carriage was on the cliff road, and though she stopped taking notice of this, he cheekily chanted, "Rook, rook! I made you look!" until she shouted for Juliette to make him go away. She stayed to have tea with May, and they were talking mechanically and about nothing when Stephen's voice called, "Where are you, May? There's somebody to see you."

"He's here!"

"Relax, dear." Juliette patted her arm. "You look lovely."

May was half out of her chair when Hal strode in ahead of the others. He stood still as suddenly as if someone had placed a hand at his chest, then flung his arms wide and roared, "Cousin May, you are beautiful! Simply beautiful!"

"Hello, Hal." He was exactly as she remembered, but also curiously different. There were the blue eyes, the same color as the sea at the equator, and his familiar, square face was dusted with the shortest of beards, but he was so much broader and burlier than she recalled, and even though he was rocking slightly on his feet in a typical mariner's stance, he seemed to be built entirely of solid power. When he stepped toward her to wrap her in a muscular embrace, she laughed with a tremble of nerves, half-smothered as she was by odors of wool, tobacco, and salt, her cheek scraped by bristles and her ribs crushed. Then, when he held her at arms' length, his gaze was loaded with such undisguised admiration that she felt herself blushing.

"Really, Hal," came Ellen's cold voice from the doorway. "There's no need to jump all over her like a Saint Bernard puppy."

"Bravo," murmured Juliette, but Hal was oblivious to both remarks.

"I nearly swapped commands when I realized how narrowly I missed being here to meet you," he said. "I wanted to claim the right to show you around, to introduce you to everybody. You've not changed one scrap, do you know that?"

"I must have done!" *He* had, she thought. Though he was only in his late twenties, he looked older, with weather-crumpled skin around his eyes and a tweed-colored mixture of gray, brown, and bleached hair brushed back from his creased forehead.

He winked at her and suddenly looked like young Hal again. "I brought you a present, from India. I hope you like it."

"Why, thank you!" She was about to open the flat package when Ellen glided up and draped a thin hand through the crook of his arm.

"It's a shawl so fine that it can pass through a ring, isn't it, Hal? What color did you choose for May? Not gold like mine or black like Grandmaire's, I hope."

May expected Hal to be embarrassed, but he said easily, "I try to choose something you ladies will like."

"And that is very thoughtful of you, Hal." May was determined not to open the gift in front of Ellen.

Juliette said, "Stephen, I suppose that you and Hal have a great deal to discuss."

But Ellen leaned against Hal's shoulder and said, "Mama is expecting us for luncheon. She has invited your family, too, Hal. Grandmaire will be there with Dora, and Jon has some exciting news he wants to share with us all."

"Well, then, in that case. . . ." began Juliette.

"Wait a minute," said Hal. Running his fingers through his hair in a gesture of helplessness, he said, "I'm sorry, Ellen, but they will have to be disappointed. I am surprised, though. You should know by now that I never make social plans for my first day ashore. There are always a hundred or more things which must be passed on while they are fresh in my mind."

Ellen's face darkened. Juliette said, "Then you must stay here and share our luncheon, Ellen. Hal would not want you to go, would you, Hal! We can send a message to Rose. She will understand the pressures of business. After all"—with a laugh—"she knows her brother of old. Once Stephen starts talking business, he loses all concept of time . . ." and still chattering, she led Ellen away.

* * *

"What did you think of all that?" May asked Daniel that evening as they bent their heads together over a dissected picture of the pyramids of Egypt.

"Of what?"

"Hal, of course. What do you think of him? Honestly, now."

"He's a c-capital fellow. A real man's man." Daniel considered a scrap of card. "Did you notice that he talked of nothing but ships? Father says that provided I'm not sick on the voyage, I'll learn more from him on the way to England than I'll ever assimilate at Oxford. He's obsessed with the Mondrich Line."

"Not *that,*" said May. "What did you think of him and Ellen?"

Daniel's ears tinged pink, but his eyes were mischievous. "He looked as miserable as a dog with a thornbush tied to his tail."

"I thought so, too." She looked smug.

Daniel said, "I'm not interested in r-romance, but Grandmaire's party is going to be really fascinating."

"I can guarantee it," said May.

Eight

Grand occasions suited Fintona. Chandeliers dripped like spun sugar under the light of a thousand candles, for Grandmaire could not abide the smell of that newfangled lighting fuel kerosene; tables glowed with the sheen of Irish linen and glittered with a treasury of silverware. Though flowers were massed everywhere, their scent was lost in the delicious aromas wafting from the kitchen. Grandmaire's parties were famous, but tonight, as she stood at the hall door, she felt confident that she had outdone herself.

Stephen bent to kiss her, murmuring compliments. She was regal in black silk shot through with gold, boned, trussed, and coiffed, her dramatic black and white hair crowned with a spray of black feathers and sequins, her chest a rivulet of jet jewelry.

She smiled, showing teeth filled with gold. "Juliette should be here. This party is not just to congratulate Jon but to bid Daniel farewell, too. She should have come." She tapped his shoulder with a folded lace fan. "She should not shut herself away. People are beginning to talk."

"But not you, Mama."

She frowned, then abruptly laughed. "You are a fool, Stephen. Oh, not in business, unfortunately, but otherwise a fool."

"If it is foolish to be happy, then I admit it." He spoke lightly, but as he turned to greet Dora, the words grated on his mind. Happy? He had not known a moment of personal happiness since he announced his decision to leave San Francisco.

Juliette was pleasant, she accepted him, but the delicate

pastels had seeped away, leaving their marriage a tone-
less, dull gray. Happy? The word was a mockery.

May was talking to Dora, thinking at the same time how
aptly yet cruelly Kendrick had described her. 'She looks as
though her face had been carved from a turnip,' he said.
Tonight she was sullen in a made-over serge gown, her
only ornamentation the mourning brooch. As May noted
the widened seams and extra band of different fabric
around her hem, she recalled Kendrick's saying that the
only difference between Dora and the Maori servants at
Fintona was that the Maoris were paid. She was moved by
pity to say, "Must you stand here all evening? Can you
come and talk to me?"

Dora's face registered astonishment only for a second.
She shook her head no and turned to the next guest.

Lena was at May's elbow, jiggling her. "I have been
waiting for *ages,*" she complained. "Come have some fruit
cup and meet the Vinton girls. They have just arrived back
from five years in Hong Kong and have some amusing
stories to tell." She lowered her voice. "Ellen sent for Hal
this evening and detained him at her house so that he
could not help escorting her here. I urged him to wear riding clothes so that she could not trap him, but like a trusting dupe, he went ready for the party. Oh, he talked about
you at such length last night that Mama pleaded with him
to change the subject."

"I thought he talked of nothing but the sea." She could
see him in the morning room, with Ellen clinging to his
arm. Her heart lurched, but she swiftly looked the other
way and pretended she had not noticed them.

"Look, there they are. Shall we join them? Oh, come on.
Surely you are not discouraged because Ellen—"

Under cover of the surrounding conversation May said,
"If Hal has escorted Ellen, then he must perform his obli-
gations. Did you not tell me that Ellen is so adoring that
Hal has grown lazy? If he is, then she will suit him much
better than I could ever do. Right now, I prefer to renew my
acquaintance with Aunt Rose. She's such a sweet lady."

"And nothing like her daughter," said Lena. "Ellen has
been so horrid to you I don't know how you can be polite to
her."

"If Ellen does not worry me, why should you be concerned?"

"Her jealousy is an illness. Oh, I do hope that Hal soon sees her for what she really is."

"I think he will," said May.

As May expected, Hal was piqued that she ignored him so pointedly. He began to grow restless in Ellen's company; she was so strained and tense that he began making excuses to leave her side willing him to return. Eventually what she had feared happened. Hal sought May out, spoke to her at length, and coaxed a smile from her. He looked so transparently delighted when that happened that Ellen's throat filled with bitterness. She tortured herself, watching while Hal took May's dance card and tiny tasseled pencil, spending what seemed an eternity writing in it.

"How could anybody consider her pretty? She's white as a corpse," said Ellen aloud.

"Who is?" asked Jon, coming up beside her.

"Oh, Jon, you startled me." If Hal were looking this way, I would flirt with him, she thought.

"Where is Mrs. Rugmore?"

"Somewhere finding an audience for her tedious stories, I expect."

"It's not like you to be unkind. What is the matter?"

She glanced at him with gratitude. Most people thought Jon cold and calculating because he went after what he wanted. There had been a tragic affair with the heiress, and perhaps he did trade on people's friendships; but that didn't mean he was unscrupulous. He was always nice to her.

She thrust her card at him. "Ask me to dance, please, Jon."

"Don't tell me I've beaten Hal." He flashed her a roguish grin that made her understand instantly why the heiress had been attracted to him. "One of my ambitions has been to be the first person to mark your card."

When music smothered the chatter, he took her in his arms, and they waltzed along the veranda. Ellen was beginning to feel soothed, almost uncaring, when Jon said, "Sorry, Hal," and she saw that they had almost bumped into May and Hal, who were not dancing, but standing close together. May talked animatedly while Hal looked bemused.

Ellen stiffened with the same unpleasant surprise as if a spider had run up her arm. In a reflexive gesture she pinched Jon's hand, and he understood the cause of her sour mood. Not that Hal could be blamed for deserting the faithful Ellen—May was so radiantly "different" that Auckland was humming about her. The local late-ripening plums were being named May plums in celebration of her purplish black hair, and the *Southern Cross* had published a spate of poems describing a maiden with petal white skin, soft brown eyes, and a voice like the strum of a bowstring—May's faintly American accent. And she was talented. Already her ambrotype portraits had been prominently featured in the Arts Institute displays. No, thought Jon. Hal could hardly be blamed for allowing May Yardley's charm to captivate him, but the real question was: How long would she be interested in him?

Ellen's pearl-and-ribbon hair decoration brushed Jon's cheek, stirring feelings of protectiveness in him. He was tempted to tell her not to worry—that as soon as May realized that Hal's veins pumped only seawater, that his reading was confined to martitime charts and his mind focused only on problems connected with ships, that as soon as she realized he had everything to offer the Mondrich Line and nothing to offer her, then she would lose interest in him.

But Jon said nothing. Why should he pave his brother's path to something he wanted for himself?

Grandmaire noticed the intense attraction between May and Hal and was instantly concerned. As soon as the bracket of tunes had finished, she dispatched Dora to fetch Ellen and bade the girl sit on the stool beside her own high-backed chair. Imprisoning Ellen's pink-gloved fingers between her withered-apple hands, she said, "You must show your courage, Ellen Forster. Feelings are to be hidden, courage to be displayed."

"I'm so unhappy, Grandmaire. I don't know what to do."

"Do? Do? There's nothing *to* do. You'd not want a man if he didn't want you. You've more pride than that."

"I love Hal, I truly do."

"Hush, child," she scolded, but with tenderness. "You might ask your Aunt Juliette what joy there is in being married to a man who doesn't want you, for she pursued my Leigh and wed him against his own will, and all it brought her was the misery she deserved. A man who doesn't love you is a man worth nothing, and I'll not see that happen to you, Ellen Forster."

"What can I do to win him back? I dreaded this, I feared it, and as soon as I saw them together, I knew it was worse than anything I had imagined. He loves her, Grandmaire. What can I do?"

"You can prove that it's my flesh and blood you're made of and hold that handsome head up high. There's more of me in you than ever was in any of my children, so show you've inherited my spirit, too. Smile. Be uncaring. Besides"—she lowered her voice—"what we *think* we want isn't always best for us, you know. The heart plays tricks, dear, and is not a reliable guide. I think you can choose more wisely than Hal." Beckoning imperiously to Jon, she said, "Dance with Jon. Enjoy yourself. Pay her compliments, Jon. Flatter my little girl. Cheer her up. I cannot bear to see my treasure unhappy."

"I'm not at all unhappy," said Ellen at once.

"That's my girl," said Grandmaire. She sighed as she watched them walk away.

Ellen was not the only guest who found others of the company distasteful. In the parlor Abigail was shifting from one tightly encased foot to the other while Samuel engaged Derwent Kine in conversation. Abby had permitted herself only a cold nod in her brother's direction before turning away to examine an ornate epergne on the mantelshelf. Abby sniffed at the roses and straightened an iris stem as she listened irritably to her brother's slurred voice. She had known he was invited but hadn't believed he would come after their quarrel. Grandmaire said that this evening would present a fresh opportunity for her to persuade him to sell Whenuahakari because Juliette would not be here, but now that she was in the same room with him, she found him so repugnant she could not speak.

91

Over the years she had made allowances for his Maorified speech and sloppy appearance, reasoning that they were regrettable eccentricities, but understandable because of his association with the tribes. Now she wanted to shrink away as if his toothlessness, his rumpled looks, and his good-natured heartiness were symptoms of a contagious disease.

It always surprised her that most people overlooked these things and actually sought Samuel out to hear his views on the "native question." They respected his views, too, which Abby considered symptomatic of the ridiculous "let's be soft on the Maoris" attitude that was in vogue.

But Derwent was on her side, and fully sympathetic with the injuries her sensitive spirit had suffered over Samuel's distasteful marriage. He was speaking bluntly to Samuel, saying, "Gullible sections of the populace will believe anything, but only the uninformed could give credence to your reasoning. The Maoris instigated the war, and from the outset they made it clear that if they won, they would take back every inch of land—land that had been bought and paid for—and then they planned to drive us all into the sea. That is fact, and borne out by their ancient laws, which decree that after a battle the winner takes all. But they didn't win, did they? If they had, I'm convinced they'd have carried out their threats to the letter, so why should we show pity now?" He chomped his jaws on an unlit cigar and continued to talk out of the side of his mouth. "By rights we should have claimed the whole of New Zealand in retribution instead of the miserable few million acres that were seized. *That* would have been fair."

Samuel was not one to bluster or lose his temper. There was even the hint of a smile in those pale eyes of his as he said, "Ah, Mr. Kine, but only a tiny minority of the Maoris waged war. Many tribesfolk fought alongside the settlers' army. They nourished and aided them, yet some of these very same people have been stripped of their ancestral lands in this supposedly just retribution. How can any of us call that fair?"

Derwent Kine took that moment to light his cigar, knowing that while there was no answer to the fellow's points, it was vital that he cut him down to impress Abigail.

Samuel said, "Actually I'm pleased you raised this question because there is a disturbing rumor I must hoe over with you. It seems that certain unscrupulous businessmen have been plying the Maoris with grog in order to inveigle them into debt and thus obtain their land as payment."

A ribbon of smoke tickled Derwent's throat. After he had finished coughing, he said, "I've not heard about that, old sport."

"And certain prominent gentlemen in government circles have been bribing the land courts to facilitate the practice." Samuel paused, noting how Derwent's eyes had begun to seek escape. "If you've not heard about *that,* then I'm astonished, nay, incredulous. I was told that you—"

Derwent moved away. Without a word or a look he propelled himself forward and marched past the grand piano and out through the French doors. Samuel watched him without surprise. He would have laughed, had the matter not been so bitter.

Dr. Adrian Forster saw Derwent Kine come into the dining room and murmured to Stephen, "He's not coaxed an acceptance out of Abigail yet, I gather. Do you know he actually came out and asked me about her fortune? Truly. I could scarcely credit my hearing. The joke is that each of them thinks the other is wealthy when in truth both are merely comfortable." He surveyed the table. "What else would Rose like? These Friday parties are a cursed nuisance. Because of our Roman Catholic customs, the roast meats have to wait until midnight and poor Rose's appetite can't last until then. She says she's already dizzy with hunger."

"A Bath bun, perhaps?" Stephen offered a silver dish. "Has it ever occurred to you that our supper tables are tributes to the glories of the empire? Consider what is offered—Indian curries, kedgeree, Adelaide puddings, Welsh rarebits, Victoria sponges, mulligatawny soup, Alma trifle . . . and all the richness shows that despite gout and a poor constitution, Mama never changes."

"She is aging, Stephen." The doctor kept a mild tone.

"You should remember that in your dealings with her. Her heart—"

"Is as sound as a dray horse's."

"You caused it to quake, with your quarrel."

He speared a piece of asparagus. "It was business, and Mama appreciates what must be said. Speaking of business, have you and Rose looked over those figures I gave you? I need Rose to vote with me. Without her support—"

"It's no use, Stephen." He looked ill at ease. "We both know that a lot of the Richmond Line problems have been caused by unfortunate decisions, but Rose says it would be disloyal to vote against her mother."

"Damn it, man! It's not loyalty at stake. This is business. I suppose you're going to say that you are also proceeding with this wool speculation. You are. Look, it is foolhardy for the Richmond Line to do it, but it would be suicidal for you and Rose to risk all your capital—"

"Those are reckless words, Stephen."

The doctor's eyes were cold behind his heavy spectacles, but Stephen ignored the warning, saying, "It is you who are being reckless."

"Are we? We buy wool for one shilling a pound and sell it in London for two shillings, and you call that suicidal? I call it stupendous profit."

"But as I explained before, the prices are artificially inflated because of the European wars. These could end any day, and when they do, the market will slump badly."

"I think the hostilities will drag on for years. The Prussians and French alone are forever slugging it out. No, Stephen, thank you for your advice, but we shall follow our own counsel, and I think the Richmond Line should speculate, too. It's time it tried something new. This might be the stroke of fortune it needs."

"Or sink the line forever," said Stephen gloomily. He tugged at his beard in frustration. Why wouldn't Adrian see reason?

"You suffer from narrow vision, Stephen. All your life you've used the same rules. You call speculation gambling, but it is not."

Stephen made an impatient gesture and, looking up, found himself staring into his mother's face. Though they

94

were separated by the width of two rooms that had been opened to make one large hall, he could see from her alert, watching attitude that she had followed the entire exchange. She's not missed a word, thought Stephen, and as if to confirm that, she smiled and leaned back in her chair.

"Mama," murmured Stephen, raising his champagne glass.

"Oh, the queen," said Dr. Forster. "It suits her, doesn't it? I can picture her likeness carved as a figurehead for one of the Richmond Line ships. Not that Mrs. Yardley Peridot would consent to something so undignified. But she'd keep the pirates at bay on the Oriental routes, don't you think?" And because he knew that given half an opportunity, Stephen would take up the worried old topic of wool cargoes again, he began to question him instead about the college Daniel would attend in Oxford. His tone warmed as he spoke. This was a wise move of Stephen's. Daniel was under a bad influence with Kendrick, and his phrenological examinations of both young men had vindicated this opinion. Daniel had a shallow upper forehead, indicating poor reasoning faculties, hollow temples showing deficient perceptive faculties, and pronounced bumps in the low "adhesiveness area," which revealed tendencies to infatuation and inability to choose worthwhile companions. Kendrick he knew well, but again his searching fingers had noted the narrowness of the skull, indicating acquisitiveness, self-esteem, and cynicism, while the ominous hollows behind his ears told of underdeveloped social proclivities. The most selfish character the doctor had ever studied.

None of his observations would have impressed Kendrick, who thought phrenology was so much horse manure and was not slow to say so. At the moment he was in the garden telling Daniel of his disgust at his friend's enforced departure. "Your father has no sense of humor," he was saying, and when Daniel began to stutter a protest, he continued, "No offense, boyo, I assure you. But if he has no sense of humor, how can I judge his motives? I measure everybody by what makes him laugh. Even the constable thought that hansom cab incident was funny—you could see that! We should have bribed him and paid for the damned horse—couldn't have been worth much."

"F-Father says we broke the law."

"So? That's never bothered me before. Oh, what the hell. I'll miss you, boyo."

Daniel's mouth fell into wry lines. He looked younger than eighteen in his formal frock coat. "I d-dread going. The voyage—"

"What I don't understand is why you have to *work*. That's a rum deal. Mama hasn't a fraction of the money your folks have, yet I'll not have to seek employment as long as there's a shilling in the bank, and then Grandmaire would see me right. Your father can hire a hundred maritime lawyers if he wants, so why turn you into one?" When Daniel said nothing, he laughed dryly. "It's because of me, isn't it? Well, sod him then. You'll be back before long, and we'll have just as much fun as we've had this summer. I say . . ." He paused, listening. "There's somebody in the gazebo, after Tawa's fireworks, no doubt. There'll be fireworks if she catches them. Let's see who it is." And he moved toward the screened gingerbread structure on the cliff edge.

All of Grandmaire's parties ended with one of Tawa's famous pyrotechnic displays, when tracks of flame streaked across the sky and fizzing galaxies whirred in circles down to the sea, while the housekeeper crouched behind a barrier with her lamps, tapers, and a covey of Maori children eager to help. Last year the "helpers" had grown impatient for Grandmaire to signal the end of the evening, and when one produced a lucifer box, they had begun anyway, so this time a temporary maid from the orphanage had been posed as a guard. With an apple and a glass of watery lemonade she sat on a cider keg in the darkness, listening to the music, so absorbed watching the dancers on the veranda that she was unaware of the boys.

"Hello there!" said Kendrick, right next to her ear.

She gaped at him silently. Daniel thought she looked like a squirrel with her clutched apple, frightened eyes, and that ugly servant's cap sticking up like gray ears.

"You don't belong here," Kendrick told her. "Grandmaire hires only Maori servants. All but dull Dora, that is.

But you don't look so bright yourself. What's your name?" When she continued to gape mutely, he grabbed her chin to force her attention and repeated, "What's your name then?"

The girl's fright curdled into defiance. While the nuns warned her to be meek and obedient to her employers, they had told her about employers' sons. She shook her head to loosen Kendrick's grip, and when he laughed, she struck upward with both hands, knocking his arms aside.

He stopped laughing. In one swift movement he captured both her wrists, and though she struggled and hissed, he held her easily. "What's your name then?" he said again. She replied by glaring at him, so he twisted both wrists until she squeaked with pain. "I asked you a question, which you will oblige me by answering," he told her.

Daniel was uncomfortable, knowing Kendrick could turn nasty when he had been drinking. "I s-say," he fretted. "Let's go back to the party."

"We've just begun! Come now, Cousin. Don't pretend that you never had sport with the hired help. There's plenty of her for both of us." He tugged the girl to her feet, then leaned over her. Despite her averted head, he succeeded quickly in maneuvering her around so that he could kiss her, but no sooner had he covered her mouth with his than he drew back, yelping an oath.

"The bitch bit me!" He wiped his face and stared with disbelief at his bloodied palm. "The bitch." He swung back a fist.

She saw it coming and tried to duck out of the way, but his knotted hand glanced off the top of her brow and smacked her back into the darkness in a soft explosion of falling packages punctuated by a tinkle of rolling bottles. When Kendrick dived in after her, she screamed with real fear in her voice.

A figure hurried along the path, skirt hems dragging in the gravel. "What is it? What is going on?"

"Nothing, Dora. It's j-just a game," said Daniel as loudly as he could.

"A game that you'd rather not join in. If my brother is involved, I can imagine what kind of game it is. Who is he

97

tormenting? Who is that crying? Kendrick! Come out here this instant."

At that moment May was leaning over the balcony rail. She had just finished a boisterous polka with Jon, and the moment they paused for breath May realized that she had overexerted herself. Her chest was pinched tight, and as she tried to smile at Jon, the room blurred.

Jon could see that she was ill. "I'll fetch your father. Here, sit down." He beckoned to Jennifer Vinton.

"No, please," said May. "Take me out to the veranda." Once there she leaned against the balustrade post, gasping. I must pass this off lightly, she thought, noting Jon's concerned expression. "I'm all right. Honestly I am."

"It's your illness, isn't it? I'd better fetch Uncle Stephen."

"No, thank you. Please don't be tedious, Jon. Father is talking business, and he'd not thank you for disturbing him over nothing. Yes, nothing. And he would very likely forbid me to go riding or on photographic expeditions, so for weeks my life would be quite disagreeable. Truly, Jon, you'd not want to be responsible for that, would you?"

His lips twitched. May thought what unfortunate coloring he had, that sandy hair and skin which, because of spots and pale freckles, always looked vaguely unclean.

"Thank you, Jon," she said, settling the matter. After flicking her fan open, she waved it slowly, breathing in time to its rhythm as she gazed out at the bracelet of lights strung on the arm of land across the harbor.

That was when the scream attracted her attention.

"There seems to be trouble at the gazebo."

"Dora's going to sort it out," said Jon.

"She may need some assistance. That scream sounded genuine."

"Dora is capable of handling anything. If she were not durable, Grandmaire would have crushed her years ago."

Dora's voice bounced over the lawn, raised high with anger. May said, "Are you sure she can cope?"

"My dear cousin, surely you're not hinting that I go out there? I'm one of life's spectators."

His patronizing tone annoyed May.

"Then I shall offer my assistance," she said, and though her chest still hurt, she brushed past him and hurried down the steps.

To her consternation she found that not only was Jon correct but Dora clearly did not want an intrusion. May found the maid sobbing against Dora's shoulder. Her assailants had fled.

"This is nothing that need concern you," said Dora in reply to May's hesitant inquiry. "The matter is closed. Don't you think that's best, Hettie? No harm has been done after all."

"If you say so, madam." Hettie gulped.

"Oh," said May foolishly, glancing back to where Jon still stood at the veranda rail. Doubtless he would say, "I told you so," in attitude, if not in words, so she could not go back that way. "Well, if I'm not needed . . ." she said, moving away along the way that led back to the front of the house via the rose gardens.

At the stone wall she hesitated. The patch closest to the house led through a long pergola thickly draped with a tangle of jasmine and clematic vines, and May had learned to avoid that because of the nuisance of drooping tendrils and the steady confetti of petals and pollen. She took the only alternative, the path near the road, and stepped out beside the low hedge to hurry to the front door, where she resolved to begin the evening all over again, by pretending she had just arrived. The cool air was heavily perfumed with roses. May had reached the drive when a horse thundered in from the road, so close that she could feel the warmth of its flanks.

"You almost knocked me down!" she called.

The rider stopped. The horse reared like a wave cresting, and the man slid off in such a fluid movement that May realized he was riding without a saddle. To her surprise he tossed the reins in her direction.

"Hold these," he said, not waiting for her to take them. Leaving the loop swinging, he loped up to the porch. May caught the reins and followed, leading the horse, while he hammered on the door with his fists.

"Well," she said, as he turned in a gesture of frustration, "I might have expected that only you would run me down,

99

though since you have such a low opinion of my driving I'm astonished that you would entrust your horse to me."

"Miss Yardley . . ." He looked at her blankly.

"Who did you think I was?" But he did not hear above the noise of his renewed thumping. When he paused, she said, "This is not the fire station."

"Pardon?"

"The fire station. You act like someone reporting a fire."

He was not listening but concentrated on sounds from within the house. Piqued, she was about to reproach him when the door swung inward and Tawa greeted him quietly. The young man replied rapidly, desperately, and not until he had almost finished did May realize they were speaking Maori. The door closed again, but instead of leaving, he stood under the porch lantern, deep in thought.

"You speak the native tongue fluently," said May, who was trying to pick it up.

He nodded.

I'm making a mess of every encounter this evening, she thought. Jon tells me not to interfere, Dora tells me the same, and now this obnoxious young man orders me about as if I were a stableboy. "Would you like your horse back now, sir?"

That jolted him out of his preoccupation. "I forgot you were there. Forgive my lack of manners, please."

"I had not noticed any variation from our previous meeting."

The remark was wasted; she doubted that he had heard her.

"I am not myself this evening, I'm afraid."

"Oh? Who are you then?"

"My mother is desperately ill. I fear she may be dying. She is weak and in terrible pain. I çannot tell you what frustration it is to be unable to ease her agony."

"I'm so sorry." May was instantly thankful that he had not heard her petty, sarcastic remarks. She did not know what to do with the information he had just given her and was groping for something adequate to say when the front door opened and Hal stepped out, slamming it behind him.

In her already shocked state it took May a few seconds to recognize Hal, for this was not the jovial young man who had danced with her. This Hal was flushed and aggressive, with murder in his eyes. But in the moment she recognized him, she also knew who the mysterious young man must be. Only Patrick Bennington would push Hal into such a stance of defiant loathing.

"Go home," he said in a voice she had never heard before. "Take your vile mother and the rest of your filthy tribe, and get back to the king Country, where all you bloody Maoris belong."

"Hal!"

He was unaware of her presence. "Get out! Go! I've had all I intend to take from you. You may be amused by parading around masquerading under our name, but to me it is a stinking insult to my dead father's name."

The young man stiffened with dignity. "He was my father, too, and he gave me the name legally."

Hal swore. "You are an upstart and usurper. You and your mother stole from my family. How did you come by that brewery? Not honestly, I warrant."

"You know I've taken nothing of yours. Your lawyer pestered me until he found out all you wanted to know. Must we quarrel?" He sounded weary. "Please let us set aside our differences just for tonight."

Hal strode toward him, roaring, "Get out! Go!"

"I shall leave when my stepfather is ready to come with me."

"Stepfather?" In the coppery light May could see Hal's neck muscles working as he struggled to contain his rage. "Stepfather! Ha! Another joke, I suppose. Your mother plays the whore to my father for twenty years, and the minute he dies you both stick your dirty fingers into my uncle's pocket. You—"

"Captain Bennington, please. It is imperative that I—"

"I could have guessed you'd try to avoid a fight. Well I have news for you, Patrick *Teipa*. I'm calling the terms, and I say we have it out now." And striding down the porch, he squared off, breathing heavily, in front of Patrick.

May dashed forward and cried, "No, Hal. Not now. You *mustn't.*"

101

"What in the world—" His face glistened like water. "What are you doing out here?"

"I was holding the horse," she said.

"What?" He was dazed by the inappropriateness of her reply.

"Please set aside your differences, just for tonight," she pleaded. At that moment the door opened again, and Samuel and Dora emerged.

At the sight of them Patrick strode forward, ignoring Hal, whose aggressiveness wilted. Placing both hands on Samuel's shoulders, he began to speak in Maori again, an anguished outpouring. Though she understood not one word, May thought his voice was the saddest and most beautiful sound she had ever heard.

"What a frightening scene it must have been," said Juliette the next morning. She rested her needlepoint in her lap. "Hal had a fierce temper as a child, and though I've met Patrick only once, he did impress me as being cold and arrogant. They say he rides around town as if he owns the place, yet nobody receives him socially."

"It must be difficult, being neither European nor Maori."

"He is a Maori, dear. One drop of acknowledged blood would make him so."

"He looks nothing like one. His features are fine, and his skin is lighter than Hal's."

Juliette glanced at her daughter. "Last evening must have been brightly lit for you to have made such a detailed study of his appearance."

May covered her confusion by bending to twitch at a fold of cashmere skirt. "There. If you stay perfectly still, that draping will catch the light beautifully. When I bring the plate out, please pretend to be stitching. That's right. The needle just so." She glanced into Juliette's face and said defensively, "I felt such compassion for him. He was in agonies about his mother. Has there been any news from Uncle Samuel yet?"

"There was a crisis in the night; but your uncle attended her, and she was much better this morning."

"I wish I could meet her," said May. "I wonder what she looks like. She must be extraordinarily beautiful."

Great heavens, thought Juliette. It sounds as though she's become bewitched by him. Next, she'll be infatuated with the gardener! But she tried to sound casual as she said, "I'm glad Samuel is happy, though his choice is regrettable. However, the marriage will certainly keep Abby away from here, so I must be thankful for that. When you finish taking your photograph, we shall go through your wardrobe and choose something especially becoming for the Queen's Birthday picnic."

"I forgot to tell you. Hal wants to escort me. Would that be all right?"

Five minutes before, Juliette would have been tempted to say a firm no. It's odd how something can suddenly appear attractive when a worse alternative is presented, she thought wryly.

"How long will Hal be ashore?"

"Four weeks. Isn't that marvelous? I'm so pleased Father decided it was time for the *Mondrich Zephyr* to have her hull scraped and refitted."

"I think the barnacles decided it was time."

"Then bravo for barnacles," said May.

And the Lord help us all, thought Juliette. Why Hal when there were so many *eligible* young men around? Why?

Nine

"I used to write you long, long letters," said May. "All about what we were doing. One was about Alcatraz Island. There was a cannon there and an enormous long pyramid of cannonballs. One ball sat by itself in a dish on the ground so that people could pick it up. I wrote that nobody could, but I thought you might be able to. And another day we went to Woodward's Pleasure Gardens. Edward was five years old and said he would kick the Chinese giant in the shins, but as I told you in the letter, we emerged from where all the stuffed animals were and there right in front of us was the giant. Poor Edward . . ."

"What letters?" asked Hal. "I don't recall those."

May smiled. They were at the wharf, waiting to board the steam ferry *Patriot*, which was to take them to the island for the picnic. "I never sent them, of course. But I kept them in a leather folder. Mother said I should keep them for a kind of diary."

"If you wrote them to me, then they must be mine. May I claim the right to see them?"

"Perhaps. But only if your promise not to laugh at them."

"You must read them aloud to me."

"Oh, I couldn't. I couldn't do that."

They had arrived early, but now the wharf was crowded, the throng thickened by the disgorging of a trainload of sawmill hands from Onehunga, who shepherded wives and children. The shrill voices sounded like sea gulls. It was a sharp, clear morning with air so still that the smoke from the ferry's funnel drooped like a sooty sock.

Miss Von Sturmer tried to keep track of Albert and Edward, who were playing tag in the crowd, careless of whom they bumped or what they tripped over. "Those two are abbreviating my life," she complained to May. "Yesterday they found the canoe that your uncle keeps for fishing, and they paddled into the harbor and threw stones at me when I tried to coax them ashore."

"Dora might help you with them," suggested Hal. "She has the right touch with recalcitrant children."

"Yes, and a touch is what they need, I'm thinking. Albert! Edward! Come here this instant!"

Edward darted out from a group of people, leaving muttering and angry glances in his wake. He paused only to pull a face at his nurse before racing off in the other direction.

May looked embarrassed. Hal raised his eyebrows but said nothing. How the Yardleys reared their children was not his concern.

The crew waited to cast off until Grandmaire and her entourage were safely aboard. In the ladies' salon Grandmaire glared at the woman who occupied the best chair until she was intimidated into leaving, then settled herself with her mohair knee rug and velour foot cushion and a list of errands for Dora.

"—and find Ellen for me. Rescue her from that dreary aunt. She can come take tea with me."

May and Hal were listening to the brass band on the aft deck when Dora moved across their line of vision. May saw her whisper to Ellen, and as Ellen rose to follow her, she cast a look of such despair at Hal that May, intercepting it, was lanced by guilt. An impulse made her tweak at Hal's sleeve and ask, "If I put a serious question to you, will you answer me frankly?"

"Of course I will."

She hesitated, aware that heads had turned and that the Vinton girls were nearby. When the music swelled with a rendition of the popular "Britannia March," she said quickly, "Have you ever declared yourself to Ellen?"

He looked so startled that she was sorry. For a moment she thought he might brush her aside, but then he took her by the elbow and steered her to a quieter place near the gangplank.

"You astonish me," he said. "Did I hear you correctly?"

"Please forget I spoke. It was wrong of me . . . really."

"Was it? Don't you feel that you have some right to ask?" His voice was firm now; he had recovered from the shock of her question. "I'm fond of Ellen. We are close, dear friends, but no more. All right?"

It was not until they were back listening to the band that she realized that not only had Hal avoided looking her in the eye, but he had also avoided answering the question. She glanced at him now, but he turned such a warm look upon her that her misgivings fled.

The harbor was especially pretty, a spread of silver and blue light, and in the distance a dozen ships drifted away like feathers on the tide. The ferry chugged on, music grinding up with the engine noises. When the spindly jetty scraped along the side, ladies gasped in pretended fright. Piles creaked. Adventurous young men in straw boaters jumped from the railings to the jetty.

Hal and May were close to the top of the gangplank and disembarked with the first group. Striding out to keep ahead of Miss Von Sturmer and the boys, they overtook Abigail, who was leaning on the arm of Derwent Kine. Daniel and Kendrick walked with them, pretending to ignore the fluttery giggles of the two Kine girls. As they passed by, Hal took May's arm and threaded it through his own. So his mother can see, thought May.

At the top of the track Hal paused. "Here we are, and this is all ours for the day. Since we are here first, do you think we could claim it for our exclusive use?"

"It's enchanting." The bay was a flat lacy-edged apron spread over a lap of golden sand. Pohutukawa trees gripped the cliffs with their twisted roots and leaned out over their own ragged shadows. Two yachts with chests like pouter pigeons' sliced through the darker waters beyond a necklace of red buoys. May glanced back over her shoulder to where hundreds of men, women, and children clogged the path in a slow-moving stream. Within minutes there would be so many people on the beach that sea and sand would be obscured from view. She sighed. "If only we *could* claim it for our exclusive use."

But May enjoyed picnics, and this one was all the more fun because she soon realized that while Hal's conversation might be disappointingly limited, he was at his best in the brash boisterousness of excursion activities. She applauded his speed in the egg and spoon race, his dexterity with the soapy pig, laughed in delight when the greasy pole pitched him into the water bath, cheered until she panted when his team won the tug-of-war, then retired to the shade to watch quietly as he participated in the archery contest and tried, unsuccessfully, to skewer a painted apple on a painted tree. The chilly breeze whipped only a faint trace of color into her pale cheeks; but her lips were pink and moist, and her eyes shone as they walked together. When he helped her climb over the warm black rocks, she bunched her skirts and he conspicuously averted his gaze. She talked eagerly of drama critics, photography, art exhibitions, the philharmonic orchestra, photography, an entertaining, instructive play called *The Road to Ruin,* and again photography.

He missed much of what she said when from time to time his attention was diverted by glimpses of one of the Oregon Line ships, a new steam and sail monster which was now in mid-harbor and coming closer. His curiosity was whetted. When it drew nearer, he would be able to read the flags and learn who was sailing her and what cargo she carried.

May folded her parasol and sat down carefully. "Hal," she chided, "I fear that I am boring you."

"No, of course not. I'm sorry if I seem preoccupied."

"I was saying that Bobby and I plan an expedition into one of the craters to photograph the old Maori earthworks. It will be enormously complicated, for we will have to carry equipment, chemicals, and a little black tent so that the plates can be processed as they are exposed. We shall go in the dogcart, trailing Te Kooti behind us with our gear."

Hal slung a shell at a sea gull. "You cannot . . . I mean, what do your parents think of this idea?"

"I haven't mentioned it to them yet. I probably won't

mention it until afterward. Bobby and I often go on expeditions. He is becoming quite capable in his own right. Last week, when we went down to the shore, I permitted him to choose a view and expose a frame of myself with his view as the background." She laughed. "A wind gusted in and snatched my bonnet away, and I could not refrain from trying to catch it, so my image is ghostly and peculiar, but the rest of the picture is excellent. Next time you come out to the house, I shall ask Bobby to show it to you."

Hal rolled onto his side and squinted up at her. "May, I want to ask you to do something for me."

"Of course. Anything you require."

"This expedition to the crater." He sat up. "I want you to put the whole notion out of your mind."

"You don't mean that."

"I'm perfectly serious."

She said carefully, "You asked me to do something for *you*. How can this be interpreted as a favor for you?"

"May, it is wrong of you to be trailing all over the countryside with a young boy as your only protection."

"Is that all that worries you? For a minute I was afraid that you were going to tell me that photography was not a suitable pursuit for a young lady. Your mother thinks so, you know. She told Lena that she disapproves of the way I spend my time."

"Mama has a lot of strong notions, but I do agree with her this time. It is *not* suitable. Wait." He imprisoned her gloved fingers. "Believe me, it is not the unsuitability which concerns me as much as your personal safety. The crater is an isolated spot, and there could be all kinds of people lurking around. Hundreds of Maoris live out near you, and—"

"Gracious, I'm not afraid of *Maoris*. They are friendly and pleasant and don't even mind posing for the camera, though they do tend to stand stiffly to attention and cannot seem to understand what I require. But I am learning. I can say *tena koe* and *haere mai* and *haere ra* and even *kapai*."

He said, "All Maoris are not friendly, May."

"All *people* are not friendly," she replied with spirit. "Gracious, you are as bad as Patrick, telling me that the

108

woods are full of fierce Maoris—" She stopped with a gasp, realizing what she had blurted out. "Hal, I'm sorry. I didn't mean to . . . I met him on the way to town one day, and he told me—"

Silence fell between them, uncomfortable as grit in a shoe. A couple with a bobbing herd of children passed close, the husband with trousers rolled to expose paper-white calves, his stout wife red-faced and wheezing. She stared at May as she went by, clearly disapproving the lack of any chaperone.

"We had better go back to Grandmaire's tent. Lena will be wondering where I am."

"So you know Patrick Teipa well, do you?"

"No, of course not."

"You were holding his horse for him."

"I happened to be there." She shivered, recalling how rage had transformed Hal into a completely different person. He was not angry now, merely cool and detached. She said, "I didn't know who he was until you spoke to him. Please leave the whole subject be. It is ruining a pleasant day."

"Very well." He looked into her eyes and smiled. She could see the effort it cost him. "I'm old-fashioned, May. Old-fashioned about a great many things: personal values, family ties. My family has suffered, and I cannot condone or accept that."

"I agree, and appreciate your feelings, but surely Patrick is the wrong person for you to hate. He could not have wished himself into existence, so none of this is his fault." And when Hal stared at her, tight-faced, she added, "I felt sorry for him. He was distraught about his mother."

"Her! It will be best for everybody if she dies, and the sooner, the better. Her death will bring an end to the hell poor Mama has lived through these last twenty years. This is not a proper topic for us to discuss, but you must fully understand. It is possible that you might see the Teipa fellow on the road, and if people saw you talking together, they could misconstrue the situation."

"Are you ordering me not to speak to him?"

"Surely there's no need of that, not now that you know the situation. You'd not want to talk to him, would you? Of

109

course not. There, that's settled," he said, though to May's mind nothing was settled; on the contrary, everything was more confused than ever.

Ellen sat on a seawall with Abby and Derwent Kine, watching Verona and Lucca make patterns with shells in the sand. Ellen saw Hal and May stroll away to be alone together. Her desire to interfere physically—to dash up and push May aside—was so strong that it made her feel ill. It seemed impossible to stay and make bright conversation, and she marveled that she could. Abby's attitude blended her usual friendliness with pity, a quality intolerable to Ellen, who desired envy and admiration.

Not a dozen yards away Hal and May paused at the foot of the bank. Hal took May's hands and helped her up to the slope, then whispered in her ear, making her laugh.

The sight, sound, and feeling that emanated from them crushed the last vestiges of Ellen's defenses. Without a word she walked swiftly away in the opposite direction, the combination of glare and tears almost blinding her.

Jon saw her go and ran to catch her alone. He reached her just as she began to sob and was at her side when she stumbled awkwardly.

"Easy there." He took her arm.

She recognized his voice with horror and ducked her head so that her bonnet rim hid her face.

"Are you all right?"

There was no escape. "It's just the heat. . . . My eyes were dazed by the sun, and I was developing a headache."

"Grandmaire will have some smelling salts. Would you like me to fetch her vinaigrette for you?"

"No, thank you." His concern was a salve for her wounded pride. "A walk will clear my head."

"It's a beautiful day, isn't it?" he said, still holding her arm, a gesture which gave her further comfort. "They say that in Wellington the weather is so disagreeable that if there happens along a day like this, they declare it a holiday."

"Of course. You're going away," she said abruptly. They were drifting to the edge of the sand now; in front of them was the clearing, where steam frittered from the humped earth ovens.

"Tonight. I'm going directly from the afternoon ferry to the *Richmond Argus,* and she sails at five. My things are aboard, and I've said good-bye to Mama and the family, so that they can stay here until the last ferry. Mr. Kine says the steam packet is a capital journey as long as the sea doesn't cut up rough. He was coming with me, but he's been delayed by Maori land court business or something, so I have the cabin all to myself. You should see it, Ellen. What a grand room it is—walnut paneling, silver and crystal fixtures. Surrounded by luxury, I feel like a Member of Parliament already."

"You'll do well." Tears itched on her cheek, and she raised her free hand to wipe them away. She had never heard Jon talk so much.

"Mr. Kine says that Wellington is a lonely place, but I expect I shall soon make new friends. People are always seeking out those in power, and no doubt I'll be moving in some influential circles, rubbing shoulders with the wealthy, but for all that I shall be lonely for genuine companionship."

"Perhaps you need a wife." They had topped the rise and were walking toward the tall shade trees which fringed the flat, grassy area where the sports were being held. A party of men was setting up trestle tables for the food.

"It's coincidental that you should mention that. Mr. Kine was adamant that the first thing any young man in government should do is acquire a suitable wife." He paused. Not once had she so much as glanced at him, and when she had spoken, her voice had been flat, listless. Grandmaire had stressed that he must speak today, before he left, but this air of indifference made his approach very difficult.

"Ellen, I realize that this is sudden, and I don't want an answer immediately. I shall be returning in six months for a long stay, and perhaps we can discuss the matter then."

"What?"

"Would you consider marrying me? I'm confident I'm going to have a marvelous future in politics. You would

111

have an assured position in society. We would complement each other splendidly. What do you think?"

She barely heard him. As they approached the trees, she stopped dead. Right in front of them Hal pushed May in a swing. A sob threatened to choke Ellen. She tugged to free her arm, but instead of letting her go, Jon gripped her more tightly and turned her to face him.

"My God," he said, "Ellen, what is the matter?"

She did not, could not reply. Abruptly she turned and with head bent began running back awkwardly the way they had come.

Jon shrugged as he watched her stumble into Grandmaire's green and white striped tent. The proposal had not been accepted, but he was patient. On his first visit home he would try again, and by then Grandmaire might have coaxed her around to thinking differently.

Grandmaire held the basin while Ellen dabbed a cold cloth against her swollen eyes. "True contentment can arise only out of acceptance," she said. "And you must accept that Hal is perhaps not the one for you after all."

"But everything was wonderful until she came along. . . . Oh, if only there were some way of spiriting her back to San Francisco."

Grandmaire ignored the outburst. "Many people were aghast when I, a wealthy and cultured widow, chose to marry Thomas Peridot, who was a rough trader and lived in appalling conditions in Kororareka. They thought I should choose a government official or a scientist, but I knew what was right. Thomas was a talented, thrifty businessman with vision and was respected by all, especially the Maoris. That was an important quality at the time. I didn't love him, of course, but we built a satisfying life together."

"What has that to do with Hal and me?"

"Don't pout at me, lass. You will be very wealthy when I am gone. No, listen, and no more tears. You must choose a husband who is shrewd, alert, and in touch with all the major decisions that are being made in New Zealand. Hal is not a suitable choice for you."

"Why didn't you say so before?"

"You are very young, and I was confident that you would come to that realization without any prompting from me. Hal is so obsessed by the sea that he would only disappoint you and make you restless. You need someone with a broader view of the world, someone sophisticated and ambitious. Unless you forget Hal, you are fated to be miserable." She raised her head. "Ah, that aroma! The *hangi* has been lifted, and I am ravenous. Emotion and fresh air work on me like a tonic. Take my arm, dear, and escort me to the tables. Let us find Jon and allow him to serve us. He's going away today. I shall miss him, but ah, what a magnificent future he has." And all the way over to the clearing she talked enthusiastically about Jon. Ellen, understanding, said nothing.

May had insisted on being there when the earth oven was opened. She watched with interest as the earth was scraped away and the layers of steaming sacks were peeled off carefully. When all was bare, she could see sagging flax baskets of food, dozens of them, containing potatoes, sweet kumara, fish, pork joints, chicken, lamb, eel, pumpkin, and pulpy-looking cabbage.

"How is it done?" asked May. "We went to a hangi at the pa at Whenuahakari, but though I tried to unravel the mystery, nobody could fully explain how it is done."

"Simple. The food is cooked on hot stones."

"Yes, but *how?* Father said it was a real art, but he was not sure of the technicalities, and Mother was trying to converse in Maori with an ancient old woman who was chewing tobacco."

"Who cares about the technicalities? I've never bothered to take any notice."

May stepped back as a Maori man with knotted arms and a tattooed face swung a basket of vegetables onto a tray. *Kapai te kai,"* he said, grinning. "Good food."

"Don't you like it?" asked May, seeing Hal's expression of disgust. "I adore the exotic, smoky fragrance of hangi food. I hope they have *puha* in there, too. Mrs. Terrill cooks it for us, and you'd never believe a wild thistle could taste so delicious."

"You like it because it's a novelty. In a year or so you'll

113

regard it as an unhygienic and barbaric way of preparing food. Look at that." And he waved an arm toward where a party of Maori children were performing a *haka*, or war dance, for queuing picnickers. "Isn't that grotesque? They prance, roll their eyes, make grunting sounds, and flick their tongues about like lizards after flies, and there is nothing beautiful in the spectacle whatsoever."

May wanted to argue that it was interesting, because a haka was designed to frighten the enemy and demoralize him before battle, but she remained silent. Patrick and his mother had soured Hal's view of the whole race. She took Hal's arm and smiled at him. "I think I saw Lena over by the trees. Do you think she might like to eat with us? I've had only a few words with her, and I should hate her to feel snubbed."

"There are so many delightful young men here. This picnic is a feast of opportunity!" Lena giggled when she joined them. "Mama has been watching *me*, so *I* must watch my step." She lowered her voice to a whisper. "Ellen has been watching you all day. Kendrick is so amused by her discomfiture. Don't look so dismayed. She has always been so horrid to Kendrick that he cannot be blamed for enjoying her misery."

"I don't want Ellen to be hurt. Truly, I—"

"Of course you don't." Lena shushed her. "You have such a sweet nature that I cannot imagine your hurting anybody. Kendrick, on the other hand, is ruled by malicious demons—or so he says."

When the afternoon ferry pulled out, only a few people were aboard: people with youngsters who had taken a touch too much sun, elderly folk for whom the day had already held its quota of bearable excitement, Jon . . . and Ellen.

She had fled to the ferry after a nasty encounter with Kendrick; he had mocked her, told her how Hal was tedious company at home because he talked of nothing but May. "It was better when he was escorting you about," he said. "At least he never bothered to mention your name, but all we have is May, May, May. He is besotted with her."

114

From the top deck Ellen saw Jon come aboard and cowered behind the funnel so he would not see her tearstained face. With arms wrapped around herself she tried to calm the raging jealousy within her. Her mouth tasted musty, making her physically ill. What can I do? she thought with dead hopelessness. It seemed to her that everybody at the picnic was pitying her, and she knew that until she was married, she would not be free of that feeling. From now on, whenever she walked into a room, someone would whisper behind a fan that she loved Hal Bennington—and he had spurned her for May. I must do something, she thought. Anything. Something to prove that I, Ellen Forster, am far above pity.

When the ferry docked at the Auckland wharf, Ellen stayed near the funnel until everybody had disembarked. Her eyes followed Jon's progress along the wharf to the next dock, where the *Richmond Argus* was aswarm with activity prior to departure. She envied Jon with a sudden, fierce wish that she could change places with him, that she could sail away to Wellington and a fresh start, away from the whispers and the unendurable pity.

Jon smoothed his hair and put the brush down, glancing at the tortoiseshell back with a smug feeling. Soon it would be silver for him—silver, suede, cashmere, champagne, and the trappings of a luxurious existence. His government salary would do him proud, and the extra commissions from Grandmaire would be so much icing on the cake. He could taste the rich life already.

He was lying on his bunk, hands crossed behind his head, savoring the feeling, when he heard his name whispered, "Jon, wake up," and he opened his eyes to see Ellen standing, looking lost, in the middle of the cabin.

"What are you doing here?" He consulted his watch. "It's almost five. We'll be casting off soon."

"We already have. Don't you feel the ship moving?"

He swung his feet to the floor and leaned out the porthole to see the wharf sliding away out of reach.

"Ellen, what are you doing here?"

She looked ill—sunstroke?—and her eyes were frightened, but she said boldly, "Did you mean what you said about marrying me?" When he stared at her as if he had missed out on some vital link in their communication, she rushed on. "If you did mean it, then I accept. I want to marry you straightaway."

"You're serious, aren't you?"

"I've never been more serious in my life."

Still, he did not give her an answer but leaned against the wall, studying her from under half-lowered lids. She tried to meet his gaze but failed. Aware that she must appear pathetic, biting her lip and wringing her hands, she edged over to his cabin chair and sat down. At once she felt more composed, more in command of the situation.

This tenuous confidence evaporated when Jon smiled at her in a most unsettling way and reached over to lock the door.

"We can't have you changing your mind, can we now?" he said.

"I won't change my mind."

There was a long silence while he contemplated her. She stared at the floor, then ventured to give him a timid smile.

"That's better," he said, and came to kneel down beside her. "So you're going to be my little wife, are you?"

His voice unsettled her. "Jon . . ." she began.

He hushed her by covering her mouth with a kiss. A kiss unlike any she had ever had before. Hal was always boisterous, but Jon's mouth was slack and moist against her lips. Disliking the sensation, she tried to pull away, but the pressure of his hand behind her neck kept her imprisoned, while with the other hand he began jerking at the buttons on her high collar.

She arrested his hand in both of hers. "What are you doing?"

"I'm making you my wife," he said, his hand now sliding up under her skirt. "This is what you want, isn't it?"

"Stop it, Jon."

He rocked back on his heels, his expression inscrutable. "You want me to stop?"

"Of course I do. You can't just—"

He was on his feet and strolling to the door. When he

reached it he turned the key with a flourish and opened the door wide. "After you," he said with a nod.

"What do you mean?"

"We are going up on deck to see Captain Perriman. He will arrange to have you put ashore on the pilot boat."

"Captain Perriman?" She had met him at a ship launching: a loud, coarse fellow with a mouthful of innuendos and a sly way of looking at a pretty girl.

"After you," repeated Jon. "I don't know what the true purpose of your visit was, but you have just demonstrated that it was not to elope with me. And you might as well understand now that I'll not be toyed with. So let's go discuss this with the captain."

"I did mean it, Jon. Truly I did."

"Did you?"

She looked terrified but resolute. And she nodded.

Jon locked the door and leaned against it. "Then, if you don't want me to remove your gown, you had better do it yourself, hadn't you?"

For a long moment she stared at him. Outside, they could hear the pumping of the tugboat and the scream of sea gulls. Slowly Ellen's hands reached up to her throat, and she began to undo her buttons.

Ten

The Yardleys were at breakfast next morning when Dr. Forster called in. He declined the offer of tea, warned them that Samuel's wife was very close to death, and almost as an afterthought told them that it seemed Ellen had eloped with Jon.

"It must have been a sudden decision," he said, his face as stiff as his tone. "She took nothing with her, and all we know is that several witnesses saw her board the steam packet just as the gangplank was being drawn up. As Jon was the only person she knew on the passenger list, we can only assume . . ."

"What a shock for you both," said Juliette.

The doctor seemed to avoid looking in May's direction. "It is not what we had hoped for her. A society wedding and the gathering of friends would have meant a great deal to Rose."

He blames me, thought May guiltily. Later, when showing her mother some of her latest batch of photographs, she voiced her worries.

"There may be a grain of truth in what you say, but no more," Juliette reassured her. "Nobody forced Ellen to elope, and you have taken nothing from her. Hal and she were not engaged. Oh, look at this picture of the boys in Samuel's canoe. What a pity Albert is turning away from the camera. It is a splendid likeness of Edward. Do you think you could pose them like that again?"

"Only if you ask Uncle Samuel for permission to use his canoe. He forbade the boys to go near it after he caught them lighting a fire under it when it was upturned on the beach."

"What a ridiculous notion! Did he tell you that? Samuel is becoming so unreasonable. . . . Still, with his wife ill one must make allowances. Did you know that he accused the boys of throwing stones at the cottage? I could hardly believe my ears. I told him that Albert and Edward would never do that—he must have been suffering from delusions."

May was not so sure. "I've chased them away from the macrocarpa hedge several times recently. They were banging tins, making a fearful noise down there one day."

"You exaggerate! The trouble is that Samuel has taken a most unfortunate dislike to them, and they realize that and respond with high-spirited teasing. Never mind. Poor Samuel will be leaving soon, no doubt. He prefers the bush and the hills and is here only because of his wife." She shuddered. "If I could just rid myself of this feeling of impending doom. It has been at my shoulder ever since we left San Francisco. How I would love to go back again."

"So would I," said May. "This place is interesting, but I find there are so many restrictions. It's so irritating to be told that I must not go here or there because it's not proper. And I live in fear of offending Hal by mentioning Patrick's name."

After a silence Juliette said, "Why should you want to mention him, dear?"

May was at the window. From there she could see the road, which all day had been busy with a slow procession of Maori people on their way to the Peridots' cottage. "I feel such compassion for him. He adores his mother. You lost your mother when you were young, too, didn't you?"

"I was eight." Juliette smoothed her skirts in a gesture that forecast her imminent departure.

"Will you tell me about her? I know so much about Grandfather Peridot and that war club—the *mere*—you gave to the museum on his behalf, but I know nothing about my grandmother. What did she look like?"

"Like me, I suppose," she said over her shoulder.

May intercepted her in the hall. "Please don't go yet. Won't you tell me about her—and about my father, too? I only want to hear what they were actually *like* so that I will feel as though I know them."

119

Juliette's eyes were enormous. With all the creases erased, she looked like the wraith of a young girl in the soft gloom. She said, "Not now, May. I'm very busy today. Mrs. Terrill is expecting me in the pantry now. We have to discuss Edward's birthday tea." And before May could plead further, she was away down the stairwell, the streamers of her lace house cap fluttering over her shoulders.

May returned to the window. She warmed her locket in the palm of her hand. It was so ironic she could almost smile. If Mother talked incessantly about my real father, I would want her to desist, she thought. Had she had not been so set against my riding, I'd not have mastered Negus so swiftly. If they had bought me a camera as soon as I wanted one, would I have been so passionate about photography? And Hal? Would he have been so attractive if the whole town had not already decided that Ellen suited him best?

No, she argued quickly. That would have made no difference. I love Hal. I've *always* loved him, and I must shake off this feeling that I've taken something from Ellen. He never declared himself to her. He told me so. Still, the tiny doubt lingered.

Over the hedgetops she could see the roof ridge and smoke-blurred chimney of her uncle Samuel's cottage. Then what about Patrick? she wondered. If he had been agreeable to her, would she be thinking of him so intensely now? All day his face had haunted her. She remembered the pain in his eyes, how distracted he had been when tormented by anxiety about his mother. She wished that there were something she could do to help him, to ease his hurt, but even while she pondered the question, she realized that after the ugly scene she had witnessed at Fintona, Patrick would probably never wish to see her again.

While waiting for the dinner gong to strike, she was strolling along the veranda, enjoying the breeze off the sea. Close by she could hear Daisy Bonny, the parlormaid, calling out to someone on the road.

"Just after two it were," came a shrill voice from the passerby. "Proper harrowing it were, too. Master Patrick is ever so cut up about it."

120

"He should 'ave been prepared for it," called Daisy from just beyond the bathhouse.

"These Maoris do go on," replied the unseen woman. "Worse than the Irish. But it's all for the best, I say. The poor wretch is out of her suffering now."

May did not pause but was along the drive and striding out onto the road before she realized what she was doing. Daisy's sister gave her a startled glance, but she hurried past her and pushed the rickety field gate ajar, heedless of the bemused stare that followed her as she picked her way across the field to the fencible cottages. High, plaintive singing reached out to her as she approached.

Inside the hedge line were groups and clusters of people, some sitting on flax mats, some standing but all very still. The singing came from a throng of elderly women who squatted around the front door. All wore head scarves and black gowns. Their lips and chins were smudged with indigo tattooing, and as they sang, they rocked sadly from side to side. Here and there around the garden, oil lamps made soft pockets of light.

Nobody took any notice of May as she hurried along the path, and it was not until she was actually inside the door which led directly into the living room that she stopped, suddenly overcome by an uncomfortable feeling of not knowing why she had come.

The room was crowded, packed to the walls with people who sobbed and wailed. There was a strong smell of candlewax and the sickly-sweet odor of jasmine. May hesitated, uncertain whether to move forward or to turn and go, when the crowd moved slightly and she found herself jostled toward the center of the room.

Here lay Rosaleen Teipa Peridot, clad in white silk, surrounded by a thicket of blossoms and lying in a polished coffin. May's breath caught as she gazed down at the serene face. Thick black hair was smoothed back from her brow, and her brown hands were folded loosely over a greenstone cross that rested just above her waist. She exuded such an air of majestic tranquillity that her death seemed a gentle thing.

She looks no older than I am, thought May. So young

and so incredibly beautiful. If only I could have met her. No wonder Uncle Samuel adored her so desperately.

Glancing around for him, she thought at first that he was not in the room, but then she noticed him near the fireplace, standing with Patrick, arm around his shoulders, almost supporting him. Her uncle was white-faced and grim with a deliberate hardness around his mouth, but Patrick wept openly. His face was glossy with tears. May had never seen a man cry before, and the sight of Patrick's unashamed grief affected her powerfully. She could not bear to look at him and know that there was nothing she could do. His mourning was something she could not share because she had not known Rosaleen, and her inability to understand made her an outsider, an intruder drawn by others' misery. Horrified by this sudden vision of herself, May turned and fled the room, not pausing until she reached the gatehouse, where she was forced to halt, doubled up by a savage pain in her chest. As she rested, gasping for breath, she prayed that Patrick had not seen her.

On the day of the funeral the Yardleys were surprised to receive an unwelcome visit from the entire Bennington family, who came in the morning and stayed right through until late afternoon. Stephen escaped by taking Hal away to inspect the graving dock that was being built next to the shipyards, but Juliette had to endure hours of cold comments and colder silences while she sat in bewilderment, trying to decide whether this was meant to be some kind of peace mission.

"Mama has forced herself to visit here today because she wants to make absolutely certain that Aunt Juliette does not go to the funeral," Kendrick told Daniel candidly.

"Oh," said Daniel, uncomfortable for fear Patrick might come into the conversation. "Come up to the archery lawn, and l-let's practice on my bicycle."

Kendrick laughed. "Practice? I can already ride from our house to Queen Street in less than half an hour."

"Then come show me what I'm doing wrong," said Daniel.

And when the penny-farthing wavered across the parched

ground, he said, "I want to be able to r-ride all around Oxford . . . oh!" He cried out as he tumbled from the high seat, the wheel tilting over him. "What did you push me for?"

"Because I'm sick to death of hearing about Oxford. You have less than a fortnight to go, and I want to make the most of it." Helping Daniel up, he said, "Let's go down to the Royal Oyster Saloon and down a few tankards, a couple of dozen oysters apiece, and see if we can find some women willing to accept the consequences!"

"I don't know. . . ."

"Come on. The sight of all those Maoris is giving me the chills. Don't know how you can stand living so close to the *pa.*"

"There are only so many Maoris because—" He stopped.

"Because of the funeral. I know. Let's go."

The boys had not returned when Abby and Lena prepared to return home. By now the funeral was long over, the mourners had returned to their village for a hangi meal, and the road was empty of all but a few stragglers. As the Bennington phaeton rumbled out of the gates, Abby declared that the visit had been a triumph for her.

"I let her understand exactly what I think of that snip of a daughter of hers," she said, heedless of the fact that Lena and May were friends. "I made it plain that I am delighted Jon has won Ellen's hand. I told her that as Jon is dearer to my heart than Hal, naturally I wanted only the very best for him. And I informed her that Hal is heartbroken. I told her that Hal is very much in love with Ellen, but that he paid attention to May only out of a sense of obligation." She nodded, frowning. "I cannot understand what he sees in that vixen."

"Oh, please, Mama . . ." began Lena.

Her mother took no notice of the timid protest. Around her hovered an acidic, sweaty tang that betrayed her agitation. She said, "I took great pleasure in informing her that Grandmaire had settled twenty-five thousand pounds on Ellen and Jon as a gift."

"What did she say to that?" Lena had already heard from May that Dr. Forster had reported the sum as five thousand.

123

"Naturally she was astounded. Much too astounded to say anything," reported Abby smugly. Prodding the driver in the back with her parasol ferrule, she said, "Drive past the cemetery, please."

She had not originally intended to go near, but her day had been so bitter in taste that she hoped a view of her rival's grave might salve it for her. When the phaeton stopped at the gap in the low whitewashed wall, Abby ignored Lena's hesitant objection and, without waiting for her driver's assistance, clambered down and strode along the broad aisle between the tombstones. Rosaleen's grave was heaped with flowers and surrounded by fresh crumbs of damp earth. Nearby, in the shade, sat three old Maori women, silently fanning themselves with squares of woven flax.

Abby did not see them. Looking neither left nor right, she made her way directly to the grave and stood for a moment glaring at the roses and lilies, the clematis blooms wilting against the stiff wreaths of green leaves. She waited for the dull feeling inside her to explode into warm satisfaction, but nothing happened. Her body was packed with cold, calm numbness.

After a time she reached out one foot and pushed a wreath aside with her shoe. Under the flowers was a flax mat, spread as if for a picnic. Abby kicked the wreath away. The women stopped fanning themselves and watched inscrutably as Abby kicked a second wreath away, then another, then walked right onto the low mound, trampling and tossing at the flowers with a mounting violence. She did not stop until all the floral tributes had been crushed and scattered. Still she felt nothing.

Lena was sitting upright in shocked disbelief. When Abby climbed, wheezing, up beside her, her face flushed from her exertions, Lena said, "Are you feeling quite all right, Mama?"

To her horror Abby burst into tears.

Eleven

Queen's Wharf extended more than seventeen hundred feet beyond the foot of Queen Street, and on a blustery day May stood at the very end of it, waving a scarf at the *Mondrich Zephyr,* which would take Hal away for six months and Daniel for perhaps as many years. The ship faded into the breath of a brewing storm. Seeing the rain coming, May hurried back to the waiting brougham. Half-penny-sized patches of wet appeared around her. Ducking her head and lifting the front of her skirt an inch, she broke into a run.

Rain rattled on the roof all the way home. After luncheon, when May went out onto the veranda, she was met by a curtain of rain. Little rivers surged around the cobblestones. Rhododendrons and ferns sagged under a barrage of water.

May felt as dull as the weather. In five weeks she had not made one single photographic expedition. Not only had Hal monopolized her time, but his disapproval had been so obvious that she had decided to resume her hobby after his departure. Stephen thought she was acting wisely. "Sailors tend to be possessive, so try to be tolerant," he said. "They spend months at sea; it's bound to affect them. And surely you've found that a lot of gentlemen think that photography is an unseemly pursuit for young ladies. Be patient. Give Hal time to get used to the idea."

But she itched to be out in search of subject material. She'd hoped to go out that evening, but this rain might mean she'd have to postpone her plans for a few days at least.

It rained all night. Toward dawn the wind increased,

gusting down on the house with sudden blasts that rattled windows and lashed the kowhai trees against the walls. May woke to the distant growling of thunder and lay for a long time listening to the hissing of waves that seemed to be right underneath her room. She worried about the *Mondrich Zephyr.* Poor Daniel would be suffering purgatory.

The barrage continued all week, forcing the Yardleys to stay indoors. Albert and Edward failed to coax their father into taking them into town to the office, so they spent the week annoying everyone at Mondrich House, venting their frustrated energy. They dogged May's footsteps and mimicked everything she said and did until she was ready to box their ears.

"They miss Daniel," Juliette offered. She repeated this to Mrs. Terrill when the mouse traps had been emptied into the flour keg, and to Mr. Terrill when he reported that the carriage horses had been let out of the stables and were wandering goodness knows where.

May did not accept the excuse when she found that all her photographic chemicals had been mixed together in the developing bath. Her patience snapped. "How long must we wait for those two to learn how to behave in a civilized fashion?" she demanded.

Juliette was offended. "When you have children of your own, you will understand," she said.

But she tried to insulate her husband from news of the boys' escapades. Stephen had troubles enough of his own. The *Richmond Margate* had been lost on Barrett's Reef in Wellington Harbor. Only the first cabled reports had been received, and no final details were available, but the losses were forecast as "heavy." Stephen paced his study, worrying. At dinner he roared violently at the boys when they kicked each other under the table. Fearing he might beat them, as he often threatened to lately, Juliette did her best to keep them out of his way. Whipping them would only harm their sensitive spirits.

By Saturday the wind had tired, the rain exhausted itself. May woke to the noise of arguing birds. The sea still sounded close; but the sky shone blue through the curtains, and sunlight trembled on the polished floor. May dressed quickly.

Negus was frisky after a week's confinement. She galloped him hard, thundering across fields, jumping a succession of low scoria walls, and loosening knots of sheep, then really extended him on the bolt home along the road. They both were panting when she turned his head toward the beach track.

The scene was magnificent. Still turbulent, the ocean dashed against the shore, spitting jets of spray right up to frost the overhanging pohutukawa trees. Great rafts of fresh driftwood sprawled along the sand, and clouds of sea gulls rose screaming as she drew near the water's edge. There was a sharp tang of rotting rish and seaweed. She was enjoying the bracing atmosphere so much that she did not see Patrick until he straightened suddenly from beside a heap of driftwood. Negus shied.

Caught unprepared, May almost lost her balance and recovered only after a frightening moment of panic. She patted Negus to calm herself as much as him.

"Is this your way of exacting revenge?" he demanded. "I almost ran you down one night, so now you seek me out."

He looked different today, rumpled, dressed in simple workmen's clothes, his hair wind-whipped and his legs encased in leather puttees. May was indignant at his attitude. "Do you realize that I could have been thrown? You frightened my horse."

"Perhaps I should apologize." He was smiling.

"You don't sound in the least apologetic."

He pulled a log of driftwood from the pile in front of him and threw it directly across her path, saying, "Really, Miss Yardley, you cannot expect us lesser beings to be on a constant lookout for you."

He's insufferable, she thought, but instead of moving past, she said, "What are you doing?"

"I'm unearthing Samuel's canoe to see if it's been damaged in the storm. I beached it and covered it when the weather turned nasty, so it should be all right." He tossed another log across her path. "What are *you* doing?"

"I'm spying out the land. It's a splendid day for photography."

"Of course, the lady photographer." He laughed.

"My work is well thought of," she said haughtily.

His response was unexpected. "Rightly so. That view of the waterfront was especially gripping, I thought. I liked the way some of the people were in sharp focus and many were not."

She was dismayed. He had singled out the one aspect of the picture that worried her, the one detail that had spoiled the scene for her. She said so.

"Oh, not at all. The blurred figures gave a feeling of movement to the scene. I'm not making fun of your work, Miss Yardley. I may find fault with you, but I admire your talent."

She picked the compliment without touching the thorn. "Do you go to many exhibitions?"

"I used to spend an occasional day browsing. Mother liked to visit art galleries. She appreciated the qualities that make a fine picture."

He's smiling, May noticed. To someone who had been reared to consider mourning a time of unmitigated gloom, this was shocking. His mother has been dead only a few weeks, and he's chatting and *smiling* about her, she thought. Stiffly she said, "Permit me to offer my condolences."

He nodded with not a hint of correct expression. "Thank you for coming to see her."

"I'd hoped you hadn't noticed. I felt like an intruder."

"Did you?" His eyes were lit with amusement. "I know that feeling well. Why did you come?"

"I wanted to see her." That sounded unfeeling, so she added, "Your mother was very beautiful."

"Yes, she was. And lovely in her nature, too."

There was no doubting his sincerity, yet May was nettled by his lighthearted manner. All that grief she had witnessed, the anguish that haunted her with concern about his happiness—had they all been empty display? Had her suffering and sympathy been squandered on a sham? She heard herself say, "I don't understand you. That day when I came, you seemed so desolate, but now—"

He had been stooping to lift another piece of wood, but as she spoke, he raised his head to stare at her incredulously.

"I thought I detected a note of disapproval—as opposed to haughtiness in your manner. You think it wrong that I can smile and laugh and that I am dressed like this, don't you? You think I should be robed to the ears in itchy serge, my arms wrapped with crape armbands. Perhaps you would prefer to see me wearing a glum face and a portrait of my mother, like that ridiculous mourning brooch my sister Dora wears everywhere. You'd approve of that, wouldn't you, Miss Yardley?"

She was flushing and would have ridden off, but now he was holding the bridle, so she had to hear him out.

"I'm a Maori, Miss Yardley. Maoris display their deepest feelings openly at the proper time, then put them away. It's healthy, and wounds heal quickly, but if it is repellent to you, that is your misfortune. Now this simple Maori lad is going to finish checking the canoe; then he is going to head for the hills behind Whenuahakari to shoot rabbits for Samuel and me to take to the tribe we shall visit tomorrow on our way south. I could simply go into the butcher shop and buy food for hospitality, but I am a Maori, and we have pride in doing things in our own traditional way. So don't let me detain you any longer," he said, stepping aside. "Good day to you."

When will I learn to think before opening my mouth to ask such stupid, tactless questions? May groaned silently. "I'm sorry, I didn't mean to give offense . . ." she began, but Patrick slapped Negus on the rump, sending her on her way. When she reached the point, she glanced back, but Patrick was flinging pieces of driftwood aside and not looking in her direction. She could hardly blame him for that.

I shall apologize properly when I see him again, she resolved.

By midday May had taken two photographs of the storm-ravaged coast and was on her way home. Suddenly she was struck by the dramatic view in front of her. Mondrich House was glistening, freshly clean, in the sunshine, but the sky behind it, from the hills to the heavens, was filled with billows and puffs and great tumbled heaps of cloud, white and dark gray intermingled.

129

"It looks like a giant's tablecloth heaped up ready for the washtub, don't it, miss?" said Bobby.

"And it will make a stunning photograph. Look at how clearly defined the trees around the house are. You can almost feel the texture of the leaves. We have one plate left, haven't we?" She noticed that Miss Von Sturmer was scurrying toward them, her apron flapping. "Set the tripod up for me, there's a dear, and I'll see what the nurse wants."

Miss Von Sturmer was frowning and squinting at the same time. "Have you seen the lads? They've run away, and the doctor is waiting to examine Edward. He kept us up half the night with his coughing. He shouldn't have been outside, but we've searched the house, and unless they're being naughty again, hiding in a cupboard or something . . ."

Bobby called, "I seen them, Miss Von Sturmer. They were down the beach there."

"When was this?"

"I ain't much good with times. Yeah, it was when we was setting up to take that picture with the dead tree. They seen us and ran away real quick. They went that way."

"Half an hour or an hour ago," said May. "But if they know Uncle Adrian is coming to see them, perhaps they are already home again?"

"No. Mary promised to hang a rug over the balustrade if they appeared meanwhile." She hurried away, and soon her cries of "Edward" and "Albert" were lost in the roar of the surf.

May said, "If I give the exposure a much shorter time, it might darken the hills and sky, yet bring out the pure white tones in the house and those marvelous clouds. Oh, dear. Not yet," for Samuel and Patrick, both on horseback, were jogging along the road in front of the house. Samuel paused when he saw the doctor's trap, then turned into the gates, while Patrick idled at the roadside. May decided to wait until he moved away before making the exposure.

"Now," she said. "The plate, please."

It was in the camera and the exposure being measured when Miss Von Sturmer ran shrieking up the path behind them.

"The boys!" she screamed. "Quickly, someone, help! The boys are in danger of their very lives!"

May finished counting the time before turning to see what was the matter. Miss Von Sturmer was easily alarmed and had made a similar fuss when the boys were stranded up a tree. She handed the wrapped plate to Bobby and called out, "What is the matter this time?"

Miss Von Sturmer was almost incoherent, but that could be attributed to the steep scramble up the path. She stopped, gasping, and flung one arm wildly toward the sea. "Out there . . . the canoe . . . capsized! Oh, they'll drown, Miss May! They can't swim more than a stroke or two."

"Are you sure they're out there?" May could see nothing but cresting, rolling waves.

"I saw them in the canoe. Two of them sitting up. Then the canoe went sideways and tipped. I could feel that something dreadful was going to happen. Last night I lay awake *feeling* it. It's dreadful."

"We must get help," said May. "Bobby, can you swim?"

He shook his head, "No, miss. I ain't half-scared of the sea. Them waves can knock you over when you ain't looking an' you come up gulping seawater. Where are they? I can't see nothing."

"Oh, my heavens," whispered May. Until now she had not been agitated by the nurse's news, assuming that the boys were really in no danger. The beach sloped gently, and even if the canoe had tipped, both boys would be able to stand up and walk ashore. Accordingly she had been looking close in for the canoe. It was out, far out in the harbor, a toy boat bobbing among the waves with a toy figure clinging to the hull—which one she could not tell at this distance. There was no sign of her other brother.

"Quickly," urged May, giving Bobby a push. "Run up to the house just as fast as you can, and shout as you go so that they will hear you immediately and come out to meet you. Quickly! It's terribly important that you fetch help as fast as possible."

"It's too late." Miss Von Sturmer sobbed, echoing May's own fears. "Mrs. Yardley could feel it, too . . . something dreadful is going to happen . . . impending doom, she calls it. And this is what she meant. Oh, those poor boys!"

"Bobby will fetch help," said May without conviction, her eyes fixed on the black splinter of canoe. It was appearing and disappearing in the harbor swell, and the tiny figure was still holding on. Where was the other boy? Where? Drowning was over and final in a matter of moments. If only she could *do* something besides watch and will them to live. If only she could swim . . . If only she were on Negus right now. He was a powerful swimmer.

Of course! Uncle Samuel was on horseback and was probably still at the house. She shaded her eyes, staring, willing him to come out now and ride toward her.

Bobby was halfway to the house; she could hear his shouts. Along the road Patrick was ambling away in the other direction, but as May watched, he stopped, turned, and galloped back to meet Bobby. A string of rabbits joggled from his saddle pommel and a shotgun was slung across his back. He leaned forward, listened to Bobby, and raised his head in her direction. Don't waste time talking, begged May. Please hurry, oh, please.

Beside her, Miss Von Sturmer screamed as suddenly as if she had been knifed. "Look!" she shrieked. "Look at that!" She immediately bowed her head and clapped both hands over her eyes as if the sight had caused her acute physical pain.

It took May a few seconds to locate the canoe again, then several more to see what had disturbed the nurse. A long gray shape was sliding over the surface of the water just yards from where the boy still clung to the hull. It seemed to roll slightly as it closed in on the canoe. Then it disappeared from view.

"It's just a driftwood log," said May as she dislodged the hands which now gripped her arm. "Only driftwood. Gracious, but you gave me a start. I almost—"

Then she saw the fin.

The sight and that understanding of what it meant were like a fist in her throat. She was only dimly aware of the shout from Patrick as he hurtled past and plunged down the steep slope. Everything seemed to slow down and fade. Was that the waves roaring or Miss Von Sturmer's muttering voice as she knelt on the fern and fumbled with her rosary beads? The canoe rose and fell with agonizing deliberation, while past it was drawn the slick gray body, gliding like a kite on a string. Sometimes it showed a foam white underbelly, and sometimes that menacing fin.

"Perhaps it's a dolphin," prayed May, knowing better. "Perhaps it's only keeping the boys company. Dolphins are friendly." She could feel the terror inside her head, freezing the lining of her skull.

"That's a shark, miss!" said Bobby.

She kept her eyes on the canoe. "Did you go to the house?"

"No, miss. When Mr. Bennington came, I thought that he would be able to fix it like. I thought—"

"You didn't think. Now do as I told you, and run to the house. Fetch everybody. Make them come at once. Especially the doctor, if he's there."

Patrick's horse was stepping out into the waves, moving with exasperating slowness. It floundered onto its stomach when it reached deeper water. Patrick gripped the saddle with his knees while he unbuckled and broke the gun. She could see him ramming cartridges into the breech and snapping the weapon shut again. He was taking ages. She wanted to shriek, Hurry, hurry, oh, please be quick.

May glanced at the canoe. Now it was bobbing in the water by itself. How could that be? She had taken her eyes off it only to urge Patrick on, and in that space of time her other brother had vanished. And now Patrick's horse had moved into her line of vision so that even the canoe was lost.

Patrick was aiming, gun butt to shoulder. She saw the recoil jerk against his shoulder and heard the crackle a split second later. Near the horse the water began to boil reddish bubbles. From where she stood May sensed the animal's panic as it thrashed to get away from the danger. Controlling it with obvious difficulty, Patrick managed to fire the second barrel. This time the threshing stopped. Using the gun butt to whack his mount into obedience, Patrick steered it into the tainted water, and soon May saw him leaning over to catch hold of something.

"He's rescued one of the boys," cried May. She tugged Miss Von Sturmer to her feet, and together they dashed, half sliding, half falling down the steep path to the beach,

133

reaching the water's edge just as Patrick's horse waded ashore with a bloodied form draped over its shoulders. The horse's flanks ran scarlet, and it whinnied in distress, rolling its eyes and flaring its nostrils, panicking at the hot scent of blood.

"It's Edward," whispered May as she took the full weight and laid him on the sand.

"I think he's alive. There's no sign of the other lad so far, but it seemed more important to get this fellow ashore. The bleeding will have to be stopped at once." Patrick glanced at Miss Von Sturmer, who was crying hysterically. "Take your petticoat off, and make a pad to place over the wound. Apply as much pressure as you can. I'll go back and see if I can get the canoe upended."

With that he whacked the horse's rump an energetic blow with the gun butt, forcing it back into the sea.

Looking back, May marveled that she had been able to remain calm, especially since the nurse's sobbing was so infectious that May's nerves were stretched between the urge to slap her face and the compulsion to lapse into helpless crying herself. With the dull roar of the surf in her ears and the sound of Patrick cursing his horse on, May worked automatically, doing by instinct what must be done, not hesitating to think about it, for if she had paused, she would have collapsed. While Miss Von Sturmer struggled out of her petticoat, May tugged gently at the shred of jacket fabric which had been wadded right into the flesh of Edward's arm and shoulder. She saw the raw pale pink of scraped bone before blood welled freshly up through the wound. "Quickly," she ordered Miss Von Sturmer.

She folded the garment into several thicknesses and, having placed it over the torn limb, pressed down with the ball of her hand until she felt the sickening movement of broken pieces of bone. "Oh, Edward, be brave," she whispered. "I don't mean to hurt you."

He could hear nothing. His face was white and still, as cold as a porcelain plate, with a smear of blood on one cheek. His lashes were bunched and wet; his lips, slightly parted. To May he looked like a sleeping merchild, too beautiful to have suffered an ugly maiming like this.

"He's dead!" cried Miss Von Sturmer, dropping his undamaged wrist and dragging out her rosary again. "Hail Mary, Mother of—"

"No!" screamed May, stopping her with the violence of her cry. "You mustn't give up! You mustn't!" She kept a constant pressure on the pad and tried not to notice the spread of color in the sand around his shoulder. She said, "You'll be right in no time, won't you, Edward? You'll be right as rain on a summer's day, won't you?" Her throat tightened until it felt as if she had swallowed something sharp. "Where *is* everybody?" she cried. "Where's Uncle Adrian? He's a doctor; he should be here by now. I don't know what else to do. Uncle Adrian should be here. What is keeping him? Where is he?"

Samuel was at the foot of the cliff path. He caught the doctor's bag and waited to catch him, too. Adrian Forster was scrambling down as fast as his aged limbs would allow, and he and Samuel were soon at May's side. Neither man expressed any shock at the sight of the torn arm, for one glance at May's terrified face told them that she was strained close to the limit of her endurance. In response to her frantic questions the doctor said, "Yes, dear. You did the right thing. You've been very brave. You helped him all he could be helped." Then he straightened and looked into Samuel's eyes without speaking. Very slightly he shook his head.

"Please do something. Please . . . I've been holding him only until you arrived—" But she must have been speaking too quietly or too late, for they had turned away to where Patrick was splashing out of the surf again. May had to squint into the bright sunshine, but she could see him dismounting with Albert in his arms. Water poured off the horse and ran down Patrick's clothes. Water gushed out of Albert's mouth. His face was upside down, and his hair hung in dark ribbons like seaweed. The men placed Albert head down over a log and closed around him, leaving her to her solitary vigil with Edward. The nurse had retreated along the beach and was on her knees again, gabbling and fingering her beads. May felt light-headed and very calm. "It's all right, Edward," she said. "Albert must be in more urgent need of help than you."

135

When the doctor put a hand on her shoulder, she stood up at once. "Thank goodness," she said brightly. "He's all right, I know he is. I've been talking to him, just waiting until you came. You'll know what to do. He won't lose his arm, will he? You can fix it, can't you?"

Before he could reply, a clear voice called, "What's going on down there?" and looking up, they all saw Juliette standing on the cliff top.

"Oh, my God," muttered Samuel. "She mustn't come down here. This will kill her."

"I'll go talk to her," said May at once. She was glad of the chance to do something else useful. Before they could stop her, she was dashing toward the cliff path.

Juliette called down to her. "What has happened? I went back into the morning room, and there was nobody there. Mary said the men had been called away urgently. Why? What's wrong?"

"May, come back!" shouted Samuel behind her.

"Don't worry, Mother. Everything is going to be all right." She was grabbing at bushes to heft herself up, and the sudden burst of exertion made her giddy. Samuel was still shouting urgently to come back. She could hear him crashing up the path behind her.

"Everything is all right," she repeated as she reached the cliff top, putting on her best reassuring smile for her mother.

To her blank astonishment Juliette's face drained to gray, and her jaw dropped. Backing away from May, she began to scream piercing, animal screams of terror.

"Mother, it's all right—"

Samuel's panting breath was in May's ear as he grabbed her roughly and prevented her from reaching out to her mother. "For God's sake, May, look at yourself," he said, then thrust her aside and hurried to take Juliette in his arms.

May glanced down at her front. All over her cream photography smock bloomed enormous poppies of blood. Over her chest, down her arms, and across the width and length of her wide skirt was a riot of bright splashes. Edward's blood.

They're dead, realized May. Both the boys are dead.

Twelve

The boys were deemed too young to have sinned and were granted a white funeral. At Mondrich House all was shrouded with crape, and silence hung heavy.

Sometimes, when May strolled along the balcony, she peeked into the nursery. Always her mother was sitting on Albert's white bed. She came down for dinner each evening but seldom spoke. No one had seen her cry. When spoken to, Juliette was vague, distracted, as though disturbed from important thoughts of her own.

Dr. Forster decreased the laudanum dose to a minimum and prescribed kindly patience instead. "The depression may take a long time to heal," he warned Stephen.

"She blames me for bringing her to New Zealand," said Stephen. "She's right. From the beginning she knew something terrible would strike at us. I refused to listen."

"But she will recover. The bone structure at her temples indicates great strength. She has the resources to accept this as the will of God."

"Accept? But you know how she adored those boys."

"Perhaps that love was so intense because she sensed that she would not keep them long."

"Do you think it would help if I took her back to San Francisco? I've offered, of course, and she only says that it is too late, but if we went anyway, she might—"

"No, that would be unwise. She would be reminded of the boys at every turn. She would see their playmates grow up and think: Albert would be that age now. Or: Edward was very like him."

"But she is so calm it terrifies me. She won't eat. I fear for her health."

"She will recover," repeated the doctor, thinking again what an alarmist Stephen was. Look at how he'd fought and argued against the wool speculation, and he had been wrong, quite wrong. He and Rose and the Richmond Line were prospering like spring lambs. Money was flowing back to be reinvested in more wool. They were rich.

In one of their rare conversations Juliette asked Stephen to build her a chapel on the cliff top overlooking the harbor where the boys had died. Occasionally a priest came to Whenuahakari to read mass for her, but every morning and evening her slight black-clad figure could be seen as she trudged to the tiny white building with the bright copper spire.

Stephen accepted that he had lost her and knew that only a miracle might restore their relationship; that acceptance pushed him into his own depression. He stayed away from home all day and visited one of his clubs each evening. He stopped going to the older clubs his friends attended, finding that the lively conversation in the more radical establishments, like the new Auckland Club, stimulated him, though on every visit his conservatism received a fresh jolt. After a time he began to wonder if the city was entirely populated by speculators. Talk was always of shares, of high dividends and dizzy profits. Listening to it, Stephen reflected that only months ago he was vainly thumping the drum to persuade the Richmond Line and Adrian and Rose against such speculation. Small wonder they had refused to heed his voice when all these feverish voices chimed. I must be getting old, he thought. I am unpersuaded that these gentlemen are astute businessmen and not greedy profiteers.

One evening, as he nursed his glass of porter and perused the club copy of the evening paper, he read about a new trading agreement said to be of mutual benefit to Prussia and France. It was such a small item, apparently deemed insignificant, but Stephen thought otherwise. This is the end of our summer of wool prices he thought. Coldness lay on his chest. Somewhere between here and England six Richmond Line ships were carrying cargoes of wool for the just-ruined market, and if boardroom gossip was accurate, Adrian and Rose had invested all their accumulated profits in yet more wool.

When Stephen arrived home, he found May alone in the morning room with magnifying glass and fine paintbrush, retouching photographs for exhibition. She stared at him and asked what was troubling him.

He kissed the top of her head and said, "Who would have thought that a friendly trade agreement in Europe could bring disaster to our own doorsteps?" And when she continued to stare owlishly at him, he said, "I hope I'm wrong. It seems I often am. We never should have come back here. Your mother was right."

May put the brush down and clasped her hands together. "Does this mean that you are thinking of returning?"

"Would you like to go back to San Francisco?"

"Oh, yes, I would love that. We had a wonderful life there, didn't we?"

"I thought you liked it here."

"I do, but I *loved* it there. New Zealand is very interesting, but I think about San Francisco more and more. Especially since . . . Will you take us back, Father?"

"It's too late," he said, echoing Juliette's words in the same sad tone. "If we could go back in time, then I would, but it's too late now."

"Why?" she asked, but he was already at the door.

For May these months of formal mourning had been lonely and boring. She felt alone in a house that, until recently, had been filled with noise, quarrels, and boisterous fun. Though people visited the house and black-edged cards were left on the hall tray, May never spoke to any of the callers. Sightseers, Stephen called them, but May copied out each name, address, and message into a blackbound memory book.

Any photography had to be done near the house, and the only time she could venture farther was when Stephen took her to Fintona or to visit Aunt Rose, who was graciously cordial to May and entertained her with stories about her dead aunts: Sarah, who had wanted to be a nun, and Jane, who had been terrified of Maoris and had been killed, with her husband, in a carriage accident many years ago. Not once was Ellen mentioned.

"She'll not tell me about my father either—and he was her brother, so she must know everything about him," May complained to Lena as they sat in the gazebo at Fintona. "Nobody will tell me anything about him. He must have been the black sheep of the family."

But Lena was in love and not interested in May's problems. The object of her adoration was arriving now, striding across the lawn with Mrs. Rugmore dangling from his arm like a shopping basket. May regarded him with displeasure, thinking that although Lawrence Ogstanley reminded her strongly of Abraham Lincoln in his tall boniness, he had nothing of Mr. Lincoln's warmth in his dull, stony eyes.

Lena was giggling. "Poor Mr. Ogstanley! Mrs. Rugmore must have met him at the door solely to regale him with more details of her forthcoming journey home. She is so excited about returning to dear Pindleton that she must bore everybody to distraction about it. Still, I'm glad that she likes Lawrence. Mama is so unreasonable in her prejudice that she refuses to allow him near our house. Every day she lectures me about Mr. Tennett and scolds me for discouraging him. She cannot abide the fact that Mr. Ogstanley receives a remittance from his family in England, and to hear Mama talk, you might infer that they pay him to stay away from them! She is so unfair!"

May said nothing. Stephen had confided that Mr. Ogstanley was wanted in Chester for questioning about a property swindle and that it was more than his liberty was worth to risk returning to his own country.

Lena lowered her voice as the pair approached. "All Lawrence needs is someone with a little faith in his genius. You must listen to the brilliant ideas he has for developing that row of derelict shops on Fort Street. And all he needs is someone with capital to invest. Grandmaire has hers tied up at the moment, so Mr. Ogstanley and I were wondering if Uncle Stephen might consider . . ."

May began to cough, recovering just as the others reached the gazebo. "Miss Yardley." Lawrence beamed, seizing her hand and pressing a damp kiss onto her bare fingers. "That cough sounds ominous, and your health is very precious. I implore you to take care."

Lena's smile said, Isn't he sweet? but May escaped to the veranda at the other side of the house, where Dora was crocheting a bed jacket from fine blue wool. She glanced up when May said, "I hope I'm not disturbing you, but I cannot endure Mr. Ogstanley's company for more than ten minutes at a time."

"That news disturbs me; you do not. Surely that man isn't here *again?*"

"I have often wondered why Grandmaire permits him to meet Lena here. Every time I come here, he shows up."

Dora was silent, head bent as she worked. May was not offended by the silence; she was used to Dora now and was developing a respectful appreciation of her steady ways.

"He flatters her outrageously," said Dora suddenly. "Don't you see why he's always here when you come?"

"No," said May, suddenly seeing and hoping she was wrong.

"Grandmaire thinks it would be a fine joke if that fortune hunter won your hand. She encourages him and keeps telling him what magnificent expectations you have. She sends for him when you arrive."

"That's nonsense, Dora. He loves Lena."

"Lena loves him, you mean. She is kind and loving, but too empty-headed to see what he is. We can. Kendrick summed him up by saying that Mr. Ogstanley is starving for money and would sacrifice anything to get it. Kendrick despises grasping. He has dozens of faults himself but wouldn't bend to pick up a shilling if it fell out of his own pocket. No, he's here to ingratiate himself with you, and poor Lena is his second choice."

"But he must know that Hal and I—"

"You're not engaged to Hal. Perhaps you never will be."

"Dora! Don't say you disapprove of me, too. I know Aunt Abigail—"

"I make up my own mind." Dora's thick wrists rested in her lap. "I like you, but you're not right for Hal. He needs a fireside wife, and you need someone to share your interests, not someone who is at sea all the time."

"But that needn't be the case! Hal has been quite long enough at sea, and soon he will want to be promoted, won't he? Father keeps saying that he needs a good administrator in the San Francisco office, so when we are married, Hal and I can go live there."

Dora looked dumbfounded for a moment, then burst into a scrape of harsh laughter. "You really have got it all worked out, haven't you? And what does Hal say about this little plan?"

"I haven't asked him yet. He's not proposed, but when he does, I will have the opportunity to raise the subject."

"Take my advice, and don't waste your time. Hal is his own man. And he'll never leave the sea." A bell tinkled in the next room. "And *she* gives the orders here. Excuse me, May."

Alarmed by what she had been told, May tried to think of some way of saving Lena from the folly of her affections, but mysteriously the problem seemed to sort itself out. In more than six weeks of visits to Fintona she did not see Mr. Ogstanley once.

"I wonder what happened to him," said May now that it seemed he was not returning. "Did he go to New South Wales perhaps? That seems to be the fashion these days."

Lena began to weep.

"When will I learn?" May put her arms about her friend. "Oh, dear. You've quarreled, haven't you?"

When Lena shook her head, her crinkly hair rasped against May's cheek. "He's angry with me. He said that I promised our family would help him, and nobody has. I truly didn't *promise*. I only said that somebody might be able to provide the finance he needs. Oh, May could you talk to him for me?"

May was silent.

"You must help me. You must." She pulled away and stared into May's face for just a second before her eyes slid away in a gesture of shame. "He was so angry, and I love him so much. I tried to persuade him that as long as we could be together, life would be far more good than bad— well, that's true, isn't it? Love is all that matters. And . . . . I permitted him to take liberties with me."

"You didn't."

"It seemed right at the time. He *does* love me, and I love him; but it didn't work. I've not seen him since that evening, and I'll *die* if he doesn't come back to me. What can I do? I can't go to Mama or to Dora. They both dislike poor Lawrence. What can I do to win him back?"

May was aghast. Her cousin's confession frightened her as much as her wretchedness did. She wanted to say that Lena was well rid of him. He'd proved himself to be an unworthy, unscrupulous, and unprincipled cad.

"I love him so much," whispered Lena pathetically.

The last of May's courage evaporated. "Ask Grandmaire what should be done," she counseled. "She has been married twice. She will understand."

A fortnight later Stephen drove through the gateway of Mondrich House only a minute behind Abigail's phaeton. She had given her wrap to the butler and was ascending the staircase when he stepped into the hall. He noticed that she seemed agitated.

"Abigail! What are you doing here?"

"I have come to see my sister." She leaned over the banister rail, endangering the stretched seams of her satin bodice. "Though I set out to see you, I now realize who must be behind this petty piece of scheming. You don't hate me enough to do this to me."

"Nobody hates you. What are you talking about?"

"Lena's marriage, as if you didn't know."

"I didn't know." He rubbed his brow, trying to recall whether he had heard anything about it, but all he could think about was the black news of today's board meeting. The Richmond Line virtually sunk, the Forsters ruined, and here was Abigail babbling about a wedding. "Whom did she marry?" he asked.

To his astonishment Abby's fury increased. "You are incredible! Mr. Ogstanley is given a Richmond Line house to live in and a Richmond Line salary—in return, it would seem, for doing nothing—and all this supposedly with your blessing, yet you calmly pretend to know nothing about it."

"It was not mentioned at today's board meeting, but considering what was on the agenda, that is hardly surprising. So she did marry Mr. Ogstanley, did she?"

Abby tried to control her fury. Of course, Stephen would deny everything, would defend his wife. "I shall tell Juliette exactly what I think of this nasty piece of scheming."

"Juliette is too ill to be disturbed."

"But not too ill to interfere in my family," said Abby, and with a twitch of her bustle she continued on her way.

"Abigail!" His voice thundered through all the hallways and into every room of the house. "If you don't come down this instant, I shall come fetch you, then throw you bodily out. I mean that."

She came, sullenly. "There's no need for coarse violence. Bullying doesn't become you."

"Nor you," he said. "Go home, Abigail. I'll find out about this Richmond Line business, but already I sense Mama's fine hand."

"How dare you blame Grandmaire!" By now Abby was on a level to look him straight in the eye, and her voice was shaking. "You and Juliette have spent your lives planning to ruin mine, haven't you?" When he began to speak, she cut across him angrily. "Don't bother to deny it. The proof is in your actions. You made a mockery of my marriage by openly giving your support and assistance to that bastard Patrick Teipa—"

"I only found him a school. That's hardly—"

"And you and Juliette talked Samuel out of selling this land. If not for you, it would be all subdivided by now and the Maoris would be in the king Country, where they belong. As it is, every time I go into town someone from her family is there, pointing at me and giggling. Filthy scum!"

Stephen was not shocked, merely disgusted. As politely as he could he said, "And are we to blame for Samuel's marriage, too?"

She looked as if he had struck her. When her voice returned, she said, "Samuel will have good cause to regret that piece of stupidity. He will also regret the way he and Patrick are conspiring against Mr. Kine's land purchases."

"In what way?"

"Don't be obtuse! But I have Mr. Kine and Jon on my side—with all the power they can wield. They'll not permit your insults and attacks to pass without some retaliation. You and Juliette will regret coming back here, I vow that you will."

Stephen handed her her wrap from the hall stand. "We

do regret coming, but not because of you. Try to overcome your bitterness, Abigail. There is ample unhappiness in all our lives."

After he had seen her out, he went upstairs. The nursery door was ajar, and he could see Juliette sitting on the bed. She must have heard every word of the exchange, yet she seemed completely oblivious.

Impatience pricked at Stephen's mind. For a moment he regretted preventing Abigail from dashing into a confrontation with her. A sharp scolding might have aggravated Juliette's condition, but it also might have jolted her sensibilities enough to tip her out of the unreal world she now inhabited. Perhaps, perhaps. Now he would never know.

Thirteen

"So we meet at last, dearest sister-in-law," said Kendrick.

Ellen glanced up in dismay. She was sitting on the cabin trunk, which took up most of the floor space beside her bunk. In her lap the baby sucked at one end of a banana-shaped feeding bottle. Ellen lifted a corner of the shawl to screen the mouth and teat from Kendrick's view.

"Do go away," she said.

Grinning with what she recognized as beery camaraderie, he said, "I must protest about the inadequacy of your greeting. After two years I might have expected a more enthusiastic welcome."

"But you are not welcome." Dismay turned to anger as he pushed in and shut the door behind him. She had seen him board at Coromandel and had fled to her cabin, hoping to avoid him. "Please go away," she said. "I'm feeding the baby. I can't talk to you now."

"Why not?" From where he had stretched himself negligently on the bunk he reached over and tugged at the shawl, laughing when Ellen jerked it out of his grasp. "Rupert, what kind of rum name is that?" he said. "And why are you feeding him out of a bottle?"

Ellen had forgotten how Kendrick unfailingly responded to a rebuff by being as offensive as possible. She tried to ignore him.

He leaned on one elbow, surveying her thoughtfully from the brim of her plain bonnet to the toes of her boots, which peeked out from under the hem of her burgundy serge traveling costume. She had seen in the first glance how he'd grown a straggly mustache which didn't suit his slicked-down appearance, made him look like a hayseed farmer dressed up for a day in town. She guessed that he'd been roughing it—prospecting at the diggings, no doubt.

Finally he said, "You've left Jon, haven't you? Oh, there's no need to be coy with me. You've run away! You have no companion, and you're behaving furtively. And I know an Ellen Forster who would never be seen in a cramped, grubby cabin like this. You've just up and bolted, haven't you? Well, well, well."

"Ellen Bennington, and in a hurry to get home."

"I prefer my theory. And don't ruffle your feathers at me. It spoils your attractiveness. I've always thought of you as a deuced attractive woman, you know."

Ellen said coldly, "Allow me to qualify that remark. To you anything that breathes and wears petticoats is a deuced attractive woman."

"Bravo. But have you ever paused to analyze the compelling attraction that exists between you and the Bennington brothers? First you were engaged to Hal." She glanced up at that, and he saw something flare in her narrow eyes. "Perhaps not *engaged*, but you would have been, the Lord and May Yardley willing, of course—"

"Go away, Kendrick." She held Rupert against her shoulder and began to rub his back.

"Then you married Jon. Why, I cannot fathom. Grandmaire wanted it, but you've never been as subservient to her wishes as poor spineless Jon is. Did he kidnap you just to please her?"

"Oh, stop this nonsense!" Alarmed by her tone, the baby began to wail. Ellen patted him, shushing distractedly.

"It can't have been the sudden passion that everybody says. You don't love him, and he's not capable of love. Do you realize that he has never feared competition or experienced jealousy? How tediously bland his life must be. Even that silly heiress chased him without managing to arouse his ardor. She fancied that he was unattainable, and she was right, of course. But why did you marry him?" When she refused to answer, he said, "Well, no matter. Now you must make the logical progression and turn to me."

"What?"

"What you need now is an adventure. An affair, and who but I should be your choice? I'm wicked, and therefore suitable, and I'm a Bennington."

"You're insane."

"Oh, you'd find it fun. I come highly recommended. And don't worry about betraying Jon. He'll be in excellent company, if a little crowded. Why, if all the husbands I've cuckolded wore their horns, some of the Associated Clubs would look like herds of prime beef."

"You're disgusting."

"I'm honest. And I'm the first one of the family actually to offer you something. Jon always said Hal was shrewd to court you since you'll end up with half the Richmond Line eventually, and—"

"Leave Hal out of this, do you hear me?"

"Well, well, I thought so. You still love Hal."

"Please go. Please." And she began to cry, but as soon as the door was shut and bolted behind Kendrick, she managed to control her emotions. "I hate you, Hal," she whispered as she scrubbed at her tears. "I hate you for everything that has happened to me. It's all your fault."

She did not see Kendrick again until the tug lines were being flung away and the lifting tackle on the docks being readied for use. Kendrick strode up behind her and snatched Rupert out of her arms before she could protest. The baby clutched at his weedy mustache, crowing.

"Ouch!" Kendrick laughed, prying the fingers free. "He has quite a grip for a tiny nipper. I wonder how much use he'll be with a cricket bat when he's older." He gazed about conspicuously. "I see the *Mondrich Zephyr* is not in port yet. You know it's due in today or tomorrow, don't you? Of course you do. Pity it's not in yet."

Ellen did not dignify his comments by making any sort of reply. Firmly she reached over and retrieved her baby, and as she did so, Kendrick arched his neck forward and kissed her full on the mouth.

"Just keeping in practice." He noticed that same flare of anger in her eyes. "Ellen." As she turned away, he detained her with a hand on her arm.

"What is it?"

"If it's any consolation to you, I think Hal's a fool."

"It's no consolation," she said stiffly.

She pushed Kendrick out of her mind, and as the hansom cab trundled her toward home, she rocked the baby in her arms and rehearsed what she would say to her parents. They must not be allowed to glimpse her despair. She would say, "Dear, generous Jon paid for my passage and insisted that I have a holiday." That would do nicely, and the apt twist of irony might even make her smile while she said it. Jon would go berserk when he discovered that she had borrowed from a parliamentary colleague (not from a friend—they seemed to have none of those) under the guise of needing the money to purchase a racehorse for Jon's birthday. "He really wants one," she had explained. "Only you know how Jon is. He will never dip into his funds for anything frivolous unless he is pushed." Jon would be furious but would not permit himself to show it.

To her mother she would describe Wellington as amusing and stimulating. "The ladies run bazaars every week," she would say. "It would not do simply to give donations, so we must stand in stuffy halls for hours, pretending that we are dying to buy each other's cakes and handwork. Dora would be a sensation there! And the fashions would make you laugh, Mother. We all are obliged to wear coal-scuttle bonnets, for the brisk wind would promptly relieve us of anything more adventurous in style. All our winter gowns must be padded and lined for warmth, so as the seasons change, slender young ladies are transformed into stout ones. It would simply not do to wear cloaks and admit to being cold."

She had even decided what she would say if they questioned why she had traveled alone. It would be truthful to say that the servants were all so sloppy that she could not endure the confined company of one of them.

It would be easy to lull their suspicions, she decided, sorting through the threepences and sixpences in her purse as the cabdriver hoisted the trunk up the path. They both were such dears that it would be simple to encourage them to believe whatever she wanted them to.

Ellen smiled as the door opened, ready to greet Mrs.

Joseph with her best face. It was not the housekeeper, but May, who stood there, pale and trembling on the doorstep.

"What are *you* doing here?"

"I came with Father." May hesitated awkwardly, then held out her arms. "Please let me help you with the baby."

"Certainly not. I must say this is a surprise." Her tone conveyed that it was not a pleasant one. "What is Uncle Stephen doing here at this hour?"

Unable to reply, May stepped back out of the way to let her in. Ellen moved ahead of her into the morning room, a dim place shrouded with layers of curtains and filled with dark, looming furniture.

"It's freezing in here." Ellen laid the baby on a sofa and straightened, rubbing her gloved hands together.

"I was going to light the fire."

"Why? Where is Mrs. Joseph?"

"She's lying down in her room. She's . . . unwell." May knelt at the fireplace, conscious as she worked of Ellen's hard gaze. "I'll have this going in a minute."

"Where is Mother?"

"In her room," said May after an awkward silence. She stretched out a hand to Ellen. "Please sit down, Ellen. Your father knows you are here. He will be here in a moment, I'm sure."

Ellen stared at the first timid flames. May was still and silent. Something was very, very wrong.

"I'm going to say hello to Mother."

"No, Ellen." There was panic in her voice.

Ellen ignored her. After scooping up the baby, she turned, then paused. Dr. Adrian Forster stood in the doorway. He was not smiling. Ellen had never imagined that he could look so old and careworn.

"Ellen, my dear," he said wearily.

"Father, don't be downcast. It's not the end of the world. I read about the wool prices in the paper, how the market has dropped. I know it's a blow, but lots of other people have been ruined overnight, too, and then go on to better times. So will we. I'm here now, so please, at least try to look happy to see me. . . ." She glanced at all their faces in turn, then sharply back to her father's desolate face. "No

150

. . . Father, please say Mother is all right. Please . . . Oh, something's happened, hasn't it?"

"It was peaceful and sudden," said Stephen. "She suffered no pain."

"I feel so inadequate," said May on the way home. "If only Ellen didn't hate me, I might have been able to offer some comfort."

"She'd not speak to Abigail or to my mother, and she has no cause to hate them, so don't reproach yourself needlessly."

"But she needs someone. Poor Uncle Adrian is devastated, and Mrs. Joseph swooning and having hysterics."

"She was devoted to Rose." He frowned. "But she does need someone, you're right. I'll send Miss Von Sturmer. She can stay until the housekeeper recovers her wits."

"Did Aunt Rose die from the shock of losing all her money?"

"It probably helped, but her heart has always been weak." Stephen stared out over the ferny hillocks. "If only they had listened . . . I urged them to reinvest only a portion of their profits, but no, they extended to the limit to buy these last shipments. Greed is an insidious thing. The Richmond Line crippled, Adrian ruined, and Rose dead. Quite a price to pay for the mirage of a few thousand pounds."

"Poor Uncle Adrian. He was devoted to his wife. I always felt a special kinship with her because of the years I was confined to a couch, too, I suppose. Did you notice how at Grandmaire's party he kept coming back to her side, checking to see if she needed anything or wanted to talk particularly to someone. She just had to hint, and he brought the person to her side. She smiled at him with such sweet gratitude. It reminded me so strongly of—" She stopped, aghast, realizing how perilously close she had come to saying, "How devoted you and Mother used to be."

But Stephen had not noticed. He said, "I couldn't help thinking how odd Ellen's sudden appearance was. Neither Abigail nor Grandmaire expected her—did you notice their surprise?—and one can't help wondering if she's come suddenly, on her own initiative."

"Left Jon, you mean? Oh, of course not. But I asked if she'd brought a nurse for Rupert, and she all but asked me to mind my own business."

"I'll send Miss Von Sturmer over at once," said Stephen.

That evening May and Stephen had supper together when Stephen returned from visiting the priest to discuss his sister's funeral arrangements. As Mary was preparing to serve coffee, a pounding noise reverberated against the French doors and Miss Von Sturmer could be heard calling out for help.

"She sounds desperate." He put down his napkin, glanced at the time—ten o'clock—and said, "It would seem that Miss Von Sturmer has been forcibly ejected, and there I was, complacent in the belief that her stubborn insistence had vanquished Ellen's pride."

Stephen spoke with the first glimmerings of humor May had seen all day, and he hurried to open the door himself with a teasing jest that died on his lips. Miss Von Sturmer was crying hysterically. Whatever had driven her home to Mondrich House was clearly more than a battle of wills with Ellen.

Stephen gave her a tot of brandy and seated her opposite May.

"Thank you, sir," she breathed, surreptitiously dabbing at her mouth with the back of a gloved hand. "Oh, it's been terrible there. This has been the worst day of my life, and I fear it's not over yet, but I hurried here as fast as I could to fetch you, sir, and—"

"Slowly, Miss Von Sturmer. Tell us about it from the beginning, if you please."

According to the nurse, she had been only grudgingly accepted by Ellen and ignored by Mrs. Joseph but had made herself useful all afternoon by turning away callers at the door. Dinner was a desultory affair of cold meat and pickles. Then the household retired early.

"It didn't seem right to me, sir, to go off to bed with poor Mrs. Forster lying dead right there under the same roof. I know as folks do it, have lying out at home, but to me it

152

seems wrong. We have undertakers to keep the bodies at their parlors, isn't that so? I beg your pardon, sir, her being your sister, but it made me feel so uncomfortable, knowing she was right there and hearing the poor doctor talking on and on to her just like he had been doing all the afternoon."

"Talking to Ellen?"

"No, sir, to Mrs. Forster." She sipped at her brandy and recovered with a shallow, floundering noise. "He was talking to her for hours, just as if she could hear him. It fair made me nervous, I tell you. After I had gone to bed, I could hear his voice droning on and on. He wasn't crying or unhappy. Just talking as though there were lots of things he had to tell her. When I fell asleep, he was still going."

"Then what happened?" asked May.

Miss Von Sturmer had not been asleep very long when a noise woke her: a sharp, abrupt noise that had faded by the time she was fully awake. She lay there, wondering if she had merely been spooked by her own imagination.

"I had the weirdest sensation that all was not right in the house. I got up to look for my rosary, and as I was turning up the lamp to brighten the room, Miss Ellen came up the corridor. She went into the study where she had asked me to fix the doctor a bed and then came out and along to Mrs. Forster's room. It was locked."

"Locked?"

"Yes, sir, locked. She stood her lamp on the hall table and shook the door handle, really rattled it, then began to thump on the door, all the while calling out to her father. I tell you, sir, it was horrible."

"I can imagine." May's scalp was tingling. She was disturbed by the story and at the same time morbidly fascinated.

"I stood there in the middle of the room all the while, trying to block my ears. Mrs. Joseph came out of her room at the back of the house and tried to stop her, and then the baby woke and set to crying. I wanted to go and pick him out of his cradle, but to do that, I would have had to go down the corridor past Miss Ellen."

"And nobody answered the door?"

"No, Miss May. Finally Mrs. Joseph came in to me and

asked me to go and fetch Mr. Yardley. 'Tell Captain Yardley that it seems the doctor has taken his own life,' she
said. Cool as you like.'' Miss Von Sturmer crossed herself.
"It doesn't seem right to repeat such a terrible, sinful notion, but those were her very words.''

May shuddered. "The housekeeper must have been mistaken. Uncle Adrian would never do that. Not with Ellen
there.''

Stephen stood up, so stiff that for a few seconds he looked
like Grandmaire's brother, not her son. "Some things are
beyond our understanding,'' he said.

The nurse followed him out to the hall, saying nervously, "Please don't make me go back with you, Mr.
Yardley. That house fair makes my skin crawl. Please let
me stay here.''

"Of course. I'll rouse Terrill, and Mrs. Terrill, too.'' He
nodded at her. "Come with me to the gatehouse. Mrs.
Terrill may need your assistance. Oh, and one thing.''

"What is it, sir?''

"This theory that Mrs. Joseph expounded: about the doctor's taking his own life. You'll not repeat that to anybody.
Do you understand?''

"I understand, sir. Not a word.''

It was not until late the following afternoon that Stephen was able to come to terms with this second tragedy.
He stood at the study window, tugging at his beard as he
tried to find enough bland phrases in which to couch the
unpalatable truths he must serve to Juliette. As he stared
out bleakly, a gig rolled in at the gate. Hal was at the
reins, flicking a long whip over the horse's back. Hal. He
had forgotten about the *Mondrich Zephyr*. Hal, of course.
For the moment he was strongly tempted to abandon the
unpleasant task he had imposed on himself and, instead,
hurry out to greet his nephew.

No, he told himself firmly. May can greet Hal. Juliette
must be told before the messages of condolence start to arrive.

May stepped out onto the veranda as Hal was tossing the
reins to Bobby. From across the cobblestones he could not
see her pink eyes or the chafed redness around her nose, so

154

he called, "And don't you look splendid! Better than any mermaid I saw on this voyage, I can guarantee that!" After dropping his carpetbag in the drive, he flung his arms wide while Bobby watched with open amusement. "I ran up every scrap of sail and stoked the boilers until they glowed. We were doing seventeen knots and a boy right across the Tasman Sea, and aye, lass, it was worth the effort. It's grand to see you."

"Hush," warned May, alarmed that his booming tones might disturb her mother.

"Hush? Why hush?" he roared, not one decibel softer.

As he strode toward her, she experienced the same repressed panic that his presence always induced after any separation. She could not decide whether it was his loud voice, his hearty smile, or his boisterousness, but he always overwhelmed her somehow. She was buffeted in a blast of exuberant affection. Today, as usual, he picked her up and swung her around until she was almost too giddy to stand. When he set her down, he was panting.

"That's better. When I arrived, you looked like that little girl lost I used to see on the veranda at the San Francisco mansion. I suppose you're lonely without your brothers."

"Terribly. If only we could go back and start again."

"Can't do that. I say, you've not been crying, have you? You don't look well."

They were walking toward the north end of the house where vines of clematis and jasmine smothered a trellis enclosing a shady, scented nook. There a cane table had been set for afternoon tea. As she rang the bell, May glanced at Hal and said, "Surely you must have heard?"

"Heard what?"

She told him about the tragedies, carefully omitting any hint that the doctor had taken his own life. If Father Markswell heard rumors, there would be a full investigation, and possibly Uncle Adrian would not be able to be buried in consecrated ground.

"I can't believe this," said Hal as she spoke. "No wonder you looked peaky. And you say Ellen is home there alone? How is she taking it?"

May waited until the maid had set down the tray and

vanished. "About how you would expect. She won't let anybody near, not Grandmaire, not your mother. I'm deeply concerned about her." She poured Hal's tea and placed the sugar bowl handy for him. "I was hoping you would offer to help her. She needs a friend right now, someone to comfort her."

"I couldn't do that."

"You'd be the very person who could," said May eagerly. "She cares about you, and she's distraught. Never mind about conferring with Father today. He's too upset to talk business. Please say you'll go. She needs you."

He raised his hands in self-defense. "Hey, there. I'd be the least suitable person. I never go near newly bereaved households, nor do I attend funerals. Never. Surely you know that?"

"Lena said something about it . . . but, Hal, this is different—"

"I'm sorry, but no. My shoulder is available only for trivial tears. Positive and cheerful, that's me."

She refused to comprehend. "Then you could cheer Ellen up. Praise the baby. Make a fuss over him . . ."

"No. Absolutely not. Look, I don't understand grief, and I hope I never do. It makes me deuced uncomfortable even to be here, knowing that your mother . . ." He glanced toward the upper story. "I know it's tragic, and I was as sorry about the accident as the next person; but there's something about crape and wreaths that makes me edgy. I feel closed in and long to be back on deck with a cold breeze gusting around me. Don't you feel that way, too?"

"No, I don't feel that way. Mourning is a mark of respect. I have noticed your attitude, though. Three times on your last leave you turned down our dinner invitations."

A look of annoyance settled, like a gnat, on his face. "I say, we're not quarreling, are we?"

"I hope not. But please, *please*, won't you put your personal phobias aside just for an hour? I'm so desperately worried about Ellen. You've known her all your life, and you could be such a comfort to her if only you would. . . ." She faltered when she met his eyes. They were cold, and there was a stubborn tightness around his mouth.

He said, "When I became a captain, I stopped doing things I didn't want to do."

Recalling Dora's words, May thought, I can't pretend I wasn't warned. She tried to smile, to show she loved him despite his refusal. "I'm sorry to have been so insistent," she said.

Fourteen

May and Hal, thought Stephen fondly, turning away from the window. It was good to have something in his life that was not fraught with problems. Everywhere else he looked, misfortunes, disasters, and disagreements seemed to rise to mock him. This was an especially bad business, coming as it did before Juliette had recovered from the boys' deaths. But she must be told.

As he walked along the corridor, the pain strummed in his hip. Bad news, he thought. It crept into his body and attacked him physically. If only he could postpone doing this. And postpone the Richmond Line meeting that faced him later this week. Even Rose's death could not put off that unpleasantness for long.

Juliette was sitting on the bed, as always, relaxed in an odd loose-limbed attitude that put him in mind of her old doll, Clarissa. *She* had mat skin and a serene expression, too.

At first she did not see him. He hesitated in the doorway, looking at her with bitter longing. For him her beauty had not faded over the years; she still had the same dark blue eyes, and her hair curled in the same childish tendrils around her face and the nape of her neck. To him she was still the essence of herself at ten years old, a wide-eyed innocent with an expression of trusting calm.

That expression did not change when she noticed him there, nor did she acknowledge his presence.

"Juliette." He pulled the nursing chair out and with difficulty stooped to sit in it so that he gazed up into her face. "I'm afraid I have more bad news. Adrian was not able to endure the prospect of living alone."

Her eyes slid away, but not before Stephen saw the pupils were wide open. He tried to talk to her, to explain the tragedy in terms that even he could accept, but the effort of controlling his grief was so great that he was scarcely aware of what he was saying.

When he finished, there was an empty silence. Stephen dragged himself to his feet and replaced the chair by the nursery table. His back was to her when she said, "You don't care at all, do you?"

"What do you mean?" he said, facing her at once.

Her eyes were enormous, almost black, and they seemed to float in the pale dish of her face. "You don't care when people die. You don't care. Your feelings are never involved. I doubt that you have any feelings."

"Sweet Olivine! In the name of Jove, be fair, please! I'm staggered by what has happened and furious with myself because I wonder whether I could have tried harder to stop Rose and Adrian from that senseless speculation. Over and over I wonder whether I could have prevented what happened."

"But you don't *care.*" She struggled to her feet, her eyes melting with tears. "When the boys died, I mourned them, but did you? No, you locked yourself in your study with all those wretched books and papers. A shipwreck was a more severe blow to you. You cared about that. I shouldn't be surprised. The Mondrich Line came first with you, just as it has always done. You didn't care about my feelings when I wanted to stay in San Francisco, and when the boys died, you didn't care about that either."

"Of course I cared!" He grabbed her elbows, refusing to let her turn away from him. "Those boys were our sons—our only children. How can you think—"

"They were more than just our sons. To me they were proof beyond doubt that our marriage was not cursed by God. They were the children your mother predicted we could never have. She said our union was cursed." Juliette choked out the words. "How she must have loathed it when they were born and how victorious she must be feeling now." She struggled to free herself. "You didn't really care when they died because you never loved them the way I did! They were nothing more than a nuisance to you.

They distracted you from your precious shipping business. If you even noticed them at all, it was invariably to roar at them for getting in your way. And now they are dead. *Dead!* And I am the only one who grieves for them."

"That isn't so. In the name of Jove, Juliette, that isn't so."

She was deaf to his denials. "Those boys were so precious to me. They were a sign that God forgave me for loving you when I was married to your brother. That He forgave me the other terrible things . . . the sins I feared were beyond forgiving. I longed to have those children, and for years I was living in terror that your mother's prediction was right. I feared that God would never listen to my penances. But He did! He heard me, and when those boys were born, I was in paradise."

"I know," he said, thinking what bitter irony it was that though she had expressed these feelings to him before, this was the first time he really understood what she meant.

Now she heard the sympathy in his voice and relaxed, slumping against him. As the anger drained out of her, all the strength seemed to go with it. Stephen drew her tenderly to him and stroked her shuddering back. He was strangely awed by her outpouring. Since that first, dreadful day, when it had taken the combined efforts of himself, Samuel, and Adrian to calm her, he had not seen her cry or heard her raise her voice above a murmur.

"Do you remember the day young Leigh was spirited away by his father?" she said, sobbing. "I knew I would never see him again. I knew I was being punished for loving you. That was the real reason he was killed. I knew it at the time, and—"

"No, it was not your fault. You cannot blame yourself for what happened," he said, his lips against her house cap. Her hair had a dusty smell. "It was the war. Hundreds of men and boys died in the war."

"No, it was my fault. I was being punished. I tried to keep young Leigh away from his father—and I even wished Leigh dead. I pretended to be a widow and wishing it were the truth. God paid me in kind by taking them both."

"I tell you, you were not to blame."

Her crying increased in intensity. "This time it was different. I know it was my fault, but how? What have I done? What? Why did this happen?" In frustration her fists beat against him.

Stephen was lost in his inadequacy. "These things happen. Nobody understands why."

"It was all so wrong, so unexpected." Tipping her head back, she showed him her raw, ruined face. "Oh, Stephen, it was such a beautiful day—a glorious day. I remember standing at the window and watching May gallop by and thinking that perhaps she was beginning to settle here, to accept living in New Zealand. I envied her.

"That morning I had breakfast with the boys in the nursery. Poor Edward had to be coaxed before he would eat his egg. I was worried about his throat. He had been coughing all night, but he wouldn't let me look in his mouth, and he refused to take any of the laudanum I had mixed with a little belladonna to ease the inflammation. But he wasn't being naughty, just trying to make me laugh so that I would stop worrying about him. Oh, Stephen, I should have made him stay in bed; but it was such a beautiful day, and I thought a touch of sunshine would do them good after all that wretched rain."

"Hush, hush," soothed Stephen, for she was growing agitated again.

"I made them promise to stay in the garden until Adrian had seen them. They *promised*, Stephen. They assured me they would stay close to the house. And they ran out, laughing . . . and I *never saw them alive again.* They never even said good-bye to me!" She paused, her breath coming in tearing gasps, and when she could speak again, her voice had diminished to a crumpled whisper. "I thought they were hiding somewhere and would spring out and shout 'Boo' at me when I discovered their hiding place. I searched the house for them, and all the time they were out in the ocean, struggling for their lives. When I came downstairs to tell the doctor I couldn't find them, there was nobody here. I was all alone, and I didn't know what had happened. Oh, Stephen, it breaks my heart that they ran away and they didn't even kiss me good-bye." She reached up with cold fingers and wonderingly touched his face. "You're crying."

He nodded. The pain in his throat threatened to choke him.

Instantly she changed. Until that moment all her sorrow had irrigated her own wounds, but the touch of his tears caused her feelings to flow toward him. She wound her hands around his neck and stood on tiptoes so that her face could press against his. Crying together, they seemed to share the same tears.

"I do love you, Sweet Olivine."

"I know, I know, and I'm terribly sorry," she cried. "All this time I have felt so isolated. I had to bear the loss alone. The shipping lines needed your time and attention, but when the boys were gone, nobody needed me anymore."

"I need you. May needs you. She finds grief as difficult as I do." He sat on the bed and drew her onto his lap. "Do you realize that these past months have almost ruined us? All this time I thought you were blaming me for the boys' deaths—"

"Why should I have blamed you? It was I who had cause to feel guilty. When I recall the terrible things I've done, I think I must be mad to imagine that Leigh's death would have been enough to atone."

"Hush, it's all over now."

"I should have died, Stephen. Why wasn't I the one to die? It's all so unfair. They'd not had a chance to begin their lives, but I—"

"No!" He was shocked. "Don't ever talk like that. Ever. I need you, Sweet Olivine. If you died, I would not be able to go on living. Life would be barren without you."

"Would it?" Her hand stole up and rested, cool and smooth, against the side of his face.

He captured it and kissed the palm roughly. "Of course, it would. How do you think it has been for me these past months, trying to go about my business, trying to unroll the thread of my life, while you have shut yourself up in this sad little room, alone with the ghosts of two dead children? You've been clinging to them, Juliette. You must let them go and come back to me so that we can proceed with our life together."

"I know. And I'm back now. My mourning is over, Stephen." She nuzzled against his neck. An elation seeped through her. She said, "Your whiskers tickle."

"I'll have them barbered off."

"No. I like the way they tickle me when . . ." And she faltered, blushing.

He stared at her for a second, then roared with laughter, a glorious, full-throated release. When she tipped back her head to laugh with him, the sunlight caught her hair and lit it with gold.

The laughter faded, leaving them looking at each other with unselfconscious hunger.

She whispered, "Lock the door."

"What? In here?"

"Yes, in here. The boys have gone, Stephen. There's only you and I now. This was a happy room once. Perhaps we can make it so again."

He sensed that she was struggling hard against the pull of past memories. The strain showed in her voice and in the tremulous little smile she offered him along with herself. It had been so long! The ache of need had tightened its grip on him by the time he turned from the locked door.

She was already lying on the white bed, her arms stretched out to him.

"I've missed you, Sweet Olivine. God, how I've missed you."

Her voice was shaking, too, and he could see the soft tears on her cheeks. "I've missed you, too," she whispered. "Come to bed, husband. Come to bed."

Fifteen

"This house is too close to the time gun, too," Lena said as she showed May around her house. "Poor Lawrence wakes in a wretched temper every morning when the boom comes."

"But it doesn't fire until nine o'clock."

Lena looked embarrassed, then said defensively, "The poor lamb is always tired because he has to stay out until so late. It is important for him to have the right social connections, you see."

"Of course," said May, wishing that she had not come. Despite Lena's breezy manner and her generous praise of Mr. Ogstanley, unhappiness shone through her face like a fever. She had welcomed May with such eagerness that May had to struggle to smother her shock at seeing her cousin's condition, very pregnant indeed for so early in her marriage. More shocking still was the poverty evident in the household. Lena's gown was a clumsily altered old one, and it was clear that she herself had unpicked the side seams and added the frills under the bustline in an unsuccessful attempt to disguise her swollen waist. The floors were bare wood, and the cheapest of reproduction prints decorated the walls. In the fireplace was a sad-looking paper fan which Lena must have made herself and placed there instead of a fire screen. Declaring with a laugh that it was the cook's morning off, Lena had served tea herself, too. May could not help noticing not only that the china was of the cheap variety sold for servants' hall use, and the cutlery electroplated white metal, but that Lena brewed the tea and cut cucumber sandwiches with a deft, practiced touch that betrayed her familiarity with the kitchen.

164

She was unable to keep from asking, "Who will help you when the baby comes, Lena?"

She was going to offer Miss Von Sturmer's services and use that as a lead to the subject of Ellen, who was the real purpose behind her visit this morning, but again Lena was evasive, whisking the conversation away in another direction.

"Dear Lawrence is going to arrange everything," she said brightly. "He is so thoughtful and says that nothing but the best will do for his little family. Just look at what he bought for me as a wedding gift." She moved over and placed her hands on the top of a dark maple piano. "Isn't it beautiful?"

"Yes, it is." May could see at a glance that it was an Excelsior, the kind advertised as suitable for schoolroom or family use, cheap and available for five shillings down and one shilling and sixpence per week. Not a splendid piece of furniture like the masculine trappings—the silver-bound cigar humidor or the elegant spirit case, the gold and ebony pipe racks or the cedarwood tobacco jar with the gold-rimmed lid.

Lena prattled on, and May tried not to look at her, tried to ignore the desperate gaiety in her voice. She gave up the purpose of her call. It would be futile to ask Lena to visit Ellen. Even if she were in a condition to visit—and she most emphatically was not—her company would hardly cheer Ellen.

"Has Hal called on you?" she asked when she could.

"Gracious, no." And Lena laughed, as if at a ridiculous suggestion. "Hal and Lawrence *adore* each other, of course, but they both are so busy with their own pursuits that they cannot find the time to be as sociable as they would like."

"What a pity," said May, pushing away the recollection of what Dora had said, that Lawrence Ogstanley was never seen anywhere but at the racetrack, in his club, or at the Post Office counter in Shortland Street, queuing with the other remittance men when the English mails arrived. "But has Hal been to see *you?* Informally, I mean."

"Of course he has, though he never stays more than a minute or two. Something always calls him away. Like

165

this morning, for instance. He was hardly in the house when he noticed that smoke coming from the *Emerald Dragon.* When he found out that I already knew about Aunt Rose and Uncle Adrian, he left right away and went down to the harbor to see what was going on."

"Wool, no doubt. Wool is prone to spontaneous combustion if it's loaded when damp, and now that wool is no longer valuable, quite a few Dragon Line cargoes may suddenly become damp. Or so Father says. The Dragon Line ships and cargoes are always very heavily insured, you see."

"Oh," said Lena. Then: "I won't be going to the funerals, of course. Lawrence says that it would be harmful for me to attend such an unhappy event in my condition. He says that I must try to think blissful thoughts all the time. He says that if I present him with a son, I can have anything I want in the whole world. Do you know what I shall ask for?"

"What will you ask for?"

"I shall ask Lawrence to take me back to England to meet all of his family. There! Wouldn't that be perfectly wonderful?"

"That would be splendid," said May gently.

"Did you know that his father is a lord? And that one of his brothers was knighted for gallantry? And that . . ."

May escaped as soon as she could. Bobby Terrill was still sitting up on the driver's seat of the dogcart, but he had turned it around to face the harbor and the great black rose of smoke.

His eyes were vivid with excitement. "There's a huge ship afire, miss, and another right beside it that looks as though it's set to join in the blaze. Twice flames have leaped aboard the run up the rigging. They look like little flags made out of sunshine."

"When you talk like that, it means you've seen a chance for a photograph."

"Couldn't we? It would look so dramatic."

She had to laugh at the way he aped her expressions. The laughter eased the ache of pity in her chest. She ruffled his hair carelessly and said, "I'm in mourning for my aunt and uncle, Bobby. It wouldn't do to be seen setting

166

the tripod up in public. I brought the camera and plates to-day only in case we saw something likely on the way in or on the way home. My intention was not to cause a scandal."

"Nobody would see us, miss. I thought it all out. We can drive down to the wharf and go around the back of the sail loft. Everybody will be on the jetty, watching the fire, and nobody will see us, and we'll have the most perfectly splendid view from the sail loft."

She stared at his bright little face, checking the plan for flaws. "How many plates have we got?" she asked as she clucked the horse into a trot. "My word, Bobby, you're a good friend to me."

"I suppose it's lonely for you, miss, now that you're the only one in the big house. Do you miss your brothers much?"

"Oh, yes. It's very quiet. They were always shouting at each other—or someone was shouting at them."

He wriggled, grinning. "Me mam used to give them what for. Not Master Daniel, though."

"He's the one I miss most. Oh, Bobby, look over there, past the chandlery. Is that Mrs. Yardley Peridot's landau?"

"Yes. There's that Maori lady, the one who calls her *Matua* all the time. What does that mean, miss?"

"It means 'old woman,' and that carriage means we'll have to go this way. If she sees us, she'll call us over, and then we'll have no chance of taking a photograph."

Bobby chuckled. Because the traffic was so thick and the road jammed with carts, horses, and carriages May had to concentrate carefully to maneuver in order to slip around to the rear of the sail lofts. After they had stopped and she had given him the reins to loop over the hitching rail, she noticed that Bobby was still laughing.

"Old woman," he snorted when she asked what was wrong. "Old woman. Me mam would fetch me a swift clip around the head, and no mistake if I called her that. Does Mrs. Yardley Peridot know what *Matua* means?"

"Of course she knows. It's not a cheeky name, Bobby. Maori people respect their elderly people. *Matua* is a fine name." She shook her head. "Hurry with that camera."

The greasy smell of smoldering wool was so intense that it smothered the sail loft's own odors of new rope and canvas, and the crackling of flames was louder than the clatter of Bobby's boots across the wide, echoing floor.

"Careful," warned May as they made their way around an enormous bolt of double-thick canvas, used for making the suit of heavy-weather sails that would be carried in the ship's sail locker. "You wouldn't want that to fall on you. A mainsail of that can weigh a ton even when it's dry."

John Heaslip, the foreman, came over to greet them, his leather apron thumping against his thighs as he walked, weighted down as it was with wooden fids, sail hooks, and a heaving mallet, a small instrument used to tighten stitches. At his belt hung a cow's horn filled with tallow, in which a collection of large sail needles kept sharp.

"Miss Yardley." He seemed confused to see her. "We stopped workin' when the fire got bad. Can't see a thing in here anyway, it's so dark with all the smoke. Dangerous, cutting and sewing in this light."

"You don't have to explain to me." She tried to smile, but the smoke stung as it caught at her throat and made her cough. "We've come to see if we can capture a picture of the burning ship. A photograph."

"Oh, a *photograph*. O' course." He cleared a window for them by shooing the apprentices away, then said, "Through the door's a better place for that," and had two of the work men open a hatch in the wall which opened down to make a platform that jutted out above the street.

"This is where we load the sails out and the canvas in. You can see it a treat from here." He rubbed his chin. "She were a beautiful ship, that. One o' the clippers on the Eastern tea run for many years. Her first set o' sails were made in Hong Kong. Cheap, nasty things, didn't last more than a few seasons, but on the fore topgallant was a bright green dragon. Splendid-looking thing it were. Fair put me in mind o' one o' them Viking ships when I first saw it. Sad to see her go."

May was coughing again when she came out from under the cape. "How long has she been burning?"

"Not so long. Two hours, three maybe. It will take all day to burn. Wool goes very slow. She's full to the decks, too. They'd just finished loading when one o' the lumpers noticed smoke coming out o' the fore hatch."

"May I please look through the camera, miss?"

"Of course, Bobby. Tell me what you think." To the foreman she said, "As you can see, Mr. Heaslip, I have an apprentice, too." When the boy emerged, she asked, "Well, then, did you translate all the shades and colors into degrees of darkness and light? Will the picture have enough contrast to make an impact?"

"It will be very gray, I think, Miss Yardley."

"I agree." She was almost croaking.

"I shall fetch you a glass of water," said Mr. Heaslip, beckoning to one of his apprentices.

Bobby was leaning out into the street. "There's a crowd of men around the Dragon Line offices, miss. They're shouting and waving their fists."

"Maybe Barge Norrimmer has decided to come out after all," said the foreman sourly. "When the fire started, he locked himself into his office and refused to give any orders to stop the fire. Not that they could do much, mind. Once wool starts to burning, there's not much anybody can do. Captain Bennington wanted to have the *Emerald Dragon* towed out into the middle o' the harbor so the fire can't spread to any other ships, but there's two other Dragon Line vessels blocking the channel with crews on board to stop anybody interfering."

"But those ships could be burned, too. Look, one of them has charred rigging already."

"That's right, Miss Yardley."

Something in his tone made her say, "I suppose they're both loaded with wool, too?"

"To the decks, Miss Yardley."

She nodded. "And if they burn, the underwriters will pay."

"That's right, miss. The full insured value o' the cargo. But it has to burn. They'll not get a penny if Captain Bennington succeeds in sinking the *Emerald Dragon* and all the wool gets is a good ducking. I think that's what's brought Mr. Norrimmer out o' his office now."

She recognized Barge Norrimmer at a glance: a small, thin restless man nattily dressed in shiny black with a tall black belltopper. Around him several bulky sailors pushed the jeering crowd back to allow him to pass through. May gave him only a second of her attention before staring again at the burning ship.

"And what is Captain Bennington doing exactly?" she asked, her voice hoarse with smoke.

"There's a fleet o' Mondrich Line rowboats out there, miss, all manned with tars and lumpers with axes. They're chopping holes in the hull, all around the waterline. It's difficult to make them out because o' the smoke. Every time they chop a hole the smoke pours out around them."

"There's a breeze stirring. I can see something now."

"Can you see enough to take a photograph yet, miss?" asked Bobby after a long interval.

"It would be too blurred. See how fast the men are swinging those axes? They look as though the devil himself were going to try to stop them."

John Heaslip slapped his knee with his leather palm and said, "They'd not be far wrong at that."

Barge Norrimmer and his escorts were climbing into a longboat which already held a score of bare-armed men who were seated all around at the oars. May could see sticks and long batons similar to those carried by the constabulary, and as she watched, Barge Norrimmer drew a long-snouted pistol from inside his jacket and held it across his knees.

"What are they going to do?" May asked, feeling dizzy.

"Have a right good go, I'd say. They're too late, though, by a whisker, no more. There goes the ship."

"Quickly, miss. A photograph!"

Even under the black cape she could hear the slow, sucking gurgle as the *Emerald Dragon* shrugged very deliberately first to one side and then to the other as though scraping out a place for herself before she settled in a leisurely fashion down into the water. The top of the deck and the crew's quarters sat above the surface like a smoking island topped by tall, stiff-branched trees. A scattering of wool bales bobbed around between the dispersing dinghies.

Bobby was jittery with excitement. "Did you capture it, miss? Did it look dramatic?"

"Indeed it did," she whispered. She felt curiously light-headed, burning, as though her lungs and throat were smoldering, too. "Take care of the plate now, please, Bobby."

John Heaslip was saying, disappointedly, "They left it too late. Would o' been a right lively scrap, that would. The Mondrich Line men all have scattered out o' the way, and Norrimmer's lot have got nobody to swing their clubs at."

"I'm glad of that." May's chest was weighted, stuffed to the collarbones with something hard. Suddenly she could not breathe. The smoky sky darkened and pressed down hard on her. She tried to cry out, to struggle, but to her amazement she could do nothing. She could not even put out her hands to catch and break her fall as she folded silently onto the floor.

She recovered consciousness to find a strange Maori woman patting her wrists. May propped herself up onto one elbow, saw that she was still in the loft, and sank back onto the folded sail.

"Where's Bobby?" It was scarcely louder than a whisper. She reached out for the glass of water on the floor nearby but flopped back, unable to reach it. "I fainted, didn't I?"

"Ae, ae." The woman held the glass while May drank.

"Where's Bobby?" Her throat hurt less this time. She frowned and dragged out the Maori words. *"Kei hea tama?"*

The woman laughed, showing tobacco-stained teeth, and said, "You speak Maori very good." It seemed to May that her efforts always met with this predictable response, mirth followed by the same compliment. This time she must have at least found the right words because the woman jerked her head and said, "Gone to get Captain Bennington."

"Oh, no." She tried to sit up. "What for?"

"For you. You *maki*. You sick."

"No, I'm not sick. I don't need Captain Bennington. What in the world can Bobby be thinking of? The last thing I want is for Captain Bennington to come here and—"

The Maori woman was shaking her head, her face a

blank of incomprehension. Beyond her, across the room, was the doorway, and through that doorway strode Hal. He looked furious.

As he picked her up, she heard Bobby's voice. "I'll take care of the plate, miss. I'll fix it for you, don't you worry."

"What's he on about?" said Hal.

"Nothing," said May. "Nothing to worry about."

"There are things which you should worry about, young lady," he told her. "Do you realize that you could have made yourself ill all over again? You should hear your voice. You sound like a warp being played out. What on earth possessed you to come here?"

"It seemed like a good idea," whispered May.

Sixteen

May dozed on a couch in the morning room, still suffering from the effects of smoke inhalation. She had been in bed for two days and would be confined to the house for at least another week. Yesterday she had been wrapped up and placed in the carriage to ride in the funeral procession, but she and her mother had remained outside, while Stephen attended the services at church and cemetery alone.

She was still in disgrace. Hal had barely spoken to her on the way home that day. He had carried her unceremoniously into the hall—like a sheep about to be slaughtered, she thought—and when her parents had met them with alarmed concern, his rage had boiled over onto them.

"She's running wild," Hal told Stephen. "She was up in the sail loft of all places, there bold as you like with no chaperone, talking away to the men as if she were one of them. John Heaslip said she encourages that young scamp—your groom's son—to act as though he were her equal, letting him use her camera and listening to his opinion. . . ."

Juliette was swift to defend her daughter. "She says he has genuine talent and a fine eye for a good photograph. And May should know what she is talking about. Her photographs have won her a great deal of praise already."

"Begging your pardon, Aunt Juliette, I know I've little grounds as yet to speak my mind, but it worries me that she's at that Arts Institute competing with men so that other men may comment on her work. That doesn't seem at all fitting for a young lady of May's standing. She should be setting herself up as an example, not a target for gossip."

May tried to speak, but her voice knotted in her throat, and all she could manage were shallow, rasping noises.

Stephen looked stern. Hal's anger astonished him; he guessed that there must be more to this outrage than indignation about May. Later he discovered that Bobby Terrill had intercepted Hal just as a confrontation with Barge Norrimmer was imminent. By tugging on his sleeve and urging him to come at once, Bobby had defused the tension and ruined the opportunity Hal had long craved— the excuse to punch the Dragon Line owner on the nose. When he heard the details, Stephen understood Hal's frustrations, yet felt like applauding May for fainting at such a perfect moment. An ugly brawl was something the Mondrich Line did not need, not when its respectability was winning customers away from the disreputable Dragon Line.

But all that he discovered later. Right now he was perplexed and annoyed. "Thank you for bringing her safely home, Hal," he said. "We thought that she had gone to visit Lena. She said nothing about going down to the wharf."

His tone chilled May. Oh, no, she thought in panic. They're going to stop my photographic expeditions. They can't, they mustn't do that. Reaching out a pale hand, she tried to croak pleadingly at her father.

Stephen did not smile. "I shall discuss this with you later," he said in a tone which made it clear that the chat would not be a pleasant one.

So May was put to bed, and the doctor sent for. Juliette plumped up her pillows and relayed the doctor's orders as if they were a judge's sentence. May thought: At least Bobby has the camera, and she wondered about her picture of the foundering ship. No doubt it would be blurred and rendered indistinct by the smoke. She had probably suffered this whole ludicrous mishap for nothing.

Even yesterday in the funeral cortege, and while they sat for hours outside the church, May had not been permitted to speak.

"Complete rest and no talking, dear," said Juliette, shushing her. "The doctor will decide tomorrow whether you are well enough for conversation."

May was waiting for the doctor now, marshaling her arguments like a general preparing battle strategy. Above all, I must be lucid and calm, she reminded herself. If I become agitated and start pleading, my voice will become a quack, and he will shake his finger at me and look horribly solemn. I must breathe deeply and speak slowly, in a normal voice if I hope to convince him I am recovered.

The door knocker chattered, and May responded immediately by biting her lips and fluffing out her frizzy bangs so that she would look appealingly healthy. She was still peering at her white face in a small hand mirror when Ellen swept into the room.

"Oh," said Ellen in dismay. She wore a long black coat with a tailored bustle and a round black hat and carried a glossy fur muff. Black heightened her thin, elegant looks.

"Don't go away," said May as her cousin backed toward the door. She tried to smile, saying, "I don't have anything catching." When Ellen still backed away, she dropped the bantering tone and begged, "Please, Ellen. I truly didn't ever want to hurt you, and if I inadvertently caused you pain, I am deeply sorry."

Ellen's chin rose. May could not read her expression behind the black veil. "I've come to see your father. Is he in?"

May sighed. "Sit down, and I shall find out for you." She rang the silver bell. Ellen sat down on the edge of a chair, and May said, "A large crowd attended the funeral. It seemed as though all of Auckland were paying its respects."

"I didn't see you there."

"Mother and I had to stay in the carriage. The doctor's instructions. How is little Rupert?"

"He's in perfect health, thank you." She paused. "I shall be engaging a nurse of my own shortly. As soon as my business matters have been completed."

"There's no need for that really. I'm sure that Miss Von Sturmer loves little Rupert. He's such a darling fellow. His father must miss him terribly."

Ellen got to her feet at once.

"Please, Ellen, how can I possibly be friends with you if you are determined not to permit me?"

Ellen answered in a light, ragged voice, not her usual

175

flat accents. May could not be sure whether she said, "I can do without you happily" or "I can do without your charity," but whichever it was, Ellen meant it to end the interview. She left the room, and a few minutes later May saw her walking up the stairs behind the parlormaid.

It was perhaps an hour later that Jon arrived. May had grown tired of waiting for the doctor, had fished a volume entitled *Photography, a Science or an Art?* from its hiding place under the sofa cushion, and was deeply absorbed in it when the French doors were flung wide and Jon strode in.

May gasped and dropped the book. It was a few seconds before she could draw breath to complain, saying, "Life in Wellington teaches people the most peculiar habits. Is it essential for Members of Parliament to introduce an element of surprise into their every entrance, or were you afraid we would declare ourselves not at home if you announced yourself in the normal way?"

"I'm sorry if I startled you, but I was told by Miss Vin what's-her-name that Ellen had come to visit you."

"Not to visit me, I'm afraid." She tucked the book away. "What is the matter, Jon? You look positively distraught."

He flexed his jaw and fiddled with the high, pointed wing collar. May noticed that the bracing Wellington climate had done nothing to improve his unfortunate complexion. He did not look at her as he said, "Of course, I'm not distraught. I came to surprise Ellen, that's all. She certainly went out of her way to surprise me."

May glanced at him speculatively. Had Ellen run away and left him, as Father had hinted? The temptation to pry was strong, but she resisted it and said soothingly, "You do realize that poor Ellen is in a dreadful state of shock."

"Grandmaire told me what had happened. She sent me a message, and I came at once."

"Of course."

He darted an odd look at her. "What do you mean by that?"

"That she will need your comfort and support, of course. I've been so worried about her. She wouldn't let any of us near her. I thought she would be glad of Hal's company, and I tried to persuade him to go see her, but he wouldn't. He said he feels uncomfortable about mourning."

"Show him a scrap of crape and he'll run a mile. Grief is a complicated emotion, and Hal doesn't understand complexities."

"And he fears things he doesn't understand," May said, realizing as she spoke that this lack of understanding was what lay behind his opposition to her photography. "But I wanted him to go and see Ellen. It worried me that she wouldn't stay with Grandmaire. They have always been such friends, yet even at the funeral Ellen wouldn't go close enough to Grandmaire's chair to touch her."

"She blames Grandmaire for the fact that—" He stopped as abruptly as he had begun, and again May had the tantalizing feeling that if she pressed him, Jon would confide in her.

"It will be better for Ellen now that you are here," she said.

He looked into her eyes, and it occurred to her that she had never before noticed how unfriendly his were, pale blue like Uncle Samuel's, but empty as a winter sky. In the second their eyes met she decided that she did not like Jon half so well as she had imagined. I was wrong about him, she thought. He *is* calculating.

What he said next seemed to confirm that opinion. "I don't know if it will be better for her, but it will be much better for me. Don't look shocked, May. Hasn't anybody ever told you that married women must never make plans alone? Especially plans concerning their property. Married women should always keep in mind the fact that they have husbands to do their thinking for them."

"It is a wife's place to be guided by her husband, of course," she began, "but don't you think that since—"

Jon was not listening. He took one pace toward the hall door, stopped, and then turned to May sharply. "That's Ellen's voice. You told me that she wasn't here!"

"No, I said no such thing. I said that she was not visiting *me,* as indeed she was not. She came to talk business with Father."

"Oh, did she indeed?" He strode out into the hallway and stood at the foot of the stairs. May could see him plainly in the diffused hall light. The smile on his face made her feel cold all over as he held out a hand to Ellen,

177

who was descending the last few stairs. "My dear wife!" he said loudly. "I came to escort you home to Fintona."

"Please, Jon," said Ellen as the coach approached the tall gates, "can't we just go home? We don't have to come here. I don't think I could face Grandmaire again."

"Because she pushed you into my arms? Come now, Ellen. That's nonsense, and you know it. Nobody made you do anything. I'll never apologize for what happened on the steam packet, so it's pointless of you to grow a long face over that. I did what any red-blooded young man would do."

"I trusted you."

Jon leaned over and grabbed her wrist, hard. "And I trusted you. All week I had sniggering remarks about my birthday to fend off, while you spent the money running away from me. I'll not trust you again."

"I shall not ask you to. I can please myself what I do from now on. I'm independent of you, Jon Bennington."

"Oh?"

"Completely independent. I'm making arrangements with Uncle Stephen."

Jon picked a scrap of lint off his sleeve and began to draw on his beige kid gloves. He sounded utterly disinterested as he said, "I trust that you've not made arrangements to sell my Richmond Line shares."

"*Your* shares?"

The beige felt topper twirled in his hands as he inspected it for marks. "Or my house or the contents of that house." He smiled at her with the same expression she had seen as she descended the stairs. "You are entitled to keep two hundred pounds of your parents' estate. Under law, the remainder belongs to me."

"You wouldn't do that to me," whispered Ellen.

He continued as if she had not spoken. "With your permission I shall set that two hundred pounds against your parents' debts. As you know, they are considerable. Grandmaire is meeting the remainder. For a consideration, of course."

"You have worked it all out between you?"

"Grandmaire thinks that I can apply myself more

wholeheartedly to her business affairs if I resign from the national parliament and merely retain my position on the Provincial Council. Of course, we shall live at Fintona from now on. The other house will be sold."

"You can't do that. I love that house. I lived there all my life until—"

"When debts have to be met, sentiment must be sacrificed. Grandmaire is looking forward to helping you with young Rupert—and, of course, our other children, all in due time."

Ellen's face was tight behind the veil. Her lips scarcely moved as she said, "Never. I told you that, and I meant it absolutely. I shall never let you touch me again, Jon Bennington."

The carriage rolled to a halt before she finished speaking, and Jon leaned out, unclasped the door, and jumped lightly onto the flagstones. He kicked the step down with one brightly polished boot and smiled as he held out a hand to Ellen. Reluctantly she emerged, her face averted coldly. Jon pretended not to notice.

"Grandmaire is looking forward to seeing you. She is deeply offended by your behavior, but you will be pleased to hear that I have smoothed everything over by explaining how great a shock your parents' death has been. Oh, by the way," he continued matter-of-factly, "I have made our apologies to Grandmaire for this evening and explained that we shall be retiring directly after dinner. She understands how fatigued I am from the journey and how eager we are to be alone together after our separation. You look very handsome, Ellen. Black becomes you, my dear."

"Well, I declare that some people need to hire those fortunetellers to help them make up their minds about anything," said Miss Von Sturmer as she brought May a cup of hot chocolate and waited, glad of the opportunity to gossip, while May drank it. "First Miss Ellen—Mrs. Bennington, I should say, though she kept insisting that I must not call her that—first she wanted me to stay, then she said she'd be hiring somebody of her own, then her husband arrives and whisks me over to Fintona without so much as a by-your-leave, and then I'm dismissed with even less ceremony. But once they do make up their minds, they waste no time. Indecent haste, I'd call it."

"They waste no time doing what?" asked May. "And are you referring to Mr. Bennington or Mrs. Bennington?"

"Neither. It's Mrs. Yardley Peridot I'm referring to. I was watching her give orders and make decisions, and I tell you, Miss May, I had to pinch myself to believe that she's an old, old woman tortured by rheumatism and gout. She acts like she owns the whole country."

"She and her family were among the first European people to settle in New Zealand. Did you know that?"

"No, I didn't, but that would explain why she has only Maori servants, all but that sullen-looking Miss Dora. Beg pardon, Miss May, I keep forgetting she's your kin."

"And what were these orders and decisions Grandmaire was making?"

"Mr. Bennington left me and baby Rupert at Fintona while he came on here, and between then and when he returned, Mrs. Yardley Peridot had arranged to have Dr. Forster's house closed up and had given orders for the sale of the house and all the furniture. It was as if she'd been planning it for days. The Benningtons are going to live with her, you see. Oh, you should have seen her face light up when she took baby Rupert onto her lap. Fair put me in mind of a picture I saw of Queen Victoria and one of her grandchildren, it did. She dotes on the wee lad already and declares that she and Dora are going to look after him all by themselves. Miss Dora didn't look too pleased to hear that, but then she never does look pleased."

May gave her the cup and saucer. "Perhaps she has very little to be pleased about."

Stephen felt that he, too, had little to be pleased about as he gazed around the table in the paneled boardroom at the Richmond Line offices. The room itself was an effrontery to his own practical business ideas. Ornate and needlessly expensive, from the specially handmade carpet to the jewelers' models of ships which were fixed all over the walls like a collection of so many priceless butterflies, the room seemed to mock him every time he entered its marble doorway. Rose had originally conceived the romantic idea of

180

building an elegant boardroom, something appropriate to the size and importance of the Richmond Line. Stephen had argued that inasmuch as the Richmond Line was essentially a family business, one of their own offices or even a parlor would do perfectly well for their meetings. Grandmaire, however, had sensed Rose's frustration at being an unimportant, minor shareholder whose views were always listened to but never acted upon, and she saw in this issue a chance to coax Rose over to her side in what was brewing up into a battle between herself and Stephen. She had just won, in court, the control of her dead son Leigh's shares—shares which should rightfully have gone to either Juliette or May—and was so fired by lust for power that she was willing to sacrifice her own frugal principles to achieve her ends. Accordingly she voted for the extravagant boardroom. Though the cost to the Richmond Line was considerable (enough to refit three ships or buy a new bark), Maire's victory had been complete. She had had forty percent of the shares and Rose's assured support with her ten percent. Such was the depth of animosity between herself and Stephen at the time that she had been prepared to do legal battle with him over every issue on which they disagreed. As these legal battles were inevitably financed by the real loser, the Richmond Line, Stephen had spent the years in San Francisco trying to ignore what was happening to the shipping line his father had founded. It was only when he could see that he had no choice but to intervene or let the Richmond Line go down that he had come home to try to save it.

And I'm going to fail, he thought despondently as he surveyed the tight, defensive faces around the table. We were in trouble before now. With these valuable wool cargoes to be somehow paid for, we face ruin. Utter ruin. And who in this room, apart from myself, really cares?

At the other end of the table his mother sipped at a small glass of schnapps. Her bosom was so heavily hung with jet that it looked like a swarm of black bees. Beside her Jon blew on the lenses of his wire-rimmed spectacles and rubbed them with a handkerchief. When Rose died, so did our chance for salvation, thought Stephen bitterly. If only he had gone to Rose and offered again to buy those shares.

If only she had agreed. But she never would have relaxed her pride long enough to sell. She'd have called it charity or flung his offer back in his face just as she had done countless other times. If only . . . but it was too late now. The shares had flown to Ellen to Jon and back to Grand-maire faster than a flock of homing pigeons.

On either side of the table sat the mediators, the sec-onds, as Stephen called them. Old Mr. McLeay murmured in a hum to his young assistant, Vincent Opal, while Ste-phen had invited Hal and Solforn Wade, an expert in mari-time law. Not that the meeting would have anything to do with maritime law, but Stephen hoped Mr. Wade's qualifi-cations might impress Mr. McLeay and gain a slight psy-chological advantage.

Stephen began by outlining the financial mire the Rich-mond Line was in and stressed that some change in atti-tude and direction was essential if a revitalization could possibly be effected.

"Our captains are too inefficient," said Maire as soon as he paused. "I have maintained for years that we should take a leaf from Mr. Norrimmer's book and hire stronger men."

This was news to Stephen. "You don't mean bullyboy captains and bucko mates, do you?"

"Those sound like derogatory terms, but I mean men who will make the crew work hard. Our ships are slack with soft discipline. And they are overmanned."

"Mama, surely you can trust us to know how large a crew a ship needs, and you can trust us to choose our own captains and mates. Install bullyboys and buckos, and within a couple of journeys we'd lose all our crews. Our sailors are almost all respectable local fellows, family men. I think we can vouch for the fact that they give hon-est work in return for their wage."

"Crews are easy to replace," insisted his mother. "And they would be especially easy to replace once word got around about the conditions on board the Richmond Line vessels. I have been comparing chandlery lists, and frankly I am appalled by the difference in cost between outfitting one of our ships and one of Mr. Norrimmer's ves-sels."

"Do go on," said Stephen.

"We spend more than double the amount they do to feed the same number of men and five times—*five times*—the amount on medical supplies."

"Let me guess. You are going to suggest that we follow the Dragon Line policy of starving the men and stocking the slop chests with extra food and essential medicines so that when the men are hungry and ill, they are forced to spend their wages on those things? Why not go one step farther and copy Mr. Norrimmer's latest idea? Did you hear about how he is cutting the fare to England down to only five pounds but proposes to charge the passengers dearly for every mouthful of food and every comfort they require on board? No, Mama. Emphatically no."

Solforn Wade glanced at Stephen for permission to speak and said, "Pray forgive me for intruding at this juncture, but it seems timely to point out that according to the Maritime Code of Regulations, there are minimum allowable levels for the manning of ships, the food, and medical supplies. Though the Richmond Line operates above those levels, the margin is humane rather than wastefully generous."

"That is not what Mr. Norrimmer tells me, young man."

"I do humbly seek your pardon and beg your discretion, ma'am, but I should inform you that at the moment the Dragon Line faces prosecutions in England and in New South Wales for the infringement of that code. The fines can be severe, and I could not recommend risking them."

"Thank you, Solforn," murmured Stephen. "Mama, do you wish to comment further?"

"Indeed I do. From your remarks I infer that you presume I wish to do something illegal. That is not so. I have never in my life done anything illegal." She glared at Stephen, who was hastily dabbing his lips with a folded handkerchief. "My suggestion was and still is that we take a practical approach. Our ships cost far more to run than the Dragon Line ships do, and furthermore, they carry less cargo and take longer on the journeys than our rivals. It seems to me, gentlemen, that we could apply housekeeping principles more rigorously for our immediate benefit."

"The Mondrich Line operates on the same time and

cargo loading limits and profits very nicely," said Stephen. "Where the Richmond Line has erred is in its ill-advised purchase of the wrong types of ships and too many of them. The growth of the Richmond Line should have been gradual and natural, not forced. We have borrowed enormous sums of money to purchase ships we do not need because we have not the custom to fill them. As a result, ships and crews stay idle, while debts await payment."

"No doubt you have a solution to our problems?"

"I do, Mama. Cut back and consolidate. Sell, say, twenty ships, enough to wipe out the debt. Concentrate on profitable routes and cargoes which suit us best, and begin a sensible long-term growth plan."

"Sell twenty ships? You must be mad!" Grandmaire snapped her fingers at Dora, who was sitting in the corner, head bent over her tapestry of stags at bay. At the command she laid it aside and brought a small vinaigrette bottle, which Grandmaire held under her nose, closing her eyes while she inhaled the aromatic salts' vapors.

"Please hear me out before you collapse completely," said Stephen. He glanced around the table. "You all will have heard about the discovery of frozen mammoths in Siberia, how these beasts have remained in such perfect condition for thousands of years that even after all this time the flesh, when thawed, remains edible."

Grandmaire said, "Not frozen meat again. You brought this up years ago, Stephen, and all of us agreed that a long journey through the heat of the equator made any venture connected with freezing meat totally impossible and impractical."

"I'm not wasting your time." He appealed to the others. "Hal has come here today to tell you about developments which the Mondrich Line has been pursuing in the study of refrigeration. I believe that this field holds the answer not just to our own prosperity but to the prosperity of this entire country. On every voyage to England, Hal goes to our special engineering works, where developments are beginning to show exciting progress. We are on the brink of . . . but I think perhaps that Hal should be the one to tell you all about it. Hal, if you please."

While Hal spoke, Stephen leaned back and watched

184

him. He only half listened, just enough to note that Hal spoke well and convincingly about the subject, but as he watched, Stephen was conscious of a poignant longing. Had the boys lived, he might one day have presided over a similar meeting to this one but instead have listened to Albert or Edward speak about the future of shipping. As Hal finished speaking and sat down, Stephen found himself applauding with more than a touch of paternal pride.

"Well done," he said, rising with a smile. "Thank you, Hal, for expressing our case so well."

"Our case?" asked Jon. "Is Hal to join us in the Richmond Line now?"

"By our case, I was referring to the Mondrich Line. We are convinced that the future of our company, and, indeed, of New Zealand, lies in refrigerated shipping, and as Hal has detailed, this is an opportunity for the Richmond Line also to share in that future."

"What nonsense is this? Refrigerated shipping—what manner of pipe dream is that?"

"No pipe dream, Mama, but an actuality. The first load of frozen meat from the Argentine has already been received with enthusiasm in the markets of England. Because of our location, we have access to the markets of the entire world. Vast, lucrative markets, well worth the cost of equipping the ships."

"Oh?" said Grandmaire. "So far cost has not been mentioned."

"Of course there will be a considerable outlay," said Stephen with a touch of irritation. "Ships must be specially built or refitted with insulated chilling chambers. The refrigeration units will be an additional expense, plus the fuel to run them and trained engineers to maintain the machinery."

"It seems to me," said Grandmaire, "that we are being asked to dismantle the Richmond Line in order to help pay for your expensive experiments. No, Stephen." She put up a puffy hand to silence him. "Before you refute that comment, answer me this: Would it lessen your expenses if the Richmond Line joined your Mondrich Line in this refrigeration venture?"

"But of course it would, Mama. Might I remind you that

in the early days we often embarked on joint ventures, and we have always maintained some measure of cooperation. This project would be no exception. Of course, it would be less expensive for us to work in together."

"Then the answer is no," she told him shortly. "You may experiment and splash your money about however you please, but no matter how it is dressed up in persuasive language, this venture is a reckless gamble. You said that about our wool buying, and eventually—*eventually*—you were proved correct. But wool cannot decay in transit, needs no expensive machinery to maintain its condition, and would not rot if buyers were not immediately available to purchase it. No, Stephen. We have already decided to hold our wool in warehouses in Tilbury until the price improves, but we have no more money to spare for similar speculation."

She's blaming me for the wool purchases, thought Stephen in amusement. To hear her talk, one would think it had been my idea.

"You will have to embark on this gamble alone," she told him. With a nod to Vincent Opal she said, "We have ideas of our own about how to salvage the Richmond Line's fortunes, a better plan than the one we have just listened to, I'm sure you will agree."

Vincent Opal was dark and cadaverously thin. Reading from notes in a bland monotone, he outlined a proposal to take advantage of the new milling concerns in Oregon by shipping pine timber and logs across the Pacific to New South Wales. He had obviously done his homework, was able to quote figures which emphasized the fact that Oregon pine would be extremely attractive on the Australian market, and repeatedly stressed how fortunate it was that their own superfluous ships could be adapted to handling timber cargoes with only minor modification.

Stephen listened to him with utter disbelief, and as soon as he had taken his seat again, Stephen jumped up to protest.

"In the name of Jove, Mama, what are you thinking of? How can you possibly propose such a thing?" he asked.

"Mr. Opal proposed it, but I consider it an excellent plan. It will certainly solve our problems with the minimum of complications. Within three years the Richmond Line could be fully solvent again. Don't you agree that such a prospect is truly inspiring?"

"Inspiring? Do you understand what is being put forward? It is recommended that we engage in a trade which will undercut if not totally destroy, Auckland's own timber trade. Do you realize that kauri timber is one of our most important exports? Now that the wool trade has slumped, New Zealand needs that timber trade. All of us, not just the handful around this table but everybody in New Zealand, will suffer if another of our leading export markets evaporates. It will be catastrophic! How can you seriously expect me to agree to such a destructive proposal?"

"Don't be dramatic, Stephen," said his mother. "We must be pragmatic, not sentimental. If this trade promises to save our beloved Richmond Line, we cannot afford to overlook it."

Mr. McLeay cleared his throat. "Pardon me for the interruption, Captain Yardley, sir, but the trade has already begun, and if we do not ply it with our ships, other companies will. I hear rumors that the Dragon Line has sent a ship to Seattle, and I can think of no other reason for it to do so. It will take advantage if we do not."

Stephen shook his head. "I truly cannot believe this. All of you have seen the timberyards, the ships loaded with logs sailing out to foreign markets, the flourishing trade we have in finished and unfinished wood, yet you propose we take steps to stifle that industry, leave it for dead. Mama, you have friends who own shares in timber holdings. How can you threaten their very livelihood?"

"All my friends have interests in many kinds of ventures. Besides, I think you exaggerate the danger."

"But Samuel is the largest timber dealer in the province, and as far as I know, he is involved in no other type of commercial undertaking." He paused, caught suddenly by the strange expression on Jon's face. He was leaning forward, almost as if he had been waiting for his uncle to make this very observation, and on his face was a curious blend of anticipation and satisfaction.

"I think I understand," he said quietly. "And if I am correct in what I suspect, then I am aghast. Before I leave, I want to say three things. First, that I vote against the Oregon timber trade, not that my vote will do much good, but in this case it is important that the vote be registered. Secondly, that if the Richmond Line is sunk by the petty, vindictive spite that I scent here today, then, though it pains me to say so, it deserves to go down." He gathered his papers together and swept them into his black leather folder. "Thirdly, that I hope I am wrong in my suspicions. I pray I am wrong."

There was not a sound from any of them as he left the room. Jon did not meet his eye as he passed by his chair.

May was waiting, leaning over the veranda rail, when he arrived home. She was wearing a black dress, and her hair was caught back into a coarse black net which was spangled all over with sequins. The severity of the color and hairstyle made her look so delicate, that Stephen felt that if he pressed a fingertip to her skin, it would leave a blue mark.

"Father," she called as she walked out to meet him, "isn't Hal coming to dinner?"

"He's coming out later. Are you disappointed he's not with me, your dashing Captain Bennington?"

"That depends entirely on what is in the newspaper. Did you remember to buy one?"

"It's in the carriage. If you wait, I—" But she was on her way to the stables, calling out to say she could fetch it herself. He followed her there out of curiosity and found her on the seat with the pages spread over her lap. When she glanced up at him, her eyes were dancing with excitement.

"It printed my picture! The newspaper liked my picture so much that it had an engraving made of it and printed it! The editor said they would, but I didn't believe him. Look, there's my name underneath."

The illustration depicted a half-sunk *Emerald Dragon*. In the foreground a longboat carried a diminutive top-hatted figure, and in the background a covey of small boats scurried away.

"I see. The picture that caused Hal to stoke his boilers. But it's splendid, dear. I'm proud of you."

188

"And I'm glad that you didn't make me give away my camera."

"Now why should I do that? You may as well get what happiness you can in life."

"Are you ill, Father? You sound odd."

"I'm exhausted by the pettiness of the world." They walked toward the house, he holding the paper and she clinging to his arm. "Today I saw an example of the kind of cheap revenge we usually associate with children. I shouldn't be surprised, but I was. Surprised and saddened. But it's not just that. I've been feeling increasingly worse lately. Your mother thinks it would be a good idea if we went to Te Aroha to try out those famous hot springs—see if I can limber up these rheumaticky old joints. And she has the notion of visiting Samuel and thanking young Patrick properly for his bravery on the day of the accident."

"An expedition into the interior!" said May. "Wouldn't it be exciting if we met the chief Te Kooti and his warriors?"

"It would be nothing short of miraculous since they all are living miles away from there. If I had a price of five thousand pounds on my head, I doubt I'd venture from safety. No, we won't see Te Kooti, but Major Mair, in Hamilton, will be able to tell you all about him."

"Oh, he's the fellow who spent years trying to trap Te Kooti, isn't he? Daniel and Kendrick used to boast about how they would run off and join his band of modern-day forest rangers. I'll write to Daniel tonight and tell him of our plans."

But later, perched at her desk, she found that letter was difficult to write. Impossible to chat to Daniel when her mind insisted on making plans of its own. She must take a good supply of plates, the developing tent, of course . . . and Bobby Terrill. He was essential—she couldn't manage the tripod without him. Oh, the pictures she would be able to take, the scenes she would capture! Maoris, living in real pas, as in Daniel's stereoscopic pictures, not Europeanized Maoris like the locals.

But as she struggled between her plans and the letter, one disquieting thought kept intruding. Soon she would see Patrick Bennington again. She drew away from the thought, from the image of his cynical face as he had told her what he thought of her. I shall avoid him, she decided. Since he so clearly disapproves of me, I shall keep away from him. I don't care what he thinks of me anyway.

Yes, I shall ignore him.

Seventeen

At the Te Aroha Lodging Establishment the party was looked after by a garrulous woman named Mrs. Larney. Everything about her reminded May of the Waikato plains they had crossed by spring cart after the train journey to Hamilton. Her hair was as gray and springy as the scrubby vegetation, her voice as penetrating as the wind, and it seemed to May that her shiny skin was poured full to bursting with the slushy swamps they had churned through. Mrs. Larney's eyes watered continuously, and she interrupted herself often when speaking to sniff heftily.

It was difficult not to like her. She was a homely soul who imposed her own rules on her guests, restricting them and spoiling them at once, chivying them to eat her gargantuan meals and scolding them to extinguish the lamps at nine o'clock at night. On their first evening they were kept awake by scratching dance music and giddy laughter from Lipsey's Hot Springs Hotel across the road, but Mrs. Larney was bright-eyed at six, cooking a huge breakfast. Her sons slept one on either porch like amiable watchdogs. Both were of courting age, and both were forbidden to cross the street after dark. "There is drinking and fighting at those dances," she confided to May. "The devil provides drink to lead folk into dark and evil things."

When she discovered that while Juliette and Stephen were taking the waters, May proposed to wander about with only a young boy for protection, the good temperance lady was scandalized.

"It's not safe, I say. Not with these miners about. I'm married to Mr. Larney, and he be a miner, so I know all about it." While she spoke, Mr. Larney knocked his pipe against the fender, showing no sign of listening. "You'll not go about alone, Miss Yardley," she said, untying her apron. "And no arguments."

The tiny settlement of Te Aroha was situated on an up-turned cheek of land between the plains and the most beautiful hill May had ever seen. Mount Te Aroha rose as steep as an Indian tepee over which a dark green knobbly blanket had been thrown, falling around the base in careless crumples. In the folds, wisps of fog snagged and were held by the fronds of the punga ferns where they seemed to wait in the sunlight for May's camera.

"It's just a hill," said Mrs. Larney, perplexed by May's patience. She could see no advantage in trudging up and down mucky tracks or along ridges to line up a fractionally better view, then in waiting and waiting for perfect light conditions. She told them that *aroha* meant "love" and that from the top one could see clear across to the ocean, but mostly she told them about herself.

Since arriving in New Zealand, the Larneys had experienced an eventful life. They had settled first south of Auckland, where their farmhouse had been razed by Maoris at the start of the wars—Mrs. Larney and the boys had hidden down a well. They moved on to Te Aroha and prospecting.

"It was a frightening time for me, I tell you, with two little ones and Mr. Larney gone, and them Maoris from across the river coming up to see what was laying around outside. I'd be scared out of me wits, I don't mind telling you. But I'd trick them. If I saw them coming, I'd put on a pair of Mr. Larney's boots and thump about the house, grumbling in a gruff voice like this, so they'd think he was home. That fooled them every time, it did."

May ventured, "I'd like to take photographs at the pa if it's at all possible to go there."

Bobby giggled at the look on her face. May might as well have suggested that they all go bathing in the river in their "inexpressibles."

May said, "I'm sorry, Mrs. Larney, but I do like the Maoris I've met. Some live near us at home, and my grandmother has Maori servants."

The sniff echoed disapproval. "Mr. Lipsey hires only Maoris in his hotel, and a bad lot they are. 'Tis best that the two peoples be kept as separate as God intended."

"That would put us all back in the British Isles then," said May, but she could see she had offended the woman and changed the subject quickly. Uncle Samuel could take her to the pa when he arrived. She said, "Where do all the people come from in the evenings? Do they live in the hills?"

"There's a gold town up the valley. Waiorongomai it's called."

"I recall the name. Was there a gold rush there recently?"

"Not twelvemonth ago, that's right. There were nigh on a thousand prospectors here. Most had taken the lay of the land, but nobody could peg out an inch until the land had been declared, and to do that, they had flags and speeches and guns firing. Everybody that wanted claims lined up in a long string, and when the signal went, they hotfooted and scrambled for the piece they wanted."

"That is the place I read about. I cut the story out of the newspaper to send to my brother in England. A friend of his—our cousin—had regrettable cause to be mentioned in it, I'm afraid."

Samuel was to meet them in Te Aroha and spend a few days there with them before they returned to Auckland for Christmas, and Patrick was expected to come with Samuel as usual. May tried not to dread the coming encounter. It would be difficult to be warm to Samuel and cool to Patrick, but she was determined to manage it.

Meanwhile, her collection of glass negatives grew. She photographed wide, bare roads where houses were set back from the clouds of summer dust. Farmers, prospectors, and children were cajoled by Mrs. Larney into posing for the camera. One day May went with her parents and captured the image of Stephen sunk to his floating chin whiskers in the hot water while Juliette sat on a bench, reading aloud from *Passion and Paregoric.*

One morning, when May and Bobby returned to the lodging establishment, a strange horse was tied up outside. It was glossy with sweat and black as licorice, and Bobby recognized it at once. Praying that her parents would not be long delayed, May went in to greet the visitors.

Patrick was alone in the "guest parlor," sitting on a shabby chair with a fawn-colored Aden helmet in his lap. When she came in, he said, "Miss Yardley," and stood up, stripping off a glove to shake hands with her.

She kept hers on and nodded awkwardly. She glanced about for a sign of Uncle Samuel, then back to him. He was dressed in the smartest of riding clothes, high brown boots that were dull in patches where mud had been brushed off and a light tweed jacket.

When she neither spoke nor sat down, he said, "Do relax, please. I never bite people before dinner." She looked startled, and he explained, "Your uncle did not come. He's ill, I'm afraid, but not seriously."

"Oh." She sat on a chair not too close to his and said, "I'm sorry you had to travel so far to convey bad news."

"It has had compensations," he said obliquely. Then: "Mother and I used to come here often. She hoped the springs might help her toward a cure."

"Oh," said May again. "Have you been waiting here long?"

"Too long, I think." He nodded toward a reproduction of Queen Victoria. "That lady has been staring at me as if she wanted me to leave, so that she could spit out whatever is causing the nasty taste in her mouth."

May laughed—it was a perfect description of a most unfortunate expression—but then said, "Oh, do be careful that Mrs. Larney doesn't hear you. That picture is her greatest treasure."

"I cannot believe it."

"It's true. And you might upset me if you insult the queen, for I'm a royalist, too, with all the enthusiasm of a new convert. Since coming to New Zealand, I have often thought what a pity it is that America has no royal family of its own. I find the feeling for queen and empire really touching."

"Not I. I must say that in America I find it delightful to be able to go into a saloon and drink a tot of brandy without glancing up to find that face staring admonishingly at me."

"Hush!" said May, in alarm this time. "Mrs. Larney will not tolerate even the mention of alcoholic beverages in this house."

"She's in for a nasty shock when she discovers that Queen Victoria is very partial to a wee dram of whiskey now and again. I believe the whole district is waiting to see her reaction to that, but nobody has the courage to tell her."

"You know her well then?"

"My mother and I were not . . . eligible to stay in this establishment."

May understood at once and could have bitten off her tongue. Surprisingly this conversation was proving to be fun. Patrick was lively and stimulating. He listened attentively, not like Hal, whose mind always seemed to be elsewhere, and he made no false pretense of agreeing with her.

"I am sorry. Every time I talk to you I make a disaster out of it."

"I'm used to such disasters," he said with a smile. That should have made her feel better, but oddly it made it worse.

He was thinking how unhealthy she appeared when she blushed. He wondered if an illness gave her skin that pallor.

"There must be some mistake, young man," said Mrs. Larney, and he saw her standing with arms akimbo, looking belligerent. He stood up at once, uttering a courteous greeting.

"I was not expecting you. Mrs. Yardley said her brother was coming to visit."

"I have come in his place."

May was on her feet, too, saying, "Mr. Bennington is related to us by marriage, Mrs. Larney."

"I know who he is, and I know how little marriage had to do with the matter," she said grimly, not looking at May. She stood aside to clear the doorway, her breath whistling in her throat. "You will find the company more congenial across the road at the hotel, young man. When Mr. Yardley returns from the springs, I shall inform him of your whereabouts."

May could hardly believe that the good-natured, chatty Mrs. Larney could be so rude with no provocation. Patrick had been scrupulously polite and even now was retrieving his helmet and wishing her a formal good day. He had not glanced at May once during the exchange, and she had the strongest feeling that if she did not make some protest quickly, then she would be a silent accomplice to this insulting treatment.

Forcing brightness into her voice, she said, "But Mr. Bennington and I had just decided to go out for a stroll to meet my parents, hadn't we, Patrick?" And to seal the proposition, she took his arm and held it while they walked past Mrs. Larney and along the path to the road.

When they were a short way from the house, he said, "There was no need for you to do that, Miss Yardley," and moved a pace away from her so that her hand slipped off his elbow.

"There was a need. She was unpardonably rude."

"Perhaps. But that is her house, and I entered it, knowing full well how she dislikes Maoris. Frankly I doubted that she would remember two people who had knocked on her door late one night, and I doubted she would recognize me again; but she obviously did."

"But she was obnoxious to you. How can you be reasonable?"

He laughed. "My dear Miss Yardley, I am a Maori with strong views of my own. How can I hope that other people will eventually come to respect my views if I cannot first accord them the same respect?"

"I would never have considered the matter in that light." She was beginning to understand why Uncle Samuel spoke so highly of this young man. May glanced at him speculatively. On his chin was a raw streak where he might have cut himself shaving. About him was a distinct essence of bay rum and the fainter smell of horses. Though of course, she could not think of him as a "young man" in the sense of dancing or parties, it still seemed wrong to be walking with him yet not holding his arm. May began to wonder why he had moved away from her. Was it accidental, or had he deliberately disengaged her grasp?

She was also dismayed when he said, "It would be best if you returned now. I think you will find that Mrs. Larney has taken your point."

"What point?"

"That you condemned her attitude. That was the only reason you offered to come with me, was it not?"

He was absolutely correct, but she denied it indignantly. "I was glad of an opportunity for some different company. Every day since we arrived, Mother and Father have spent each morning at the springs and have returned there after high tea most days. The most exciting thing I have done to date is to play squiggles with Mother. All the rest of the time I have been accompanied by the sound of Mrs. Larney's voice."

"How tedious for you."

"I'm not complaining. I came here to take photographs, and this has been a real adventure for me apart from the dearth of company." Before he could repeat his suggestion that she return, she continued hastily. "You are interested in photography, too, are you not? You spoke very knowledgeably about it when I met you at the beach. I wondered if it was a diversion of yours."

"I've been interested in it ever since my father gave Mother a Bible which had photographs as illustrations. They were the first I'd really studied."

"Frith's photographs? Of the Holy Land?" She stumbled on a loose stone and somehow found herself holding his arm again.

"You know them? I used to gaze at them for hours. Later I read about the difficulties the photographer had overcome —the sand and flies gumming up the plates, the heat so intense that developing chemicals actually boiled in the tent. But my interest is only theoretical. I've never attempted to take a photograph, though Samuel had an old camera he was going to give me at one time. Mother was ill then, and I'd not have had time to learn to use it properly anyway."

"He gave it to me," she said, remembering guiltily that the camera had been more appropriated than offered. To make amends, she said, "You must permit me to show you how to use it. How long will you be staying in Te Aroha?"

"Possibly only a few hours. Until I've seen Mr. and Mrs. Yardley."

"Oh, Mother will be pleased to see you. She often says how grateful she is to you about the heroic way you acted that day when the boys were killed. She hoped you would call on her, but you've not been near."

"I've not been to Auckland since then."

"Are you like Uncle Samuel and find the city distasteful?"

He glanced at her in amusement. "I never feel perfectly at ease anywhere. I've begun to look on that as an advantage—I'm more objective and everything seems clear and sharp to me. But I like the city as well as most other places. Samuel detests it and says nothing will induce him to return. I think he should. He's not well and needs to spend the summer recuperating. Oh, don't look alarmed. He had a heavy cold and throat infection during the spring, and he's not managed to shake it off completely. I'm hoping that your parents will write to him, insist that he come to Auckland for Christmas. If they agree of course."

"You need not worry about their reaction. They will regard everything you say with sympathy, as I do."

He smiled at her earnestness. All Auckland was in raptures over her beauty, but for the life of him he could see nothing appealing about that pallor. She was pretty enough, with good teeth and a beautiful smile, and her eyes had an unusual quality of glowing innocence; but for all that she was hardly what he would term a beauty. What did surprise him was the glimpse of a straightforward yet sweet nature. Before he met her, he had imagined she would be as haughty as her superior cousin, Ellen Forster, and his first meetings with May had confirmed this prejudice.

Now he was confounded when May said, "I must confess that this encounter has been different from what I expected. Until an hour ago my opinion of you was at such variance with my present estimation that I dreaded meeting you again."

He began to laugh at that. When she asked why, he

198

would say only, "My sentiments exactly," and laughed again.

She looked stricken. After withdrawing her hand from its snug position against his jacket, she hurried on ahead, moving swiftly despite the restriction imposed by her bustled skirt. He caught up to her at the foot of the long path which led up to the hot springs gate and stood in front of her, holding her by the upper arms and willing her to look into his face.

"I was laughing not at you but at myself. Please, I do mean that."

She hesitated, then said, "I apologize for getting upset. Are we friends?"

He glanced at the black-gloved hand that was held out to him and peeled off his own glove to clasp it in reply. His hand was brown and strong. She could feel its pleasant warmth as he took her fingers and tucked them back into the crook of his arm.

"I should thank Mrs. Larney," he said. Then almost as if to cover over that statement, he said, "Do you know of whom she reminds me? The fierce cannibal chief Hongi Hika. Do you think that an odd comparison? They are not similar in ferocity, of course. Some historians estimate that Hongi Hika was responsible for the slaughter of more than fifty thousand Maoris from opposing tribes. In his youth he went to England and met the king, who gave him a suit of armor and many other gifts, which he exchanged for muskets. Whenever he went into battle, he wore the helmet and chest piece of the armor, until one day when he was taken by surprise and shot in the ribs."

May was frowning, not sure how this could connect with Mrs. Larney. Patrick continued. "The musket ball entered his lung and didn't kill him outright. He lingered for months, but the story goes that from that moment on Hongi Hika made a mournful whistling noise with every breath as air was drawn in and out of the hole in his chest."

"But wouldn't the wound have healed over?"

Patrick grinned at her and said, "Don't ask me. He was not one of my ancestors—not unless he was, as he claimed,

199

the sum of all the warriors he had eaten. Quite a few of my tribal ancestors went into his hangi ovens."

"Is that May with that young man?" asked Stephen. "I must be mistaken. It couldn't be."

"You are not mistaken," said Juliette, coming through the gate ahead of her husband. "She is with Jack Bennington's boy Patrick."

"I had no idea that they knew each other so well."

"I had no idea that they *liked* each other so well," said Juliette in an odd tone.

"Fine lad that. Instead of giving in to circumstances, he makes the best of things. Fine head for business, too. Do you know he built that brewery up out of nothing?" He smiled at her vinegary expression. "Shipping's commerce, too, you know, and there's money aplenty to be made in ale. Still, it's a shame he'll never fit in anywhere. He and Samuel are the mavericks of our little world. They are wise to stay together. Hallo there, lad!" And waving his walking cane, he set off down the path toward them.

Juliette, who noticed that May did not relinquish Patrick's arm until she had to, tried to smother her disquiet. Patrick was more handsome and better spoken than she remembered. The American education had polished his manners and injected a warm burr into his voice. Despite her own prejudices, she liked him and said so to Mrs. Larney later.

"Of course, May should be polite to someone who is, after all, a relative of ours," she told her. "Now, if you would be so kind as to excuse me, I must begin my packing. Mr. Bennington will be escorting us farther inland to see my brother tomorrow, and we hope to have an early start."

"I still think that Maoris are not fit company for a young lady like Miss Yardley. To be seen walking arm in arm with him in public! I tell you that—"

Though Juliette agreed, she said, "Excuse me, please. I have things to do."

"You'll find you're not welcome farther inland, especially if you're seen with that young man. He's developing a shady reputation in this district—he and your brother, Mr. Peridot, as well. Not just as Maori sympathizers—

200

which is bad enough, for the wars will never be over in some folks' eyes—but as a double-dealer. Dishonest, that's what he is."

"What did she mean?" asked Juliette that night as she braided her hair into two long ropes, ready for bed.

Glancing up from the folder of Mondrich Line papers, Stephen said, "Has Samuel never told you what he and Patrick are up to? It's a wonder. You'd probably approve."

"Tell me then, and see if I do." Already she was deciding that she didn't.

He clipped the folder shut and went behind the screen in turn, talking to her while he changed out of his dinner clothes. "The pair of them are seeking to undo what Abigail's swain—that Kine fellow—is trying to do. Did you know that Mr. Kine is aiming to set himself up with a huge estate?"

"Abby did drop hints about Mr. Kine's having a castle built for him in the country. Is it somewhere hereabouts?"

"There's no sign of any castle yet. Nor will there be if Samuel and young Patrick have their way. Mr. Kine has employed agents who lure the Maori owners into debt by extending what promises to be unlimited credit, sell them quantities of what they cannot resist—usually grog—then foreclose on the debt."

"But surely that must be an illegal practice?"

"You'd be surprised how many extensive landholdings have come into European hands by that route." Stephen climbed into bed. "I shall be glad of a different bed tomorrow night. This one has more lumps than a sack of potatoes. I think the floor would be more comfortable."

"But how does my brother come into this scheme?"

"He and Patrick are stepping in just in time to pay the debts and secure the land. Mr. Kine is thus neatly frustrated in his ambitions—and very angry, too, I hear. He is laying out money to pay agents and obtaining nothing in return."

"But the Maoris still lose their land. Really, Stephen, it seems to me that Mrs. Larney was perfectly justified in what she said—"

"Wait, Sweet Olivine. I've not finished. Samuel told me

201

that Patrick was inspired by the way his tribe gave away yet held onto Whenuahakari. He is doing the same kind of thing here—making himself a guardian of the land, as it were. The Maoris keep the use of it, but his name goes on the deeds. And there is a splendid irony in all this."

"What might that be?" she asked, thinking that Patrick sounded too noble to be true. The observation made her tingle with alarm.

"The land frauds are based on the liquor trade, and Patrick is preventing them with money earned by his brewery. Jack Bennington was right when he told me that Patrick has a most unorthodox outlook on life. The young men at the clubs only want to deal with scraps of paper and use borrowed money to make their paper pyramids. The principle seems to be to buy with the sole expectation of finding some fool to sell to. Nothing is valued or kept. No work is done. I find it refreshing to hear about someone like Patrick, who—"

"Stephen?"

"What is it?"

She was lying on her back with her eyes closed. "I'm very tired, and we have a long journey tomorrow. Could we please let the subject be?" And when he kissed her brow, she added sleepily, "And please don't discuss this with May. She is so terribly impressionable."

Eighteen

Samuel waited for them at a Maori pa some half day's horseback ride beyond the next town, a settlement considerably larger than Te Aroha with a church, a race-track, and even an unpainted wooden courthouse. Patrick was familiar with the place and gave them a tour before showing them to a guesthouse for the night, an improvised business where the landlord's children were evicted from their quarters to make room for May and where Bobby and Mr. Terrill had to sleep on hay in the stables.

"Make the most of the luxury," Patrick told them before leaving for an unrevealed destination. "You'll have rougher lodgings tomorrow night."

They discovered soon enough that he was not exaggerating. All morning they trekked in single file along a valley floor. Occasional breaks in the overhead vegetation showed hilltops gray with clouds. Eventually they splashed across a stony stream bed and, in a fine, warm drizzle, climbed a muddy track to a small plateau where a cluster of dwellings huddled miserably inside a low enclosure at the foot of a tall black cliff. The gray dreariness of it all was lightened only slightly when the weather cleared and sunshine slanted out from between the clouds.

May drew her horse alongside her mother's, reaching out to her in dismay. This was not at all how she had imagined the pa would look. "Is this the place?" she whispered.

"Does it look a little too primitive for you?"

May's nose wrinkled. "It looks dismal."

Several large yellow dogs stood in the gap in the crooked fence and lifted their muzzles, barking mournfully. Patrick snapped something at them, and they stopped the noise but now circled the party at a cautious distance, shoulders hunched. Their thin coats rippled over corrugated ribs.

"It's nothing like I'd visualized," said May, still disappointed. "I imagined high carved archways and tall, sharp-toothed palisades with trenches, to repel enemy attackers."

"The Maoris don't fight each other now, so there is no need for fortification. And as for carving, I read that most valuable artifacts had been removed to the king Country for safekeeping during the war. But look, that large building at the back. All the red-painted trimmings are carvings. That's the meetinghouse. It looks identical to the one at the pa we lived by when we were children. Our cottage was just like one of these huts, with a packed-earth floor, walls of sticks and rushes bound with flax, and a thatched roof."

"I remember your telling me about it. Somehow it sounded colorful and romantic, not poor and drab."

"It was poor, all right, I can assure you of that, but we were happy enough. Definitely not drab. And I'm sure you will find this an interesting adventure. Country Maoris are very hospitable and friendly; you'll like them."

Patrick was swinging down from his saddle, but he called to them to stay on their horses until he found Samuel. No point in their having to wade through the mud. He, however, squelched through the mire to the nearest hut. Clusters of brown faces stared at them from all the sack-screened doorways.

May said, "Perhaps we can persuade Uncle Samuel to come back with us today, so we won't have to stay overnight."

"The experience will be good for you," said her mother cheerfully.

She sounds as though she's prescribing medicine, thought May, but then Stephen rode over and said, "This will not be what we are used to, but regard it as an education, and try not to show disgust at anything you see. These people are courteous and deserve our respect."

Patrick emerged from a doorway, drawing a wake of

children after him. "Samuel is in the meetinghouse," he said, taking the bridle of Juliette's horse. May kept up alongside, and as they ambled across the compound, Patrick explained that normally visitors were welcomed with the flinging down of a ceremonial challenge and speeches and songs, but because the tribe was scattered, the chief and many elders being away in the king Country, he hoped they would accept an informal welcome instead.

They stopped some distance from the meetinghouse, beside a high-roofed tin shelter where a fire burned on the ground at one end. At the other end firewood was stacked below a bundle of woven flax baskets. Two enormous coiled mesh eel traps hung from the smoke-stained rafters.

Children darted around them to hold the horses. May gave her reins to a little girl with oily braids and a tweed jacket, on which twisted balls of wire served as buttons. May smiled at the child, who ducked her head, giggling.

An old woman emerged from the meetinghouse to stand in front of the porch. Raising both hands, she began to wail a monotonous chant. Her hands trembled like leaves in the wind. As the song gathered momentum, she moved her fluttering hands away, then back toward herself in a gesture that seemed part beckoning and part benediction.

Patrick said to May, "She is asking you to go forward. She'll probably kiss you in the Maori style. It's called a *hongi.* Don't be nervous of her."

The woman was ancient. Even the red rug draped toga-style over her long black dress was dull with age. Her *moko,* or chin tattoo, had faded to a faint smudge, and her eyes glazed with cataracts; but there was bony strength in her fingers as she grasped May's head and pulled their noses together, hard. While she did so, she inhaled a long hissing breath through her nostrils.

May stepped back a pace when she was released. *"Tena koe,"* she ventured timidly.

"Aaah!" cried the old woman, much impressed by being wished good day in her own language. She grasped May's hands fiercely and turned to Patrick, speaking rapidly to him in a loud, authoritative voice.

He looked angry. *"Kao, Matua. Kao."*

She jabbered back more emphatically, stopping only

when Juliette stepped up to her for her greeting. May moved over to where Patrick stood and asked him what the old woman had said to him.

"She is a silly old woman. A real *kuia.*"

"What did she say?" persisted May. "You said no to her, but I couldn't understand what she was saying."

He shrugged and said, "It was nothing of any importance."

Juliette interrupted the exchange. "We shall go in now, May. Mr. Bennington, would you be so good as to arrange suitable accommodations for Mr. Terrill and the lad? They would probably appreciate something to eat and drink after the journey."

"Certainly, Mrs. Yardley."

As she followed her mother across the porch, May wondered if it was a coincidence that every time she struck up a conversation with Patrick, her mother contrived to separate them. Last evening at the lodging house they had been in the middle of a spirited exchange, discussing the current theories about the beginnings of the world. He prescribed to Darwin's evolutionary ideas, while May was firmly of the opinion that the catastrophe theory was the right one. She was expounding why she felt it much more likely that the world had been thrown together in eruptions of enormous violence and was enjoying herself immensely when predictably her mother appeared on the porch and asked if Patrick would please be so kind as to go out and see if he could procure some apples or pears for her. She felt that she absolutely had to taste something fresh and crisp, and there was not one piece of fruit to be had at the lodging house. May first felt suspicious then. It was not like her mother to have sudden cravings, and May had never known her to ask specifically for fruit before. In any event, the discussion with Patrick was ruined because by the time he returned the subject had cooled.

As she stepped aside to allow her mother to go into the meetinghouse first, she wondered whether these little intrusions were deliberate or coincidental. Her mother smiled sweetly at her, and at once she felt ashamed of her suspicions. Why in the world would her mother want to stop her from conversing with Patrick?

Inside, the meetinghouse was dim and cold, with a sour odor of smoke that rasped in May's throat. The room was enormous yet windowless, and the only light slanted in from an oblong hole in the center of the roof, directly above a pit of blackened stones in which a fire crackled. The chute of light was filled with sparkling dust particles, all constantly moving, while fumes from the fire seemed to curl out toward the corners of the room. The far wall and part of one side were covered with decorative panels of woven reeds, and the unlined remainder had been used as a display for rows of *piupius,* the native skirts made of rolled flax. They looked like black and brown bead curtains.

Though there were more than a dozen groups of people here, the room was large enough to accommodate them easily without losing the feeling of space. In one corner a mat had been spread on the dirt floor, and around it sat young women, cards fanned out in their hands. They were so intent on their game that they did not glance at the Yardleys.

Samuel was sitting on one of the benches near the fire. He saw them and limped over, beaming.

May was shocked by her uncle's appearance. She knew that he was a year younger than her mother, but now he looked at least twenty years older. His flesh seemed to have shrunken and hardened onto his bones, leaving the skin of his face and neck loosely wrinkled. He moved stiffly, as her father had a few weeks earlier, but his voice was cheerful.

"I had to wait in here," he explained as he kissed his sister and niece. "It was more than my life was worth to come out and spoil Ruihi's little performance." He held out a pitifully thin hand. "How are you, Stephen? Did the magic waters work for you?"

"I'm a new man. But you look as though you might benefit from a few long immersions yourself."

"Nothing wrong with me. I'm as fit as a grasshopper and twice as springy. Come sit by the fire," he continued, shooing some bare children off the benches. "You, too, Stephen. Warm yourself. It can get very chilly after a long ride."

"Patrick tells us you are not well," said Juliette, trying to keep concern out of her voice.

"The boy exaggerates. He has a sound heart but tends to be too concerned about other people's welfare. I keep telling him that he should consider himself occasionally."

His sister said quickly, "But you don't look at all well, dear. Does he, Stephen? Now I don't want any arguments. We are taking you back to Auckland with us. You can stay at Mondrich House and Mrs. Terrill will feed you broth and posset and other such nourishing delights." She laughed as he grimaced at the idea. "You hated them as a child, too, as I recall. Samuel, I will not accept a refusal. You are coming with us."

He looked relieved but joked to Stephen, "If you had said that, I could have resisted. I know better than to argue with our Juliette."

"So do I."

Juliette poked Stephen's arm reproachfully, and they exchanged a tender glance.

Samuel said, "Could we please wait until our messengers return? We sent two men to the king Country to try to negotiate a purchase of the remainder of the Maori land between here and the border. It seemed much simpler to buy it now, before Kine's agents move in on the owners with their grog and promises. So much land has already been lost for virtually nothing that we hope the Maori king will appreciate the sense of our proposal—and our price, of course. As long as he has confidence in Patrick's motives, all will be well, but there's the snag, I'm afraid."

"Why? Surely King Tawhiao would believe him without hesitation. He is one of them after all."

"Unfortunately Patrick is not one of anything. Years ago, when he applied for a bank loan to make improvements on the brewery, he was turned down flat. I investigated and was told that the 'black quarter,' as they put it, was all they could see and on those grounds he had no chance of obtaining finances anywhere in the city. When he deals with Maoris, the opposite thing happens. They distrust his white blood. But these negotiations with the Maori king would be complicated anyway. You know how

208

the Maoris love drama and oratory and how they seize on any chance to have a weeklong debate."

Juliette said, "Surely you don't have to be here personally to hear the messengers' stories? Couldn't Patrick take care of the negotiations himself? He does speak Maori, doesn't he?"

"Yes . . ." began May.

Samuel spoke at the same time. "He knows it fluently, which is amazing, since he's picked it up only in the past few years. When Jack died, he knew fewer than a dozen words."

"Why was that?" asked May, but her voice was lost in a burst of shrieking laughter from the cardplayers.

Juliette said, "Then it's settled. You come back with us tomorrow. Patrick can stay to see your messengers."

"It will have to be the day after, if you don't mind an extra day. The minister is calling tomorrow for a wedding. I must be here because the bride is one of my hundreds of godchildren. As it is, the wedding will be disappointing for poor Katerina. So many of her uncles away, and her father dead—"

May leaned forward impulsively. "I know how it can be improved—if you agree, of course. I shall take a portrait of the bridal couple and their families. Do you think they would like that?"

"Like it? It would make their day. That's very generous of you. Ah, here comes the tea. I wonder what is delaying Patrick? The lad should be here with us."

"Shall I pour?" offered Juliette.

On the tray were six chipped enamel mugs and a porcelain teapot painted with forget-me-nots and sprays of tiny leaves. The tea was milkless and very strong, and though they all stirred in several spoonfuls of sugar, it tasted vile.

"The tea will be tainted, I'm afraid," said Samuel, who was the only one drinking. "The one huge go-ashore pot is used to boil up all manner of things, and the flavors tend to linger in the pot and give the tea a definite accent. One thing I look forward to when I go to town is a good cup of tea, yet I always forget to bring a new billy back with me."

"You must have our kettle, and begin using it at once," said Juliette hastily.

"We'd best wire the lid down first," said Stephen, "or they might use the thing to boil eels in. This tea has a distinct aroma of boiled eels."

"Which is probably a hint of tonight's dinner menu," said Samuel, showing his gums as he laughed.

But a hangi was being put down especially for the guests, and at last May was able to learn all the intricacies of the process.

"Mmm. It smells so good," said May to Patrick. "I hadn't realized how hungry I was."

"I'm glad you like it. A lot of *pakehas* detest the smoky taste. They want to know why the Maoris go to so much trouble to end up ruining the food."

"It does seem a lot of complication, to build such a huge fire, heat the stones for hours, then bury everything for more hours. Why go to such trouble?"

"Simple. The Maoris had no pottery and no heatproof vessels to cook food in. They had to devise some special way of cooking or else eat everything raw. At least, that's what Samuel says."

"I find it curious that Samuel rather than your mother has explained so much about Maori culture to you."

He turned his head toward the hangi pit. May could not gauge his expression and was beginning to understand that once again she had been tactless when Patrick said suddenly, "My father was a bigot."

Jolted, May wondered if she had misheard, but he continued in the same unemotional tone. "He forbade my mother to tell me anything about Maori ways. It's odd because he adored my mother, and he certainly loved me, but prejudice was something he never managed to conquer—if he tried. He disapproved of the way my mother's relatives continually visited us, and being Jack Bennington, he never tried to disapprove silently." He glanced at May, wondering if he was shocking her, and saw, instead, sympathy in her face. "I'll never forget the day Father came by unexpectedly and found Mother searching my grandmother's head."

"I beg your pardon?"

"For lice. Kooties, as they are picturesquely named

here. They are a fact of life, and the Maori style of hugging and cuddling puts everybody at risk, so . . ."

"You don't need to be defensive. I had them once." She had never confessed this to anybody before and was astonished to hear herself. "The daughter of one of the city councillors in San Francisco became infected and passed them on to me. What a fuss there was when Miss Von Sturmer discovered them. I couldn't understand it."

"Neither could I. Father almost burst his boiler. I shall never forget his rage—the way he thumped the table and demanded that I be shielded from all the disgusting, repellent aspects of Maori life—and the way Mother sat in utter calm as though she were unaffected by the slurs. Shortly after that, I was sent to school in America." He smiled. "That was interesting, but a lost cause. Father saw me being accepted as an Englishman or an American when I returned. A hopeless idea, but I know he meant well."

"Why hopeless? When I first saw you I had not the slightest inkling that you were—"

"Dabbed with a tar brush?"

"That's a horrible expression."

"Quite flattering, compared to some things I am called. You should hear my half brothers on the subject." He laughed. "I see that you have. Or Derwent Kine. He'd like to nail my hide to a wall, but never mind that. Perhaps he will have his chance one day. Ah, they are calling us to come eat. I hope you know how to eat with your fingers, Miss Yardley."

"Very, very cautiously, if the food is hot. This is such fun. Do you know, I was dreading meeting you again, and I've enjoyed your company so much. You're not at all arrogant, are you?" And she tucked her hand into his elbow.

"Have you ever tried to be just a little less frank?"

"Would you prefer that? I can speak at length and never once say what I really mean. Would that please you?"

"Indeed, no. I find you delightfully refreshing."

They were smiling at each other, and he was thinking how the white clematis in her hair flattered her pale skin when her mother came out of the meetinghouse to look for her.

The sight of the two close together raised another

211

prickle of alarm in Juliette's mind, but she kept silent until much later. They had said good night to the menfolk, all of whom were to sleep in the meetinghouse, and had retired to the gloomy little hut she and May would share. As her daughter unlaced her stays for her, she said, "So you still find Patrick amusing company, do you?"

The casual note was not lost on May, nor was the slightly disparaging use of his Christian name, as if he were a servant or native hawker. She replied, "I like him very much. I feel at ease with him somehow. Do you understand what I mean?"

Juliette was afraid that she did understand but said lightly, "It wouldn't really do to become too friendly with him, though, would it now?"

"Whyever not?" She eased the loosened stays over her mother's head and began unpinning her hair.

"Hal would be extremely angry if he heard about your friendship with Patrick."

"Hal is a good deal too sensitive about Patrick. I don't see why he should bear such hatred toward his half brother. Mr. Bennington cannot help who his father was. Why, he had no more say in the matter than I did."

"May!"

"Oh, Mother, I am sorry," said May unhappily. "What I intended to say was—"

Juliette interrupted firmly. "I think we shall leave *that* subject to rest there and return to the original topic. You owe considerable loyalty to Hal, which means you should respect his feelings whether or not you consider them reasonable."

May knew better than to argue against that firm tone but had to offer a token protest, saying, "I thought that you liked Mr. Bennington."

"I admire his courage. I'm grateful for what he did in trying to save the boys and for his concern for your uncle Samuel, and I admire what he is doing here—" She stopped, annoyed with herself for saying too much. Continuing on another tack, she concluded, "Of course, I like him. He is a fine young man, for a Maori."

May was sitting on the iron bedstead they were to share. She looked up from the task of unbuttoning her boots and said, "What is he doing here that gives you cause to admire him?"

Juliette sighed. "Really, dear, you make my head ache with your questions. And to think that you were such a quiet wee girl. Would you please hunt out the jar of chloroform embrocation for me? I think I shall dab some on my temples and see if that will ease my pounding head."

The bed was hard and damp and smelled strongly of mildew. Before dawn May woke, stirred by the sound of her mother's soft snoring, and once awake, she was unable to doze off again. This was in part because she was fixed into the habit of rising early to check the lighting conditions for the day. She was dressed with her hair pinned up in a matter of minutes. Juliette did not move as May quietly slipped out of the hut.

It was going to be a clear, hot day, perfect for the wedding photographs. May picked her way carefully across to the center of the compound, squinting up now and again at the sun, which was a dazzling blur rimming a low saddle in the mountain range. She was standing with arms akimbo, frowning thoughtfully at the front of the meeting-house, trying to decide how far forward of the porch she should pose her groups so that she could capture as much background as possible, when gradually she became aware that someone was watching her. She turned abruptly to see her uncle leaning against the enclosure fence.

May went over to him, scolding. "You should have told me you were there."

"Why? I was having myself a puzzle, trying to decide what my ladylike young niece was doing, standing and waving her arms about in such an unladylike fashion."

"I do look silly. Bobby Terrill has often told me so. I was trying to decide how to arrange the bridal couple. I want to get the meetinghouse in the picture, too, but not so that the carved center pole thing looks like a hat or horns."

"Is the camera working as well as it should?"

"It takes excellent pictures. Thank you so very much for it. I didn't realize at the time that you had promised it to Patrick."

"He would never have been interested."

213

"But he is. He knows such a lot about photography. I was impressed."

"He may know a lot, but he'd not have the patience to follow all the chemical processes through."

"I shall find out today. I promised to show him how to take and develop a negative plate. But why are you up so early, Uncle Samuel? You look as though you were alone with your thoughts."

"I'm listening to the birds—the tuis and the bellbirds. Savoring the quiet shadows, that's what I call it. You know, lass, your father came to see me with what he expected would be bad news for me. I suppose you've heard that a trade in Oregon timber is being developed across the Pacific, and soon its cheaper wood will close many of our timber mills? Your father said it has been in the newspapers. Well, lass, instead of being upset, I welcome the move. We've plundered these forests for far too long, and for what? So that people can use these magnificent kauri trees to make fowl houses, dog kennels, stables. It's obscene."

"Then why did you become a timber merchant?"

"When I began, the logs were used to make ships' spars. Your grandfather Thomas Peridot started the trade, and I took over from him. There was a dignity in that, but to cut the logs up for all manner of trivial uses doesn't seem respectful. Do you know what the Maoris did? When they wanted a tree, they prayed to *Tane*, the god of the forest, and begged his permission to kill one of his children. When you consider that a large kauri takes a thousand years to mature, it's not inconceivable that they have souls of their own. No, it will be good to have the trade slowed down. Perhaps it couldn't have been done earlier—so many thousands of people were arriving every year, and they all needed houses. And we had the men from the mills to consider. This Oregon trade will mean that the harbor sawmills will stay open. The pine will come in as logs and go out as dressed timber, ready for sale in Australia." He paused. "I think I hear Juliette calling you."

She was sorry to end the encounter. Most of the time her uncle seemed like an alien being to her, but this morning he was warm and human. But Mother needed her to brush

214

and pin her hair, so she could not linger for much longer here.

"Would you please tell me before I go," she said, "what exactly are you and Patrick doing here? Why are you buying more land when you already have so much and Patrick told me himself that he has no intention of living here? He wouldn't tell me what you both are up to."

"I'll tell you the details when you've seen to your mother. That is, as long as you'll not be bored."

"I won't be," promised May.

The minister was an elderly man with a smooth, gentle face and slumbrous brown eyes that moved as though suspended in heavy fluid. He wore tattered trousers with layers of darning at the cuffs and a tight black coat with a stand-up collar. On the gold trimming were embroidered the words *Ringatu Church.* May read that and wanted to ask him about Te Kooti. The minister had arrived on a shambling bay horse, his grandson behind him. Evidently the minister was an old friend of Samuel's. May photographed the two of them sitting comfortably on the ground in the sun. Standing beside his grandfather, the boy made a great show of stuffing and lighting the pipe, and when the exposure was over, he grimaced in delight, poking out his bright berry-stained tongue at Bobby.

Bobby chanted insolently, "Whose tongue is red and bleared his eyes? Who in the gutter often lies?"

May heard this while she was under the cloak, focusing camera and attention on a row of scrubbed children, shiny-faced in starched sailor suits, dressed exactly like Queen Victoria's royal children for this special occasion.

She heard Patrick say, "That should be 'Whose *nose* is red,' shouldn't it? And what temperance dragon taught you that?"

"You know very well who," said May, emerging with the wrapped negative. She gave it to Bobby with the automatic instruction to keep it damp. "He's repeated that dreadful rhyme only to tease, aren't you, Bobby?"

"I believe Mrs. Larney has a temperance rhyme for every occasion," said Patrick.

"We heard quite a number."

May wiped her hands on a small towel, then handed it back to Bobby.

"Are you going in to watch the ceremony?" Patrick asked her.

"Soon. I must paint a few more plates with solution ready for when the bridal party emerges, but right now I am waiting for Katerina. I looked in on her a few minutes ago, while she was getting ready, and oh, she looks lovely. Here she comes now. I don't think I've ever seen a more striking-looking bride. Bobby, could you please ask her to pause for a minute when she is halfway between the cottage and the meetinghouse? Ask her if she'd mind looking down at her bouquet while I take the picture. Could you count the time for her. Thank you, dear."

How regal these Maori women are, thought May. The crinoline gown had served dozens of brides in the ten years or so it had been owned by the tribe, but Katerina's graceful bearing bestowed freshness on the out-of-date style as she posed obediently, head bent over the ferns and starry clematis.

While the first hymn rose inside the meetinghouse, May quickly finished her preparation. She said to Patrick, who alone kept her company, "Why didn't you tell me about your little scheme here—buying the land, I mean?"

"Why should you be interested? Look, Miss Yardley, I'm no avenging angel, no matter what Samuel has told you. What I'm doing is striking a balance among what I want to do, what my mother expected of me, and what my conscience dictates. Because the last two forces are more powerful than the first, here I am. Not because I like it here." He grinned at her. "Sorry to disappoint you."

"But Uncle Samuel was telling me how it was before the wars—how there was a grain mill here to make flour, how the Maoris grew fruits and vegetables, all kinds of cash crops. And now they don't bother any longer. Aren't you trying to inspire them again?"

"Do you really think I could? It would take more than my efforts or Samuel's wishful thinking. All I'm trying to do, Miss Yardley, is to stop what I consider a crime. Not right a wrong or save my people, because they must do that themselves and frankly I doubt that they have the heart. The war killed their spirit. That's not overstating the case. Since the wars they've lost their *mana*, their pride. They no longer bother with carving, tattooing, all the crafts that once were so important. They're the way Samuel has been since Mother died—drifting without direction. *That's* really why their land is slipping away from them."

"But surely they appreciate what you're doing for them?"

"Why should they? Benefactors do not require thanks, and anyway, their *true* benefactors are the people who buy my ale. No, Miss Yardley, if anything, they are suspicious of me. I hear that King Tawhiao calls me *Tauhou,* which means 'stranger.' They have an old prophecy which goes like this: 'A stranger is standing behind the tattooed face. He is the white man who owns the earth.' I don't flatter myself that the prophecy talks about me. I rather think it alludes to Christ. But the fact remains that they are suspicious. Now, if you have finished, let's slip into the meeting-house. I'd like to see Katerina take her vows."

After the feasting that evening a concert was held, an impromptu program composed of songs and poems brought back from town and grafted onto more traditional material.

A battalion of sparrow-chested little boys with piupius wrapped around their thin hips stamped out a racous haka. Two poppets sang "Rule the Waves, O England" with shy Maori words, and then all the women, including Ruihi in her red toga and Katerina in her bridal gown, performed a graceful poi dance.

May sat beside the groom, a solemn figure in a stiff collar, with hair draped from a center parting like buffalo horns. On her other side Samuel explained that the poi was a fist-sized ball of fiber covered with dried flax and attached to a long or short string, depending on the dance. In the short poi dance the balls whipped and snapped around the dancers' wrists to crack out a sharp rhythm. Then the girls fastened the short pois to their waistbands and loosened the long strings while the music changed to a slow dipping melody. May sat bemused as the pois swung in a perfectly orchestrated pattern, swooping and soaring in

217

loops and arcs, while everybody sang the haunting song and the dancers' bare feet flapped a beat on the earth floor. Their piupius rattled like rain on the roof. May was enraptured.

During a break she saw Patrick standing near the door and went over to talk to him. "Yes, thank you, I'm enjoying myself immensely," she said. "Those dancers are so deft, so clever—" She broke off as Katerina came by, pushing her veil up off her face. She pressed noses with Patrick, then with May and thrust the pois she had been using at May.

"For you," she said.

"Thank you . . ." began May as she vanished in a swirl of white satin. To Patrick she said, "Will you show me how to use them?" Holding the pois out to him, she preceded him through the doorway.

Outside, it was bright moonlight, washed with a yellow glow from the heaped bonfire. Someone had mentioned that Samuel was providing fireworks in honor of his goddaughter's marriage, and there were two kerosene tins of boiled sweets to be distributed yet. The party was far from over.

"The long ones are easiest," Patrick told her, swinging one and then putting the string in her hand. "Twist your wrist very slightly as you feel it pull on your hand. Good, that's the way."

"This is a lot harder to do than it looks," May decided as she tried unsuccessfully to change direction. A child darted past, running between them, with another child in pursuit.

"We seem to be standing in the middle of the highway," said Patrick. He put out a hand to draw her to one side, and as he did so, the whirling poi hit him just below one eye.

"Oh, I am sorry," said May, reaching out and touching his cheek with her fingertips. "I am sorry, Patrick. I don't know how that happened."

"It was worth it." Her fingers had slipped and were now resting on the tweed of his shoulder.

"Why?"

He placed a hand over hers. He did not reply. He was standing very close to her, smiling in that unreadable way.

"Why was it worth it?" she whispered.

He did not reply but watched her silently. She tried to smile back at him but felt foolishly nervous. The moment seemed to solidify around them.

"Patrick . . ." she heard herself say. The skin of his neck was smooth and gold in the firelight. She wanted to place her palm on it, but her hand was still lying flat under his. Her breathing sounded loud and clumsy. She wished that she could say something entertaining, something that would make him toss back his head and laugh that delightful free laugh of his. He must think I'm a fool, she thought. I hit him in the face and knocked all the wit out of my own head.

"We'd better go in," she ventured, tugging at her hand.

His expression changed at once. "No," he said, and pressed her fingers together tightly. Bending his head forward, he kissed her.

She was not surprised. As soon as his lips touched hers, she realized that this was what she had been waiting for, this was why she had been unable to think clearly. At the same time the kiss was so sudden that she was caught off-balance and staggered against him. His arms wrapped around her, firmly but gently, steadying her. She could feel every one of his spread fingers between her shoulder blades. And just as his arms were gentle, his mouth was tenderness itself—a kiss that caressed and savored her. She closed her eyes. He tasted of warmth—clean, human warmth spiced with a faint tang of bay rum. She felt safe. Serene happiness enfolded her.

Nineteen

For the first few weeks after Christmas Samuel spent most of his day sitting in a wicker chair on the veranda, his mouth open as he dozed. When May had completed her work on the scores of photographs from the journey, she captured a likeness of him sleeping unawares, with one of the stable cats held like a cushion in his lap and another curled at his feet.

In those first weeks May was confined to the house, too, as a punishment. When her father came out of the meetinghouse and found May tangled in Patrick's arms, he had retaliated with the whole armory of weapons she most dreaded—disappointment, disapproval, and dismay. He had been coldly courteous to Patrick and had accepted immediately May's offer that it was all her fault. As indeed it was. Hal was right, he said later. Hal had stressed that May needed a chaperone, and if she could not be trusted alone, then she would have to have one.

Fearing that Miss Von Sturmer would be charged with her protection and dreading the thought of having to go everywhere with her, May stayed quietly at home, hoping the threat would be forgotten.

She shrank from what her mother would say. Ever since the tragedy of the boys' deaths May had felt protective toward her, and the aspect of this that hurt most was the knowledge that she had let her mother down. Implicit in May's behavior that night had been the suggestion that Juliette had not brought her up properly. May waited in trepidation for the lecture from her mother.

To her humiliation the lecture came, instead, from Uncle Samuel. May was reading the paper to him one morning, when Juliette joined them with a basket of letters she was sorting. She and Samuel looked at each other, Juliette nodded, and then he stopped May's reading in mid-sentence and began immediately to tell her how inconsiderately, unfairly, and wrongly she had treated Patrick. May was aghast. Her uncle spoke kindly; but the speech had obviously been rehearsed with Juliette, and they both seemed to think so badly of her that May was crushed.

"You don't understand," she pleaded. "I like Patrick. I trust him and feel so happy when I am with him. It was only one little kiss."

Juliette tore a sheaf of letters partway in two to indicate they had been answered and tucked them at the back of the basket. She said, "Do you give little displays of affection to all the young men you happen to like?"

"Of course not! Well, only to Hal, but that is different."

"Quite," said Juliette, marveling at how attractive Hal was growing in her eyes.

Samuel's expression was grave. "Patrick is a fine young man, but he has serious drawbacks which affect his eligibility. He has Maori blood, and he earns his living in a way which is unacceptable to the social circles you move in. He is also well on the way to making enemies with important people. Mr. Kine, for example."

"And I say bravo to him for that."

"We all do, dear," said Juliette, skimming a letter.

"The fact is that many people would leap at an opportunity to harm Patrick. Not just the Benningtons but all their friends. His birth has made him a pariah. You must realize all the implications of that."

"But that's not fair. He can't help his birth—"

"Nor can he alter it. Jack Bennington may have legally adopted him, but it didn't help him much. In the eyes of Auckland he is illegitimate. Even a knighthood from the queen wouldn't make him one whit more acceptable to your friends."

"Why are you telling me this? Are you saying that it is wrong for me to be friends with him?"

"I'm trying to protect Patrick, to stop him from being hurt, and you could hurt him very deeply. You are a beautiful young woman, and Patrick is not made of stone. If

221

you should unwittingly encourage him to become fond of you . . ."

"I see." May twisted her hands in her lap.

"Patrick has a generous nature, a fine intelligence, and a tender heart. It would grieve me to see him harmed any further. He has already suffered so many slights, so many insults . . . There, dear," he said in alarm. "Don't distress yourself so."

But May was crying in earnest now. She shook her head as her uncle tried to put his arms around her and pushed him away. "You don't understand," she said, weeping. "You don't understand at all. I wasn't playing with Patrick's affections. I wouldn't hurt him. You're telling me that I'm a selfish, shallow flirt, but I'm not. I *care* for Patrick. I really do. I wouldn't hurt him for anything in the world!"

Unable to bear any more scolding, she rushed out of the morning room and did not stop running until she was in the orange orchard, where she flung herself down onto the warm grass, still sobbing. Her uncle's words goaded her like a hot spur. She pressed her face into the soft green lap and thought bleakly: They're right. I am a selfish, shallow flirt. I encouraged Patrick to kiss me. I *wanted* him to, and I never paused to think how carelessly I was playing with his feelings; but then I never thought that he might *have* any feelings toward me anyway.

She rolled onto her side. Through her closed lids the sun was a hot orange blur. Suddenly she remembered San Francisco and how she used to lie in the sun like this, imagining that happiness was flowing into her body through those warmed eyelids and spreading through every part of her. The desire to go back to her old life was so physically intense that it took her breath and pushed it back down into her lungs until her chest burned. Fresh tears welled under her lids, and she gave in to them with a sense of hopelessness. Life here is too complicated, she thought. I don't fit in. I don't understand, and even when things are pointed out to me, I cannot see their logic. In San Francisco I had a place in society, just as I do here, but the difference is that there I was comfortable in that place,

222

and here I am bewildered and unhappy. Oh, how I wish that I could go back to San Francisco!

Patrick was not mentioned again. As a sign of good faith May took care not to talk about him, but she was secretly disappointed when her uncle avoided the topic, too. Once a letter arrived from him, but the contents were never discussed, unlike most other correspondence, which was shared, as were the ecstatic letters from Mrs. Rugmore, now back in Pindleton. May wondered what Patrick was doing. She searched her photographs and was furious with herself when she discovered that she had not included him in one single frame.

But now that Samuel's health was better, May had other things to occupy her mind. Samuel became her chaperone, giving her freedom again, and several days a week the dog-cart rolled away from Mondrich House loaded with Samuel, May, Bobby, and the camera equipment.

May photographed a wagon which had been pulled completely in half after being stuck in a deep mud hole. When they arrived on the scene, the horses were being dragged out of the mire. May's picture encapsulated so much drama that the newspaper made an engraving of it and featured it on the front page. A week later she was featured again. Samuel took her into the Waitakere ranges to see the last of the logging operations at one of his camps. May photographed a double team of eighteen oxen hauling a single gigantic log along a dry stream bed. The log was wrapped about with chains, like a trussed whale. Each link was thicker through than May's waist. It was Bobby's idea that Samuel should stand on top of the log to give scale to the monumental girth.

Under the engraving the newspaper ran a story called "Colossus of the Forest, Doomed to Extinction," which told how the timberworkers would soon join the thousands of unemployed in the city. The story made Samuel angry enough to dictate his first-ever letter to the editor, stating not only that it was commendable that the forest would now be saved, but that all the Peridot timberworkers were assured of continued employment, either in the harborside sawmills which processed Oregon pine or in jobs found for

223

them elsewhere. After the letter was published Samuel found himself something of a minor hero. When he appeared, cheers rose from the loose clusters of jobless men who clogged Queen Street's intersections.

Despite the swelling numbers of unemployed, the city flourished. Factory chimneys exhaled as much dense smoke as ever, carts jostled one another in the streets, bearing movable mountains of goods, and shoppers abounded. Only the newspapers grumbled, warning of dire times.

"The editors are like old women caught without their flannel petticoats," said Stephen, lighting an after-dinner cigar. "They can feel the chill wind blowing up from the South Island, and it's nipping their ankles. The situation is desperate down there. Naturally, I suppose, considering that all their wealth rides on the sheep's backs. This slump in wool prices has hit the whole island, for if farmers go down, the rest plunge after them."

"But we'll not be so badly affected here. Our trade is diversified," said Samuel, nudging his empty glass.

Stephen reached for the decanter. "So they say. I feel uneasy about this situation, but Jon Bennington is living proof that money can be made out of almost nothing. Ellen had very little left after the debts were paid, but he's spun it into a small fortune by playing the stock market. He struts into the Richmond Line meetings very cock-a-hoop in his vicuna velour frock coat." Stephen's long whiskers fluttered against his shirtfront. "I'm not tempted to dabble. It seems like putting your hands into fools' pockets and taking their money."

Samuel said, *"I'm* tempted to sell my shares, the prices are so high now. I've stock in most of the finishing industries—doors, furniture, window sashes, that kind of thing. But if I do sell, I'll have no say over placing my surplus men in good jobs. There'll be five hundred or more when the last bush camps close. Patrick is taking more than a hundred for this new brewery and soft-drinks factory he's building near Hamilton, but that still leaves me with a problem. Once they're placed, I may sell everything and retire. I don't like the atmosphere lately either." He downed the last of his port. "I'll tell you who's unaffected by all this: your mother. She's bright-eyed as an eagle, never misses a trick, and she's not speculating."

"You surprise me. Mama can't resist the scent of money."

"Yes, but she'll deal only in solid things. Land and buildings. My, but she's shrewd, too. You weren't here when she acquired that land south of the city, were you? The government issued a twenty-pound bond note to any man who had paid his own passage from England. The catch was that it was good only for the purchase of some rather scrubby land, but your mother could see the potential and hit on the idea of exchanging goods from the Peridot Emporiums for half the face value of the bonds. Well, ten pounds bought a tempting pile of goods, and since those goods cost Grandmaire only five, she soon had all Auckland chuckling in admiration over the way she had accumulated an enormous tract of land for virtually a quarter of its value."

"She's got claws like an eagle, too," said Stephen. "And nobody would have objected either."

"She's Auckland's royalty," agreed Samuel. It was clear from their tone that both men were fond of Grandmaire. "Even though she soon sold the land for a massive profit, nobody murmured. She's never bid against at auctions, you know, and it's a wonder that anybody has the temerity to shop anywhere but at the Peridot Emporiums. Actually, Stephen, I think she's softening with age. Saw her with that great-grandson of hers today. She dotes on him. Dandles him in her lap, doesn't mind when he almost garrotes her with her necklaces. He's not even an attractive child as far as babies go, but she thinks he's perfect."

"Because he's Ellen's," said Stephen, adding coolly, "Ellen always was my mother's favorite grandchild."

"There was no sign of her today. Kendrick was visiting, which may have had something to do with it. Those two have always been with daggers drawn. Don't know why."

Stephen said to Juliette later on, "It's a miracle that he doesn't know why those two dislike each other. He seems

225

to know everything else that happens in this town. We could almost cancel our subscription to the newspaper while he is in residence."

"It's true, he does like to gossip," conceded Juliette. They were in her boudoir, where silk-shaded lamps painted everything with rose light. "But I'm grateful to him for it. I hear a surfeit of gossip, but nobody ever tells me anything about our own family. Until Samuel came to stay, I knew nothing about poor Lena and how disastrous her marriage is, nor did I know that Ellen was expecting another happy event."

I wonder how happy she is about it, thought Stephen, recalling how desperate Ellen had been that day she begged him to help her escape from her marriage to Jon. It seemed that she was properly trapped now, poor lass. But instead of commenting, he picked up one of Juliette's visiting cards and said, "Why don't you have some fancy ones made—ones with your picture?"

"*Cartes de visite?* I think they are vulgar, that's why."

"Samuel showed me one of Abigail's cards. Kendrick gave it to him and confided that the artist at Reading's Studios was made to retouch the photograph over a dozen times until it flattered her sufficiently to suit her. It does, too. She looks twenty years younger."

"And I can see no advantage in having a *carte de visite* which appears to be twenty years out of date, no matter how it might flatter me," said Juliette tartly. She sighed. "All these nieces of ours having babies, Stephen. Abby a grandmother soon . . ."

He said, "How would you feel about sharing grandchildren with Abigail? Are you still completely opposed to the idea?"

"May and Hal?" She frowned, her face pink and crumpled in the light. "Oh, Stephen, I don't know. . . . I've always been unhappy about the idea, yet since that unfortunate incident with young Patrick, I can't help thinking that we should try to settle May as quickly as possible. She is ready, don't you think?"

"So long as she's happy," said Stephen.

"Of course. It would be lovely if she could be a contented

wife like Ellen. It's a shame those two are not good friends. Ellen would be such an encouragement to her."

Pity help us all, thought Stephen.

As summer faded, Samuel began to talk about returning to the tribe. "Te Kooti has been very quiet lately. Too quiet. I think I'll go on down to the king Country and see what's brewing up."

"You wouldn't!" said Juliette, pausing in the middle of buttering a triangle of toast.

"Of course I would. Did you know that there has been a petition, taken before parliament, asking for a pardon for the old fox?"

"That would be condoning all he has done, surely?"

"Not exactly, May. But I think we judge old Te Kooti a bit too harshly. He's a step out of time, that's all. Sixty years ago Hongi Hika was behaving far more atrociously, and now he's a kind of folk hero. Te Kooti is rebelling valiantly against a tide which has come in too far to ever be reversed. Like it or not, the country belongs to the pakeha now. Almost two-thirds of this island and virtually the entire South Island are European-owned."

"That's sad when you consider how it must have been —or even how it was when we were children. Remember how Auckland looked when we first saw it? Rolling acres of brown fern and the ghostly volcano cones, and the only sign of habitation were brave little tents dotted where their owners hoped to buy land."

"And now it's a city. A place to get away from as swiftly as possible. Not that I haven't enjoyed your hospitality and your daughter's company, but I must return."

"Can't you stay until Queen's Birthday at least?" asked Juliette. "Hal will be home, and we have a family dinner planned. Everybody will be here. Even Grandmaire, would you believe it! It's going to be a special occasion."

"She's coming *here?*" asked May. "Here, to our house?"

"I invited her, and she accepted," said her mother. "I'm as astonished as you are."

Samuel sucked at his cup of tea, wiped his mouth with a dash of the napkin, and said, "If you ask me, her nose is a mite out of joint. More than a mite, in fact. People are talking about *your* dinner parties now, and your Mrs. Terrill is gaining a fine name for herself. I suppose you know how Mrs. Lancaster has been trying to bribe her away from you. Not that she'll succeed. Mr. Terrill won't go. He says that Mr. Lancaster is a terrible taskmaster."

"I prefer to hope they stay with us out of loyalty," Juliette began before a glance at her brother's face showed that he was only teasing. She said, "I'm glad you feel better again, but we will be sorry to lose you. I shall miss hearing all the inside news."

Samuel chuckled. "Now that you're so chummy with Grandmaire, you can get all the news from her."

Samuel called on each of the family in turn before he left. May accompanied him as usual, watching and listening with interest at Abby's house. Her coldness made him react with extra-loud joviality, which in turn made her frostier still. It's more distaste than dislike, May decided. Aunt Abigail sees the rough surface manners, not the soul underneath. Samuel seemed incongruous in that dainty parlor among the spindle-legged furniture and porcelain ornaments (Abby had tried to usher him into the morning room, but he would not be guided), and Abby was plainly ill at ease, as though his raucous laughter and sweeping gestures were a threat to her possessions. While the two exchanged remarks, Kendrick lounged in an armchair, openly amused. He saw them out and shook hands with his uncle.

"Look after your mother, lad," said Samuel.

Kendrick raised an eyebrow. "My dear sir, it is *her* vocation to look after me, though when that Kine fellow is about, she does neglect me shamefully. Perhaps you should speak to her."

When they drove away, May said to Samuel, "Kendrick always gives me the uncomfortable feeling that he knows what I am thinking. What do you think of him, Uncle? Is he a bad hat?"

"Probably, but then Abby's ruined him. She and Grandmaire both doted on him, and I'd guess that your brother was the first male friend he ever had. Exclusive feminine company can warp a fellow's personality, or so my father

228

used to say when he took me off to logging camps with him to get me away from the womenfolk." The dogcart was turning into the street where the Ogstanleys lived. "Ah, but you should have seen Abby as a young girl. She was blond and beautiful and so bonny that everyone adored her on sight. Her daughers have been so disappointing by comparison."

"Dora and Lena are both fine young ladies."

"True, but they don't have their mother's spirit. She would never have let anybody trample on her. It doesn't do to be too biddable, my pet. Remember that."

"Are you trying to tell me something?"

"Gracious, no," he said as he handed her down at the gate. "You are not the kind of young lady who would let other people make up her mind for her, are you now?"

They found Lena on the back porch, pounding clothes with a dolly peg. She was startled when she saw them, and her greeting was a mixture of dismay and guilt. May expected her uncle to ask why there was no servant to do that work, but he ignored the incident and asked to go inside. Though they had not taken tea at Abby's and were thirsty, Samuel declined refreshments and said they had only come for a quiet chat.

He held Lena's chafed hands while they talked in the gloom of the parlor. May stood at the window, restless as she always was in that house. It reeked of unhappiness. Gazing down at the harbor, she listened to her uncle's plans with envy. How exciting it would be to see the old tattooed chiefs all gathered together. She waited to hear if Patrick would be going, too, but here, as at Mondrich House, his name was not mentioned.

When they were leaving, Samuel pulled a packet from his jacket pocket and wrapped Lena's hands around it.

"It's for you. You and the baby. I may not be back here until the little fellow is several months old, and it would hardly do for his great-uncle to neglect giving him a christening gift, would it now?"

"How can you be so sure it will be a boy?" She unrolled the brown paper, her movements awkward, for she no longer had a lap to rest things on.

"Of course it will be a boy," he said as she opened the red

229

leather pouch and drew out the money. "But only a little of that is for him. The rest is for you, my dear. For you." And in case she was too obtuse to understand the full meaning, he added. "It's not to be spent on that dashing husband of yours. He has a beautiful wife and should be content with that, don't you think? No, my dear—"

"A hundred pounds?" Lena's eyes were red-rimmed, and her voice was thick. "You've made a mistake, I think. A hundred pounds . . ."

"It's nothing."

"I can't possibly accept—"

"Yes, you can." His voice was suddenly fierce. "What else am I to do with money? I have no family, nobody except Pat—except the Maoris. But even if I had twenty children, it would make no difference." He put his arms about her shoulders and gave her a quick hug before standing up. "Now take care of yourself, won't you?"

"Of course." She seemed dazed as she showed them to the door. When they rolled away, she was still framed in the doorway, gaping blankly at the folded notes.

Samuel said angrily, "It won't do any good, you know. He'll have it by this evening, and the bookmakers and the taverns will have it all by the end of the month. I shouldn't have done it."

May said nothing. She was thinking about the look on Lena's face, staring at the money as if it were a million pounds instead of a hundred.

Kendrick was at Fintona when they arrived. He was sitting in the middle of the morning room floor, rolling a striped blue ball to Rupert. Ellen was seated in Grandmaire's chair, keeping a suspicious eye on him while she worked at her tapestry frame. With her black gown and white lace cap she looked so much like a younger version of her grandmother that May gasped when she saw her.

Ellen glanced up and said, "Oh, I thought you would be alone, Uncle Samuel. Kendrick said—"

Kendrick laughed. "If you can break your ironclad rules by being civil to me, you can surely do the same for May, even if she is not going away." He beckoned to May. "Come help me play with my nephew. Isn't he the prettiest thing you ever saw? At least, that's what Grandmaire says, and who am I to argue with her?"

"Where is Grandmaire?" said May, noticing how quickly Ellen bridled at the implied criticism of her son's looks.

"I offered her some snuff, and she had to leave the room rather suddenly."

"Really, Kendrick!" Samuel tried not to laugh.

"He is disgraceful, isn't he?" Ellen rang the bell and stood up, saying, "When Tawa comes, you may like to order tea. Good-bye, Uncle Samuel. May."

"Are you going to say good-bye to me, too, Ellen? After all, it could be a year before you see me again." Kendrick tweaked at the hem of her skirt as she passed. Ignoring him, she walked out, very straight-backed, and closed the door softly behind her.

Kendrick said, "I console myself that one cannot hope to win universal affection."

"And I suspect there is a strong reason behind her attitude," said Samuel. "Now what's all this about going away?"

"Grandmaire thinks it would be a good idea if I were to see something of Europe. She seems to think that it is time Daniel came home and has suggested that we make the journey home together. We can keep each other entertained."

"In trouble, you mean. What do the Captain and Mrs. Yardley think of the suggestion?"

"Uncle Samuel! I am weary of your suspicions. The only reason Ellen remained in the room was that she would not leave me alone with her son, and I resent her suspicions, too. Anybody would think I planned to dip his pacifier in whiskey. And now you accuse me of leading Daniel astray. Why, the very idea is preposterous. If you must know, Grandmaire thinks that—"

"Grandmaire does not need to think," Maire Yardley Peridot snapped as she entered the room. Dora supported her, though she leaned heavily on an ebony and silver cane. As she jabbed her way toward her chair, she grumbled, "Grandmaire does not need to think because Grandmaire can see right to the truth of the matter. This rascal would have me believe that after all this long time, he misses his cousin so much that he must be with him. He thinks that I am so old that I no longer understand his mind. Do you know that when the Amalgamated Pie and Biscuit Company collapsed last week, it took Abigail's new phaeton and four grays with it?"

Kendrick looked abashed. He had no idea how she could have known that. "It seemed a sure profit." He shrugged. "I sold them on impulse for a fine parcel of shares and expected to have them back within the week, with lining for my pockets besides. When the company crashed, I hoped Mama might be tolerantly amused, but she found out an hour ago and chased me out of the house, threatening murder if I return."

Grandmaire rested her feet on a burgundy hassock. "We can't have our poor Kendrick murdered, can we now?" she said, not to the adults but to young Rupert, who began crowing and stretching out his arms to her the moment she entered the room. Now that she was settled, Dora placed him in Grandmaire's lap. At once he snuggled against her bosom, plucking at her jet necklaces, cooing.

Grandmaire pinched his cheek affectionately. "Who's my boy then?" she said.

"It always used to be me."

When she looked at Kendrick, her eyes were shrewd. "You always get what you want, so don't complain," she said.

"I'm longing to see Daniel again," said May on the way home. "I almost wish I could go to England and meet him, too."

"Not I," said Samuel. "You'd not catch me aboard a ship."

"Daniel doesn't mind ships so much, now that he's outgrown his seasickness. I wonder if he's changed? He's doing so many interesting things. I'll hardly know how to talk to him. He'll be so sophisticated."

"And what you do isn't interesting, I suppose? How many photographs of yours has that newspaper taken? Nine? Ten?"

May wondered if she could broach the subject now. Samuel was in an expansive mood, and it was a lovely day. The sky was a sheet of blue spread with a loosely fluffed white eiderdown. Soon the gray roof of Mondrich House would be in view.

"Could you please stop here for a moment, Uncle?"

"What is it, lass? You don't feel well?"

As the cart glided to a halt, she said, "I may not have another chance to talk to you alone, and I want to ask you your opinion. Your honest opinion." She unpinned the locket from her collar and thrust it into his hand. "About him. Look inside."

"Hal? Oh, lass. I can't say whom you should marry, though I know your father thinks—"

"Sorry." She took it back and pried out the top picture. "There. Ever since I put in the second photograph, I have forgotten that this was Hal's locket originally. Please tell me your honest opinion of him."

Samuel stared at the picture, his lips pursed. Finally he said, "Where did you get this?"

He doesn't sound pleased, thought May. "Grandmaire gave it to me. She told me not to show it to anybody."

"Aye. That's her style. Sow the seeds of trouble."

"No, Uncle! I was touched by her kindness. When we came to New Zealand, the one thing I most wanted was to find out about my real father. But nobody will tell me anything, and I was hoping you might. You must have known him, and—"

"Aye, I knew him right enough." He glanced at May's eager face, then back at the picture. "That beard was a late addition. He was a dandy lad, as handsome as you'd see anywhere. A trifle weak at the chin but handsome. Ladies always turned to look at him, even later, when he'd grown portly."

"And what was he *like?* What kind of person was he?"

"Charming. Yes, charming. He had a way about him." He handed back the locket and unhooked the reins.

"Is that all you're going to tell me?"

"Yes." He clucked at the horse, then changed his mind and dragged on the reins again. "Don't be upset, lass. I don't think you'd really want to know more."

"But I do! He was my *father!* If you don't tell me what

233

happened, then surely sooner or later I will find someone who will. It shames me to have to ask people, but I vow I will do it."

"Very well. Though I don't agree with this, I suppose it's best that I tell you. Leigh was . . . how shall I put it? Your mother did not want to marry him because she feared it would be a mistake. It was. He neglected her, just as Mr. Ogstanley neglects Lena. Leigh spent most of his time at Fintona, and finally he went away altogether, leaving your mother virtually destitute, with you and your brother to care for. In the end he came back to steal young Leigh away. Grandmaire and Abby both had a hand in that, to their eternal discredit." He glanced at May's bowed head. "You can see why even they are reluctant to discuss him. It's a sad little story with an unhappy ending. Nobody saw your father and brother again. They were killed in the wars, near New Plymouth."

She closed the locket. "You make him sound so unpleasant."

"No, lass. But he was wrong for Juliette. She loved him once, but they both were so young. She idolized him so much that she could not see he was wrong for her. May I give you some advice?"

"Of course." She looked up, and he saw moisture on her cheek.

"Put that picture away. You're better off now, you know. Stephen loves you. He's as proud of you as if you were his own daughter. He *is* your father now."

"I know." She could no longer see him through her tears. Her soul ached with disappointment. The information she had longed for was so bitter that she wished she could spit it out of her mind. She would not destroy the photograph, for she could not hate the solemn faced soldier in it; but he had failed her, and all her dreams of him were dying. She would never look at him again.

She said, "All the way to New Zealand I thought about my father. He was my reason for wanting to come. Everything seems to turn sour for me here. I make mistakes. I suffer such terrible disillusionment. Have you any idea how much I wish I could go back to San Francisco again?"

"Would that make your life any different?"

"Oh, yes. Auckland is interesting, but San Francisco is elegant. And fun. I have such happy memories of my life there after I began to get well again."

"Perhaps you're right, but I'm thinking that the trouble lies not with New Zealand but with you," said Samuel as they rolled toward home. "You're growing up, and that hurts. Your longing for San Francisco is nothing more than a longing to be a child again. Most of us wish at times that we could return to that happy state, but none of us can. None of us can ever go back there again."

May glanced at her uncle, thinking how wrong he was. He's never lived anywhere else but here, she thought. How can he know?

Twenty

"What a magnificent gift, Hal," said Juliette. "I don't think I've ever seen such an elaborate sewing basket before. Not that it could be called a basket when it's such a substantial piece of furniture."

Hal looked gratified.

"Isn't it beautiful, May?" Juliette nudged her.

It's hideous, thought May. "Thank you, Hal," she said. "It certainly is a surprise."

Hal said, "I had it made specially for you. The cabinet-makers in Hull are outfitting the cabins in the new refrigerated ships. When I described what I wanted, they made this, using first-grade ebony with silver ornamentation."

"Dora would love to own something like this," said May.

Juliette frowned at her and said, "Look, May, all the drawers have been lined with velveteen, and there are compartments for everything. All these scissors and every pair different—"

Hal said, "I counted fifteen pairs, and there are three full trays of needles, crochet hooks, thimbles, every kind of implement you could possibly want."

If I ever decide I want to sew, thought May. "That's very thoughtful of you, Hal. *Was* it your idea to buy me this?"

"It was Mama's actually. She and Grandmaire thought that it would be the perfect gift for you."

"Did they indeed?" She opened a drawer. Dozens of bright spools of silk nestled in tight-packed rows.

"I'm so glad that they were right. Lena said that you wouldn't want this because you never do any needlework, but Mama pointed out that you didn't take photographs

236

until you were given a camera and that this might help you develop an interest in something more—"

"Ladylike? Suitable?"

Hal flushed. "Mama and Grandmaire don't mean to be critical, but half of Auckland thinks that photography is not an appropriate hobby for you. I thought, I hoped . . ." He was floundering, embarrassed. "If you tried something else, you might find it equally interesting."

He meant well. It was cruel of her to be ungracious. Impulsively she reached up and kissed Hal's cheek.

"You do like it then?"

Juliette exhaled a small, silent sigh. When she met her daughter's eye, she smiled at her in approval. May kept her voice low and her smiles tight, and it was not until Hal had gone to join Stephen in the upstairs study that she collapsed, laughing.

"It was either laugh or cry," she said, "and a silly workbasket is not worth tears." She ran her hand over the gleaming lid. "What do you think, Mother? Could this find a home in your boudoir? It's time you threw that ghastly wicker basket of yours onto the scrap heap. The wretched thing has been in tatters for years."

"I could never part with my mother's sewing basket. You know better than to suggest that."

May flicked a cupboard door open and pushed it shut again. "Perhaps I can store photographic equipment in here. I wonder whatever possessed Hal to bring me a gift like this? He usually brings everybody some small trinket, but this monstrosity must have cost him a fortune."

Juliette said, "I think Hal is going to declare himself to you. It might be well to have your answer ready for him."

"Oh." She swung the door again. The knob and hinges were made of silver and chased with a delicate pattern of roses.

"Your father dotes on Hal," said her mother resolutely. "I'm sure he is hoping that your answer will be yes." When May remained silent, she continued. "His health is slowing him down more and more. Daniel will be able to help him with business but he has such *confidence* in Hal. They think alike and understand each other. Your father was hoping that the boys might have grown up to take re-

237

sponsibility. . . ." She faltered and cleared her throat. May was still apparently intent on examining the little cupboard. "May, dear, your father and I are concerned only for your happiness and security. You know that."

Your father. Your father. The words plucked a chord of pain inside her. Samuel was right. Stephen *was* her father. If she married Hal, he would become a son, replacing the boys who had died.

"We love you, May. We want you to be happy."

She felt guilty. "I love you, too."

"And Hal? Do you love him?"

May bit her lip, suddenly confronted by the image of Patrick lowering his face toward hers. She said, "I've adored Hal for as long as I can remember. When I was younger, he seemed like a god." As she spoke, she heard the echo of her uncle, saying, "She loved him once, but they both were so young." She looked up at her mother and said, "I'm confused about my feelings. When you told me Hal was going to declare himself, I felt no happiness. Perhaps I should tell him I'm not ready yet."

Juliette began nervously smoothing her skirt. "Often a woman's feelings do not deepen until she has been married for quite some time. Dear, I must be frank with you. Your father would like to see you settled with Hal. Happily settled, of course. We both think that Hal is the perfect choice for you."

"But I don't *want* to be married yet."

Juliette walked to the window and turned to face her daughter. She listened with obvious exasperation as May explained that she would be tied down if she married, that she was enjoying photography, and that she knew once she was a married woman, she would be expected to give up her freedom.

"Then have a long engagement," said Juliette. "Take two years, or even three. But when Hal speaks to you, please accept him. In return there will be no pressure for an early wedding date."

"Then why an engagement? There seems little point—"

"We don't ask much of you, do we, dear? Please try to oblige us now. It would make your father so very proud

238

and happy if you and Hal could make an announcement at the family dinner."

"I'm sure it would," said May.

This is inevitable, May rationalized later as she and Hal sat alone in the parlor. Again May had the same crazy desire to laugh and cry as she waited for Hal to string the question together.

As usual on his first night ashore he was bubbling with news of the voyage. Everything that happened must be recounted, it seemed, and tonight he insisted on telling her all about the two new refrigeration ships, relating the overheating problems they were having with the chilling plant and telling how dangerous it would be unless a way of controlling the temperature were found. Fortunately the ships would not be ready for use for at least a year, so there was ample time to solve the problem.

May had heard all this before but pretended to be interested as her concentration wilted and her thoughts drifted inward. Her lack of emotion astonished her.

Of course, she loved Hal—she had never doubted that. Marriage to him was something she had dreamed about for years, and here was the magical moment when all her girlish longings would materialize, yet she felt no excitement at all. Were the dreams stale? Was her contrary nature pulling at her, willing her to resist something that everybody else expected of her?

Aware that Hal had stopped talking, May raised her eyes and studied his strong, open face. He looked nervous, intense, and anxious. May smiled, thinking how very handsome he was.

"Hal," she said, "would you please pose for my camera one day on your leave? I know you don't approve," she hurried on, "but if you indulge me, I shall show you how photographs are made. You might change *your* mind then or at least understand my interest."

He looked annoyed. "Must you, May? I'm trying to propose marriage to you, and you persist in introducing the one bone of contention between us."

"I'm sorry." She raised her voice as he rose and strode across the room. "I must be honest with you, Hal. If you wish to become engaged to me, then you must make allowances for the things I want to do. I don't wish to deceive you."

He strode back and seized both her hands. "I love you, May." ·

"And I love you." It was so easy to say she was surprised.

He took a deep breath. "Usually, when people marry, they find that they must make sacrifices."

"Of course." She was looking up into his face. His expression was that of a loving parent who must say no to a child.

He was choosing his words with care before he spoke. "It is very important to me that my wife be above reproach, and what is perfectly all right for you to do now may be impossible when we are married."

"I agree," she said. "But I also wonder how anxious you are to marry me if the first thing you do is tell me what I am not permitted to do when I become your wife."

He sat down beside her. "Anxious? May, I've loved you all my life. I used to look forward to seeing you when I came to San Francisco, and when I heard that you were returning to Auckland, I was over the moon with joy. I knew the moment I saw you again that one day we would marry. And I know it's what the captain wants, too. He's dropped so many hints lately." He beamed at her. "Shall we call him in and tell him that he can open that champagne now?"

No, she thought. No. "Just a minute, Hal." She freed her hands and rubbed them together. "You talked about sacrifices and giving things up when we're married."

"We'll discuss that later. Let's make this official first."

"Please, Hal, there's something I want from you, too."

"Anything. Just name it, and it's yours."

"You must be growing weary of life at sea, and to be honest, I'm growing weary of life in New Zealand. When we are married, I want us to live in San Francisco. Father keeps saying that he needs a good man for that office, and over there you wouldn't have the pressure of your mother disapproving of everything I do. Don't you see that—"

Hal listened to her, dumbfounded. He realized that if he argued with her, refused this totally impossible request,

240

there would be no engagement. What had the captain said? Promise her anything she wants, son. All you'll be doing now is making public something we've all known for years. It will be a long engagement, and you'll have ample time to settle the details.

"Anything," he said, interrupting her by thrusting his arms around her. His kiss was firm and vigorous, and he rubbed his mouth against hers until she felt consumed by the sensations of skin, springy bristles, and the tarry smell of tobacco.

She smiled, breathless, when he let her go. Her lips were numb.

"I love you, May."

"I know." Her mouth would not move quite properly when she talked, and she was apprehensive that he might kiss her again, so she said, "Then it's settled, and happily, too. Dora said you would never leave the sea, and I'm glad she's wrong. You've really given me something to look forward to."

"Not for two years, at least," said Hal. "You do want a long engagement, don't you?"

A week later May and Hal stood in the hall, flanked by Juliette and Stephen, welcoming guests to the Queen's Birthday dinner party.

It was cold for autumn, one of those evenings when the elements tune up for an orchestrated rehearsal of what the following months will bring. Every swing of the door sent an icy gust across the hall and afforded a glimpse of the night outside, where veranda lamps illuminated a billowing tent of rain. Guests scurried in with sodden hems and dripping umbrellas.

Juliette said, "I had expected a flurry of regrets when the storm broke, but it would appear that everyone is coming to share our celebration." She whispered to May, "Thank you, dear, for bringing us so much joy."

Hal rejoined them, saying, "There's no sign of Mama yet."

"I think she is coming with Grandmaire," said May. "Don't be nervous, Mother. I'm sure they will be absolutely charming. Hal says they both are delighted about the engagement."

"Enraptured," Hal told her. "But it was hardly a surprise. Mama has accused me for years of belonging more to the Yardley family than to the Bennington." He put his arm around May's shoulders and gave her a hug. "You're not afraid of Mama or Grandmaire, are you?"

"Nor am I," said Juliette quietly, "though I fear what they may say. I want tonight to be perfect, with nothing to distract attention from you both." She nodded toward the parlor where sherry glasses clinked like wind chimes. "Everybody is so pleased for you, May. Are you happy, dear?"

May paused, glancing over to where Hal was peering out into the dark rain. "It's all so strange and new that I don't know what I feel yet."

Stephen turned from talking to one of the guests and said, "Hal's a fine fellow, May. I want the best for you, and they don't come any better than Hal." He looked at her searchingly and added, "Your happiness is very important to us both."

For a moment May felt foolishly ungrateful. "I know," she whispered.

Juliette tugged nervously at her gloves. "I wish they would arrive. I feel so apprehensive."

"Be your usual serene self," Stephen advised her. "You must show Mama who is the lady of this house."

But the party from Fintona did not make its entrance until the receiving line had dispersed among the guests in the parlor. Juliette was muttering to Stephen that she feared they were going to be snubbed when he nodded toward the door.

A lull settled over the chatter as Maire entered slowly, stooped and heavy on Dora's arm. Behind her Abby clutched Derwent Kine's elbow. Both their faces were garlanded with smiles. Accompanying them were the Kine girls, precociously dressed in long bright pink gowns with their hair pinned up in sausage-shaped clusters.

Hal said, "It seems that Mama has taken over the girls' wardrobe." He repressed the small feeling of unpleasant surprise that struck him whenever he saw his mother in a gathering of other people. In her home surroundings she never appeared quite so gaudy. He stepped forward, saying, "Good evening, Mama. We feared you must have been delayed and had begun to wonder at the reason."

Ignoring both Hal and his rebuke, Abby cried out, "My dear child! My dear new daughter!" and rushed across to fold May into a perfumed embrace. "My dear daughter! Isn't she beautiful? Isn't my Hal the luckiest man in all of New Zealand? Look at her, so modest as well as so beautiful. That is a blush on your cheeks, isn't it, dear?"

"Mama, *please,*" murmured Hal.

May was cold, chilled through by the expression in her aunt's eyes. She hates me, she realized. She's pretending to approve only because there is nothing she can do to change the situation.

"Thank you, Aunt Abigail," she said.

Abby let go of her as abruptly as she had embraced her. "We all are so happy," she announced to the room. "This has been the most blissful day of our lives!"

"Don't you think she's overdoing it a trifle?" said Stephen in an undertone.

"Hush," said Juliette with a smile. She stepped forward to greet her sister.

"Mr. Kine and I have news of our own," said Abby gushingly. "This afternoon we were married. Isn't that exciting? Oh, Juliette, I do hope you don't mind, but we will have to claim some of this evening's attention. This will be our wedding feast after all."

"It's the Queen's Birthday dinner, and I don't think she'd mind sharing it in the least," said Juliette pleasantly.

Dora had left Grandmaire seated by herself and was hissing in Hal's ear. "I could strangle Mama, I really could. She promised Kendrick that she would never marry that obnoxious fellow, and look at what she's done now that he's away in England. It's Grandmaire's idea to have the wedding today, of course. She wanted to ruin your engagement party. I am sorry, May. Grandmaire just wanted to spoil things for Aunt Juliette."

"Please don't fret, Dora. Mother will be so gracious that

243

any intended slight will pass completely unnoticed," said May soothingly.

But Dora was still fuming. "How could Mama have married that revolting fellow? Kendrick will be *incensed*. He loathes the man. And as for those daughters . . ." She shuddered.

May looked at the girls' bright young faces and at Dora's sullen expression and felt a wave of pity for her. She said, "I have marvelous news, Dora. Hal has agreed to leave the sea when we marry and to take me to live in San Francisco."

To her astonishment Dora's face opened to emit a shrill laugh. May stood by, feeling foolish at not knowing what the joke was. When she recovered, Dora said, "Hal told us it was to be a long engagement, but we had no idea he meant *that* long. Ah, don't mind me, May. Come. Grandmaire wants to talk to you."

"I am an old woman, and old people do not like to be kept waiting. At my age one must measure one's time with great care."

"I'm sorry, Grandmaire—"

"So I may offer my felicitations at last. Hal was very remiss in not bringing you to receive my blessing."

"I'm sorry, Grandmaire—"

"Hush. I have lived on this earth long enough to know what to expect and what not to hope for. You are your mother's daughter after all. Show me your engagement ring, my dear."

"I don't have one."

"No betrothal ring? Dora, fetch Hal this instant."

"No, Grandmaire. Dora, don't fetch Hal. He offered to buy me one, but I refused."

"How curious. Most girls look forward to having an engagement ring." Her eyes were as sharp as the edge on a greenstone chisel, and a pattern of lacy shadows moved over her skin as she regarded May shrewdly. "You are reluctant to commit yourself, aren't you? Just like your father," she said with satisfaction. "Your mother grabbed at marriage with unseemly eagerness, but you are like your father. Cautious. Leigh was always cautious."

People were listening. May edged away. "Excuse me, please, Grandmaire."

The beringed fingers were hard on her wrist. "Where is your locket, child? You promised me that you would always wear it."

"I did not think it suitable for this evening."

"What nonsense. Tonight you announce your betrothal to the world. What more fitting occasion would there be for wearing your father's picture? Now do as I say, child, and run along upstairs and—"

"Mama, if you please," said Stephen, suddenly in front of her. "May I escort you in to dinner? The meal is ready to be served."

As May had predicted, Juliette coped easily with Abby's attempted scene-stealing. By asking Stephen to announce a toast to the newlyweds before the soup was served, she tidied the subject away and permitted the remainder of the evening to focus on the engaged couple. But as she reflected later, forces other than the weather and her sister seemed determined to sabotage the evening.

Barons of beef were being carved at side tables, and potato puffs served from silver trays, when suddenly the double doors flapped open and a cold draft circled the room, causing the candles to gutter like a missed breath.

May glanced up to see Lawrence Ogstanley framed in the doorway. His face shone, and his hair was a wet ragged cap. At first she thought he was smiling, so twisted were his features, but when he spoke, his voice trembled with hatred. "A fa ily dinner! Ha! What a fine family you are!"

Heads swiveled. Napkins fluttered. Stephen and Hal rose from their places.

"Stay where you are. Don't get up on my account," he said, flinging his arms in a gesture that all but made him overbalance. "Sit down and listen. Listen to me, all of you!" An unnecessary command, for he had everybody's full attention. "I've come here to tell you all what I think of you."

"He's *intoxicated!*" whispered Juliette. "He can hardly stand up. Oh, Stephen, we must get him out of here quickly. This is disgraceful."

"You, all of you, are bastards," said Lawrence with another extravagant gesture. "Selfish, stuck-up, arrogant
bastards, the lot of you."

"This is a family party," said Stephen as Hal's chair
scraped back.

"Family? Then what am I?" bellowed Lawrence, sway-
ing on his feet. "What am I if I'm not one of your miserable, pompous family, hey? Answer me that then."

Hal was moving toward him as Stephen said, "Jon is not
here because he is where he should be, home with his wife.
And you've not been invited because you should be at
home with Lena."

"You do know who *she* is?" said Hal in a dangerously
quiet voice. "Lena is your wife, in case you've forgotten."

Lawrence's arms flailed as Hal stepped close to him.
"You keep away," he cried, staggering backward.

Hal's fists were up. His arms pumped, flexing for a
punch; but as he closed in to strike, Lawrence's knees
buckled, and he slumped forward to fall full length onto
the carpet.

Hal pushed at him with the toe of his elastic-sided boot.

Stephen was standing up. "He's in no condition to ride
home. We'll take him out to the gatehouse and have him
bedded down in the grooms' quarters for the night." To his
guests he said, "Please excuse Mr. Ogstanley. I doubt that
he is responsible for any of his utterances this evening."

"Bad business that," said Derwent Kine loudly. "Fellow
needs horsewhipping. Did you hear about that snip of a
milliner gel who called on poor Lena and kicked up a
ruckus, accusing him of—"

Grandmaire tapped him sharply on the wrist with her
lorgnette and said, equally loudly, "No character, no back-
bone, no ambition, and, it would appear, no head for whiskey. What in the world can poor Lena have been thinking
of?"

An astonishing remark, thought Stephen, considering
that she had probably been the engineer of that sad mis-
match. He glanced at his mother, but she was gazing
straight ahead with her most righteous expression. It was
Abby who met his eye, Abby with a look of pure venom.

"Poor Lena," whispered May. She was waiting at home,

246

huge with child, while her husband carried on his disreputable life as if she did not exist, as if her devotion did not matter.

"Don't upset yourself," murmured Juliette, squeezing her daughter's hand reassuringly.

You would understand, thought May with a fresh surge of pity. "How could you endure it?" she said.

"What, dear?"

But May did not reply.

As Grandmaire's carriage pulled away into fresh volleys of rain, Stephen said, "Sweet Olivine, you were magnificent. The evening could have been a disaster, but you made it a triumph."

"But how was the food?" she called over her shoulder as she hurried to join May at the fireside. "Ah, that's better. It's freezing out there by the door. What a night this has been! I couldn't taste a single mouthful. Was it acceptable?"

"It was memorable, truly memorable," said Stephen, pouring himself a fresh cup of coffee. "And if they don't remember the food, they will never forget the disruptions."

"The food was perfect, Mother." May spread her hands to the flames. "It was an inspiration on your part to serve so many local dishes. Aunt Abigail said she had not tasted those tiny freshwater crayfish since she was a child, and that dish of wild pork with a touch of puha in the sauce kept everybody guessing."

"So did the glaze on the fruit tarts," said Juliette, pleased. "Some thought it was made from honey, but nobody guessed flax nectar simmered down until it was thick enough to spread. I was sure Abby would guess what it was, for heaven knows we spent enough hours collecting flax nectar in jars when we were children." She leaned back in the arm chair. "I'm glad that the food, at least, was adequate. This has been one of those evenings we will shudder about for weeks, then look back on with amusement."

May said, "I wish that Daniel could have been here. And Lena and Ellen, too, of course. And Kendrick would have added something amusing to the evening, provided he wasn't too cross about his mother's becoming Mrs. Kine. But oh, dear, I had not realized until tonight that Aunt Abigail is going to be *my* mother, too. That prospect is positively—"

"Delightful?" offered Stephen wickedly. They all were laughing when Stephen cocked his head to one side. "That's a carriage. Who could it be at this hour?"

"Somebody who has forgotten something perhaps," said Juliette, toasting her hands in the warmth. "Mmm, what a lovely feeling, knowing I can lie abed in the morning as long as I want to."

"I wish I could, but Hal is taking me to luncheon at his mother's house. I'm not looking forward to it much."

"Don't worry, dear. When Hal is away, you can easily avoid her politely by—"

"In the name of Jove!" shouted Stephen from the front door. "Quickly, Juliette. May, fetch Mary!"

"What is it?" They both were in the hall, peering out into the driving torrents, when Stephen staggered across the porch under Lena's sodden weight. Her face was gray as it lolled against his shoulder, and her arms hung loosely.

"My heavens!" said Juliette.

"She's collapsed," said Stephen unnecessarily.

May dashed off to the kitchen, while Juliette and Stephen walked Lena over to the fire. Water dripped all around her, and her hair streamed in crimped orange ribbons over her forehead. She was shivering so violently that she could not speak.

Juliette glanced at her husband and mouthed that they needed a doctor. "But don't you go," she added swiftly. "We can send someone over to Terrill, and he can rouse a groom."

"In the name of Jove, what is she doing out alone in this storm? Sweet Olivine, see if you can get any sense out of her. That husband of hers wants—"

"Hush, dear, please." Juliette was draping a dry shawl over Lena's shoulders. "Can't you see she's upset enough already? What was it, dear? Why did you come out here?"

"L-Lawrence said he'd be home for supper, and I waited and waited for him." She huddled closer to the fire, which

Juliette was prodding into renewed life. "Then I began to be afraid, and—"

"You didn't know he was coming here?" asked Juliette.

"Had he left you at home *on your own?*" asked Stephen in a dangerous voice.

She nodded. She looked like a newly hatched chick with feathers still wet from the egg.

"Well, don't you worry about a thing, dear. We shall soon have you dry and into a snug, warm bed. The doctor will come and give you something to ward off a chill. We can't have you getting sick with your time so close, can we?"

"But that's just it, Aunt Juliette." She began to sob. "My time *has* come, and I'm so afraid. I've been driving around, looking for Lawrence . . . I was positive that he must have fallen off his horse again . . . I was all right until the cramps began, but then I didn't know what to do."

"You did the right thing," Juliette said soothingly. "Here's May, and she and I will help you with your things. Can you manage the stairs, do you think?"

She shook her head. "No, Aunt Juliette. Thank you, but I cannot stay here, not when Lawrence could be lying at the roadside somewhere, injured. I know that the poor lamb must have had an accident of some kind or he would surely have been home by now."

Stephen thought of her "poor lamb" sleeping off his excess of alcohol in the grooms' quarters and did not trust himself to speak.

May said, "But Mr. Ogstanley is here—"

Juliette interrupted. "He insisted that we not worry you; but he has a stomach upset, and your uncle would not hear of his riding back home through this terrible weather. He has been given a bed for the night. There, now." Lena slumped forward, her face contorted. "Was that a bad one?" she asked when Lena relaxed again. "See if you can stand up, dear, and May and I will help you upstairs."

Lena pushed her hands away. "Lawrence! I want to see him now."

"No," said Juliette firmly. "Not until the doctor has attended you. We don't want to worry Lawrence, do we now? Up you get, there's a good girl."

"I feel so helpless," wailed Abby the next afternoon. "A mother should be with her daughter at a time like this. Ask her again, Dr. Nunn. Make her see that I should be in there."

"I assure you, Mrs. Kine, that nobody has turned your daughter's mind against you. She refuses to see anybody but her husband."

"And he has vanished," said Juliette. "My husband saw him to bed last night, but this morning, when Terrill went in to check on him, there was no sign of him at all. Captain Yardley has sent men out to look for him."

Derwent Kine tugged at his wife's arm. "Come, Abigail. If she won't see us, we might as well go home. That screaming is unearthly, Doctor. Can't you do anything to calm her?"

"We are doing all we can, but she has not responded to saline cathartics, and mustard plasters are giving no relief either. I bled her this morning and administered chloroform inhalation, but most of her agitation is mental, not physical. The presence of her husband would greatly soothe her, I think."

But all of Stephen's efforts failed to find Lawrence, and it was not until the following morning that he appeared of his own accord. He rode up to the front door and tied his horse to the veranda rail. The house was still. Lawrence's eyes were dark-rimmed, and his tongue was clumsy.

"Where is he?" he asked the butler, who emerged, yawning, from the office beside the front door. "Where's my son?"

Drawing back out of reach of his breath, the butler said, "Mrs. Ogstanley has not yet been delivered, sir."

"She's been in labor long enough to produce a dozen infants. What does that damned doctor think he's doing?" He went to push past, and the butler immediately blocked his way.

"Sir, I regret that I cannot—"

Juliette's slippers pattered down the stairs. She looked exhausted, with red-rimmed eyes and blotchy cheeks.

250

When she noticed Lawrence's condition, she stopped, still partway up the staircase.

"Please, Mr. Ogstanley, do try to keep your voice down. Lena is dozing, but only fitfully. She has had a dreadfully distressing night."

He snorted. "Song about nothing if you ask me. My mother always said that this business was simple nature and no need to make a fuss about it."

"If your mother had spent the night here, she would have had ample cause to change her views." She watched him retrieve his hat and coat from the hall stand. "What are you doing?"

"No sense in hanging about here if she's asleep. Though sleeping won't help to produce my son. You might be so good as to tell her that when she wakes."

He's worse than he was the other evening, she noticed with distaste. Striving to be pleasantly brisk, she said, "You will go no farther than the dining room, and that is an order. I shall order coffee for you, and you are to drink as much of it as you can and sit quietly until your poor wife calls out for you again. If Lena considers you a 'poor lamb,' then that, Mr. Ogstanley, is what you will be, for today at least."

He nodded, bemused.

An hour later Dr. Nunn sent down for him, but Lena was tossed by a storm of fierce contractions and did not recognize him, even though she shouted his name and dug her fingernails into his hands. The midwife muttered in a low, unheard voice as she sponged Lena's face and arms with cold water. The room had a fetid smell. Lawrence shivered. The backs of his hands were striped with blood. He recollected descriptions he had heard of madhouses. When the doctor sent him downstairs to wait, he strode out the front door and over to the stables. Terrill spoke to him, saying apologetically that instructions had been issued to keep his horse and saddle there. Lawrence could easily have knocked the man down with one blow of his huge fists, but to Terrill's relief he seemed to sympathize with his predicament and turned without a word, setting off toward town on foot. When he was almost to the coast flats, a cart piled high with tree fern logs stopped for him, and he rode the rest of the way into town.

That evening searchers were sent out after him, again unsuccessfully. Downstairs at Mondrich House Abby waited anxiously, Jon, Hal, and Dora now keeping her company. May sat with them until past ten, then crept upstairs. The doctor was standing outside the nursery door, his thin arms folded, his face like crumpled paper in the light of the hall lamp.

"Please let me sit with her now that she's quiet. Just for a short time. Until her husband is found."

"She is extremely tired, Miss Yardley. I really don't think—"

"May," came a weak cry from the bedroom. "May, is that you?"

Protesting, the doctor followed her in. Lena tried to smile. The room was suffocatingly hot. The mirrors were fogged with steam. Lena's skin was raw with blotches. There was a strange phosphorescent light in her eyes that frightened May. Distilled eagerness, she thought, but then Lena closed her eyes and immediately looked very old.

"Lawrence . . ." she said.

"He was here," said May.

"Dora. Is she here? May I see her, and you, May. Just the two of you."

Dr. Nunn said, "She must not be permitted to overtax her strength."

After he had gone to fetch Dora, Lena whispered, "It's no use, May. I'm dying. I can feel it. I know."

"What nonsense," said Dora, alarmed, when Lena repeated the remark. "All you need to do is obey the doctor and—"

"Listen, please." Lena's voice was tranquil. "If I am delivered of a boy, would you please christen him Lawrence? Will you look after them for me, Dora? Both my Lawrences?"

"Lena, stop this talk. The doctor says—"

"If she is a girl, I want you to have her." Lena grasped her sister's hand and stared into her face. Her hands were slippery with sweat. "Lawrence would not know how to look after a little girl, so you must take her to Fintona and

252

bring her up there." She paused, gasping, until she could continue. "A little girl needs a secure home. And will you name her Dorinda, which means . . . which means 'a gift,' just as your name does? Will you do that for me?"

"Why? Why ask me?"

Lena was breathing in shallow, dragging sounds. "Promise. I want you to have her. Not Mama, nobody but you. Promise, Dora. Promise me."

"Oh, very well. I shall humor you, but let me assure you that none of this is necessary. You will be well in no time and will call your child Thomas or Emily."

"Dorinda." Lena's smile shone with phosphorescence. "I have an intuition it will be a girl. Will you make her lots of pretty little gowns to wear?"

"Yes, but I shall allow you to choose the patterns and colors." And when Lena shook her head, she said, "Lena, for goodness' *sake.*"

"I warned you not to tire her," said Dr. Nunn, coming to shoo them out.

May reached for her cousin's hand and noticed with a jolt that her grip was slack and, despite the sweat, icy cold. Overcome by the sudden, awful premonition that Lena knew what was going to happen, May was unable to reply with more than a nod and when Lena whispered, "I asked you to stay so that you could witness the promise. Please, May. Make Dora keep her word."

"Out you go," said the doctor. "Mrs. Ogstanley must rest."

Twenty One

Toward dawn May woke in fright, jarred bolt upright by harrowing screams. She lay rigid with fear long after the piercing echoes had died away.

Then the silence seemed endless and even more frightening. Oh, Lena. Poor Lena, thought May, realizing what had happened.

She began to cry.

It was midmorning when Lawrence Ogstanley ambled up the drive on a borrowed horse. The groom who emerged from the stables to assist him noticed that though he was freshly shaved, his clothing was rumpled and the stale odor of whiskey much stronger than the smell of soap.

Looking at him askance, the butler murmured, "If you would be so good as to wait in here, sir, I shall fetch somebody to speak with you."

"What do you think you're playing at? Wait in here, nothing. I've come to see my wife."

"I'm sorry, sir, but I have my orders. The family is not to be disturbed. I shall fetch somebody to speak to you if only you will be so good as to wait here—Sir! I must insist—"

But Lawrence pushed past him and trod purposefully down the hall, his cloak swirling around him. At each room he paused only long enough to fling the doors wide and glance inside.

Everybody around the dining table looked up blankly at the thud of the doors. Nobody expected to see him; in fact, as Juliette described it to Samuel later, most of them had quite forgotten his existence.

Lawrence strode in and thumped the table with his fist.

All around the perimeter cups clattered in their saucers. "What are you playing at?" he shouted. "I've come to see my wife, and some stuffed shirt at the door tells me to wait and be spoken to. What's going on?"

Stephen was on his feet, saying, "Now then, old fellow. You can't burst in here like that."

"I can't be kept out either. As I keep reminding you, this is my family, too, no matter how unpalatable that fact may be to you." As he spoke, he scanned the faces around the table. Yardleys, Benningtons, nobody from Fintona. Nobody who might take his side . . . ah, there was Dora. Head bent, as always. He'd not noticed her at first. She might stand up for him. "Dora," he said roughly, "Dora, you tell them I've got my rights."

But Dora kept her head bent. Cowardly, he supposed. Beside her May put an arm about her shoulders as if in support. Stuck-up little piece, thought Lawrence. Imagined she stood on a higher step than anybody else. Then, belatedly, he noticed Dora was crying. So was May. Mrs. Yardley's eyes were red, too. And there was Lena's stupid sow of a mother snuffling into a handkerchief. . . .

His gaze swung back to Stephen, who was saying, "Be reasonable, old man. This is no time to make a scene."

"She's dead, isn't she?"

Stephen nodded.

"And my son? What about my son?"

There was a pause. "You have no son," said Stephen, trying to keep the contempt he felt out of his voice.

Lawrence heard it anyway and reacted with belligerence. "I want to see my wife's body. I demand to see it. I'll claim it and take it away now. It's my right. I'm her husband, damn it. In the eyes of the law she's mine, not yours."

Stephen could see the futility of it all. For the last hour this gathering had been arguing over the future of the tiny baby girl upstairs, quite forgetting that they had no right at all to decide her fate. She belonged not to Dora nor to Abby but to her father. He would take her. Nobody would be able to stop him; not even Lena's last wishes could be respected in a matter of family like this. Stephen stared at Lawrence with mounting frustration. He would claim the

255

girl, take her away, and from now and forever would continue to blackmail them all into paying his exorbitant living expenses while his daughter grew up alone, unloved and neglected, just as his wife had been.

"In the name of Jove, no! I'll not stand for it," he said aloud.

"You can't stop me," declared Lawrence, turning to go.

"That wasn't what I meant," called Stephen. "Come back, old man. I meant that she's not ready to be removed yet. Do be quiet, Abigail. Try to control yourself. Come here, Lawrence. Come sit down. Juliette, could you please pour a cup of tea for Lawrence?"

Stephen was aware of shocked and questioning glances but reasoned that there was nothing he could do but play for time until a solution occurred to him. Could the baby be hidden? Not for long. One of the servants might talk, or a visitor to the house might say something. Neither this house nor Fintona could offer a safe concealment. If they were caught, Lawrence would be the type to rush directly to the police with a charge of kidnapping. Could Lawrence be persuaded to go away to another country? No, that was equally impossible. Not while that remittance kept coming from England, the insurance that kept him here, a safe distance from his family and English law. He could possibly be paid to go to Canada or America, but Stephen rejected that solution. Now that Lena was dead, he would not permit another penny of shipping line funds to go into this wastrel's pockets. Then what was the solution to be?

Hal unwittingly provided it. All morning he had grown more visibly uneasy. Every moan from Abigail had caused him to shudder; while the others wept, he grew more markedly marose. Clearly he longed to be out of there, and now Lawrence's arrival provided him with the excuse he needed. He pushed back his chair, saying, "Take my chair. Let him sit here. I'll not stay in the same room as a man who treated my sister so dispicably. Be grateful, sir, that there are ladies present, or I would be obliged to do much more than merely snub you." To Stephen he said, "Please excuse me, Captain. I must get back to the ship. Tom Isherwood said that we must be out on the tide by noon if we hope to beat the *Scarlet Dragon* to Sydney." He hesitated. "Should I go, or would you prefer me to stay and leave on Friday on the *Mondrich Fairbreeze?*"

Stephen paused, glancing from Hal to Lawrence. In that moment he knew what must be done. "Of course, you must leave now. But a word with you before you go." He nodded to Lawrence. "Excuse us, please."

Closing the double doors behind him, he said to the butler, who had been hovering in the hall, "Quickly, fetch Terrill. We shall need his help."

"What for?" asked Hal.

Stephen told him.

A few minutes later Stephen looked into the dining room and beckoned to Lawrence. "I shall take you up to see her now," he told him.

Mollified, Lawrence came out, saying, "I knew that you would see reason. After all, I am Lena's husband, and I have every legal right to claim her body—"

"Yes, yes," said Stephen, ushering him along the corridor. The fellow still bristled with belligerence, and no trace of grief or remorse showed in his face or his voice.

As they reached the hall, Hal stepped out in front of them, and Terrill, after striding around behind Lawrence, grabbed both his arms and pinned them behind his back. Lawrence's reflexes were so impaired by his hangover that he had no time to shout or struggle before Hal's packed fist smashed into his chin. Lawrence sagged without a sound.

"Quickly," said Stephen. "Let's carry him over to the stables."

Ten minutes later Terrill drove a cart out of the shed. On the cart was a crate, and inside the crate, trussed, gagged, and cushioned on a bed of straw, was the unconscious Lawrence.

Hal shook his bruised hand to help restore the circulation. "I'll transfer him to the brig as soon as we reach open sea, and he can stay under guard until Tilbury. I'll see he's put ashore when we sail again for Hull. The mood he'll be in when he wakes, he'll like as not be out to kill me. Are you sure he'll not have the law onto us for this?"

"He'll be keeping well away from the law, I should think. No doubt he'll stay very quiet until he can find a passage to some other safe haven. Oh, one last thing: We'll keep this incident to ourselves, won't we? Let my mother and yours wonder what has happened to their friend. Mama detests mysteries, so let this be a little medicine to help cure her meddling."

Hal laughed. "It will be a pleasure."

"Bon voyage," said Stephen.

"Why wasn't I informed about Lena's death straight away?" complained Grandmaire after the funeral. "And why did Hal leave when he should have been here supporting you? He is your eldest son. It's disgraceful that he wasn't here."

Abby said, "The shipping schedules must—"

"Nonsense. I know that Hal hates funerals, but this was his own sister! Stephen should have delayed the ship a few days. I'm astonished that you didn't insist on it."

"Even if they had delayed, I doubt that Hal would have come."

"But he would have been able to exert pressure on Mr. Ogstanley to attend. This is a scandal. Poor Lena buried and not a sign of her husband!"

"But nobody knows where he went," protested Abby. She accepted a glass of sherry from the tray Tawa held before her and waited until Grandmaire had sipped at her schnapps before tasting it. "Mr. Ogstanley appeared at Mondrich House several times during Lena's dreadful ordeal; but he always vanished again, and nobody knows where. This time, though"—she leaned forward confidentially—"we think that Stephen had a hand in it. Mr. Kine has a theory that Stephen has paid Mr. Ogstanley to stay away."

"Really?" said Grandmaire coldly. "And what possible reason could Stephen have for doing that?"

Abby was alarmed. She guessed the real cause of her stepmother's displeasure but had not reazlied how deep that displeasure was. It was taking her such a long time to dredge the matter up.

"Would *Matua* like another drink?" asked Tawa, picking up the glass.

Abby said, "I have always done my utmost to keep you informed of everything. When Mr. Kine and I decided to get married, you were the only person we consulted. I always tell you everything I know, but—"

Grandmaire rapped her cane furiously on the floor. Abby started, and sherry splashed onto her black glove.

"You are patronizing me, Abigail, and I will not stand for that. Why was I not informed as soon as Lena was delivered? And why was I not called to Mondrich House for that so-called conference about the infant?"

"I don't know," mumbled Abby. "I expected that you would be there, but at the time I was so distraught that Dr. Nunn had to give me laudanum."

"Very well. I accept that, but you must make amends. This nonsense about Lena's baby. You must take it and rear it at your house."

"I offered to, but Dora refuses. She said that Lena—"

"How can she refuse? *She* knows nothing about babies. She is clumsy and stupid with Rupert. And where is she planning to keep the wretched creature? Not here at Fintona surely."

As if on cue, a wail rose from some distant part of the house, and Ellen's voice could be heard, uttering soothing words.

"Nobody thought to consult me," said Grandmaire. "And I must say, Abigail, that I am staggered by Dora's lack of consideration. She has not returned here once since Lena died, nor has she thought to ask my permission for what she plans to do. Not that I have any intention of granting it. Ellen will soon be having another child, and two children about the house are quite enough for someone of my age. Besides, Dora's time is fully occupied in looking after me. You must order her to hand the child over to you and put a stop to this nonsense at once."

"Aunt Maire, I have tried to make her see reason, but she is behaving so oddly I cannot fathom her at all."

Grandmaire sipped her drink. When she spoke, it was with a flat calm. "Dora has been with me for more than twenty years, and all that time you and I have maintained certain financial arrangements."

"You have been extremely generous."

"Not only that, but when she came, we spoke of legacies, did we not?"

"I believe we did," said Abby. She could feel the tight anticipation in her throat, of someone who stands on a gallows trap and waits for the lever to be pulled.

"I always paid you instead of Dora because I knew that if I put money in her purse, she would grow independent and begin to think for herself. It seems that she is doing so anyway, and it is up to you to stop her. Her wages have ceased, of course, but if she persists with this folly, you will have far greater reason for regret. Wills can be altered just as easily as they are written."

"Please, Aunt Maire . . . there is no cause to be hasty. I am doing all I can to persuade the stupid girl. Of course, she is not in her right mind now. Her reason is clouded with grief. I mean, she was always very fond of Lena, and at the moment . . . When she has had time to think this through in a practical light, she will realize that she could not possibly adopt a child, not someone in her position. . . . And perhaps if you could discuss—"

"I have no intention of dignifying the notion by discussing it with her."

"I only suggested . . . She thinks the world of you, so perhaps—"

"She barely tolerates me, and you know it," the old woman retorted. "Not that I mind. Why should I? Dora is sensible, quiet, biddable, and eminently useful—all the qualities I needed twenty years ago and still do. I do not need to stress how very angry and disappointed I shall be if I lose her services. That is all I have to say." And to emphasize her point, she rang the bell to summon Tawa. "I shall see you again when this has been settled, Abigail."

"I shall call as usual tomorrow, Aunt Maire."

"*If* Dora has been persuaded to see sense. Not otherwise."

Abby stared at her in dismay. "But I call on you every day. I have always called on you every day."

Grandmaire sighed. "You *used* to call each day. Now if you will please excuse me, I have a headache. As a rule I enjoy funerals, but this one has had a bitter aftermath. Good day, Abigail."

* * *

At the center of the controversy Dorinda Ogstanley seemed inappropriately tranquil, considering the tragic and disruptive elements that had surrounded her birth. Juliette marveled that she was so healthy, that the tortured delivery had left no ill effects whatever.

May adored her and hung over the end of her crib for hours at a time, admiring her sweetly serene face and ruff of soft marigold hair. She complained to Juliette, "Dora won't let me pick her up. You'd think I was hamfisted or destructive, to hear her talk."

"Never mind, dear," her mother reassured her. "She accused Miss Von Sturmer of incompetence, too. I'm afraid the baby has brought out the worst of Dora's nature. I never suspected that she was so possessive and overbearing."

"I did," remarked Stephen later. "That woman has taken over our household completely."

Juliette sighed. "I have to be constantly watchful for signs of unrest among the servants. Dora has managed to antagonize all of them, it seems. And the wet nurse threatens to leave so often that if I see her coming toward me now, I quickly move in the other direction. She protests that it is insufferably embarrassing for her, trying to feed Dorinda while Dora sits right beside her, watching every minute."

"What I want to know is, how much longer is this to go on? When can we hope to be rid of them both?"

"Oh, Stephen! The baby is only three months old. Far too young to be moved. And where would they go? Abby is furious with her, your mother refuses to have her back at Fintona unless she gives the child up, and she has no financial resources of her own. How can you suggest . . ." She paused and shot him a suspicious glance. "You're teasing, aren't you?"

"I wish I were. I find her intolerable, I'm afraid."

"You will feel more charitable toward her when you come back from Te Aroha."

"Perhaps. I wish you could come with me."

"And leave Dora alone with the staff? She would have the whole house completely reorganized by the time we returned, and only commands issued in her voice would be obeyed. We would find our requests ignored." She laughed. "I can see why Fintona ran to such a rigid discipline."

"If only Mama would take her back."

"But Dora has committed the unpardonable sin," said Juliette. "She has made a decision without consulting Grandmaire. Isn't it silly? She belongs at Fintona, and I know she wants to be there, but unless Grandmaire unbends . . ."

"She never will," said Stephen gloomily.

Twenty Two

Between the stables and the macrocarpa hedge which sheltered the fencible cottages was a small paved yard, surrounded on three sides by a whitewashed wall. May had found the yard when looking for a suitable place in which to build a holder for her glass printing frames. It was a perfect location. The white walls reflected the light so well that even on a gray winter's morning she could set out a rack of negatives and be confident of achieving crisply contrasted prints.

One afternoon in mid-December she was peeling back the corner of one print to check progress when she saw someone walking across the field toward her. She straightened and wiped her hands on her apron while she squinted through the dazzle of her own little oasis of light. Was it? Yes, it was!

"Patrick!" she cried at once, and untied her apron as she hurried to meet him, laughing with pleasure.

His arms were heaped with packages, but he grinned at her over the top of them. "Forgive me for not doffing my hat to you. I'm an errand boy today. You may call me Saint Nicholas if you wish."

"Let me help you. Here, set them down in the corner. I cannot leave these frames until the pictures are ready, and you are not going up to the house without me. How long has it been since I saw you? It seems years."

They could not stop smiling at each other. "It is a year. Just. I was disappointed when you did not come to Te Aroha this time."

"Were you?" He had not, of course, been mentioned.

263

"But you are as busy as ever with that camera, I see. What is your subject here?"

She laughed self-consciously. It was so *good* to see him. "This is a hansom cab, of all things. I was trying to capture its exact nature: the glass, the shine of the harness brasses, the texture of the horse's coat and mane." She peeled a print away from the negative to show him. "That's not one of the better ones, but it will give you some idea."

"But it's very good. You've caught the character in the driver's face, and those flowers in the vase look half-wilted just as cab posies often do. And is that young Billy inside? He's grown up in a year."

"Bobby."

"I admired those photographs of the bridal party that you sent with Samuel. Katerina was delighted with them."

"She wrote me a little note of thanks. This is my niece, Dorinda," she said as she removed more prints. Most she placed immediately into a lightproof box, ready to be taken inside and fixed with chemicals, but this one she handed to him. "I had hoped that it would be a clearer portrait, but it is almost impossible to coax her to keep still for long enough to make the exposure. But never mind this. Tell me about yourself. What have you been doing? I read in the newspaper that you were building a brewery in Hamilton. And a soft-drinks factory, is that right? Oh, you must have so much news, and I'll not let you go away until you have told me everything."

"Very well." They walked back toward the house. "I know what would interest you. I met the Maori king. You'll never guess what he was doing."

"I don't know. Conferring a knighthood?"

"No. He was going shopping."

"Surely kings don't go shopping. Not even Maori kings."

"It's true. It's perfectly true. Samuel and I were at the nearest store—a real outpost of civilization it is, too—with the intention of choosing gifts for me to deliver to your family for Christmas. We arrived to find the storekeeper putting up the shutters. He told us he was sorry but that nothing could be sold until King Tawhiao and his party had been served, so we waited, and soon they arrived all on

264

horseback. I've never seen so many tattooed faces, green-stone earrings, or kiwi feather cloaks in one gathering before. First everybody sat outside on the ground and drank tea with enormous quantities of sugar and ate sweet biscuits. Samuel and I enjoyed ourselves immensely, but the storekeeper's wife, who served us, was extremely nervous and jumped when any of the old warriors spoke to her. Then, over a period of several hours, small groups went into the store and chose what goods they wanted, brought them out, and the storekeeper wrote down the prices in a ledger. This continued until everybody had chosen his own particular treasure, and then the storekeeper totted up the amounts. I thought his voice shook when he said, 'Sixty-five pounds, sixteen shillings, and fourpence,' but the king's steward didn't blink an eye. He opened a carved box, pulled off the dogskin cover, and underneath was more money than you could imagine: banknotes, coins, gold pieces. He paid the storekeeper, and in silence the party mounted up and left. After they had gone, the store-keeper went inside and put the money in his own strong-box without even counting it. Samuel asked him why, and he said that if he did, and the money was wrong, some hint of discontent might creep into his attitude the next time the entourage came."

"And their custom was too valuable to risk losing?"

"That's right."

She noticed that he was watching her face, smiling to himself, as if at his own inward thoughts. "You're teasing me. You made all that story up."

"It's true, I swear it. I would cross my heart if I could reach it."

"I am sorry. I'm treating you more thoughtlessly than I do poor Bobby. Here, set your packages down on the ve-randa. I have to fix these prints before they darken too far. Would you like to come see how the process is finished off?" She helped him unload his arms. "Are these things which were left on the shelves after the king's party had been through?"

"There was nothing left. Their pillaging was total. That is why I had to do the shopping here, in Auckland on Sam-uel's behalf. I hope you approve my choice."

265

"I know we shall. And before you go, I must give you our gifts for him." Still chattering, she took his arm, and together they walked around to the back of the house.

Upstairs in the study Stephen was listening to Derwent Kine with a mixture of impatience and distaste. Because the fellow was Abigail's husband, and virtually family now, he tried to put his prejudices aside and accept him, but it was difficult. Stephen viewed him across that chasm which separates those who have worked hard to achieve what they have from those who have gained everything by manipulating others. Not only could this fellow boast that he had never done a day's work in his life, but he was a politician with a politician's deviousness.

This was his fourth visit since Stephen's return from Te Aroha, and only now was Mr. Kine getting to the point. The first call had been entirely social, the second had brought a small hint, and on the last visit the groundwork had been prepared.

He need not have bothered, thought Stephen, listening without sympathy to his woes. So many similar tales had been told at the club that with no effort of imagination Stephen could have exchanged roles with Mr. Kine and unfolded his troubles for him. At last the boom in stock and share speculation had peaked and begun to topple. All around Auckland companies were collapsing like the fragile card houses many of them were, and because these elaborate structures had been shored up with borrowed money, their fall was dragging respectable businesses down with them. Clothing workshops, potted meat, biscuit and shoe factories, were closing their doors, and if the rumors were true, many more would soon be turning their workers out onto the streets. While nobody gave the workers or their families a second thought, the speculators who had caused the crash were loud in their wailing and glum with worry.

"Jon is ruined, too, you realize," said Derwent, reaching for his coffee cup, which he had drained sometime previously.

Stephen refilled it for him from the silver Georgian coffeepot. "Is that so?" he said politely, though he doubted that news. Jon was too cunning to allow himself to become completely caught by a situation beyond his control.

"When the prices began to fall, he held on, thinking the situation would right itself. Then, when the downward trend accelerated, he panicked and threw all his stocks onto the market. Suicide, of course."

"Of course." Perhaps there was some truth in what he said. At the last Richmond Line meeting he had been struck by the resemblance between Jon and Dora, a likeness he had never noticed before. On reflection he realized that it was not a facial similarity so much as the fact that Jon's expression had fallen into the sullen cast Dora used to wear.

"But Jon is protected, no matter what happens to him," Derwent Kine continued. "At Fintona, and, since he is married to Mrs. Yardley Peridot's grandaughter, his future is assured, of course."

"Jon works very hard for my mother, make no mistake about that. She tolerates drones when she finds them amusing, but Jon is there because he is of real use to her. He is capable, efficient, and no doubt loyal, but you should be aware of that since he once worked for you."

"Please, Captain Yardley, I meant no offense. I'm fond of Jon. Very fond of Jon."

"But you didn't know I was," said Stephen shrewdly. "I'm not, but I'll not hear it said that he's making use of my mother. Not that anybody could, of course."

Derwent stroked his stiff beard. This conversation was not flowing into the correct channels. Every time he began to steer it in the desired direction Stephen blocked it off by challenging one of his remarks. He was being damned unhelpful altogether, downright rude. The way he kept pulling out his fob watch and looking at it was unsettling, and his refusal to pick up any of the hints about whiskey was nothing short of inhospitable. From where Derwent sat it was difficult to see why Stephen was so universally well regarded. He was nothing but an arrogant snob.

"Anyway, I prefer not to discuss members of my family."

"I assure you that no offense was meant," said Mr. Kine, dragging out his tobacco pouch and tapping his pipe on the rim of the ashtray. "My point was merely that Jon is pro-

267

tected from feeling the bite of hard times. Your wife's sister and I are in a precarious situation with no resources to fall back on."

While he stuffed his pipe, Stephen's contempt deepened. The tobacco pouch Derwent Kine used was notorious, made as it was from the tattooed buttock skin of a slain Maori warrior. Stephen had seen it many times before at clubs and in smoking rooms and had viewed it with distaste, but now he had to struggle with the urge to sweep it to the floor. With an effort he fixed his gaze away from it and said, "I do not understand. I cannot reconcile penury and extravagance."

"I beg your pardon?"

"Captain Aulde drew my attention to an unusual piece of cargo last week, an intriguing device which was set aside for inspection because its crate had been damaged in transit. It was a Hercules horse action saddle, a mechanical substitute for horseback riding. We found a book of instruction which claimed the device would stimulate the liver, quicken the digestion, and reduce obesity. It looked expensive, all silver trimmings and embossed morocco leather. We wondered what manner of person would want to own such an object." He sighed and ruffled a corner of a stack of papers with his thumb. "Captain Aulde sent a note to the store along with the mechanical horse. Apparently the device had been imported especially to fill an order."

"What of it?" said Derwent, reddening.

"Nothing," said Stephen. "Except that the price of that frivolous piece of extravagance approximated what it would cost to stable a real horse and pay a groom's wages for one year."

"That has nothing to do with you," said Derwent, on his feet in anger. "How dare you criticize the way I spend my money? What right have you to pass judgment?"

"None. None at all," said Stephen easily. "Except if you were to ask me for money or for some form of financial assistance. *Then* I might consider it my right to criticize or pass judgment. But you have not done that, so it was remiss of me to comment. Please accept my apologies, Mr. Kine."

How had this happened? thought Derwent in bewildered rage. How had the conversation upended and spilled all his hopes away? Ignoring the outstretched hand, he said tightly, "I hope that Dora's conscience rests easy with her. It is her stubborn behavior that has brought hardship to my wife."

"If that is a reference to the way Abigail has been pocketing Dora's wages all these years, then I am disappointed in you for mentioning it. But perhaps I misunderstood. I have noticed increasing deafness on one side this past year and find I often misunderstand when people tell me things."

Derwent stumped down the stairs and snatched his hat from the stand. He flung the door open and strode out onto the veranda, seething with frustration. Just as he stamped down the steps, May walked around the side of the house, talking to a young man.

At first Derwent did not recognize him, and at second glance he disbelieved the evidence of his own eyes. That illegitimate Bennington fellow, here being chummy with the captain's daughter? Impossible. But as he stared, May glanced up, saw him, and placed a warning hand on the young man's arm. Yes, it was he all right.

Derwent stiffened. Rage and anguish squeezed together in a hazy red mass behind his eyes. No wonder Captain Yardley scoffed at his problems. He was harboring Derwent's worst enemy under his roof. Aye, and probably giving him financial assistance, too. If the stories were true, then this scoundrel had already amassed more land than the acreage of the Firth and Morrin estates combined. He couldn't have done all *that* solely with brewery profits. Abby was right. The Yardleys were out to sabotage them any way they could, and here was proof.

Striding forward, he planted himself in their way.

"Good afternoon, Mr. Kine," said May. Patrick said nothing, and it seemed to Derwent that his expression was pure arrogance.

Derwent Kine raised his hand and slapped Patrick across the face with his bunched gloves.

"Mr. Kine!" said May.

Patrick gave May's elbow a slight push. "Go up to the house," he said. "Don't be afraid. Just do as I say."

"I'll fetch Father," she whispered.

"No. Wait by the door."

"Issuing orders to the young lady of the house? You really *are* one of the family, aren't you? I suspected that this family wished me nothing but harm, and now I know I was right."

"If that is what you suspected," said Patrick, "then I think you did yourself an injustice by marrying into it. Or perhaps the marriage is not such an advantage as you had hoped."

"You . . . bastard."

Patrick's expression did not alter. "Good day, Mr. Kine," he said.

Derwent swung with the gloves again; but Patrick stepped to one side, and the fingertips whistled past his ear.

"Excuse me, sir. You are barring my way."

"Are you a coward as well as everything else? Don't you know what a challenge means?"

"It means that you are displeased about something, but since we are not friends, nor are we ever likely to be, your displeasure does not concern me."

"I am calling you out," insisted Derwent.

Patrick hesitated. He had heard that Kine habitually wore a pistol under his frock coat, and at the moment his legendary vicious streak seemed very close to the surface.

"I demand an answer, sir."

Patrick said, "I do not accept your challenge. According to the rules of gentlemen, you are unable to challenge me unless you have been provoked. I am not sufficiently interested in you to wish to provoke you into a duel."

"Not provoked! Why, you insolent . . . upstart!" He glanced at May. Lowering his voice, he said, "You steal parcel after parcel of land from right under my nose, then have the gall, the utter gall, to claim that you have done nothing to provoke me. That is ridiculous!"

"Is it? Then I must beg your pardon. I understand that I was buying the land from under the noses of credit merchants. Did you know that there are more than a dozen men who have actually sworn in court that *they* were the would-be purchasers of my land?"

Patrick spoke with careful calm and the unpleasant sensation that he was fencing on a thin line. This stocky man was known for his temper and his bullying nature; but he was also a politician, and Patrick gambled that he would not lose control of himself while May was there watching.

"You know full well that it was *me* you were swindling," said Derwent with a bulldog thrust of his lower jaw.

At that point Patrick was aware of a softening of the older man's aggression. His gaze had wavered slightly, and the voice was less strident. It was like that moment in arm wrestling when the opponent relaxes for a fraction of a second to shift his grip and the match is in no doubt from then on.

Patrick spoke loudly so that Derwent Kine would know that May could hear every word. "As it happens, nobody was swindled. But if I was dealing with you, then you must have been using agents, and you of all people would be aware of the illegality of such a practice." He paused and added softly, "And dueling is illegal, too, is it not? Good day, Mr. Kine."

"You were magnificent," repeated May. "Absolutely magnificent. He is a loathsome little man and you put him to rout perfectly." She shivered. "I was afraid that he would shoot you."

Patrick laughed; but his back was covered with cold sweat, and his body felt detached from his mind. "I think he wanted to."

"I'm sure he did. I was *aghast* when he hit you with his gloves. I truly thought he had taken a fit. Oh, Patrick, I am so glad that you didn't hit him back. You could have knocked him down easily, but I'm so glad you restrained yourself."

"Why?"

"I loathe violence. I utterly detest it." She sat on the porch swing, and he seated himself beside her.

"There must be some reason for such a strong view."

"We had a stableboy once. His name was Young, and he was a friendly, cheerful boy with a smile for everyone. I couldn't help liking him until one day I saw him thrashing

271

one of the dogs for stealing a piece of bread and cheese that he had left out on a low bench. I screamed when I saw him beating the dog, and I was so upset when I found out the reason. It was the boy's own fault if his lunch was eaten for him. But I remember it all so clearly because that was the first time I ever asked Father to do anything for me, and I was so apprehensive about approaching him."

"You wanted the boy dismissed?"

"No. Just taken away from the animals. He was the gardener's assistant after that. But Father agreed with me. He said that violence is a mental aberration which feeds on itself. But do you know the strangest thing? After that I never could feel any liking for that boy. Every time I saw him all I could think of was that wretched, whimpering dog." She noticed an odd expression on his face, so she said, "You don't share my views, do you?"

"I agree with what you said about the dog. Cruelty to animals is despicable. But about violence generally, no. I must be honest with you, Miss Yardley. If Mr. Kine had insisted upon really hitting me, not swatting me with his gloves, but actually punching me, I would have been obliged to knock him down. I did not want to—he is smaller than I am—but yes, I would have fought him if I had had no choice."

"Oh." He could not read her expression because the rim of her sunbonnet screened her face. She did not look up at the sound of a carriage rolling into the driveway. Finally she reached out and touched his arm. "Thank you for your honesty. Most of the young men of my acquaintance would have agreed simply for the sake of being agreeable."

He had to laugh. "Most young men would not have had to find out the hard way that the only way to rout bullies is to call their bluff. For some reason I seem to attract bullies."

She colored. "I am sorry. Every time I see you I say something tactless sooner or later."

"You are too sensitive. There is no need to be so concerned about what I think." He noticed that Mrs. Yardley and another woman were alighting from the carriage. "I must go." He gave her hand a quick squeeze. "I'll tell you what, Miss Yardley. Because you disapprove so strongly, I shall promise never to brawl in front of you. There, does that make you happy?"

May did not have a chance to answer because her mother was ascending the steps, a bright smile fixed behind a thin fog of azure veil. "Mr. Bennington, how kind of you to call," she said in her most formal voice. And as Dora, stout and matronly in gray teffeta, came up the steps, she said, "Dora, dear, have you ever met Mr. Patrick Bennington?"

"Teipa," said Dora coldly.

"As you wish," said Patrick. "How do you do?"

"None the better for your asking." She looked him up and down with frank distaste. "I've seen you in town. Well, we've met now." And she marched inside.

Patrick said, "I really must be going, Mrs. Yardley. I came only to deliver Christmas gifts from Samuel."

"How extremely kind of you," said Juliette in that same dangerously courteous voice. "I thought perhaps you might have called to offer May your personal congratulations."

"For the photography award? I read about that sometime ago, and I was delighted for her."

"Not the award," said Juliette.

"Mother, please. . . ."

"I was referring to her engagement," said Juliette steadily. "Samuel did tell you that May is now engaged to marry Hal, did he not? I thought you must have come to offer her your wishes for her future happiness. We all are so thrilled for them both."

May was almost crying. "Did you have to tell him like that?"

"But, dear, I assumed that you had broken the news yourself. You were chatting so intimately." She stared at her daughter closely. "You look tired. Remember that you must guard against strain. Your lungs are weak, and you must always consider your health." She unpinned her hat, glancing at her daughter in the hall mirror as she did so. "One more thing, dear: Patrick's mother died of consumption, and we all know how highly contagious that is."

273

"But Patrick is perfectly healthy. Uncle Samuel told us that the doctors—"

"Doctors can make mistakes." She kissed her daughter's brow. "Perhaps I am being overprotective when I warn you to keep a little distance from Patrick, but your health is so fragile, dear."

May said, "I suffered no ill effects when he kissed me."

To her astonishment her mother responded sharply. "Don't be impertinent, May," she said, and holding her hat in white-knuckled hands, she swept past and up the stairs.

Twenty Three

After she had knocked, May stood on the doorstep, hugging her upper arms, tense with nervousness. She knew that Patrick was in there because the window nearest her was glowing softly through the screen of drawn curtains. There was no reply to her first knocking, or the second. She hammered again, harder but with less confidence. Obviously he had seen her coming up the path and was refusing to answer the door, but she tried once more and waited for a long interval before reluctantly giving up.

Though the sky was as silver as water, the garden was deep in silent shadows when she turned to go. All she could distinguish was the faint strip of path at her feet and the ragged black tops of the towering hedge. It had rained last night, and now after the heat of day the scent of warm, damp earth still lingered.

May was approaching the gap in the hedge when she heard the gate latch rattling, and a second later Patrick stepped out of the darkness.

She gasped and said, "You did startle me. I was so certain that you were at home."

"No, Miss Yardley. I was down at the beach."

"I see." She had braced herself for a chilly reception but was dismayed to find him even colder than she had feared.

"You shouldn't be out at this hour," he said.

"I know." She tried to joke. "It's not safe, you told me so yourself. Fierce Maoris are everywhere."

Her attempt at humor failed utterly. He said, "There is not enough light for photographs now," in such a tone that she knew he wanted her to go home.

"I came to talk to you," she said.

"If the subject is what I imagine it to be, then please be assured that there is absolutely no need—"

"Please," she said. "Please."

"Very well." He said nothing more until he had opened the door and stood back so that she could enter the front room ahead of him. He nodded toward the wing chairs that bracketed the fireplace and said, "Sit down. Make yourself comfortable."

The room was tinier than she remembered, with a low ceiling and a dark varnish over the paper on the walls. It was difficult to believe that so many people had been crammed in here around the coffin. Now the few items of furniture seemed to fill the room: two bookcases, both packed with what looked like encyclopedias and textbooks, a brass wood box, a draped table on which the lamp stood, and a high-backed sofa opposite her chair. Patrick sat casually on the sofa with his long legs stretched out in front of him. He was lightly dressed, with a blue silk shirt open at the neck and rolled up at the sleeves, twill trousers, and bare feet. May watched him unroll his sleeves and button the cuffs and was suddenly stifled by an awareness of intimacy. His hair was tousled and damp at the ends. A tinge of blue shaded his jawline. She was reminded, forcefully, of an occasion when she had seen Stephen first thing in the morning, bare-legged and still in his nightshirt, with the atmosphere of bed clinging to him.

"Well, Miss Yardley?"

She began quickly, saying, "I have been so unhappy since you left this afternoon."

"Oh? I thought I left you in a happy frame of mind."

"I've been miserable because of what Mother told you. She shouldn't have—"

"Told me about your engagement?" he interrupted crisply. "No, she should not have done that. You should have told me, May. Why didn't you?"

She shrugged helplessly. "I don't know. This sounds stupid—improbable, too—but I didn't think about the matter at all. Not once while we were talking. Not until I realized that Mother was about to break the news, but it was too late then."

He said nothing. Leaning back with his arms folded, he regarded her impassively.

"All right," she said. "I shall accept that you don't believe me, but that is the simple truth of it. I was so pleased to see you and enjoyed your company so much that I did not give a moment's thought to my engagement. But that is not as ridiculous as it sounds. You see, I seldom think about the matter at all."

"You don't sound like someone desperately in love."

"I'm not," she said, and hastily amended that by adding, "At least . . . no. I don't want to sound as though I were making excuses. You probably think badly enough of me as it is."

"No. Go on. Say whatever you were about to say."

"Mother asked me to accept Hal when he proposed. I intended to put him off, but she said that it was very important to both her and Father that I accept. She said that there would be no pressure put on me to be married until I felt ready. There. That is how it all happened; but saying it out loud makes me feel shabby and disloyal, and that's not true. I'm not being disloyal—just trying to explain how I feel."

"What you *are* saying is that you are happy about being engaged, is that so? Then why did you feel miserable this afternoon, so miserable, apparently, that you had to come to see me?"

"I don't understand why, but I felt desperate. I still do." She looked at him as though pleading for help, but his face still showed no emotion whatsoever. She said, "It seemed to matter that you not think badly of me, and it seems more vital than anything else in the world that I not hurt you."

"And you thought you had hurt me?"

"I was afraid I had. At the same time it hurt me, too. I couldn't bear it. The pain drove me to come and see you. Does that make any sense to you?"

He nodded, but she could not read his expression.

She sighed. "I know I should not be here, yet I had to try to explain. I don't know what to say, and there is no reason why you should want to hear me out, but I'm so sorry about my behavior." She faltered and stopped.

He stood up. "Please don't worry about it anymore. Still, thank you for coming. I do appreciate the thought."

She had the helpless feeling that she had expressed herself so poorly that somewhere between them the meaning had been lost. "Patrick." She touched his sleeve hesitantly. "Patrick . . ."

He looked down at the oval of her pale face, marveling that he could have ever considered her pallidly unattractive. The desire to kiss her dragged at him like a powerful undertow, but he pulled against it and stepped away from her.

"Patrick, please. I can't leave like this."

He rounded on her abruptly, saying, "My God, May, what do you expect from me?"

He noticed how she flinched at his tone and how her eyes swelled with tears before she swiftly ducked her head.

He was instantly contrite. "Here," he said, "I'm not angry with you. Here, sit down." After guiding her to the sofa, he sat beside her and took her hand. Immediately she burrowed around in his palm until her bare fingers and his were entwined. The sensation was so provocative that he had to struggle with impulses either to scoop her close in passion or to thrust her away from him, but he could see that she was seeking comfort and quite innocently unaware of the effect she was causing. He breathed deeply to steady himself and said lightly, "You do care about me, don't you?"

"Oh, yes, yes, I do. That's why I am so confused. Being engaged to Hal is something that I always knew would happen. Everybody thinks it is the right thing for me. It's taken for granted. What I cannot understand is why I feel so uncertain myself."

"Was this engagement the aftermath of our last meeting? Was your father very angry with you because of me?"

"Oh, no. Uncle Samuel was the only one who was angry."

"Samuel?"

"It's surprising that he didn't tell you about the engagement. He knew Hal and I were planned for each other; that's why he was angry. He made me feel dreadful when he pointed out how wrong and inconsiderate I was to flirt with you."

"He said that?"

"Not in so many words, but that is what he meant. He implied that I was being a heartless flirt, but he was wrong." She looked him in the eye, saying, "A flirt plays with people's feelings for her own amusement, and I wouldn't do that to anybody. Truly I wouldn't."

When he said nothing but sat staring at the entwined brown and white fingers, she said, "You still think badly of me, don't you?"

"No," he replied, and after a long pause said, "You will marry Hal eventually. It will be just as everybody says. There will be an enormous wedding. Half the city will attend, and everyone will wish you happiness. You will live in a beautiful house like Whenuahakari. Your friends will flock to visit you. None of them will ever snub you or make cruel, hurtful remarks about you. Some may be slightly critical of your dedication to photography, but once you have children of your own, you may prefer to pack your cameras away and become a typical society lady. Your parents will be proud of you. They will praise your husband and admire their beautiful grandchildren. Those children will have happy, uncomplicated lives. Nobody will taunt or make fun of them. They will have countless friends to play with. Miss Yardley, your life will continue to be as beautiful, as insulated, and as comfortable as it is now." Very gently he disengaged her grasp and helped her to her feet. Tears were flowing freely down her cheeks, but he resisted the almost overpowering urge to fold her in his arms. Instead, he ushered her to the door, saying, "You have a wonderful life ahead of you. Most young ladies would envy your good fortune."

On the step she turned back to him. "Then why do I feel so wretched? I came to you hoping that you would give me the answer."

She thought that he was not going to reply, but just before the door clicked shut, he said, "That, Miss Yardley, is something you must discover for yourself."

She was quite alone, staring blankly at the peeling paint on the closed door. It looked like bark in the darkness.

Reaching home, she stopped beyond the pool of veranda light and circled the house to the long flight of steps that led up to the top balcony. The white-painted nursery was golden in the soft light. May noticed that the boys' old stuffed toys had been unpacked and replaced on the long white shelves. They looked like a row of bright story creatures sharing in the game Dora was having with Dorinda, thought May, watching as Dora tickled the girl and cooed to her on the white counterpaned bed.

May tapped on the glass and went in. The room smelled of dusting powder and warming oil.

"Where have you been?" said Dora, clearly annoyed by the intrusion. "Aunt Juliette has been looking for you."

"Mama . . . Maaaa . . ." gurgled the baby, waving chubby arms. Dora picked her up and held her against her shoulder.

May knelt beside her and reached out, saying. "Please could I hold her for a moment?"

"Be careful." She relinquished her grudgingly and watched as May held her gently in the crook of her arm. Cooing at Dorinda, May stroked the bright hair with a fingertip.

"She's going to have lovely curls, don't you think?" said Dora approvingly.

"Yes," said May, and to the astonishment of them both she burst into fresh hot tears.

"Whatever is the matter with you?" asked Dora, rescuing the baby and joggling her to soothe her wails. "Hush, dearest, hush. Auntie May upset you, didn't she? There, there, Mama will make it better." And to May she repeated, "What is the matter with you?"

May shook her head. She had buried her face in the counterpane and was crying with great, tearing shudders.

"Are you ill? Because if you are, I can't have you in—"

"No," May said, sobbing.

"What is it then?"

"I don't know. I'm . . . I'm so dreadfully unhappy, and I don't understand why."

Dora nuzzled the baby's neck. "You have no reason to cry," she told May. "You have everything in the world to be happy for. Look at me. Why, I've been unhappy for most

280

of my life, but it never occurred to me to wail about it. You're spoiled, that's your trouble. You have every advantage and nobody to consider but yourself." She kissed Dorinda's cheek. "Wait until you have children of your own. That's when you'll know what it is to be happy and content. Just you wait and see."

Twenty Four

"It's h-hardly appropriate for an engagement gift," said Daniel. "But when I saw it, I couldn't resist it. I was going to s-save it for your birthday, but that's such a long way off."

"Daniel, it's lovely," said May, lifting the collapsible field camera out of its box. "A Thornton-Pickard Instantograph. Oh, Daniel . . . I read about these, and I longed to ask Hal to buy one for me, but he is so set against my photography that I dared not ask. Do you realize what you have done for me? Now I don't have to take that clumsy developing tent everywhere. And this camera is so light that I can easily carry it by myself. I'll give the old one to Bobby, and he'll be thrilled, too." She flung her arms around his neck and kissed his bearded cheek. "I'm so pleased to have you home again."

"So you keep saying."

"And all these weeks you've had this camera hidden away? What a tease you are."

"Not only this, but a ton and a half of dry plates. They m-must be kept somewhere cool and used within a year. The dealers thought I was insane to buy so many, but I said, 'You d-don't know my sister. She'll use them up without any trouble.' "

May held the camera in her lap. "It's *exactly* what I wanted. And it has everything. Turntable, tripod, focusing cloth, and a time shutter, too. And plate holders—"

"It takes ten-inch by eight-inch plates. There were larger ones, but I thought you'd prefer something manageable."

"It's perfect. And I'm glad you waited until we had a free

day before you gave it to me. What pandemonium it's been since you arrived home. Meetings every day with Father, Richmond Line and Mondrich Line business, and, after the work is done, so many invitations to suppers and socials and glee clubs that if this keeps up, you'll have seen the inside of every house in Auckland by the end of summer. Everybody is curious about you. You've been away so long that most people have forgotten what you look like. Not that anybody could tell now," she added, tweaking his chin whiskers. "Why did you grow a beard? You have such a handsome face."

"I have been told that I look distinguished," he told her loftily. "And that I have butter dripping from my chin, so take your choice. Either description will suit." He stood up and smoothed his hair flat, studying himself in the mirror. "Kendrick will be here soon. We plan to go cycling this afternoon."

"He is still staying at Fintona?"

"He vows he'll n-never go home while Mr. Kine is there, and since he lost his seat in the last election, it looks as if Mr. Kine is home to stay."

"Aunt Abby gained a new family and lost her old family all at once," said May. "Jon is at Fintona, and Aunt Abby is not welcome there until Dora returns—and inasmuch as Dora has been here for seven months now, I doubt that she ever will go back to Grandmaire. And now Kendrick is out of her reach, too. She'll take that hard."

"N-Not as hard as Kendrick has." Daniel pulled the curtain aside and peered out before saying, "I'm worried about the depths of his hatred toward Mr. Kine. When he heard the news, I thought he'd g-go berserk. Now he's all right when he's sober, but when he drinks, he turns vicious and unpredictable."

"That sounds frightening." She squinted through the viewfinder. "You'd best treat him with caution until he comes to terms with everything."

"He's my friend. I have to stand by him."

They had covered this ground before. "But not if it means trouble for you. You stood by him and were thrown out of Oxford. It's all right. Father can't possibly hear. Anyway, what does it matter? You passed your finals, and that's all Father worries about. He's had so many problems lately that sometimes I think he hardly notices us at all. I'm so glad that you are home to help shoulder the load with him."

Daniel flushed. "He d-doesn't let me do a thing. Oh, I go to all those meetings, but Solforn Wade is the only person permitted to speak. There's really n-nothing for me to do here. I'm going to ask Father if I can go to the London office or to Sydney. I'd be m-much more use there. Besides, this town is dismal. I remembered it as a happy place, but it's so depressing. Everybody looks so poor. And all those unemployed."

"This is only temporary. Everybody says that things will improve soon and there will be jobs for all. Please don't talk about leaving."

"I'm serious, May. I need to work, and I know I c-can be useful to the Mondrich Line. I could practically run it if I had to. It's frustrating to be spending week after week just sitting in on meetings."

"You are impatient, aren't you? Why don't you ask Father for more to do? Tell him how you feel?"

"I'll ask Hal's advice. H-He'll be home in a few days." He grinned at her. "I suppose that's why you've been moping about. How dense of me. I thought the camera might cheer you up, but of course, you're pining for Hal."

"Not at all. This camera is just the medicine I need, but I'd best start learning how to use it right now because as soon as Hal arrives, I'll have to pack it away again." She sighed. "I wish he could learn to tolerate lady photographers."

Every February, when the rose gardens around Fintona were ripe with the full glory of summer color, Mrs. Yardley Peridot entertained friends, family, and people of importance at a garden party. This year more than two-hundred-fifty had accepted with pleasure, and as usual, a few uninvited extras arrived with them.

Dora Bennington was one.

As May helped her down from the victoria, she said, "This will be the first of Grandmaire's parties that you

284

will have attended as a guest. Quite a novelty for you, Dora."

"The first party I've ever been to uninvited," she remarked, rocking Dorinda in her arms while she waited for the ornate wickerwork perambulator to be unloaded. "And the first party I have not had to arrange, though I doubt I shall enjoy it." She stared critically about her. "Look at where the marquee has been erected! The ground is like a swamp over there. And look at the archery targets. Ellen placed them, no doubt. She would never consider that everybody will have to fire arrows into the glare of the afternoon sun."

"I expect that she is so busy—"

"Grandmaire would see to that." Dora's smile was sour. "And I say she's welcome to all of it."

Ellen was closing the bedroom door behind her when her husband came striding up the corridor. He stopped.

She nodded coldly without speaking.

He said, "What are you playing at now?" The space between them was covered in two swift strides. "Where is that new dress I bought you to wear today?"

"Hanging up in the wardrobe with all the others."

"Why? Why, in God's name? Surely you cannot appear at the garden party in that rag?"

"Indeed I will. If my memory serves me accurately, you once told me that I looked extremely handsome in this dress. 'Black suits you, my dear,' you said."

"But that was years ago." He grabbed her wrist and twisted her arm around to show her the cobwebbing of darns at the elbow. "You can't greet all those people wearing this. You look hideous. Always in black just like *her*. You're turning into her, do you realize that? You look like her, you sound like her—"

"Excuse me, please."

"No. Do as I say, Ellen. Go put on that pretty dress that I bought for you. Heaven knows I could ill afford it, but I wanted—"

She cut him short. "Then take it back. Take them all back. I'll never wear them. This is my dress. Mine. Bought with my money. I'll wear it until it rots, and then I'll patch it and go on wearing it."

"What will people think? They're probably all talking about you, whispering behind their hands, saying—"

"That I'm poor. Which I am. Or that I'm in mourning. Let them talk." She shook her arm. "Would you please let go of me? And lower your voice or you'll wake Roseanne."

He held fast. "I would have expected you to have more pride. You always cared what people thought. You were proud."

"That is the trouble. I am proud. Far too proud to be bought with gifts. Now, if you will excuse me, Grandmaire wants me to check progress in the kitchen."

With his left hand he grabbed her collar and slipped his fingers into the neckband. She grew rigid at his touch but continued to glare at him, her thin face set, her narrow green eyes unafraid. He said, "If I pull hard, this dress will tear right down the front. Then you will be forced to wear the dress I chose for you."

Her voice was perfectly calm. "If you do that, I shall put a black shawl around my shoulders and carry on with my tasks. Would you please let me go?"

This time he did.

"Thank you," she said. As she walked quickly away, tears burned behind her eyelids, but she held them back with fierce determination.

Grandmaire was on the veranda overlooking the archery lawn, keeping a watchful eye on Rupert, who was riding a realistic-looking rocking horse. The horse was covered with dappled ponyskin and had large brown glass eyes and bristly eyelashes. She stopped talking to her other guests when her son walked down the path. "Stephen!" she called.

He paused and looked up, leaning on his stick. In the harsh light furrows showed plainly across his brow, and when he doffed his top hat, a glint of scalp shone through the hair on the top of his head.

"You will forgive me," she said to the guests, "but I must talk to my son alone. Business matters, you understand."

"Business is all that matters to you, Mama," he said. When she frowned uncomprehendingly at him, he spoke more loudly, "In the name of Jove, use your ear trumpet if you need to. What is the use of being vain if you cannot hear the compliments people pay you?"

"He *is* a fine boy," agreed Grandmaire as she picked up the silver hearing aid from behind her chair and settled comfortably. "Sit down, for goodness' sake. Or are you afraid you'll not be able to rise again? We are a pair of old crocks, aren't we? You with rheumatism, me with gout. We're like a pair of battle-scarred old cats, limping and battered, but certainly not beaten."

"And with a fight or two left in us yet. Well, Mama, that timber deal with the Oregon lumber company saved the Richmond Line, just as you predicted. I don't suppose you could conjure up a cure for what ails the country, could you? The outlook in Auckland is bleak, and prospects in the rest of New Zealand are just as grim. The trade depression seems determined to squash us all. I've ordered notices posted in all the Mondrich Line offices abroad, warning people not to come here. Not that many are foolish enough to. The ships coming in are empty of passengers but I have people clamoring to leave on every vessel."

"I know, I know. But I'll not discourage anybody from coming, not when they've money to pay their passage and I've got houses to rent." She reached out a withered hand to grasp the rocking horse bridle. "Not so hard, dear," she warned, ignoring the boy's pouts. "You might fall off and land, crash! on poor Grandmaire, mightn't you?"

"No, I won't. I won't hurt you," said Rupert. He was a fineboned dark child with Ellen's pointed chin and full pink lips.

His great-grandmother did not hear him; she was cupping her ear to Stephen as he said, "We are having disappointing problems with the refrigeration plants. It is taking far longer to outfit the vessels than we had bargained for. All manner of delays have plagued us."

"Yes," said his mother. "And then you were beaten to the first blow by the Mainland Shipping Company."

"That was extremely frustrating. Especially since we didn't even know they were working along the same lines.

The first thing we knew was when a shipment of frozen New Zealand lamb was unloaded at Tilbury. I heard that it was as fresh as when it was packed on board."

"A complete success. And when is your first cargo to leave?"

"Hal is taking the *Mondrich Pioneer* to Christchurch the day after tomorrow. They should be on their way to England in less than a fortnight, with luck."

"Hal? I thought he had gone already."

"He should have; but there was further trouble with the temperature control, and it took the engineers longer than expected to get it working properly again."

"Then you must send him to me without delay. I want to wish him luck before he goes." She uttered a dry laugh. "Here was I, ready to take offense because I thought that he had left without bidding me farewell."

"You know I wouldn't do that, Grandmaire," chided Hal as he settled beside her. "Didn't Captain Yardley tell you that I stayed especially for today? You've done well to choose such a dazzling warm day for it, too, or did Ellen do that for you?"

Hal spoke lightly because Ellen was in the third chair on the veranda, sitting on the far side of Grandmaire. Whenever he looked up, Ellen intercepted his gaze with a cool expression that made him uncomfortable. Since becoming his brother's wife, she had acquired a kind of gloss, a new aura that sometimes made him wonder whether he had ever really known her. Who would have imagined that Ellen would have become so domesticated that Grandmaire remarked frequently how happy and maternal she was? And whoever would have expected her to become so conservative in her dress? Again today she wore a fittingly modest gown with high neck and respectably bustled skirt. Though it was black, a color he disliked, he had to admit that on her it was striking.

Grandmaire was saying, "And when are you planning to be married? You've been engaged far too long already."

Hal murmured something noncommittal and glanced across the lawn to where Kendrick and Daniel were showing the Kine girls their new velocipede bicycles.

Grandmaire said, "Engagements are foolish nonsense anyway. I can see the sense for them as an aid to help poor or less privileged folk save money, but in a family like ours there is no need at all. I always say that . . ."

Hal stopped listening and began mentally ticking off the arrangements to be made before the *Mondrich Pioneer* sailed. They were needing another officer, and this would be the chance to train one of the engineers as a supervisor, but the problem was to decide which one had the most leadership potential. He was considering the possibilities when something Grandmaire said snapped his attention back to her.

". . . even if Jack Bennington did legally adopt him, I don't think it gives him the right to the name, so he's Patrick Teipa as far as I'm concerned."

"Quite," said Hal, totally lost. He looked to Ellen for some indication of what had gone before, but she was suddenly absorbed in feeding Rupert pieces of peeled apple.

"Stephen probably wouldn't think to mention it to you, and I did only because I think he is a totally unsuitable companion for May. And you should know what goes on while you are away. You have a right to know."

"Quite." He hoped that she would say more to elaborate; but that ended that subject for her, and it was not until Ellen rose to go inside that Hal saw a chance to find out what he had missed. He caught up to her as she entered the dining room and stood beside her while she opened a drawer of the dresser.

"I don't think I can say anything," she said in reply to his question. "Even though it is firsthand from Mr. Kine, it is gossip and none of my business."

"It's my business, and I want to know. What did she mean by saying May is not a suitable companion for that. . . ? Never mind. She implied all kinds of things. You have to tell me." When she said nothing but continued poking among the invitations, visiting cards, toys, and pieces of a child's puzzle in the drawer, he lost his temper with her. "Very well, if you won't oblige me, I shall have to ask Mr. Kine for some illumination on the topic, and no doubt he'll relish the pleasure of telling me what's been going on behind my back."

"I'll tell you," she said, "but only to spare you humiliation." She closed the drawer without having found whatever it was she had searched for. "Mr. Kine seems to think that May and Patrick Teipa are more than simply good friends. He saw them together at Mondrich House, walking arm in arm, laughing in a very intimate fashion. When Mr. Kine sought to reprimand Mr. Teipa for the trouble he has put in his path, May defended her friend and forbade Mr. Kine to say one word against him."

"Where was Captain Yardley?"

"Right there, at home. Apparently this friendship has the full consent of May's family."

"I don't believe it."

Ellen could see that he did. "I wish I hadn't told you. It *is* only gossip."

He cupped her face in his hands, just as he used to do long ago, when he was the only person she ever dreamed of and when in bliss she believed he loved her, too. Now she jerked away from his touch, stung by the reminder of all that she had lost, all that May, it would seem, did not appreciate. She moved to the window, where a table held a collection of scrimshaw work. Above the table on one side was a mirror, and on the other a framed photograph of Maire's second husband, Thomas Peridot, dressed in a kiwi feather cloak and holding a Maori spear trimmed with tufts of dogskin.

Hal hesitated awkwardly. Because the mirror's surface was bloomed with age, he could not read her expression. "I'm grateful to you, Ellen."

"What will you do? Will you ask May about Patrick and tell her that you heard it from me?"

"I'll not mention your name."

She'll deny everything, of course, thought Ellen. Bitterly she said, "You'd be advised to forget the whole thing. May conducts herself as she pleases, and to me it seems a miracle that there has not been a full-blown scandal about her. Of course, I don't know how much basis there is for all the rumors and stories about her and Patrick."

"Rumors? Stories? Has it come to that?"

"Aunt Abigail has been keeping her friends well entertained. You know how she enjoys a tantalizing tale."

"Then the gossip will be spread all over town."

"Your mother means no harm. But nobody can resist a story about Patrick." She shrugged. "He is universally known as Mr. Bennington, you know. Jon says that even his fellow provincial councillers ask if Patrick Bennington is his brother. They all are intrigued with everything he does. The whole town talks about him. He is quite the man of mystery, didn't you know?"

But Hal did not wait for the last words. As she had hoped, her remarks spurred him to action. When the French doors from the morning room crashed open and slammed shut again, she followed to see what would happen.

Verona Kine missed being pretty by a half inch which, in the right place, would have transformed a snub button into a pert nose, but she was an appealing little creature with huge dark eyes which were fixed in clear adoration on Kendrick.

Daniel felt uneasily sorry for her and apprehensive about the attention Kendrick was paying her. He knew that Kendrick's loathing of his new stepfather extended to his stepsisters as well. He never referred to them without contempt and always called them the parrots, a reference to their harsh voices and shrill laughter and to the gaudy ensembles in which Abigail dressed them. Today Lucca was garbed in watermelon pink while sixteen-year-old Verona wore a gown the sickly green of new grass. Both dresses were decorated with so much buttercup gilded *passementerie* that Daniel wondered if his Aunt Abigail had been struck color-blind. He had seen her earlier clad in a gown which seemed to have been made entirely of scarlet beads and black ribbon.

Now Kendrick was paraphrasing a remark he had made to Daniel at that time. "I said how very gratifying it would be if my mother would only confine her excruciating taste to her wardrobe, and now I see that she has extended it to yours as well."

Verona looked puzzled. She heard "excruciating," but his tone was so honeyed that she wondered whether perhaps he really meant "exquisite." She waved the champagne glass airily and said, "Thank you. We think it is such fun to have a mother to dress us."

"What about a brother?" asked Kendrick with a sly look at Daniel. "What could *he* do for you?"

Lucca spoke up. She was a boyish thirteen-year-old. "Mama says that we must be as charming to you as we can, so that you will be reconciled to the idea of having us in your family."

"Is that so?" asked Kendrick, looking at Verona. He took her glass. "Let me fetch you some more fruit punch."

Lucca said, "We are not allowed to have anything with alcohol in it."

"Nor shall you." Kendrick smiled. "Not when you have two gentlemen to look after you. Isn't that so, Daniel?"

"I'll come with you," said Daniel.

The band in the gazebo was playing "Home, Sweet Home." All the bandsmen wore white jackets and navy and white striped trousers. Their leader wore a shako with a white pompon on the top. Explosions of sunshine bounced along the instruments as they played.

Daniel hurried to keep up to Kendrick. "Do we have to stay talking to them?" he asked. "I w-want to find somebody interesting. Lucca is far too positive, and every time I look at her I see her father."

"Exactly." Kendrick stopped. "And *that* is why I want you to stay with me for an hour or so. That's all. You can chat with Lucca for that length of time, can't you?" And when Daniel frowned, he said strongly, "It's important. Call it a favor. But when I take Verona down to the beach, you keep Lucca up here."

"Why? What are you going . . ." But before he could finish, Kendrick had walked away and Hal was there in his place, asking if he had seen May.

"Is s-something wrong? You look upset."

"I have to talk to her." Hal gazed about distractedly. "Damn. It should be easy enough to see her. She's the only one here dressed in her nightgown."

"Easy there, I say. Those Liberty gowns are all the s-style in England. You should know that."

"I've seen them and been shocked by them, I don't mind admitting. I thought May would have more sense. It seems

292

that every time I assume she is too sensible to do something she proves me wrong." He was craning his neck, scanning the crowd. Daniel saw her by the marquee, holding out her arms to show someone the loosely draped sleeves of her flimsy garment. He said nothing, but Hal noticed her, too. "Ah, there she is," he said.

Daniel put a hand on his shoulder. "I say, go easy, won't you? May never did like to be told . . ."

"And what are you dithering on about?" asked Kendrick as he approached with two slopping glasses. "Here, this is Lucca's. You take it. Wouldn't do to get them confused, would it now?"

Daniel took the glass absently. He was watching Hal as he spoke to May, wondering what had made him so angry. It could not be just the gown. They had already quarreled about that yesterday, and afterward Daniel consoled May by theorizing that Hal feared what the new style represented, accessibility, vulnerability, and freethinking, all anathema to Hal. He was old-fashioned and would have to be educated gradually into the new ways, it was that simple.

"Come on," Kendrick was saying. "You can't let me down now. Not when my taste buds are already tingling with the sweet taste of revenge."

Daniel asked him, "D-Do you think that May's gown is shocking? Anything to make a fuss over, I mean?"

Kendrick grinned. "If she wasn't your sister, I'd answer that. No, of course not. Now come along, or the parrots will have flown away."

May was conversing with a woman in a blue dress, whose plaited wheat straw bonnet had a sheaf of artificial bluebells pinned to the side. They jiggled as she nodded to May. Hal heard her say, "I agree that in every photograph something should be left to the imagination," so was not surprised when May introduced her as Mrs. Wey, a fellow Arts Institute member. He excused himself courteously to her and led May over to the shady trees, where a large group of conservatively dressed Maori people were eating ice cream out of willow-patterned custard cups.

293

"Tena koutou," said May, smiling. "Good day to you all."

They nodded shyly, and the men began to get up from the flax mat on which they all sat, but Hal stopped them with a gesture.

"No, carry on, please." And he drew May away out of earshot.

"That ice cream looks delicious," she observed. "Apparently the QCE restaurant makes it to Grandmaire's own recipe. It is twice as rich as their own ice cream and too expensive to be made commercially. Shall we have some now?"

"I want to talk to you first."

At his tone she colored. "If it's about my gown, I'm sorry, but I *like* this style. Liberty gowns are just coming into fashion, and when more people are wearing them, you'll not be so disapproving. But I think I should be able to choose my own clothes. You'd not want to spend all your shore time at the dressmaker's with me, would you?"

"It's not your dress, though you know what I think of that. I want to talk about that Teipa fellow. Mr. Kine is spreading gossip about you, gossip which delights my mother, as you can imagine."

"There is no reason for it." She glanced up and saw such restrained anger in his face that she was afraid. "Patrick came to our home to deliver Uncle Samuel's Christmas presents. Mr. Kine insulted him and tried to call him out."

"But you were walking arm in arm with him, chatting in a friendly way. I warn you, May, that I'll not tolerate you making us a target for malicious gossip. Apparently all Auckland is agog."

She flared up. "And I want to know why you *want* to marry me. If everything I do is unacceptable, then why should we continue this engagement? Sometimes I wonder if you even *like* me."

"That's unfair. I love you. You are the one whose behavior is bewildering. You will not listen to my opinion on any subject. You refuse to wear an engagement ring. You won't agree to fix a date for our wedding—"

"That's not fair. We have discussed the matter several times, and each time I have repeated that as soon as you

294

agree to take over the San Francisco position, we can be married. You are the one who will not agree."

Hal looked uncomfortable. "But what if the San Francisco position no longer existed?"

"What do you mean? Father has never found anyone satisfactory to stay there. The man in the office at the moment is waiting to retire if Father can find someone capable to take his place, and—"

"May, listen. This is all highly confidential, and Daniel doesn't even know yet; but the captain wants to place him there. No, please listen." And he hushed her with a gentle touch of his palm to her cheek. "Daniel is desperate to have something important to do, and this will be a real challenge. Both the captain and I think he will be ideally suited to the position."

"But what about us?"

"Please, May, try to see this as reasonably as you can. I love the sea. The thought of leaving it is abhorrent to me. I love you, and I hope you can try to understand how I feel."

His face had blurred. Disappointment blinded her. "But you promised to take me back to San Francisco. You promised."

"Is it so important? We can go there on our honeymoon if you like. . . ."

But May did not hear him. She had turned away and was walking swiftly across the lawn. Soon she had disappeared into the crowd.

Ellen saw her go and paused in mid-sentence. They had quarreled. It was a tiny gain, but all her triumphs were small these days. When she glanced back at her aunt, she realized that she had dropped the thread of their conversation.

"Ellen," prompted Juliette, "you were telling me what good fortune you have with your babies, both with such placid dispositions. It must be a family trait, and a happy one at that. Dorinda is positively angelic, and Dora is making a splendid mother. Nobody would guess she was fostering her."

"Then there is no chance that she will give her up?"

"I would doubt it. Abigail keeps trying to persuade her,

but there is such a bond between her and the baby now that nothing could break it. Why, does Grandmaire want Dora back? She has never given any indication—"

"It is I who want her back." Ellen glanced about so swiftly that her black bonnet ribbons caught at her chin, and she had to brush them away before she spoke. "It's dreadful here without Dora. You have no idea. . . ."

"I'm astonished. I had no idea that the two of you were such good friends."

"We're not. But she was so good with Grandmaire—far better than I am. They *suited* each other. She read to her, coaxed and cajoled her, and never seemed to mind no matter how awkward or obnoxious Grandmaire could be. Now that she's gone, I am expected to spend practically every minute of every day in Grandmaire's company. I urged her to have this garden party, even though people said it was wrong to put on a grand show when there is so much hunger and need in Auckland now."

"Yes," said Juliette, who was also shocked by the extravagance and waste. "My dear, it might be good for you to come and help us at the soup kitchen. Once you have seen for yourself how appallingly poor some of the people are, your own situation will be bliss by comparison, no matter how much Grandmaire irritates you."

Ellen said, "You've asked me before, Aunt Juliette, and I told you that Grandmaire will not spare me. And frankly I fail to see how comparing my lot with that of others is going to improve conditions for me here. I'm sure that if you and Uncle Stephen really try, you can persuade Dora to return."

"I don't know that I can, dear. We would like to see her here where she belongs, reconciled with Grandmaire, and in fact, your Uncle Stephen . . ." She paused. "I don't think *we* have any control over the matter. It's up to Grandmaire to invite her to return."

"She won't." Ellen sighed. As she turned her head to glance about guiltily again, Juliette noticed fine lines like scratches cut into the skin on either side of her mouth. "It's all so trivial really. If only Grandmaire had been consulted about the baby in the first place."

"We didn't give her a moment's thought at the time.

Other details were more pressing. But of course, we at Mondrich House are accustomed to running our lives without Grandmaire's supervision."

"And she can't bear that. She doesn't care what happens to any of us, or how unhappy we are, just so long as she feels that *she* arranged everything."

Shocked by the naked bitterness in Ellen's voice, Juliette said, "But, my dear, you are her favorite!"

"Then I would sooner not be." Realizing that she had said far more than she had ever intended, she added pleadingly, "You won't repeat any of this, will you, Aunt?"

"Of course not. Come, dear. Take me inside, and show me this darling baby. You should bring the children to Mondrich House when you need a little air to breathe. We would always welcome you, you know."

Once they were out of sight of the gazebo, Kendrick tugged on Verona's hand and began to run, forcing her to trot after him as nimbly as her hobbled skirt would permit. She was giggling, stumbling, and when he stopped, she collapsed against him in a burst of bubbling laughter.

"Oh, Kendrick, you are *wicked,*" she said chidingly.

"I've been told that before. You must be more original."

She opened her eyes very wide, as though it took an effort to focus them. Then she laughed again. "This is fun."

"I was hoping you'd say that. Come on."

"Where are we going?"

"I'm going to show you something a real brother never could." He tugged at her hand. "Come on. This will be fun like you've never had it before."

When Lucca and Daniel returned to the gazebo with the fresh drinks and found nobody waiting, Lucca was philosophical. "She's always thinking up excuses to get away from me," she said, putting the glasses down on the rim of a stone birdbath. "But I do wish she hadn't gone off with Kendrick. I don't like him."

"Most people find him amusing," said Daniel, trying not to gaze too obviously toward the cliff path.

"Verona has a sweet nature; but she's too trusting, and sometimes I worry that she may be a little too dim for her own good. Did you hear what Kendrick said about her smile? That it reminded him of the saying 'All sunshine makes a desert'? Verona took that as a *compliment*. She didn't see that he was making fun of her. I don't know why she has to make a fool of herself with him when you are so much more attractive."

Daniel raised his eyebrows. "I s-suppose I should s-say thank you."

"It's a pleasure. That wasn't flattery, Mr. Yardley. It was a simple observation. You have a kind face and a deferential manner. It is my hope that my sister will also observe those qualities in you. Whether she has the wit to appreciate them is another matter again." She sipped at her drink. "Ah, this is much nicer than the last two. They had quite a bitter aftertaste, I thought. What is yours like, Mr. Yardley? Well, though it is pleasant talking to you, I suppose I must make some effort to find Verona. Papa gave us the strictest instructions to stay together. I wonder where she and Kendrick have gone? Do you think they might have strolled down to the beach?"

Hastily Daniel said, "Look, there's Kendrick," and when she followed the line of his arm toward the house, he added, "He's gone around there, by the r-rose arbor."

"Was Verona with him?"

"No, he was quite alone."

"Then perhaps we should go ask him where Verona went. Papa will be furious if he sees her wandering about by herself."

"She might be with Aunt Abigail," offered Daniel.

"Then we must find her, too."

Feeling wretched and silently cursing Kendrick for making him an unwilling accomplice, Daniel allowed himself to be led away

At all social gatherings in Auckland there came a time when the ladies tended to drift together to discuss gowns, illness, and other people's business, and the men congregated to mull over commerce, horse racing, and other people's business. Today the gentlemen were clustering on the veranda, and the talk was depressing. All of them had lost money recently, a few had lost everything, and most derived a morbid consolation from the feeling that they had been trapped on the same sinking ship. Not one of them suspected that greed might have had something to do with the collapse of the business community, and because the nonspeculators like Hal and Stephen kept a tactful distance, there was nobody to point this out to them.

"It's all right for you," Derwent Kine was saying to Jon. "You've got it soft for life, here in this mansion. Things are not so easy for your mother and me, you understand."

Jon tried to mask his impatience with geniality. "Where is that bluff, confident spirit that I remember so well? You can stand for Parliament again in the next general election. You told me often enough that one defeat was not a setback."

"It's different for you. You're a young man, with your whole career spread out before you. With Mrs. Yardley Peridot and all her fortune behind her, you could never fail."

"She's feeling the pinch, too," said Jon, guessing that his stepfather was leading up to something. "Grandmaire has a whole street of houses in the Surrey Hills area, and of that street only three of the houses are occupied."

"But she has no mortgages to worry about. It's well known that the Yardleys never borrow. That's where I've come undone. I borrowed to buy land, and thanks to that Bennington—sorry, Teipa—rascal, I'm properly in the stew, left with several hundred acres, which is not enough to begin to do anything with."

Jon had heard all about the encounter with Patrick and could not resist saying, "If you approach him in the right way, he may agree to purchase the land off you and combine it with his several thousand acres. I hear he's growing hops and wheat there now."

"I doubt that he would do anything to repair the damage he has caused, but I do think it would be fitting if someone in the family would make some small sacrifice to compensate me for the loss."

He's serious, thought Jon. He's serious, and he wants me to make the small sacrifice, or he'd not waste his breath discussing it with me. "Let me get you another drink," he said, reaching out for Mr. Kine's glass. "Whiskey, was it, sir?"

"Not just yet. We were talking about the family."

"Oh. I thought you meant Mr. Teipa's family. But they all are Maoris, aren't they?" And after a short silence he said, "What exactly did you have in mind?"

"You *are* interested in what I have to say? You are not entirely intent on making snappy remarks to belittle my predicament?"

"Nobody is belittling you, sir."

"Good, for I've had all of that I could stomach from your uncle. I've been looking about here, and it has occurred to me that with all the work you do for Mrs. Yardley Peridot you are fully occupied, wouldn't that be so?"

"She does keep me busy, but I like that. Work is my only recreation. It always has been so."

"As I recall. But with her business keeping you fully employed, you really do not need the extra pressure which the Provincial Council must place upon you. Everything together must add up to quite a strain."

He wants me to get out of my nice safe seat so that he can claim it back, thought Jon. Soon he will hint that I was meant to have it only until he wanted to sit in it again.

"It's the custom with newcomers to allow them to have something easily contested to begin with," said Derwent Kine. "Just until they find their feet, of course."

"Oh, of course," said Jon. "I couldn't agree more. And now you are interested in coming back on the Council, is that it? I thought those days were behind you?"

"They were, but in these hard times one must do whatever one can."

"And *whoever* one can," said Jon with a laugh. Before Mr. Kine could take offense, he added, "There's a by-election coming up in the Ponsonby electorate. Old Horvathen is planning to retire earlier than expected. An infection in the bloodstream, nasty business. I'll tell you what. I'll put your name forward at the nomination committee on Friday week. Glad to do an old friend a favor. There's Hal. I must have a word with him. He's off again in

300

a couple of days. Excuse me. Splendid talking to you. Splendid."

"But Ponsonby's a marginal seat. I'd never be able to win that one," protested Mr. Kine after Jon's back.

Jon did not appear to have heard him.

As the dusk was sliding a shade over the sky, Daniel and Kendrick pedaled home toward Mondrich House. The velocipedes transmitted every bump in the road through their solid rubber tires, and they had to steer carefully and watch the ground in front of them in order to avoid the worst ruts and potholes.

Kendrick was in such an exuberant mood that when they reached the crest of a steep slope, he did not bother to dismount. With a whoop he clutched the handlebars, stuck his legs out sideways, and flew down. The bicycle's fixed pedals whirred around so fast that they became invisible in the scatter of road dust. By the time Daniel scrambled to the bottom of the hill Kendrick was sprawled on his back in the long roadside grass, gazing up at the sky and lustily bellowing a song which had echoed in taverns since the era of the Maori wars:

We'll let the bottle pass,
And we'll have another glass,
For the men of merry, merry, merry, merry England!

Then with an upside-down grin at Daniel, who stood puffing above him, he said, "Aren't you going to ask me about the little parrot I plucked? You've not said one word about it all afternoon."

Daniel propped his machine against a tree trunk and sat down. "I don't think I want to know. Verona seems like a d-decent girl."

"Decent, ha! I've never had it so easy, boyo, as the Welshman said. Hardly ruffled her feathers. You saw her when she came back to the party. All smiles and sunshine."

Daniel said, "I don't understand how you could seduce a girl out of spite."

"When it comes to the moment of contact, it never mat-

301

ters what the original motivation was. I forget what I saw in the woman, where I am, everything. A glorious feeling." He flung his arms wide. "But you're very prim this afternoon. Who cares if it was out of spite? No, I prefer to call it revenge. Spite sounds so triflingly petty. And revenge it was. Daniel, old son, I'm going to relish that moment for the rest of my life."

Snapping off a dry grass stalk, Daniel said, "I don't see why you had to be avenged for anything. Miss Kine's done nothing to h-harm you."

Yesterday Kendrick would have reacted angrily. Now his voice was blissful as he said, "Her father turned me out of my home. He married my mother, and I shall hate them both forever, but now, whenever I think of it, I shall have the memory of today's little revenge to comfort me. It's perfect, Daniel. It's absolutely perfect."

"But what if she tells her f-father?"

Kendrick laughed. "Why would she want to do that? She's as terrified of him as you and I."

Twenty Five

"I thought that you and Hal were going to the Vintons' after the party?" said Juliette when she, Stephen, and Dora arrived home to find May reading a book on the veranda.

May waited until Dora had taken Dorinda inside, then said, "Hal and I had a disagreement, a serious one."

"It is serious only if you permit it to be," Stephen told her. He sat beside her on the porch swing, while Juliette settled on a cane chair.

"It *is* serious," said May.

"Then I'm sorry to hear it," Juliette said. "Your father and I were thinking that it really is time you two began to plan for a wedding date." She stared at May's tense face. "Would next July be rushing you?"

"Mother, we've had a *disagreement.* Of course, I don't want to set a date now."

Stephen took her hand. "What your mother means is that every engaged couple has differences of opinion. It doesn't mean that they stop caring for each other. Can you tell us about this quarrel and see if we can help?"

She stared into her lap, then burst out, "I promised to marry him on the condition that he take me to live in San Francisco, but now he says that you might be giving that position to Daniel. He told me in confidence, and I know that it will be marvelous for Daniel, and I feel so selfish being upset about it; but I had my heart set on going, I really did. Dora warned me that Hal would never give up the sea; but he was so insistent on *my* giving things up that I decided to ask him anyway, and he agreed so readily at the time that I thought everything would be wonderful. . . ."

Stephen said, "Then each of you inflicted wrong on the other. No, my pet. If your engagement was conditioned on both of you sacrificing things you value, then it was no fair bargain. It sounds as though you deceived each other. I cannot imagine that Hal would willingly give up the sea, and you love your photography. But what surprises me is your anxiousness to go back to San Francisco. I thought you were happy here."

I've hurt his feelings now, she thought. Aloud she said, "I do like it here. It's interesting, and I've made lots of friends, but . . ." She gazed at him appealingly. "I keep doing the wrong thing here. I meet with so much disapproval."

"You'd find the same thing in San Francisco," Juliette pointed out. "It's true that here in the colonies people are extremely conservative, but I think that even in California you would want to be in the vanguard of fashion. It's your nature, May, and you will be criticized for it no matter where you go."

"Your mother is right, pet. You must learn to choose. Follow the safe path and have society's approval, or do as you please and hang the consequences!"

"Stephen, I don't think we should be *encouraging* her. . . ."

He laughed. "Why not? She gets some of this rebelliousness from you, you know. Sweet Olivine, you always had more courage than any dozen other young ladies put together. But this quarrel with Hal worries me," he added seriously. "You haven't got doubts about marrying him, have you?"

May stared at her hands in her lap.

Juliette said quickly, "Of course she hasn't, have you, dear?"

"Then, if your heart is set on San Francisco, would you like to live there for two or three years? I could spare Hal for the Pacific run for that long, and if Daniel is there, you'll not be entirely alone while Hal is at sea. Would that please you?"

"Very much." She looked searchingly into his face, then

into her mother's. "This marriage means a lot to you, doesn't it?"

Juliette said, "It does, dear. Especially to your father."

"It will make Hal my son," said Stephen. "But above all, we want you to be happy. You know that, don't you?"

"Yes, I do. And I appreciate it."

"Then it's settled," said Juliette happily. "A winter wedding then. Hal can come to dinner this evening, and we'll discuss all the details. Oh, this *is* exciting, isn't it?"

Shortly before ten o'clock the next morning a hansom cab stopped outside the gates, and Verona Kine alighted. She stood for a few moments, then squared her thin shoulders and walked toward the house.

May was discussing Bobby Terrill's first independently taken photographs with him on the gatehouse porch. He saw Verona's hesitation and said, "Excuse me, miss, but there's young Miss Kine, come here all alone."

"It can't be," said May, but she set out and caught up to her near the veranda.

"Oh, thank goodness," said Verona. "I was so afraid that I might have to explain my mission to the butler. Is Kendrick here? I went to Fintona, but Tawa said he had not stayed there last night, so I hoped to find him here."

"He was here at breakfast time," said May, noting the girl's unhappy expression and the nervous tremor in her voice. What had Kendrick done now? "I think they might be in the stables. Daniel said something about adjusting the handlebars on one of their velocipede contraptions. If you wait on the veranda, I shall see if I can find him."

"No. Please let me come with you. He might not come back with you if he knows it's me. And I must talk to him. I *must*."

"Has Aunt Abigail sent you on a peace mission?" asked May, taken aback by Verona's vehemence. When Verona bit her lip and did not reply, May continued, "I suppose she saw how well you were getting on with Kendrick yesterday and thought that you might be able to persuade him to return home. Well, good luck to you, but don't be afraid of him. Kendrick wouldn't harm you."

Verona's face paled, and she looked even more frightened.

Kendrick and Daniel were in the stables workshop. Smoke from their cigars made a gray haze in the small room. Their laughter cut off abruptly when they saw Verona. Neither of them spoke. Because both looked guilty, May assumed they had been interrupted in the middle of a smutty conversation.

Verona said, "May I please speak to Kendrick alone?"

"Of course," said May.

As Daniel made to leave, Kendrick grabbed at his arm, but Daniel shook himself free. "Good morning, M-Miss Kine," he said as he stepped into the sunshine.

Verona did not look at him. She moved into the dim workshop until she was very close to Kendrick. Her eyes were enormous, and her low voice shook.

"You took advantage of me, Kendrick, and you shouldn't have done that to me. You are going to have to marry me now," she said.

"That boy is downright irresponsible," declared Stephen as he scanned the note that had been left beside his breakfast plate. "He's been home only ten minutes, and now he's dashed off again, without so much as a by-your-leave. It's Kendrick at the back of this, I shouldn't wonder. What do you know about it, Dora? What trouble is your shiftless young brother in now?"

"Stephen, please." Juliette glanced from Dora's passive face to her husband's annoyed one. He was taking less and less trouble to conceal his dislike of the woman, but Dora seemed unaware of it so far.

Dora said, "I don't mind, Aunt Juliette. But you'd best ask Grandmaire why the boys have run away. Wherever they've gone, you can be sure she will have put money in their pockets to help them. Very generous to some, Grandmaire is," she added bitterly.

Stephen slapped the letter down. "Daniel says he doesn't know how long they'll be away. Weeks or months, he says. What does he think he's playing at? I spend a tidy sum to have him educated, and now that he could be of some assistance, he dashes off. Well, whatever the trouble is, they both can come back and face up to it like men. I'll send someone after them and have them back here before you can say 'Kendrick Bennington.' That I promise you."

But discovering their whereabouts was not as straight-forward a process as Stephen had anticipated. Grandmaire would not help; she assured him that even if she did know, she would not tell him. All she would do was hint that they had been driven away for reasons that meant "life or death" to one of them.

And that means death to Kendrick, I'll be bound. And much deserved, no doubt, thought Stephen.

A survey of the shipping offices turned up nothing, and though Stephen sent men to question all the sailors along the waterfront, he knew this would be fruitless. There were hundreds of coastal vessels coming and going; it was easy for anybody to slip aboard one of them. Almost all these vessels were Maori-owned, and all were crewed by Maoris, many of whom would not answer questions on principle.

Still furious, and chafing with frustration, Stephen gave up the search.

It was not until May that Daniel arrived back in Auck-land, alone. It was gusty, blowing in damp breaths, and as he walked along the wharf, the gaslights were being lit. The streets downtown were noisier than he remembered, and empty warehouses had been turned into temporary housing barns for the homeless unemployed. Despite the wind, the stench of drains and urine filled the air. Children with rags wrapped around their feet tugged at his jacket and begged him to buy tobacco or shoelaces, matches or apples. A tout from the Stone Jug Inn matched stride with him and began to talk about an illegal bare-knuckle boxing match between the local champion and a huge Maori who was tattooed on face, thighs, and but-tocks. Daniel thought of Derwent Kine's tobacco pouch and shook his head. The tout kept after him until they were halfway up Queen Street, where a uniformed consta-ble was checking that shop doors were secure. Daniel paused to ask the constable the time, and the tout disap-peared.

At Wellesley Street he boarded a horse-drawn bus. It was cramped and smelled of sweat. Dirty straw was scattered on the floor for the passengers to spit on if they wanted. The driver stared when Daniel spoke. People with accents like his seldom rode on buses. Daniel sat at the back. He stared out of the window at the luminous gaslights, the dark buildings, and the pale spreads of tent camps, lit from within. When the bus passed near Fintona, he shouted to the driver to let him out.

Twenty Six

Early on that morning in February Daniel and Kendrick had wangled a ride aboard a coastal freighter, a twelve-ton scow carrying oil and candles up the coast. The skipper, a genial Maori, had been amused by their predicament. He put them ashore at a tiny settlement called Waimaori, or Freshwater, telling them that if they struck inland, they could soon find a profitable occupation digging for kauri gum, which was exported and used in the manufacture of varnish.

"It's hard work, but there's good money," he told them. "And nobody will find you there. Just a few Maoris and a dozen farms, maybe, and Mrs. Tucker at the store. She'll tell you how to get started."

Mrs. Tucker was blowsy and beaten, with three toddlers tied to her dirty apron strings. "So they don't fall in the fire," she explained. "Lost one that way an' don't aim ter lose another. Gumdigging, hey? Good lark if yer work hard. Yer can harvest the gum from cuts in the bark or climb up inter the treetops ter see if there's chunks of it there, but the best way's digging. Land hereabouts is swampy and soft. Good, easy going. I'll buy all yer can bring me, as long as it's scraped clean. Got ter have every speck of rust off ter fetch the best prices. Some of them Maori kids come in with a sack full an' only the top layer's scraped proper. I tip it out an' they swear because I'll not give top price for that. No use ter anybody if it ain't properly scraped."

She sold them two shovels, knives, long metal probes for feeling in the ground for chunks of gum, buckets, pannikins, and enough food for a month. "If we survive a month

309

on a diet like this," said Kendrick glumly as Daniel packed the flour, salt, and potatoes into flax baskets.

Mrs. Tucker hobbled out into the yard and banged on an old tin bucket. Almost immediately a young Maori boy appeared, listened sullenly while she berated him in his own language, then led a swaybacked horse around to the door and loaded it up with the baskets of goods.

"See that he brings the baskets back, will you?" Mrs. Tucker said. "He'll take you up inter the valley. If you stay with the Austrians after that, you'll not go wrong."

"What Austrians?" asked Kendrick, but Mrs. Tucker had already shuffled back inside.

From that moment they were virtually on their own. The Maori boy managed to tell them that his name was Honi, or John, and clearly indicated at the end of the journey that he expected payment, refusing to unload the baskets until they had doled out enough coins; but beyond that basic communication he could tell them nothing, and they discovered soon enough that the Austrians could not speak English either.

There was nobody at the camp when they arrived, giving them a chance to see what had to be done. By evening they had fashioned a thatch and sacking tent and had made beds of heaped fern fronds and a fireplace from round river stones. While Daniel stowed the goods away in a rough safe, Kendrick surveyed the valley—a wide and desolate swamp, covered with tea tree scrub. And all around the edges, stretching as far into the distance as they could see, was a vast kauri forest, battalion after battalion of tall thick-trunked trees.

"They're beautiful, aren't they?" said Daniel, tipping his head back and looking up to where the bole swelled out into branches. "There's n-nothing like this in England. How far do you suppose it is from the ground to where the branches begin. S-Sixty feet? Seventy?"

"Who cares?" said Kendrick.

"All that smooth trunk and not a bump or a branch. No w-wonder they make such magnificent timber trees."

"Best thing for them," said Kendrick, slipping a cigar from his inner pocket and biting off the end. "This place gives me the bloody creeps. Trees, trees, and more trees.

It's almost enough to persuade me to submit myself to Mr. Kine's tender mercies." He laughed shortly. "On second thoughts, no. Any one of these trees looks a damned sight better than the determined Miss Kine. When she stood there and told me I had to marry her, I could feel the cold rim of her father's pistol at my temple."

The Austrians arrived in camp just after dusk. There were seven of them, all men and all middle-aged, dark, and swarthy. While one lit the fire and cooked their evening meal, the others tipped their haversack loads of gum out and set to scraping it. Their chatter was loud, continuous, and unintelligible. They ignored the newcomers. When the food was ready, they sat in a circle, all eating out of the one deep pot, scooping up the hot food with stiff rags of bread. Nobody spoke until the pot had been wiped out.

"I wish we could talk to them," said Daniel. "I'll wager that they could tell us some interesting stories."

"They're savages," said Kendrick scornfully. "Consider their manners. Listen to that belching. And their language sounds primitive."

"I think it sounds pleasant," said Daniel, stretching out on his springy bed and gazing up at the silvery-barked moonlit trees. "Have you ever considered how we plunder the land and the sea? Nothing is safe from us, not coal, not minerals, not gold, and n-not even humble kauri gum. Did you know that the Maoris used kauri gum for all sorts of things? Uncle Samuel told me that they used to burn it in their kumara plantations to keep the m-moths from laying their eggs on the plants. They used the gum smoke for tattooing pitch, and they even used to ch-chew it."

"It would break your teeth. That stuff's like iron."

Daniel was pleased that he was even listening. "N-not the soft, fresh gum."

"Go to sleep," said Kendrick. "I want to dream about women, and I don't want Maori *wahines* intruding. Especially gum-chewing wahines."

Kendrick planned to stay away three months; then Daniel would return to Auckland to find out if it was safe for Kendrick to come home. He figured that if Derwent Kine were baying for his blood, he might as well plan on never returning, but if it were quiet, he would risk coming back.

They had only been on the gum field a short time, however, before Kendrick declared that he was bored, frustrated, and utterly miserable.

Daniel refrained from pointing out that if Kendrick did some work, he might actually find it enjoyable. He himself was past the stage of aching muscles and hideous fatigue. Now that his body was accustomed to tough physical exertion, Daniel discovered that he relished the new sensations of strength and fitness. He was pleasurably conscious of his own body, and though the changes were slight as yet, he was aware that his arms were thickening, his shoulders broadening, and his chest was beginning to deepen.

"It's been only six weeks, and we're doing so well," he argued. "We're h-halfway there already."

"I think I'll go back to Fintona and ask Grandmaire to hide me. If I look at another pot of beans, I'll throw up. I've been hallucinating about food, and when I go to sleep at nights, I don't think about luscious ladies, but luscious joints swimming in gravy. It's a desperate situation, I tell you. Let's go home."

"You're not serious. You c-can't be."

"And why not? What is more serious than a man's stomach, apart from his—"

"You can't go back yet. The servants would tell Mr. Kine, and he'd have you out of there in no time at all. You don't s-seriously think that Grandmaire's servants would protect you surely?"

"Perhaps you're right." He recalled some of the things he had said and done to the comelier of the young Maori help at Fintona. "Yes, on reflection you would be right. Ah, well. We stick to our original plan, and I learn to love bean stodge."

But soon even Daniel was wishing they could return. The weather soured. Cold rain soaked the camp. The flour mildewed. Gum digging in the rain was no fun. All the novelty had gone, and with it most of Daniel's enthusiasm. Every morning they left after the Austrians and were back well before them in the evening. Now their gum hoard grew with depressing slowness. Kendrick turned morose. He was lazier than before. Often he would plead illness and send Daniel out into the gray dawn alone, staying behind on the pretext of scraping gum. The heap of un-scraped gum never seemed to dwindle.

One evening he showed Daniel what he had been carving on those days in camp. Very pleased with himself, he produced an amber statuette some ten inches long and three inches thick.

"What do you think of this?" He beamed. "This will make the Auckland girls sit up and take notice, don't you think? How would you like to have a member like that, hey, boyo?"

"It's . . ." Daniel could not think of anything to say. "You're not going to show that to ladies, are you?"

Kendrick ran a forefinger along the length of it and over the bulbous tip. "Ladies won't know what it is, but if they're *not* ladies, they'll be impressed. Don't look shocked." He rolled the statuette into a square of sacking and tucked it into the side of his swag roll. "I'm starting to look forward to going home," he said happily.

A few days later a new group arrived: a man in his thirties with two children, a boy of about ten, and a girl of fourteen or fifteen. They were no friendlier than the other Austrians, but the girl smiled at Daniel and Kendrick occasionally, until her father noticed and cuffed her. She wore black stockings and a black skirt topped with a faded red jacket. Daniel liked her because in the evenings, while the men sat smoking, she perched nearby, a goat-skin fiddle balanced on her knee, and sang to them. Her songs were simple, repetitive, and mournful, but Daniel was impressed that even those could be played with only one string and a short fiber bow. While he listened, he remembered the Gypsies' campfire he had sat by on a holiday on the wild Cornish coast.

One afternoon Kendrick pulled himself up out of the trench in which he and Daniel were working.

"It's my stomach again," he said. "This griping pain is crippling me. It kept me awake all night."

"Sit there and rest awhile," said Daniel, straightening and wiping his sweaty brow with the back of his hand. "I'll work on only another couple of hours; then we can knock off."

Kendrick grimaced. "You stay here. I'll go back to camp

313

and dose myself with some of that ipecac. When I feel better, I'll come back."

"Are you sure you'll be all right?" The ipecac tasted so vile that Kendrick would usually take it only after heavy persuasion. He *must* be feeling ill.

"I'll be back soon." He grimaced again, then hobbled away through the scrubby manuka toward camp.

Daniel worked for another hour and stopped to eat. He had wiped the worst of the mud from his hands and was pulling the stopper from his water bottle when he heard Kendrick shout. He paused, bottle at his lips, and was frozen like that, waiting, when a high, tearing scream rolled over him and on down the valley.

Daniel dropped the water bottle. There was something so chilling in that scream that he could feel his limbs draining as the sound penetrated his body. Something unspeakable had happened to Kendrick.

Abandoning his tools and haversack, he sped across the marshy ground. Coarse manuka branches slapped at his legs and scratched the arms; all the while his mind raced faster than his pounding legs. What can have happened? he wondered, his thoughts frantic. He guessed an accident; Kendrick could have somehow slipped and fallen into the fire, badly burning himself. That would explain the shout, the interval, and then the scream when the pain struck him. But why the silence now? Had he passed out?

Daniel was scrabbling in his mind for the best ways to treat severe burns and wondering how best to get his friend to a doctor—if there *was* such a person within treating distance—when, some fifty yards from camp and still out of sight of the sacking tents, he was stopped short by the sound of the girl crying, overlaid by the noise of the Austrians arguing.

Oh, God, no, thought Daniel, dropping to all fours. Creeping forward swiftly and keeping under cover of the scrubby vegetation, he moved up until, by raising his head, he could see into the clearing.

At first he was confused by the activity. The Austrians were milling about, jabbering and gesticulating excitedly; the tense atmosphere reminded Daniel of a pack of hounds before the hunt. At one side, just outside a tent, the girl sat crying. Her brother hovered behind her, patting her hair in an effort to calm her, but she wailed on, ignoring him, rubbing her eyes with both fists.

And then Daniel saw Kendrick.

He was sprawled on his back on a bumpy hillock between the tents. Daniel caught only occasional glimpses of him as the group of men tightened and loosened, but he saw enough to tell that Kendrick was either unconscious or dead. Though nobody appeared to be guarding him, and he did not seem to be physically bound in any way, Daniel knew instinctively that he was the Austrians' prisoner. They had caused his scream.

Daniel tried to think calmly. If Kendrick were just unconscious, he could come to at any time, and if Daniel were close by, he would be in a position to help him. He could not possibly rescue Kendrick while he was immobile, of course, but even a few whispered words of encouragement, a plan of escape could cheer Kendrick. It was obvious that he was in a nasty situation. That girl was still wailing, and the men were ignoring her. She and Kendrick must have been surprised in a very compromising situation.

Cautiously Daniel made his way in a semicircle around to their tent. Under the back corner peg was a leather pouch containing what remained of Grandmaire's contribution to their journey. With the idea of retrieving it, he dragged himself along on his stomach, keeping the hulk of the tent between himself and the Austrians. With both hands he wrestled the tent peg, forcing it until the sweat ran into his eyes. It refused to budge.

"Damn," he muttered under his breath. For a few moments he lay there, panting, and then remembered the all-purpose knife they kept up under the tent ridge. Taking enormous care not to rustle the sacking, Daniel slithered into the tent by lifting up the lower edge and sliding his body underneath. He crouched in the tent, trembling with tension. In front of him the flap bulged open so that he could see the Austrians' boots as they tramped around the clearing. Kendrick was out of sight, and though he could have seen him by stooping to peer through the crack, he did not dare move.

With the knife in one hand he slid out again, and

crouched behind the tent. The Austrians were still arguing loudly, and the knowledge that they were absorbed in their conversation gave Daniel enough confidence to take a quick peek around the corner of the tent, where manuka bushes partially screened him from the clearing.

Kendrick's face was visible now. He appeared to be calm, and Daniel was relieved to see that his chest was rising and falling. He was not dead. Something had been spread on the front of his body. It looked like the girl's red jacket. Daniel looked more closely, then realized with mounting horror that the front of Kendrick's trousers had been torn away. His lap was a puddle of blood.

Now the chill that had gripped him with the sound of the scream returned to freeze him to the ground where he lay.

He was unable to move, unable to think, not even able to drag himself into hiding. All he could do was watch numbly while four of the Austrians picked Kendrick's sagging body up and carried him away toward the east rim of the valley. Two of the others followed, both carrying thick bundles of rope, while the remaining two stood talking in the center of the clearing.

Soon Daniel's senses thawed enough for him to realize that these two were arguing about him, and from their gestures and tone he gathered that they were trying to gauge how far away he was working and whether he might have heard any of the disturbance. He now knew that he himself was in very real danger.

Abandoning all thought of digging up the money, Daniel crawled away, then struck out in the direction the men had taken Kendrick. While he moved across open country, he was able to follow their tracks easily on the swampy ground. Once he stumbled and almost fell in a spongy hollow. He stretched out his hand to grab for something to steady himself and saw to his horror that he had almost fallen into a bright splash of fresh blood. Sick with apprehension, he hurried on.

At the edge of the valley the tracks stopped. Daniel was sure that the men had taken Kendrick into the bush and feared that they planned to hang him there. He stood in the gloom, surrounded by the tall silver trunks, listening for some sound that would indicate which way they had gone, but the forest had absorbed them without trace. The silence was frightening. Daniel waited, indecisive, listening, until what seemed like hours later, when he heard their voices.

As soon as they passed by, he came out from the clump of fern in which he had concealed himself and pushed in through the undergrowth, trying to retrace their steps; but it was already beginning to grow dark, and in the thickening dusk his eyes played tricks on him. Bodies seemed to materialize, dangling from branches, only to turn into saplings as he approached. When he dared call out to Kendrick, his voice echoed back to mock him. He floundered around in a nightmare until he collapsed, exhausted, at the foot of a tree.

When he woke next morning, he realized that his nightmare was very real. In the distance he could hear the Austrians shouting to each other as they tramped through the bush toward him. It was immediately clear to Daniel that they were searching for him; he had not returned to camp and therefore knew what they had done to Kendrick. If their search were successful, he would not survive it.

Dazed with fear, he fled, somehow making his way to the coast. Traveling by night, he followed it south until he reached the next settlement. A coastal freighter brought him back to Auckland, where he stumbled into the servants' entrance at Fintona, ate an enormous meal, and fell asleep with his head on the kitchen table.

The next afternoon Grandmaire, Ellen, and May listened in silence while Daniel told them what had happened in as much detail as he felt was fit for their ears.

Grandmaire frowned when he had finished. "Did you just run away and leave without finding out what had happened to poor Kendrick?"

"He m-must have been dead, Grandmaire. I called and called for hours, and if he were alive, he would have answered."

"The men would not have come hunting Daniel if Kendrick were alive," May said. "They must have murdered him and would have done the same thing to Daniel, too."

"Don't talk of death and murder. I'll not believe that

Kendrick is dead. He's probably wandering about in the bush, lost, since you abandoned him."

He'd not wander far with those injuries, thought Daniel, but said nothing.

Ellen had been standing with her back to the others, staring out across the archery lawn while the story unfolded. Now she turned and said, "This fate would have befallen Kendrick sooner or later. I'm sorry he's dead, and it's terrible that he was murdered; but sooner or later someone would have killed him."

"What nonsense are you talking, child?" Grandmaire rapped her cane for emphasis.

"Kendrick was an unscrupulous womanizer."

"He was a rascal, but a decent young man for all that," protested Grandmaire. "I know you never liked him, Ellen, but that gives you no cause to make unpardonable accusations."

"Are they?" countered Ellen. "Let me tell you that he even tried to force his attentions on me when he met me on the ship on my way back from Wellington. Me, a young wife with a babe in arms. And now he is dead. Though Daniel is being tactful about the reason for this sudden violence against our Kendrick, we know him well enough to guess."

"Ellen, please! I insist that you stop this at once." Grandmaire rang the silver bell, saying, "You are making me feel ill."

"You should know everything about this, Grandmaire. Why he and Daniel ran away in the first place, for example. What he told you about a gambling debt may have been true enough, but there was more than money behind his urgency to get away. At your garden party he gave Verona Kine alcoholic drinks, and when she was as silly as a fowl, he enticed her down to the beach and seduced her."

"Surely Kendrick wouldn't . . ." began May. Then she recalled Verona's white, unhappy face.

"Oh, it's true enough," persisted Ellen in her flat tones. "Verona told him that he would have to marry her, so being the gentleman that he is, he ran away. It's true, isn't it, Daniel?" she demanded when Grandmaire's cane rapped to shatter the line of her story.

He looked bleakly at Grandmaire and nodded.

Ellen's voice grew bitter. "And now Verona is going to have a baby. Yes, a baby. Kendrick's baby. You can imagine the state of terror she is in that her father will find out. And of course, he will. She cannot hide a thing like this for much longer. That's why she keeps coming here, Grandmaire. She hopes that there has been some word of him, that somehow she can find him and persuade him to marry her and save her from ruin. Who will tell her Kendrick is dead? Who will tell her that her life is over, that she might as well be dead, too, for nobody will ever want her now?" In the awful silence that fell she stared at each face in turn, and May was shocked by the hardness in her eyes. Finally Ellen said, "If he's alive, I'll be happy for him, and if he's dead, I'll be sorry; but if he's being punished for his sins, then it's no more than he deserves."

As she reached the door, Tawa entered. Ellen said, "We have just received some bad news. *Matua* would like a drink. Would you please fetch her a glass of schnapps?"

Outside, Bobby waited for May in the dogcart. Daniel paused out of earshot and said, "You g-go home alone. I'll come later."

May was afraid his courage would evaporate. "No, Daniel. Please come home with me now. I doubt that Father will be angry when he hears what you have been through. We've all been so worried about you." She shrugged. "My wedding has even been postponed. It was supposed to be on Hal's next shore leave, but of course, we couldn't make arrangements with you missing. Father will help find out what has happened to Kendrick, I know he will. Please come home now. Once you've told him everything, I know it will be all right."

"No. I'll come home later. I'm g-going to see Miss Kine."

"Verona? Are you going to tell her?"

"It's best if I do. I feel responsible for what happened. I tried to stop Kendrick, but I didn't try hard enough."

May said, "I feel so sorry for her. Ellen was right, you know. Her life *is* utterly ruined. All she can look forward to is shame and disgrace."

"That's why I'm g-going to see her father, too."

319

"Why? Whatever for?"

He was walking away from her, as if anticipating that she might try to dissuade him. She noticed that the jacket he was wearing did not fit him properly across the shoulders, then realized it was one of Kendrick's. Of course. He had none of his own clothes with him, and all of Kendrick's were at Fintona.

"Daniel!" she called. "Why are you going to see Mr. Kine? You're not going to cause any trouble, are you?"

He turned and swept Kendrick's shooting cap off his head in an extravagant bow. The sunlight seemed to dissolve into his buttercolored hair. "Me, cause trouble?" he said. "Most certainly not. I'm g-going to ask Mr. Kine for his daughter's hand in marriage."

Twenty Seven

People said that the worst of the depression would not reach Auckland. It was too prosperous, too healthy to be affected. They went on saying this despite the signs all around them. For three years the misery had been steadily increasing.

Poverty scarred the city. The factory section was occupied by squatters and rats. Samuel's sawmills had been forced to close. A temporary measure until new orders come in, he told the men as he paid them off. He felt like a traitor, but even Patrick's flourishing breweries could employ only so many workmen and delivery wagon drivers.

The few small workshops that managed to remain open soon found that they were facing a new enemy, industrial unrest. Caught in a vise between rising costs and falling profits, many factory owners tried to keep going by cutting wages. Trade unions formed almost overnight, it seemed, to fight this injustice. The new Bootmakers' Union struck so often in the futile attempt to preserve wage levels that the newspapers began to call the members the Fighting Bootmakers. Nobody smiled. Life was grim. The Auckland City Council employed old men to break rocks for the roads, but many more starved to death. Bodies covered with sacks and old newspapers were found in doorways and huddled in alleys.

People stopped being shocked. It was worse on the South Island, they kept saying. There it was freezing cold, and there were thousands more unemployed. When the touring Welsh rugby team played the Canterbury side at Christchurch, many of the players kept their overcoats on throughout the game, so bitter was the wind off the mountains. When the newspaper suspended publication for a few days, hundreds of old men died in the parks, frozen without the wadding of discarded papers inside their jackets. In Auckland people read about it and shook their heads.

Stephen stopped going to his clubs. Inside, the conversation was unrelieved gloom, and outside, beggars waited. Once Stephen asked a strong young man why he was reduced to this, and the man sneered at his ignorance. Nippers are the only ones with jobs now, he said. Nippers and women. Why hire a man when a child does the work for a quarter of the money?

Have faith in the future, Stephen wanted to say. Cargoes of frozen meat were already being shipped to Europe and sold as fast as they could be unloaded. A time of great prosperity was at hand, he felt certain.

But he said nothing. The young man with the outstretched palm was not interested in the fairy-tale future. His ears were deaf to words of encouragement.

Stephen employed a hundred jobless men to landscape twelve acres of sea frontage to make a park for the city. They worked by day, and at night vandals came in. Young trees were uprooted. Fountains were smashed. Walls and paths were ripped out, and the flagstones scattered.

Stephen could not understand how people could behave destructively toward something of their own; he posted guards at Whenuahakari, young men to sleep in the orchard and gardens. It provided work, Stephen told Juliette when she protested the fortification of Mondrich House. Every single job was a patch to help hold Auckland together.

With this in mind, he closed the San Francisco graving dock so that all Mondrich Line refitting would have to be carried out in Auckland. Daniel wrote in protest, saying that the idea was needlessly expensive. The San Francisco dock was more modern and better equipped.

Stephen proudly showed Juliette the letters, saying, "I never thought the day would come when my own son tried to tell me what to do. I must say that I had doubts, serious doubts, about the wisdom of sending him off after that

322

tragic business with Kendrick, but he knows what he's about. He's making a splendid fist of that end of our Pacific operations. We're managing to cut the opposition and turn a tidy profit *and* keep up our reputation for safe respectability."

"I hope his marriage turns out as happily." Juliette sighed as she put on her coat. "Verona seems so shallow. Her letters contain nothing but descriptions of clothes and hairstyles. There is never more than a passing mention of the baby. Benedict Yardley. I do wish she could have chosen a simpler name. Or called the boy Stephen."

"Cheer up, Sweet Olivine. They might have chosen Derwent."

Juliette shuddered. When she finished tying her bonnet, she said, "At the time I was horrified by the suddenness of everything: Daniel appearing home, the tragedy, then the marriage and Daniel going away. And that very premature baby . . . It all seemed indecently hasty."

"Sometimes things are best done quickly," said Stephen, not meeting her eye.

"But now I think it's all for the best. Abby would never have given Daniel a moment's peace. She is still convinced, despite all the searches, that Daniel invented that story about the Austrians and that Kendrick is staying away to spite her."

"He's dead, all right. Daniel would never have offered to ma—" He broke off, then resumed, saying, "Are you off to the soup kitchen now?"

"The chore we all dread," she said with a smile. "Never mind. We must do what we can to help."

Along with other society ladies, those from the Yardley household took their turn serving bread and stew to long queues of needy at the Society of Ladies' soup kitchen, which was operating at the foot of Queen Street near the railway station. Juliette helped on Tuesdays and Thursdays, while Dora and May did their service every Friday and Sunday.

May loathed the work. She had begun with the optimistic view that because she would be giving assistance to the poor, she would find this an uplifting, satisfying experi-

323

ence. In her mind she pictured the poor as an endless mass of hungry people who would smile gratefully at her as she filled their bowls and pots with nourishing food.

The reality was disillusioning. They worked in a stark, drafty hut with an open counter along one side. There was nowhere to sit down and no time to rest. The stew was watery and had an unpleasantly oily smell. Dora speculated sourly that it was whale meat, or horse flesh, and May, not sure whether she was serious, felt nauseated whenever she leaned over the top of one of the huge pots and caught a strong whiff of the aroma. It astonished her that the people not only came back day after day to receive it but seemed to *like* it. Many brought spoons with them and, once they were served, leaned against the wall across the street, eagerly scooping stew into their mouths. Just to watch them made May feel ill.

The poor people did not behave as May thought they should. Instead of lining up patiently, they pushed and jostled. They never thanked her but argued she had not given them enough. They squabbled with each other, accusing each other of cheating by coming back a second and third time in the same day. May listened incredulously, but Dora laughed.

"What do you expect? That they say, 'Please, ma'am, thank you, ma'am, after you, ma'am'? Why should they be gracious to each other? They hate what they have to do, coming here like beggars to fill their children's bellies."

"Dora!"

"You don't know a thing, May Yardley. *You* expect to be happy, and *they* don't even expect to have food on their tables. They hate us, did you realize that?"

"Of course they don't," she said nervously. "We're helping them."

"If you don't believe me," said Dora in the authoritative manner May found intensely irritating, "look into their faces."

But May did not believe her until one afternoon when they were preparing to close. The day's rations had been exhausted, and as usual, there were still throngs of people pushing hopefully up to the counter. One woman thrust a battered tin billycan at May and said, "Please, miss, can't you find a little somethin' to scrape from the sides of the pots? Anythin' will do. Please, miss."

The "please" attracted Dora's attention. "Why, I know you, don't I?" she said. "Hettie, isn't it? Hettie Ireland?" And in the beaten-looking face May recognized traces of the young girl Kendrick had intimidated that long-ago night at Grandmaire's party. Almost seven years had elapsed since that evening. Young Hettie Ireland had looked about fifteen; this woman had the face of a forty-year-old. She wore a dirty winter-weight coat and a sagging felt hat, and she looked so embarrassed at being found out that May took her container and turned away out of pity, scraping what congealing scraps she could from the stew containers.

Dora was not so reticent. Ignoring the angry clamors from the other customers, she said, "Are you married, Hettie? Do you have a family?"

"Four wee ones, Miss Dora. Three girls and a baby boy."

"And is your husband out of work?"

"He ran off, Miss Dora. We was turned out of our home, an' there ain't no places in the Charity Hall for men or for children with fathers, so he ran off. He said it were better this way. At least we got a corner to sleep in an' food if we're lucky. Oh, thank you, miss," she said to May. "The good Lord bless you."

She pushed her way through the crowd and disappeared. It was then, gazing after her, that May was aware of the hostility on the other women's faces as they drummed their empty containers on the counter, moving away only when she and Dora and other women together lifted the counter and swung it up like a shutter to block off the gap.

"There," said Dora. "And thank goodness that's the last of them until Sunday. I'm glad we work Sundays. That's the one good thing about this job. It does beat reading the Bible all day."

The other women looked at each other without comment. Since emerging from the shadows of Fintona, Dora was gaining quite a reputation as an outspoken "character."

May was silent, too. She shivered, frozen to her core by what she had seen. All her life she had been careful to respect the privilege of her position, as she had been instructed. Now, for the first time, she was seeing the unbridgeable chasm that stretched between herself and these women. They did not look up to her but saw her as someone to envy and despise.

Though this revelation jolted her, May smothered the unpleasant feelings. On her workdays she dressed soberly and went off in the trap with Dora, conscious that she had much to be thankful for. She was happy and comfortable and had interesting friends at the Arts Institute. This year it seemed likely that she would win the Silver Distinction Award for the fourth year in succession. And Hal—albeit reluctantly—had agreed that marriage would not put an end to her photographic activity.

The wedding, which had been postponed after Daniel and Kendrick's disappearance, had been postponed still longer while searches were made for Kendrick. Now, at last, preparations were being made for a small New Year's Day wedding. Juliette took May to the dressmaker's to look at patterns for opulent wedding gowns and hid her disappointment when she chose a simple ready-made silk dress instead.

As the year waned and December approached, May grew more and more depressed. Juliette could see that she was unhappy and tried to bolster her with anxious attention. Every day she mentioned how delighted she and Stephen were about the wedding and how prewedding nerves were nothing to worry about. After all, she had seen so little of Hal last winter, what with his having to help on those searches for his poor brother. They would be able to make up for the separation with the lovely long American honeymoon that was planned. What a pity that Daniel and Verona could not be at the wedding, but May would be able to describe it all to them when they went to settle in San Francisco on their way back from New York. And perhaps in a year or two Juliette and Stephen could visit for a holiday and really enjoy the grandchildren. Stephen would be so proud. ... .

May tried to laugh but was suddenly confronted by the vivid recollection of Patrick's speech about her future.

"What is it, dear?" asked Juliette anxiously. "You look as though something had walked over your grave."

"Someone once described how my life would be when I married Hal. It seemed unreal at the time, but now I can see how accurate the description was."

"That's nice, dear."

Is it? thought May. The memory disturbed her. After dinner she took a lamp up to her room and rummaged through her desk until she found the leather folder that held her long-ago letters to Hal. As she read about the outing to Alcatraz Island and the day at Woodward's Pleasure Gardens, she was touched by the intense feeling of adoration shining through the words. I loved Hal completely then, she thought wistfully. I worshiped him and dreamed hopelessly of becoming his wife. And here I am now, almost on the eve of the wedding, twisted inside with a discontent I cannot fathom.

After taking her locket from its hiding place behind her handkerchief sachet, she prized it open. That Hal she had adored stared solemnly back at her. She felt nothing, save mild regret. Oh, Hal, this is not what I wanted for us both, she thought in despair. I wanted excitement, rapture, delirious happiness. . . .

She wondered, as she often did, whether her discontent was somehow connected with Patrick, then pushed the idea away by reminding herself that Patrick never thought about *her*. Since that evening at the cottage she had not once set eyes on him. From town gossip she knew he had been to Auckland several times, but there was never any sign of life at the cottages. It hurt to think he avoided her, but she listened for news of him just the same. Most of the gossip about him was based on envy. He was flourishing in these hard times, for the poorer people were, the more they drank. Patrick was now reputed to be one of the wealthiest people in Auckland.

In mid-December Samuel arrived, chirping with news about the farming ventures in the Waikato. The Maoris were moving back onto the land and beginning to make profitable use of it. Hops and barley were supplying the new factories at Hamilton, and not only were the ales and soft drinks doing well on the local market, but a scheme

327

was being investigated to export bottled mineral water to Europe. Someone was going overseas to establish market contacts. May wondered if the "someone" was Patrick, but he was never personally mentioned in any of Samuel's chatter.

One afternoon, after May had returned from a Christmas shopping expedition, she hurried upstairs to where Samuel was basking quietly in the sun.

"I thought I saw Patrick today," she said. "Dora and I were coming out of Merrington's, and I thought I saw him riding past in a cab. Is he in Auckland?"

Samuel kept his eyes closed as she sank into a chair beside him. "He's staying at a hotel before he goes off to Europe."

"So it is he who is going."

"Yes, and soon. We plan to have a quiet meal in his room on Christmas Eve. Then he'll be away a day or two later. He'll be gone before your wedding day, lass."

"Oh."

Samuel flapped a newspaper at her, saying, "Read me something exciting but not too depressing."

"Uncle Samuel . . ."

"Read to me. There's a good girl. It's time I learned a little more about what is going on in the world."

As she folded the paper, she said, "I have a favor to ask. Would you please ask Patrick if I could see him before he leaves? He could come to the cottage and I could meet him there."

"No, May." He opened his eyes. "As a rule I don't tell folks what they should or should not do, but what you propose is to ride hell-bent to disaster. Both you and Hal are fine people. Jack Bennington always said that Hal was a good, honest lad. He'd be proud to see you marrying his son."

Proud, proud, thought May. All I get is proud. "I know that Hal is a fine person; but so is Patrick, and I want to say good-bye—"

"Then write him a letter," said Samuel bluntly. "Patrick is special, and frankly he's fonder of you than he should be. I'll not have you hurting him, and that's what would happen if you arranged a meeting. Let him go to

328

Europe and find someone who will care about him and appreciate all his fine qualities, someone who would suit him. That's not you, lass."

"You sound as though you were telling me that I'm not good enough for him."

"Why should I do that?" retorted Samuel. "You've made up your mind to marry Hal, and it seems to me that Hal is the only person in the world you should be thinking about right now, what with the wedding so close." He patted her hand. "You should be bubbling over with happiness, lass."

"And if I'm not?"

"That's for you to sort out for yourself," he said, closing his eyes again. "Read me some news now, there's a good girl."

Late on the Thursday before Christmas the *Mondrich Pioneer* docked at Queen's Wharf. Instead of proceeding directly to Mondrich House, as he usually did, Hal took a cab to his mother's home. Abby saw him striding purposefully up the path and called to Derwent, warning him that Hal looked angry.

"You must have guessed that he would find out as soon as he arrived," she wailed to her husband. "And you know how the slightest mention of the Seamen's Union brings Hal out in a rage. Why couldn't you have waited until after the wedding before you agreed to that appointment?" She rushed to the front door ahead of the maid and flung it open. "Hal, dearest! Isn't it exciting? Only a fortnight until the wedding?"

Hal stared at her and said, "Last time we spoke you had nothing nice to say about May at all. What has brought about this change of heart? It wouldn't be anything to do with your husband, would it?"

"Derwent does think the marriage is a splendid thing . . ." began Abby, hurrying after him as he strode into the parlor.

"I don't give tuppence for what Derwent thinks," said Hal. "I've come to gnaw a bone with him, and what I think is more important than— Ah, there you are." Derwent was pouring whiskey into glasses. "You'll know why I'm here. The moment the pilot stepped on deck this afternoon he be-

329

gan rattling on about your being hired by the Federated Seamen's Union. Is that true? Have they employed you to address their meetings and to plead for them in Parliament?"

"And if it is?" said Derwent, handing him a glass.

"Then I could cheerfully knock your head off. Do you realize what a threat that union is to the harmonious running of the Mondrich Line?"

Derwent Kine smiled. "Cheers, lad," he said, as mildly as if Hal had paid him a compliment. "Do *you* realize what a lot of hard talking I had to do to get that job? Oh, yes. The union looks on me as being one of the Yardleys now, you know. In two weeks' time I'll be father-in-law to the Mondrich Line heiress herself." He nudged Hal and winked. "And don't tell me that you'll not be getting a hefty bundle of stock on New Year's Day. I've heard tell that May Yardley's dowry is enough to bring tears to a banker's eyes."

"I'll not discuss it," said Hal.

His mother was at his elbow, patting his arm. "But you'll be generous to your poor mother, won't you, son? I was hoping that you'd dip into your savings to buy me a really handsome carriage for Christmas. I've not had a smart vehicle to ride in since Kendrick lost my beautiful phaeton in that dreadful misunderstanding. Really, I get upset whenever I think of it. Poor, dear Kendrick . . ."

Derwent said, "Give the lad a chance to breathe, Abigail. Of course, he'll be generous, won't you, lad?" With another wink he said in an undertone, "Your mother has been under such strain this past year. This wedding has given her something to look forward to."

"And you wouldn't want Mr. Kine and me to arrive at the cathedral in that shabby old thing in the stables, would you, dear? After all, you won't need your savings now."

How did this happen? thought Hal, bewildered. I came here to blast the fellow for a traitor, and within one minute he's put me on the defensive, and within two both are dripping in my pockets.

"I feel so frustrated," he said to Stephen later in the evening. "I went there to have it out with Mr. Kine, to make

330

him see that he had no option but to resign, but he wriggled out of the subject every time I tried to hang it on him."

"He's a politician," said Stephen. "You grab for him with both hands and always come up clutching empty air. But never mine that, son. The union was bound to employ somebody, and as I see it, they could have employed someone far more dangerous than he is. And Mr. Kine is accessible to us. If we ever want to talk to him, we can." He picked up the top document from a pile on his desk. "This is a much more serious matter. This maintenance report from England. It alleges sabotage."

"One hold had to be jettisoned completely. Thousands of pound's worth of meat flung to the Indian Ocean sharks. We tried to repair the refrigeration plant, but the damage was beyond our abilities to put right. When we reached England, it was found that vital parts of the machinery had been sawed almost through, so that they'd break after so many days at sea. It was sabotage, all right, and Barge Norrimmer's hand is behind it."

"Easy there. If you've no proof, you've nothing."

"It's because of that collision in Wellington Harbor between the *Mondrich Explorer* and the *Silver Dragon.* Norrimmer puts inexperienced men in charge of steam packets—men who don't know anything about the maneuverability of clippers. Of course, there will be trouble."

"We're taking them to court over that," said Stephen. "And half of a Dragon Line crew was jailed in Brisbane last month. They attacked a group of tars in a saloon, apparently thinking mistakenly they were off one of our ships. Oh, they're harassing us, all right; but they always have, and they always will. Remember this, son: Don't attack them without proof, and keep your temper under control. Anger dulls a man's thinking processes. Tell Sheridan to keep a full guard around that refrigeration plant all the time."

"You'd better check for damage last thing before you sail," said Hal next morning. This was proving to be an unhappy morning for Hal. For the next two years Sheridan would make the run—*his* run—to Europe, while Hal as-

331

sumed command of the *Mondrich Southern Cross* on the Pacific route out of San Francisco.

"I'll look after her for you," said Sheridan.

"The box of damaged engine parts is down in a locker beside the refrigeration plant. The maintenance engineer in England thought it might be a wise precaution to carry a full set of spares in case something similar happened again."

"Yes, so you said." And Sheridan laughed. "Hal, old friend, you remind me of a mother sending her child off to school for the first time. You don't want to part with her, do you?"

"I like the refrigeration run," said Hal. "It's a challenge."

"Marriage will be a challenge, too. You should look on this as a price you have to pay to become the captain's son-in-law."

"I do. And a price I pay reluctantly, I might add."

"We can't have talk like that just before your wedding day," said Sheridan. "I've a bottle of the best Scotch here, and I'll not hear any protests. Maybe I'll miss your wedding, but I'm damned if I'll be cheated out of the celebrations altogether, so drink up, my friend."

Hal drank up.

Meanwhile, May had arrived with Dora at the soup kitchen. In a token of Christmas goodwill the fare had been extended to include one apple per "customer." The stew, however, was as foul-smelling as usual, and May was grimacing as she lifted off the caldron lid when she glanced up to see an urchin grinning and aping her expression from a glassless window across the street. When their eyes met, the child waved. Impulsively May picked up a red apple and waved that.

Today promised to be a busy day, with long queues forming already. Within minutes May was so busy occupied with measuring out the two ladlesful per container that she had forgotten the child and was startled when a grubby face appeared over the edge of the counter and a voice said, "Where's me apple, miss?"

"Oh, it's you." May hooked the ladle onto the rest and

rubbed an apple onto her apron to burnish it before handing it to the child.

Instead of thanking her, he snatched it and said, "What about one for Pirate?"

"Pirate?"

"This 'ere is Pirate." And a ginger and black kitten was produced from below window level and plonked onto the counter.

"Pirate? Oh, of course, the black eyepatch. But kittens don't eat apples."

"Pirate eats anything when 'e's 'ungry enough."

A florid-faced woman nudged the child with her elbow. "'Ere, you, get that mangy thing out of 'ere. We want ter be served."

May ignored her. To the urchin she said, "How would you like to have your photograph taken?"

"We want ter be given us food," snapped the impatient woman.

"Dora, I won't be a minute," said May, untying her apron.

"You can't go now," said Dora. "Look at how many are waiting! Can't you take your photographs later, when we've finished?"

"We want us dinner!" shouted the woman.

But May had snatched up her case containing the camera and folding tripod and was gone, saying, "I'll not be a minute. Just as soon as I've captured that unique face . . ."

"Or that unique sunset, or that unique building, or that unique pohutukawa tree," muttered Dora, slopping a dollop of stew into a chipped enamel bowl.

Whenever May conceived an idea for a photograph, she became oblivious to everything around her, focusing her entire attention on the composition of the scene.

She posed the child in a doorway, knees hunched in front of him, bare feet spraddled on the step and the kitten clutched in a tight hug up under his chin. Concentrating as she was on the picture in the viewfinder, she did not notice the shouts of abuse from the women waiting in the queue across the road. Head under the black cloth, she was aware only of the child and the kitten.

She had exposed two negatives and was fitting a third into the back of the camera when something brushed with a whooshing noise against her skirt. She thought nothing of it and bent to look into the viewfinder. "Apples out of sight," she told the child. "And don't smile now. Pretend that someone has taken the apples away. How would you feel then?"

To her consternation he suddenly shrieked and clapped a hand to the side of his head. The kitten wriggled free and dashed away in a ginger blur, and May straightened up, saying. "What's the matter?" as a stone rattled to the pavement beside her feet.

When the urchin took his hand away, she saw a scrape on his cheek, a dirty smear of blood darker than the other smears on his face. He pointed to the women across the road. "It's them, miss. They's throwin' stones at us."

Indeed, they were. More stones dashed against May's skirt and skittered over the pavement. When she looked around, a stone struck her on the neck, just below the point of her chin. It felt as though someone had swatted her with a hot twig, but when she put a hand to her throat, she felt moisture and pulled her fingers away. They were red on the tips. What was happening? Utterly bewildered, May gaped at her attackers.

Now they began to shout at her, though they stayed where they were, keeping their places in the queue. From the distance across the street May could see the hatred in their faces.

"Rich trollop!"

"Playin' with 'er luxuries while we starve."

"Oo does she think she is, makin' us wait like this?"

May's strongest impulse was to continue with what she was doing and not allow them to cow her into returning to the soup kitchen, but the scattering of stones that kept raining around her doused that impulse immediately.

Then one woman walked several paces into the roadway, a stone cocked menacingly in her fist.

"They'll get yer, miss!" wailed the child from behind her. "Run fer it. Run as fast as yer can!"

May grabbed the camera and case and looked around distractedly. She could not go back to the soup kitchen, for

334

the way was barred by this hostile crowd, and to reach safety, she would have had to dash through a forest of angry faces and threatening arms. Turning in the other direction, toward the railway station, she began to run.

This was just the signal the women needed for their rage to erupt. With shouts and howls they began to follow, scooping up stones as they went. May ducked her head and quickened her pace, aware of the thickening wake behind her. She was too frightened to cry. Stones slapped her on the back and clattered on the roadway in front of her, and her ears dinned with the sound of pounding feet not her own.

"Trollop!" shouted a woman at her elbow. May glanced sideways and recognized the florid woman who had scolded her before. The woman was strong and fit; despite her bulk, she easily overtook May and grabbed at the empty camera case.

Still running, May struggled to hold onto it, but when the woman dragged at it persistently, May looked back and saw to her dismay that the rest of the mob was gaining on her. With all the force she could muster she thrust the camera case against the woman and pushed her so that she stumbled and fell sprawling into the roadway. May darted around and ran faster, hoping that some of her pursuers might pause to help their friend.

The ruse did not work. Another frantic glance back showed that the pack was closer than before. Some of them were laughing, showing gap-toothed grins as they panted after her. Others shouted encouragement to each other in between the abuse they hurled at her.

"We'll show yer what we think of rich ladies!"

"Yer camera won't do yer no good when we catch yer!"

A stone caught May right between the shoulder blades, pitching her forward with an involuntary cry of pain. Fear blinded her. Her breath was scraping raggedly in her throat as she forced herself to run faster, and faster still. To her right the railway station loomed ahead. She swerved across the path of the sprinting women, hoping to dash in there for sanctuary.

Her chest was beginning to cramp, and she stumbled over the rolling pebbles in her path as she raced for safety.

A red haze was filling her head as panic drove her on. In her desperation she did not see the hansom cab pulling out from the station bay until the horse had almost run her down.

With her free hand she clung to the harness as the horse tossed its head away from her, snorting at the scent of her fear. She shouted up to the driver, "Help me! Help me, please!"

He did not understand the reasons for the chase but could see at a glance that the lass stood no chance against so many enraged women. Twenty, was it, or thirty? More than he could beat off, even if he was foolhardy enough to climb down and face them. He called out, "Get into the cab. Quick, and you'll be away in a second." As he spoke, he dragged on the reins to swing the horse around.

Sobbing, as much from pain and exhaustion as from fear, May scrambled for the cab door. As she grasped the handle, she was seized from behind by aggressive hands. Her bonnet was ripped from her head. Someone punched her. The tripod, still with camera attached, was wrenched out of her grasp. Not daring to look around, May hung on to the handle and scrabbled for a foothold as the cab increased speed. The women dropped away. She swung on the door and almost fell inside.

Stones thudded on the window frame. May stared out, gasping through the hot pain in her chest. A few women chased after the cab. Some looked angry. Most were laughing as if the whole incident had been nothing more than a bit of sport. May placed a trembling hand against her bleeding throat and wept as she watched one of the women dash her precious camera again and again onto the road. She turned for one last agonized glimpse and did not see someone leap onto the platform in front of the cab. Too late she realized that the door was swinging open. She screamed.

"Hush, May," said Patrick. "It's only me."

"Only you!" She grabbed both his hands, whimpering in relief. "Only you! Oh, I've been afraid for my life . . . I . . . ." The pain in her chest stopped her, and she doubled over, gasping.

"Don't try to talk." He put an arm about her and drew

336

her carefully against his chest. The top of her head tucked under his chin, and she leaned against him gratefully, feeling safe.

He said, "Your breathing sounds bad, May. I'll take you to a doctor. It is Dr. Nunn, isn't it?"

"There's . . . no need." She concentrated on breathing through her mouth, slowly, slowly, waiting between breaths until her lungs ached. "This happens . . . sometimes," she said when she could. "It's almost . . . better now."

He held her at arm's length, and she tried to smile at him. "I'm so glad you came along. Why were you there?"

"I wanted to see you before I went away. Samuel was completely uncooperative, but I found someone who told me where you would be. I was on my way along Fort Street and saw the riot, never imagining you were at its center. What happened?"

"The women were angry with me. They tried to frighten me, I think."

"That's serious 'frightening.' Are you hurt?"

"My camera is." Her eyes filled with tears. "They smashed it, Patrick. Smashed my beautiful camera. It's all in pieces now, broken all over the road. . . ."

"Hush, you silly thing. Cameras are replaceable. You are not." He tipped her chin up with his fingers. "You *are* hurt. That looks like a puncture wound."

"Someone threw a stone at me. Lots of them did. They pelted me just as they stoned wicked women in the Scriptures." She tried to turn it into a joke, but he would not smile. "I think that was their intention, but I would not stand still and be their target."

"Is that the only damage?" He ran his gaze over her chest and arms.

"Most of the stones hit me on the back. When I began to run, they all came after me, jeering and shouting and calling abuse. It was very frightening at the time, but exciting, too. Once something similar happened in San Francisco, and I felt like this when I almost had that accident the day I met you."

"At least your voice has suffered no damage, Miss Yardley," he said teasingly.

337

"Oh, Patrick, it is so *good* to see you. I feel better just for being here with you. I have often wondered what you were doing. I even hoped to hear from you, but all these months and there has been no word at all."

"Years." He tugged at his cream silk cravat and drew it from around his throat. As he folded it lengthwise, he said, "If you unbutton your collar, this might be easier."

"What is it?"

"A tourniquet for around your neck. Nice and tight, as you deserve." At her startled look he said, "A bandage to keep the dust out of that wound. I don't like the look of it. Does it hurt?"

"Yes, it does."

"Good."

"You're angry with me, aren't you?" she asked, watching his face as he wrapped the cravat gently around her throat and tucked the ends into her collar. He did not reply, so she said, "If you are angry with me, why were you coming to see me?"

The driver opened the roof hatch and asked, "Where to, sir?"

"Mondrich House," said Patrick.

"Why? Why were you—"

"You ask too many impossible questions."

"Patrick," she said in a low voice, "are you going away because of my wedding?" When he turned his head away again, she said, "You are, aren't you?"

When he turned back, there was real anger in his eyes. "Some questions should not be asked."

"I think these should." She astounded herself. Still shaking from her experience, she was in a strange careless mood, able to speak with a frankness extreme even for her, to voice things she had previously shied away from. "I think that if you are angry with me, you should tell me why and not go away with unsaid truths hanging between us."

"What difference will it make? We shall never see each other again. You know that, don't you?"

"Oh, Patrick . . ."

Instead of consoling her, he shrugged at her tears. His eyes were still hard and bright. "What do you expect? All

338

right, if you must know, I am angry because I never thought this wedding would take place, and I'm angry because I should have gone to Europe a year or more ago. If I had been sensible by now, I'd have completely forgotten you." He glanced impatiently at the hand placed so timidly on his sleeve. "My God, May, what do you want of me?"

The hansom was slowing down as the horse began the long, slow pull up Hospital Hill. May stared at the arch of bells swinging on the harness and said, "I think I want you to tell me what I should do."

She could not tell whether he laughed or snorted. "I can't do that. Even if I was Martin Vinton or Hugh McLennan or even Hal Bennington, I doubt I'd have the right to give you directions on how to run your life. It belongs only to you, Miss Yardley, and if you don't know what you want by now, there is little point in asking me."

"I do know what I want," said May.

"Good for you," he said in a flat, unencouraging tone. He was staring at a hansom cab which was striding out swiftly to overtake them. As it passed, the driver signaled to their cab and swerved into the curb, forcing them to stop.

"I thought that was your fiancé," said Patrick as Hal sprang out and strode toward them. "He must have been looking for you."

May scrubbed at her face with her wadded handkerchief. "He'll be pleased to hear about the camera, at least," she said.

Twenty Eight

Minutes earlier Hal had arrived at the soup kitchen to find the ladies in hysterics and Dora manning the counter alone. While she served the now silent queue, Dora told him what had happened, assured him that May had not been hurt, and said that presumably she had been whisked home in the cab.

"If only we could go home," wailed one of the women. "Our lives are in danger now, Captain Bennington."

"Thanks to Miss Yardley," said Dora, grimly ladling. "She provoked the women into teaching her a lesson. She often deserts her post when she sees something she wants to photograph."

That damned camera again, thought Hal as he ordered the cabby to make for Mondrich House, and hurry. She'd probably say she was so shaken up that the wedding would have to be postponed again, and he'd not stand for another postponement, especially if her photography were the reason behind it.

He was too soft, that was his trouble. Grandmaire hinted often enough that May needed a firm hand, and his mother was forever nagging at him about May's outrageous behavior. They seemed to think that it was his fault, that he should be able to control her. Perhaps he should. Perhaps if he were more positive with her, she would respond with affection. Heaven knows, she was anything but affectionate these days.

Hal sighed with frustration as the cab stopped to allow a nurse pushing a perambulator to cross the street. If only all this were over—the wedding, the fuss, the family chafing at him—and he were back at sea again. On the ocean he was in charge, but on land he felt swamped, overpowered, unable to cope.

His mother was the worst, with her barbed remarks about May. It was wrong that she should be saying openly that the only redeeming feature May had was her money, so thank goodness there was plenty of that. Hal shuddered to think of how his mother would blow today's misadventure into a scandal and delight in every malicious retelling of it. Unless his Christmas gift managed to sweeten her into a charitable mood.

Sheridan's whiskey had mellowed him sufficiently to make him generous, and before he'd gone looking for May, he had visited the coachbuilders' and purchased a smart new gig, a fancy red one with gold-trimmed wheels and scarlet leather seats. It had cost a large chunk of his savings, but if it made his mother happy, it was worth it.

He was thinking expansively about the pleasure on her face when the gig was delivered later and wondering if he could arrange to be there and see it when his hansom pulled out into the middle of the road to overtake another cab. Glancing across, Hal saw May inside. He rapped on the hatch and shouted at the driver to halt the other vehicle, but it was not until he was out and striding back toward it that he noticed May's companion.

He hesitated for only a moment while shock gave way first to blank disbelief and then to explosive rage. His fiancée in a cab in public with that bastard? His anger surged over his curiosity, and he burst the cab door open and reached in with both hands to drag the scum out into the road. He saw a startled expression on Patrick's face and horror on May's as she scrambled out of the cab and tried to stop him.

He had every advantage, of course. When someone is flung out of a cab onto the dirt, he has no chance of landing the first punch or even the second, and by that time Patrick was too groggy to do anything. The cabbies wisely looked the other way and let Hal get on with it, and only May screamed at him to stop while she pushed and tugged at him, trying to get him away.

His actions became blurred. He was struggling in the grip of a cold determination with a task to be thoroughly

341

executed. Only after he had shoved May into his cab and climbed in after her did he see his fists smashing into that arrogant, detestable face. Only when he sat nursing his hands was he aware that he had accomplished his aim at last.

Hal smiled. A warmth of triumph spread from his mind through his body. He did not notice that May was rigid beside him, her shoulder pressed to the window, her face averted. Hal dropped one hand over hers, and it was not until she pulled her fingers out of his grip that he noticed anything was wrong.

"Sorry," He held his hand before his eyes and studied how the blood threaded along the knuckle creases. A satisfying pattern, he thought.

"Sorry?" Her voice was tight. "Why did you do it?"

He grinned, euphoric with the sensation of power. "I've wanted to do that all my life. Ever since I found out who he was."

"But he's done nothing to harm you. Nothing. Not ever, at any stage of his life."

"He has harmed me by his very existence. Believe me he has. I'd have thrown him into the road and driven the cab wheels over his neck if I thought I could get away with it. He's harmed me, all right."

"I can't believe you mean that." She glanced at him suspiciously. "Have you been drinking?"

"What if I have?"

She shook her hand off his arm. "Please don't touch me, Hal."

"I'll touch you if I damned well please." Anger began to ebb back into his brain. "And you can stop defending Patrick Teipa. What were you doing in the cab with him anyway? Haven't you made enough of an exhibition of yourself already today?"

"What? What did you say?"

"I'm going to be your husband, May. You had best make your mind up to the fact that I will give the orders in our house. I'll not be ruled by a petticoat. It's time you began to conduct yourself like a respectable young lady, not causing a riot by flaunting yourself, then hobnobbing with scum like him. If this is any example of how you choose to spend your time, then it's no wonder I hear stories about you every time I return to port. When we are married, things will be very different, I can promise you that."

"You may tell your mother to stop repeating the stories because we are not getting married," said May.

"And you can forget this photography nonsense, too. Mama showed me the newspaper where you were reported as having won a prize for classical studies. Classical studies indeed! I may not know about photography, but I know what classical poses are. I cannot fathom why the captain would permit such goings-on, but I tell you right now that I never shall."

"We are not going to be married, Hal."

"I thought we'd come to that. I suppose you'll say that the experience today has unsettled you so much that we must have yet another postponement. It won't work, May. On New Year's Day we *will* be married."

She continued to look straight ahead, her head erect. "I'm not going to marry you, Hal. Not on New Year's Day or on any other day."

"But everything is arranged. You can't just change your mind."

"Yes, I can." He could see from her expression that she meant it. "I decided back there that I will never marry you."

Anger swelled, filling his head to bursting. "It's not because of *that* surely? Not because of *him?*"

"He didn't deserve it, Hal. You were brutal and ugly. No matter what you may think of him, Patrick is a fine, decent person, and he has never once—"

"Stop it! Stop it at once, do you hear me?"

She was silent, looking out the cab at the treetops and beyond them at the wide, glimmering harbor.

"I'm sorry," said Hal, struggling for a normal tone. "It was bad enough to see you with him, but to hear you praise him is intolerable."

When she did not respond to that, Hal grew alarmed. Surely she didn't mean what she said. He couldn't allow her to abandon everything, not now. Not after she had kept him dangling for so long—saying she'd marry him and then using one excuse after another to put the wedding off.

"We've been engaged a long time, May. We should have been married years ago."

She said, "You wouldn't agree to live in San Francisco. Not that it matters now. I shall go on living at Mondrich House and you will be able to go back to your real love. Your ship."

He couldn't let her do this to him. It would wreck his life. His whole future plan depended on his admission to the Yardley family. A stake in the Mondrich Line was there, waiting for him in less than a fortnight. He'd earned that. It was his by right. It was ludicrous, impossible, to think that he could lose everything all because of a trivial upset over a nobody like Patrick Teipa.

"You'll feel better when you've rested," he said, touching her arm.

"I'll feel better when I've told Father and Mother that the wedding is off," she said.

"May, this is so senseless."

In an unsteady voice she said, "Don't touch me, Hal."

Rage expanded inside his skull again. He was too meek, too willing to let her call the shots. He mustn't, couldn't, let her do that this time. Not when the marvelous future was so close.

Action was called for, the anger told him. Action would be the answer. He would talk to her and not permit her to go home until he had extracted fresh promises from her. It was imperative that she see their marriage was important—not just to him but to everyone.

Hal rapped on the hatch, and the cab rolled to a stop.

"Sir?" The hatch opened, and the driver's face looked in through the wedge of sky.

Hal thrust a half crown piece at him. "Wait here for us," he said as he jumped out.

May began to cry when he handed her down. Her body was beginning to ache from the peppering of stones that had been pelted at her, and her throat burned under the makeshift bandage. Her feet were so tender that she winced when she landed hard on the ground and felt the stony road through her boots' thin soles.

"We're going to walk along the beach," said Hal, keeping his voice low but making it plain that a few tears would not help her.

"No, Hal, please. I feel terrible. All I want to do is go home."

Go home and wreck my life, thought Hal. Not while I'm able to prevent it. He said, "We're not going on until this whole matter is settled." And as if to seal the statement, he picked her up in his arms and marched off across the tussocky sand hills and down to the beach. Over his shoulder May saw the cabdriver watching in bemusement. Then the road and the cab and the driver were hidden by a screen of pohutukawa trees as Hal carried her along the beach. The sand was hard and wet from the retreating tide. Hal's boots left crisply outlined impressions on the surface.

He set her down on a rock, where foliage arched like a scarlet and green roof overhead. As soon as he let go of her, she huddled her arms against herself with an involuntary shiver.

The movement did not escape his attention. "So I'm repulsive to you now, am I?"

"I'm hurt. And tired. And disgusted. And sore. Hal, I want to go home."

"When you've listened to reason. We *are* being married, and there's an end to it. Everybody expects it. My family, your family—"

"No Hal."

He tried again. "I understand that you may be distressed, and I'm prepared to make allowances for that; but don't you see that you can't change your mind over a silly trifle?"

"It's not silly. I could never marry you after seeing you act in such a brutal fashion. And I'll not stay here and be browbeaten by you either." She braced her hands on the rock, ready to make the short jump down onto the sand.

Hal grabbed her wrists and leaned against her. His body was pressed hard to hers as he covered her mouth in a bruising kiss.

The instant he relaxed pressure on her lips she turned her head away in a repeat of the shrinking gesture.

345

Hal said, "I love you, May."

"It's no use."

"I'll do anything to make you happy," he heard himself say. "I'll let you take as many photographs as you want. I'll not criticize your choice of clothes. I'll even leave the sea . . . for a time."

"Please, Hal. Don't degrade yourself any further."

"But I love you. You can't do this."

"I'm sorry, I truly am. But it's no use."

"I don't believe you." He seized her shoulders and gave her a sharp shake. "I don't believe you. You couldn't love me yesterday and last year and the year before that and now suddenly say it's no use."

"It's true. I am sorry, very sorry, but it's true."

"Damn it, May, I'll not let you make sport of me. We belong together, and I've no intention of letting you go."

Wearily she said, "I don't blame you for being cross or for thinking that I've made free with your affections, but I haven't, Hal. The way you acted today opened my eyes to the fact that I could never—"

What happened next took her so completely by surprise that it was over almost before she realized what was happening. Hal kissed her again, savagely this time, as if to cut off what she was saying with a more positive statement of his own. When she struggled to pull free, he increased the pressure, ignoring the fists flailing at his head, fiercely smothering her with his mouth, while one tightly cramped arm held her pinioned against his chest and the other hand scrabbled at his clothing.

Suddenly he lifted the front of her skirt and grabbed at her underclothing. She beat harder at his head, frightened now that she was beginning to understand, but he overpowered her easily. In one sudden movement he seized her upper thighs and pulled her forcefully down across his lap. There was a hot, tearing sensation and a powerful punch up into her body. Then another, and Hal slumped against her for a moment. She stopped struggling.

After turning away to straighten his clothing, he faced her again, but this time there was no euphoric sensation of power. He could not even meet her shocked eyes; his tone was defiant as he said, "That's settled the matter then.

346

I've claimed you, and you're mine. We'll be married on New Year's Day as planned."

May was too stunned to reply. She knew exactly what he had done, and why, but as he carried her back toward the cab, she could scarcely believe this had actually happened to her. The pain was still there, but it was simply an addition to the accumulation of hurts and aches that clustered all over her body. Hal had raped her. He said he loved her, and then he had taken her without love, as violently and abruptly as a slap across the face.

Sick at heart, she huddled in the carriage. He told the driver to take her home, that he would walk back to town along the beach to get some fresh air in his lungs. He's ashamed of what he's done, she thought, uncaring.

Hal paused a short distance from Fintona. Ahead of him he saw Ellen walking along the high-tide line. She carried Roseanne on her hip and was watching Rupert throw pieces of driftwood at the sea gulls. There was an air of forlorn hopelessness about her that echoed his own mood.

All the way along the coast he had forced a brisk pace and adopted a jaunty manner, but for all the pretense his soul was permeated with self-disgust. He was angry with May for fencing him into the desperate situation and furious that she had given him no other choice, but his common sense kept quietly reassuring him that he had done the only possible thing. It would have been madness to allow her to go home, determined to break off the engagement. By claiming her like that, he had taken irrevocable steps to ensure that the wedding would proceed.

At the sight of Ellen he stopped. His despair intensified as he watched her. In her dark old-fashioned dress she had such an air of simple dignity that he found himself wishing that May would emulate her. She was a lady. Unquestionably a lady.

Rupert darted in his direction to snatch up a piece of wood, saw him, and shouted, "Uncle Hal! Uncle Hal!"

He had to come forward then. After he had swung his nephew high in the air, he said to Ellen, "I thought you disliked sand and water. I'm surprised to see you down on the beach."

"We come down often. The children like it here, and it gives me a chance to get away by myself. Away from . . . everybody."

"Grandmaire is not easy to live with."

"If only Dora would come back." She glanced sideways at him out of her narrow eyes. "You've quarreled with May, haven't you?"

"How can you tell?"

"I know you well enough to tell almost anything. You look like an avenging angel. You've lost your temper, and now you don't know whether you've gone too far."

Abashed, he stooped to pick up a handful of powdery sand. It streaked in a fine mist from between his fingers. Ellen was staring at him, and he tried to keep his face impassive. Finally he said, "It's nothing. Prewedding nerves, that's all. Nothing serious."

"She doesn't suit you, you know. And you don't suit her."

Her tone annoyed him, and the fact that she was indubitably right annoyed him still more. "We'll settle our differences," he said, more curtly than he had intended.

Her expression was odd, a mixture of sadness and affection, like a mother watching her child leave home. "Good luck to you then," she said.

Twenty Nine

"Stay by the table, Hal. You're not to come one step closer."

May was lying on a daybed in one corner of the morning room. Her face had a bluish tinge, but he could not see her clearly in the shadows. He stood behind the table with the vase of red roses, feeling like a schoolboy called to task.

"I've told them, Hal. I've talked to Mother and Father."

"What have you told them?"

"That I cannot marry you. It was less difficult than I had anticipated because they both were horrified that you would let me come home alone after I had been stoned by those women."

"Stoned? But—"

"I told them that Patrick had rescued me from the possibility of serious injury and had wanted to call a doctor, that he had been escorting me home when you dragged him out of the cab and beat him senseless right in front of me. I told them that I tried to stop you, but you pushed me out of the way and continued to punch him as he lay in the gutter."

The scent of roses clung to the inside of his mouth and nose. He felt ill. "What did they say?"

"Mother defended you. She said you were upset and so was I, and we should calm down before making any final decisions about the wedding."

"I think so, too," he agreed quickly. "You'll feel differently soon—"

She shook her head. "Father understands. He knows how I feel about brutality. In fact, I think he abhors violence as much as I do. I think he's even guessed that we've never really loved each other."

"What do you mean? I love you, May."

"Stay where you are. I don't think you do love me. You may not have known I had been stoned, but you did know there had been a scuffle, yet not once did you ask if I had been hurt. How did you put it? I had been flaunting myself? Making an exhibition of myself? I had been *stoned*, Hal. I was hurt, but you didn't care."

He flushed. "That's not fair. I had other things on my mind."

"Yes, hatred toward the person who tried to help me. I am being fair, Hal. Do you ever care if I am happy? Or are you concerned only about making me obey you, making me conform to your ideas of what a lady should do? Or are they Aunt Abigail's ideas? And would you be so desperate to marry me now if it were not for the Mondrich Line?"

"May, really!" He took a step toward her.

"It is the sea that you love. Not me. Dora was right when she said you needed a fireside wife and I needed someone who could share my interests. She didn't think the wedding would ever take place. Neither did—" She stopped and began again. "Do you realize that yesterday you taught me a great deal about the nature of love? It's not idolizing people or worshiping them, but it's putting concern for their happiness and well-being ahead of your own. We don't have that concern for each other, Hal. Our wedding has been canceled."

He sat on the arm of the sofa and leaned toward her. "You've forgotten something, May. You *have* to marry me now. You've got no choice in the matter."

Silently she studied the backs of her hands. One was marked with a purpling bruise, a pansy-shaped blemish on her white skin.

Hal persisted. "Don't you know what might happen as a result of yesterday?" His voice made it clear that he hoped it would happen.

"I might have a child." Her glance flicked to his face before returning to her hands. He could sense the fear.

"You didn't think about that when you dashed off to cancel our wedding, did you?"

"Yes, I did, and it makes no difference. If there were a dozen children, it would not be enough. No power in the world could ever make me marry you now."

If May had scraped all her courage together to face Hal, he needed all his to approach her father.

When he entered the study, he began to blurt out a mixture of apology and explanation, but Stephen stopped him with a gesture. He looked at Hal, thinking how strange it was that while Juliette had had to be persuaded to accept the match to begin with, now she was far more disappointed than he. Oh, he loved Hal like a son, with a father's acceptance of his faults and pride in his good qualities, but deep down he was not surprised that May had decided against him. That temper of his was ugly. When Hal was a lad, Stephen had regarded it as an exuberance, a friskiness of youth, and though it flared less often now that he was older, when it did, it caused more damage. He opened his mouth to say: I warned you about it only yesterday. I warned you about that rage of yours.

But he reconsidered and said regretfully, "May is precious to me, and there's nothing I want more than to see her happily married. Happily, you understand. It seems that it's not to be, and all I can say is that your Aunt Juliette and I are bitterly disappointed. We'll not place blame or criticize, but I'm deeply sorry, son, whatever the cause. We'd have liked to welcome you into the family."

"I'm sorry, too."

"Sit down, lad. I'll not keep you long." He pushed an official document toward Hal, saying. "This is a counter claim for damages filed in court by Norrimmer. He's stating that the *Mondrich Explorer* deliberately rammed the *Silver Dragon* and that he has witnesses to swear to that before the judge."

"I wonder what *they* cost," said Hal.

It can't be over like this, he thought. A few sentences of regret and all my future sunk in fifty fathoms. How had it happened? It couldn't have been that squabble with Patrick, for that was such a little thing, and him someone of absolutely no account. Was it really too late? If he confided to the captain what had happened yesterday, he might insist that the wedding go ahead. But how could he tell a man he had raped his daughter? Hal stared at the document gloomily. Fate seemed to have wrung his neck for him while he stood, dumb as a rooster, and allowed it to happen.

Stephen said, "You might like to take this document to Barge Norrimmer and let him have it with my compliments. You'll be able to think up a suitably apt instruction to go with it." He smiled at Hal. "Cheer up, son. Life's not meant to be easy, you know."

It was not until the interview was over that Hal understood. As he was coming downstairs, he saw Samuel in the hall, hanging up his hat. Hal had stepped down from the top landing when the morning room door opened below him and May, unseen, called out, "Did you see him, Uncle Samuel? Is he all right? Oh, I do hope he's not badly hurt."

Hal stopped. Samuel was saying, "He's battered and bruised and not near so pretty as he was yesterday morning, but he's all right. No damage done but a few teeth loosened. The chemist said they'll set firm again as long as he doesn't try eating one of the hotel's steaks."

May said, "Oh, thank the Lord for that! I've not had a wink of sleep worrying about him. Did you give him my note? Did he read it while you were there?"

Hal's boots had turned to masonry. This was insane. Impossible. Yet in some grotesque way it made perfect sense. It explained May's outrage over his treatment of Patrick. She had pounced on that as an excuse—not only to break the engagement but also to put Patrick in the best possible light. Hal's outburst had been extremely convenient for her. She wanted a convincing reason not to marry him, and like a fool, he had provided her with one.

"He read your note," said Samuel, walking out of sight toward May's voice.

"Did it cheer him up?" she asked eagerly. "Did it make him laugh?"

Hal's heart froze.

Patrick lay on his hotel bed, staring at the bright reflection of his room in the large wall mirror. He wondered how many similar reflections of similar rooms he would see before his tour of Europe was over, and neither the question nor the likely answer gave him much pleasure.

When the drum roll of thumping sounded on the door, he guessed who it might be. Though he had given instructions at the desk that he was not to be disturbed, he had also resigned himself to the fact that he could not hide from Hal. As the thumps gave way to booming kicks, Patrick got up off the bed and stood in the center of the room, tense but ready.

With a splintering crash that shook the portrait of Queen Victoria on the adjacent wall the door flung open. It *was* Hal, and one glance at his face was sufficient to warn Patrick that here was not only danger but the most lethal kind, drunken danger. Judging from his disheveled appearance, Patrick assumed that Hal had already warmed his aggressions this evening. A bruise stained his forehead above one eye, and when he spoke, his voice slurred through lopsidedly puffed lips.

"You bastard," he said.

"An entirely predictable remark. But then I should know not to expect anything original from you," said Patrick, who then wished that he himself had begun differently. He recalled their father warning him that nothing riled Hal more than a belittling remark about his intellect. "He's not only poorly educated but poorly equipped to be educated," Jack Bennington had said. "If you ever tangle with him—and you will—make allowances for that."

"I've come to finish you off," announced Hal, strolling into the room.

Patrick watched him carefully. While his own injuries looked bad, he had sustained little damage except to his face. Almost all the blows had been inflicted while he was lying on his back with Hal leaning over him. In that position Hal had been unable to strike with much force, so although Patrick's face was distorted with swollen cuts and bruises, his body was fit and strong, and his mind perfectly clear.

He said, "I have no wish to fight you, Hal. We had a

scrap yesterday—hardly a fair fight, but a scrap nonetheless. I have no desire for a rematch."

"I gave you the thrashing that's been itching at me for years, ever since the boys at school taunted me about the black bastard in our family."

" 'Nigger bastard' was the term they used to me," Patrick said politely.

"I'd have finished you off yesterday, if she weren't there."

And if she weren't there, I'd have fought back, thought Patrick, but he said nothing, concentrating on Hal, noting his unsteadiness, the sudden blurting of his speech.

"You've spoiled my wedding. It's your fault that it's off. You needn't think that you can meddle between May and me and live to boast about it."

"So she won't marry you?" Patrick was visibly elated. May's note had been maddeningly vague, and Samuel had said that it would be best to wait until she was recovered before anything final was said. He'd not dared hope that the wedding was actually canceled. Without thinking he said, "My God, she's dumped you, hasn't she? She's seen the light at last and jilted you."

Hal dropped an inch in height as his knees flexed. Patrick readied himself for the punch, but instead, Hal said. "Oh, she'll marry me, all right. She's going to have to whether she wants to or not."

"What do you mean?" He kept his eyes on the pulse in Hal's neck.

"She may have fancy notions about you, but I've put paid to them, I can tell you. She'll have to marry me in another month or two." He made a generously sweeping gesture that almost unbalanced him. "She's mine now, you smug-faced bastard. I've made sure of that. Claimed her in the most reliable, time-honored fashion. Oh, she's not a pure little flower any more. She was until yesterday, oh, definitely, but not any longer. I've had her, had her good and properly in a way that you never will. Ha! I thought that would make you squirm."

"You're a contemptible liar."

Hal laughed and said something obscene. At the sound of filthy phrases rubbed up against May's name, Patrick's restraint snapped. He sprang forward, drawing back his fist, and pounded it right into the center of Hal's smirking face. Hal gasped with surprise and staggered back, but Patrick was there, matching him step for step and pounding his fist into him again and again. With a final jerk Hal's head snapped back against the huge mirror. Instantly a crack leaped from behind his head and raced up to the top edge of the glass. More cracks fanned out in a swift black spider web.

Patrick stepped back and watched himself reflected a dozen and then a hundred times, until, after hanging in that crazy pattern for what seemed ages, the design crumbled, sliding in a thousand shards of light over Hal's slumped body.

Half an hour later Patrick was in the lobby, paying his hotel bill and supervising the removal of his luggage into a cab. His hand hurt ferociously. The lobby doors stood open to the warm night. A horse-drawn tram rumbled by along the center of the street. A light shone in front of it, and in the beam moths danced. Inside the tram a jammed crowd of people laughed and talked animatedly for all the world as though they were at a party. Trams were still a novelty. People rode to Ponsonby just so they could ride back again.

Patrick and the clerk both watched the tram pass by. Then, as he picked up the change with his left hand, he said, "Was it you who gave Captain Bennington my room number?"

Abashed, the clerk said, "He is your brother, sir."

"Only in the sense that Cain and Abel were brothers."

"I beg your pardon, sir?"

Patrick's voice was pleasant. "Captain Bennington must have paid you well to discover my room number and even better to ensure that he was not disturbed while he wrecked my room."

"Wrecked your *room?*"

"Did I forget to mention it? I'm checking out because I cannot stay in the midst of destruction like that. One word of advice: I'd not plan how to spend the money Captain Bennington paid you. Putting the room to rights

355

will take every penny of it, plus considerably more, I would imagine. But do inspect the damage for yourself." As he turned to go, he said, "And remember that both of you are responsible for the destruction. All but the damage done to the captain's nose. That was my pleasure."

Thirty

"What a glorious day," said Samuel, leaning on the veranda balustrade beside May. "I can understand why our immigrants never get used to the idea of celebrating Christmas in the middle of summer, for it seems a pity to waste such beautiful weather on a festival designed to cheer the miseries of the northern winter."

"I've never really thought about it."

"You're still feeling depressed, aren't you lass?"

She nodded. "It's not just my aches and bruises—they're much better. I feel guilty about letting everybody down. Mother is so disappointed, and Dora is furious that I rejected her brother. She thinks the world of Hal."

"But your father understands. Take comfort in that. He'd be far more upset if Hal left the Mondrich Line."

"Aunt Abigail has threatened to use her influence to make him go. I still shudder when I think about that ghastly scene with her and Mr. Kine here last night. Did you hear all those things she said about me?"

Samuel lit a cigar and flicked the match into the ruffled pink azalea bushes. "Everybody on Whenuahakari would have heard them. I applauded everything she said. Not that I agreed, but because with every insult she uttered your parents must have become one degree more positive that you had done the right thing in staying out of her family. I know my sister well and have been unable even to feel much compassion for her. Her overriding selfishness has dragged her from one unpleasant situation to another. Oh, she's furious that she's no closer to the Mondrich Line wealth. She'd have been expecting a steady flow of it to

357

move in her direction once you and Hal were married. I'm being uncharitable, but that's the blunt truth."

"I know." She sighed, inhaling the cigar scent with pleasure. "But once I made my stand against Hal, it seemed that suddenly I was quite alone. I hadn't expected Mother to be so displeased. She didn't want me to marry Hal at first, and it was not until Patrick—" She glanced at her uncle, her face flushed. "I thought he would have answered my note. You took it to him the day before yesterday, and there's been no reply. You did give it to him?"

"I'd not deceive you, lass."

"But you want me to leave Patrick alone. I cannot blame you because it seems that I bring him nothing but harm. But I do care about him. I care more than I realized. Not that there is any point to my caring," she added in a flat tone.

Samuel said, "Caring is never wasted. There's not enough of it in this world. But I hope you appreciate why I feel so protective toward Patrick. He's had far more knocks than anybody should in one lifetime. I've got some news for you now, lass, but"—and he regarded her shrewdly—"I want a promise from you before I tell you what it is."

"News about Patrick?"

"I want you to promise me that you'll not give Patrick any false hope. He's in a queer mood—I can't make him out—and I'm wondering whether he's going to declare himself to you. He loves you, lass. Maybe I shouldn't tell you that, but I want you to be prepared. You must refuse him, you know. Let him go away to Europe and forget all about you. It's the only way this can end. The best thing for him, for you, for everybody."

May listened to the pain in Samuel's voice, and the flare of joy died. He's right, she thought. He's right, but it doesn't matter anyway. She said, "I'm never going to marry anybody. I can't. Not now. So you can tell me what the news is."

That's odd, thought Samuel, who had been expecting her either to radiate joy or to spark with indignation. He whispered in her ear.

She pulled away. "He's at the cottage?"

358

"Yes. He left the hotel on Saturday night and has been there ever since."

"I wondered . . . I thought I saw a light there when we were driving back from late services last night; but I glimpsed no more than a flicker, so I decided that I must have been imagining things. And he wants me to go and see him?"

"He asked me to give you the message at a time when you could slip away. So off you go. If anybody comes looking for you, I'll say that you've gone down to the beach. Take your time. I don't mind how long I sit here warming my bones."

She patted her netted hair. "I'll make myself tidy."

"Go as you are. Pop your bonnet on, and go this minute. Anybody who sets eyes on you will see at once that something's boiling up inside you. And, lass, remember what you promised: no false hopes."

Again that mystifying reaction. Deadening of light in her eyes. The flat comment that she would not be marrying anyone. Ever. What can have happened? he wondered as he watched her blue-sprigged gown until it floated out of sight. Knowing her as well as he did, he'd have expected her to rise to the challenge. He frowned. There was more to her depression than the ugliness of the other day. Something else had affected her—and badly, too. Samuel hoped that whatever it was, Patrick's company might help. I'm hoping for a lot more than that, though, he thought as he settled down to wait. I've tossed the fish into the pot, and I've given it a good stir and set it over the fire. Now we'll just have to be patient and see if anything starts cooking.

One of the stable cats came rubbing around his legs. He set it in his lap, stroking a loud purr out of it.

"Life's much simpler for you and me, isn't it, cat?" he said aloud.

Unused and neglected, the garden was overgrown, and the lawn a tangle. May had to tug hard at the gate to pull an arc through the long weeds, then was forced to stoop under the overhanging hedge as she made her way in. The cottage looked deserted, but Patrick opened the door as soon as she knocked.

Because she had recovered so swiftly, she expected to see him looking better, too, but dark bruises smudged his eyes and iodine marked one cheek.

He smiled crookedly at her expression. "The inside of my mouth sustained the most damage. I shan't enjoy food for a week or two, so it's as well that I haven't planned a large Christmas dinner."

"I don't know how you can joke about it," she said, touching the side of his face. "Oh, Patrick. I am sorry. None of this would have happened if you had not been so concerned about me."

As he shepherded her into the front room, he said, "There was far more to his rage than simply seeing us together. He's brooded about me most of his life. It's ironic. I used to brood about *him*—being the legitimate older son— until I decided that poisonous thoughts were both danger- ous and wasteful of good energy. But don't blame yourself for the beating. It's been coming a long time. You stopped him once, remember?"

"But you did nothing to defend yourself, and afterward, when Hal had taken me away, all I could remember was that you promised never to brawl in front of me. Is that why you did not retaliate?"

Patrick laughed without bitterness. "He took me by sur- prise. One minute I was talking to you, and the next he had me in the gutter. I never knew how it happened. But let's forget about Hal. There's no harm done. My face will mend, and you've come to see me, so suddenly it's a mag- nificent day. You know"—with another careless laugh—"I wasn't sure whether you would come or not."

His tone was so warm that she had to jolt herself into an awareness of her resolution. Instead of looking at him, she moved right into the room, gazing around at it. All the fur- niture had been polished. Flowers were banked in the open grate, and more were arranged in vases around the room. On the mantelpiece was a silver-framed photograph of his mother. May noticed with a wrench that though expen- sive, bought flowers had been massed elsewhere, Rosaleen's picture was placed carefully between two tiny vases of mauve wild flowers.

"I'm glad you came," said Patrick. "If you hadn't, I think I'd have braved your father and come to the house."

"He wants to thank you for helping me, so he'd have been pleased to see you." She took a deep breath. "I had to come see you. You are going away soon, and I would have hated to think that we had only ugliness as a last memory of each other." There, she thought. My voice quavered, but I got it out bravely enough.

He said, "Last memory? I hoped you might have come to tell me about your change of plans." When she said nothing, he went on cheerfully, "Come sit down. I have a gift for you. Something special."

On the table was a large box wrapped in vivid yellow paper and tied with orange ribbons. She could tell by the clumsy bow that he had wrapped it himself, but as he handed it to her, she noticed something else. His right hand was badly swollen.

"It's nothing," he said in reply to her question.

"Nothing? It's like a melon. I'd guess you've cracked at least one bone in your knuckles. How did it happen?"

"I bumped it," he said, and laughed again with evident pleasure. "Don't look at me like that, for I'll not tell you any more. This is far more important. Here, see if you like it."

The wrappings peeled away, and she opened the cardboard carton inside. "Oh, Patrick. *Patrick.*" She gazed from the camera to his face and her vision blurred.

He was like a child, thrilled with her reaction and still anxious to make sure that the gift was perfect. "It's not exactly the same as your other one. I went back to where you'd lost it, and some child had scavenged the pieces, so I took them with me when I went to search for another."

"When did you do that?"

"Later that day. Why, is something wrong with it?"

She was crying. "You went back all beaten up and spent the evening finding me another camera? Oh, Patrick, if you knew how touched I am . . ."

"I told you that cameras are replaceable." He tried to make light of it, obviously touched by her gratitude. "I'd planned to do the rounds of all the city photographers until I found one who would sell me a spare camera, but at the first studio the fellow looked at me askance, no doubt sure that I was a brawling ruffian. He practically shoved this one at me and quickly retreated to his darkroom."

"Who was he? Which studio were you at?"

"Premier, I think. It's written on the box of negatives."

"So it is." She wiped her face and tucked her handkerchief into her sleeve. "That must have been Mr. Albertson. He *would* have been alarmed. And won't he be astonished when I arrive at our next Photographic Society outing with his camera? Patrick, I hardly know what to say."

"You don't need to say a word. All the thanks I could want are right there in your eyes."

"I feel ashamed. You have been so generous, so thoughtful, and I have no gift for you."

"Think nothing of it. I could see how upset you were when you lost your camera. You were shaken and injured, and all that mattered was that camera. Naturally I had to do what I could to replace it. But don't thank me, May. It's not thanks that I want from you."

He spoke in the same intimate tone that had alarmed her earlier. Now he was leaning back on the sofa, stretching his long legs out in front of him in such a comfortable at home attitude that she thought: When I think of him, I shall always picture him like this.

Then she noticed that he was watching her more closely, with a soft, expectant expression, and her alarm intensified. I must not hurt him, she thought. I must stop him from saying anything too personal to me. But what can I say until he asks me? I must say something. Anything. It's better for me to make a fool of myself than to risk hurting him after he's been so kind and loving to me. With that idea half-formed in her mind she burst out, "I suppose you know that I'm not to be married after all?"

"Not to Hal," he said softly.

Her heart squeezed up into a hard lump in her chest. "Not to Hal. Not to anybody."

He smiled. "That sounds like quite a decision."

"It is." She put the camera carefully on the table and walked to the window. Dust hung on the lace curtains. It

362

made powder of her breath when she spoke. "I've made up my mind that I shall never be married."

He was about to laugh, to say, "What rot," but her tone stopped him. Her voice was emotionless, dead. Suddenly his scalp and neck began to prickle with a horrible suspicion. He recalled Hal's boasting words—the obscenities, the taunts that he'd had May in a way that Patrick never would—and the prickling suspicion spread like a rash over his shoulders and back.

Still, he couldn't believe it. Hal's bragging was empty bravado, sour grapes of the rankest variety. *Nobody* would do that to May Yardley, especially not Hal, who professed to love her.

But even with his doubts it was an effort to say, "You would need a powerful reason to make such a decision."

"I have a reason," she said in the same wooden tone.

He strode over to her, placed his hands on her shoulders, and turned her to face him. She ducked her head at once, but not before he saw that her face was scarlet.

It *was* true.

"May, oh, May," he said helplessly, and drew her against him. He hoped she hadn't sensed anything in his voice. He hoped his heartbeat did not betray his feelings. The concentration of dismay and disbelief sickened him, yet he knew that somehow he had to feign ignorance, try to speak normally.

Holding her against his chest so that she could not see his face, he said, "A quarrel with Hal is not a reason to turn against all of us." My God, I should have killed him, he thought.

"It was more than just a quarrel."

After a pause he said carefully, "May, if he harmed you in any way, would you please—"

"No." She pulled away, her face still flaming. She tried to meet his eyes but failed. "After he attacked you, I told him that I could never marry him. We had a violent quarrel. Very violent."

I had the chance to break his rotten neck, thought Patrick. He said, "I'm sorry if I was the cause of any trouble between you."

"No, Patrick. I simply realized that I didn't love him."

363

"That must have been some realization if it has sworn you away from men for life." He spoke with care, trying to capture delicate butterflies of meaning. "We're not all like Hal, you know."

"I know, but it's too late." He could see that she was struggling, torn between the need to lie and the desire to be honest. Moving to the mantelpiece, she stared at the photograph for a long moment. Perhaps it gave her the strength she required, for she faced him with dignity and said, "Hal was personally violent toward me in such a way that it is no longer possible for me to marry anyone. No matter how I feel or how much I might . . . love someone, I have resolved never to get married."

God, she's courageous, he thought. I wonder if she knows how explicitly she has described what happened? Yet she's told me with decorum and grace. No apology, for it was not her fault, and no bitterness toward Hal, though he royally deserves it.

"I'm telling you this only because Uncle Samuel said that I must not give you false hopes. He said that you had to go away to Europe so that you can find someone who is right for you. Someone who—"

"Look at me, May."

"I can't." It was a small, broken voice.

His admiration dissolved into compassion and swept away his anger. She's told me the ugly truth, and now she wants to go away and hide, he thought. Standing beside her but not touching her, he said, "Perhaps I don't need to go to Europe. Perhaps the right person is here beside me now. You do love me, don't you, May?"

She nodded, and he said, "I knew I loved you that day in Te Aroha when you bravely faced the dragon and walked off holding my arm. I was rocked when you became engaged to Hal, but I never thought you'd go through with it."

"Why didn't you say something? Why stay away for so long?"

"Because this whole thing—you and I—is so impossible that I'd have been insane to try to court you. All I could do was wait and hope that you would make up your own mind

364

and not fall in with the plans your family had made for you. And I was right. Eventually you did."

"It hasn't done me much good," she said, fumbling for her handkerchief. "Now I'm in a worse situation than before, and you must go away. . . . No, Patrick, you *must* find someone else."

He laughed. "I'm not going anywhere, Miss Yardley. I'm going to stay right here and marry you, no matter what you say."

"No! I meant it, Patrick. I can't possibly marry you. You don't understand at all, do you?"

"Don't I?" If he could have spoken frankly, he would have told her that it didn't matter what had happened with Hal. It must have been rape, forcible rape, an experience to be forgotten as speedily as possible. There was no stain on her and no permanent harm done, unless . . . unless she feared she was with child. Of course! That was why Hal was confident that she would "have to marry him in a month or two."

And as if to confirm that, May was saying, "You *must* go away and forget me, Patrick. I shall stay right here with my family. Oh, perhaps I'll go to San Francisco soon to stay with Daniel and Verona. I've always wanted to go back. Since I won't be living there, an extended holiday might be nice."

"You'll go alone?"

"Why not?" she said, too brightly. "But it's only a possibility at this stage."

She's got it all worked out, he thought, and pain filled his mind. What agony she must be going through because of a few minutes' selfish violence. He wanted to cry for her.

"Sit down, May," he said tenderly, and, with an arm about her shoulders, led her to the sofa. "Do you trust me?"

"Of course."

"Really trust me? Blindly, unquestioningly?"

"I'm not sure what you mean."

"I'll try to explain. When I was little, my father used to balance me on the mantelpiece. He would stand back a pace, put his hands in his pockets, and tell me to jump. The distance to the floor seemed terrifying, but Father would

365

order me, very sternly, to jump. 'Trust me,' he would say. I can still hear him. I would launch myself into space, expecting to land with a painful thump, but instead, his arms wrapped around me, and his laughter boomed in my ears." He squeezed her shoulder and began, suddenly, to laugh.

"What's so funny?"

"I shouldn't tell you this, but I will. The first time my father did that to me, I was very young and extremely frightened, so much so that when he caught me, I wet my pants with relief. All over him."

"You didn't!"

"Yes, and it tells a lot about him that he was brave enough to try the same stunt many more times after that. There! I made you smile. Quickly, before it wears off, May, will you marry me?"

The smile faded instantly. "I told you . . ."

He held up his swollen hand to stop her. "Do you really trust me now? Without question?"

"I think I trust you with my life."

"Good. For I have something else to tell you. My father was bigoted, and I think that from that fact I gained most of my strength against bigotry. He gave me my best advice, too. It was he who trained me to be extremely cautious. 'Make up your mind slowly,' he said. 'Don't rush at things, or you'll only break your nose.' " The image of Hal flicked into his mind, and he dismissed it by continuing, "But he was emphatic that once I had made up my mind, I must pursue my ambition. You are my ambition, May, and I am determined to marry you."

"Oh, Patrick, please listen—"

"No, *you* listen to me. If you get up and go home now, I shall follow. If you go on this mad jaunt to San Francisco, I shall be on the same ship. If you change your mind and meet Hal at the cathedral, I will come and disrupt the service. I promise you that I mean this, May. So why not accept me gracefully?"

"But I can't . . ."

"If you trust me, hush." He placed the swollen hand against her cheek, and his skin burned her. "Come with me," he said.

Wondering, she allowed herself to be led into the next

366

room, a white-painted bedroom where the sun splashed gold over the high iron bedstead. The quilt was embroidered with silver ferns and clematis blossoms, and May guessed that Patrick's mother might have made it, over thousands of quiet hours.

"Sit down," said Patrick, drawing the curtains to screen the sunlight. When he came back, he sat beside her and kissed her gently. "I'm going to make love to you," he said.

"Patrick . . ."

"Hush." And he kissed her again. Then, as he loosened the strings on her bonnet and lifted it off, he said, "Please don't be afraid of me or what I am doing. I promise not to harm you." And bending his head, he kissed the white skin below the bandage on her throat, where her pulse was pounding.

It doesn't matter, she thought as his fingers twisted the buttons loose. He loves me, and I love him. We cannot be married, but for this once we can be together. I can pretend that we are married, that this is our home, our room, our bed. And I can allow Patrick to cancel everything that happened with Hal. All the ugliness will be smoothed away and forgotten.

She looked at the face bent close to hers. He was frowning as he concentrated, the sore hand impeding his progress. His lips were curving slightly; she wondered what he was thinking. Impulsively she raised her face and pressed her mouth adoringly against his. "I love you," she whispered.

All his planning disintegrated. He had decided to make love to her in a quiet, leisurely way, with great care not to hurt her. It had begun as a tense, nervous business, but that unexpected kiss touched off his emotions' fuse and transformed him with an explosion of delight. Suddenly this became something they shared, something they both were doing, with joyful kisses, tender murmurings, and the easy shedding of garments. It was not until he had slipped their bodies between the cool of the sheets and fitted himself between her silky limbs that anxiety inhibited him again. It was so supremely important not to hurt her, and he was so afraid that he might. She was frightened, too, her face tight against his neck, her breathing

367

rapid. Though he caressed her with tenderness, she did not relax.

"Please try not to be afraid," he told her. "I would die rather than cause you pain. Remember this. Right now you are lying in the arms of someone who loves you more than anything in the world."

"I know, and I love you," she replied, but despite herself, she was braced, waiting fearfully for that thrusting hurt. It did not come. Nothing happened, nothing more alarming than a warm, moist sensation of something firm rubbing between her legs.

"Trust me," he murmured, bending his head to kiss her mouth. As he did so, she felt him slide into her. He paused, perfectly still, kissing her.

"Is it over?" she asked timidly.

He laughed, a genuine, ringing delight.

"What's the matter?" She could tell that he was not making fun of her and found herself caught up in the laughter, too. "What are we laughing at?" she whispered.

"At something gloriously funny. Ourselves." He looked into her eyes, and suddenly all the humor dropped out of the situation. With a moan he brought his mouth down over hers and kissed her again, but fiercely, while at the same time his body moved within the clasp of her legs, stroking, thrusting, and caressing her.

For a few seconds May felt like a swimmer, floundering, sinking, with the waters closing over her head. Her limbs were too heavy to paddle, her arms too weak to splash. That panic and faintness were almost immediately swept away and followed by a feeling of gentle excitement and then in turn by a more intense excitement until she felt that she was being washed by a succession of waves, each more powerful than the last until the end, when he surged into her with one final, shuddering thrust and she clung to him, trembling, her body shaken by the sensation that he had been lifted by a curling breaker and dumped softly onto a beach to lie helpless and gasping.

She opened her eyes. Patrick was gazing into her face with the tenderest expression she had ever seen.

"I love you," he said. "As if you didn't know it. Now, Miss Yardley, will you marry me?"

She closed her eyes again. If only he had waited. If only he had allowed her to savor these luxurious feelings for a few minutes before it was all dashed away.

"I won't permit you to refuse me," he said.

It was not fair of him to do this when she was exhausted and vulnerable. "I can't," she whispered, and to his horror she began to cry. "I can't, I can't, so please don't ever ask me again."

He was beside her now, propped on one elbow, kissing at her tears, trying to calm her sobs. It seemed they would have to have it right out in the open, but he tried a light approach first. "You've decided that you don't love me after all."

Choking laughter mixed with the sobs. "Of course not."

"It's because of Hal."

"Please, Patrick."

"He took you against your will, didn't he?"

"Could you tell?"

"*You* told me, more or less. Haven't I just proved to you that what Hal did makes no difference to us, to you and me?"

She nodded.

He tipped up her chin and waited until she looked at him. "You are afraid that you might have a child. Am I right?" When she nodded again, he said seriously, "If you do, then it will be mine. Mine, from just now. I will never have a moment's doubt about that. Never. And I don't want you to either. Is that clear? Please, please, don't cry."

She was sobbing in earnest, spilling out broken bits of sentences, while he rocked her gently against him. "The only reason I let you . . . love me was so that . . . if I did have . . . a baby, I could always think it was yours. I'd look at it and see you in it . . . it would make everything all right . . ."

"Of course, it's all right. Hush, hush."

She clung to his neck. "You don't know what you're doing for me . . . protecting me, loving me, taking away my nightmares. Patrick, I don't know what to say."

"Just say you'll marry me," he said.

Thirty One

A dark brown phaeton was in the drive when May arrived back at the house. Still glowing, she called to Bobby, "Who is it? Who is visiting?"

He glanced up from polishing a saddle. "It's your grandmother's, miss. *Matua.*" And he smirked. The name still tickled him.

"Of course. I didn't recognize the horses." And she strolled on inside, humming to herself.

Grandmaire had evidently just arrived, for Dora was helping her out of the small storeroom which was used to house her commode when she visited. May paused, surprised both by Dora's deferential manner and by the sharp affection in the old woman's voice. "That's the way, Dora," she said. "You know just what to do. Sometimes I think that I'm surrounded by fools at Fintona. Clumsy fools and half-wits."

"Ellen is no fool," said Dora.

"Ellen is never there," snapped Grandmaire. She hobbled forward, stooped over her cane. "Ellen spends all her daylight hours avoiding me, avoiding everybody. Don't know what ails the girl. She has everything she wants —Ah, there you are!" she said accusingly. "You are the girl I have come to see."

"Me, Grandmaire?" May hurried to kiss her corrugated cheek. "Why me?"

"All in good time. Settle me down, Dora, and fetch my son. I want him to hear what I say. Where's Tawa? Where is that lazy slattern?" she asked, gazing around piercingly. "She is never there when she's wanted either."

"She's emptying the slop pail," said Dora bluntly, but

with a twitch of her lips. "Here, will this chair suit you?" she asked, steering Grandmaire toward the high-backed chair near the window.

"Yes, it is far too hot in here," she complained, not having heard properly. "Open a window, Dora. The French doors, too. And speak up when you talk to me. Don't mumble like that."

"Would you prefer to sit in the parlor?" Dora shouted.

"I can't see a thing in parlors. Always too dark." She glared at May. "What are you grinning about, child?"

"I'm happy," said May.

"Hmph!" sniffed Dora, sweeping past to complete her errand. "No conscience obviously," she remarked as she left the room.

As soon as she had gone, Grandmaire confided, "She used to be a splendid girl once. Really splendid."

May wondered if the purpose of this visit was to entice Dora back to Fintona. Knowing how pleased her father would be to be rid of her, May said, "I'm sure you miss each other. Why don't you ask her to come back?"

Grandmaire straightened in indignation. Her cheeks pouched, and her jaw bulged, making her look so much like the queen that May almost laughed aloud. "Nonsense, child!" said Grandmaire. "I can't ask her back. She's become *independent.*" She pronounced the word as if it were a contagious disease, as if she had not based her entire life on being independent.

And that was what Stephen swiftly pointed out to her after he and Juliette had listened to a lecture about the fatal mistake they—meaning Juliette—had made in allowing May to become too independent also.

Grandmaire dismissed her son's comments with the wave of an age-spotted hand. He reflected that she had come without her ear trumpet on purpose, though he fancied that she could hear well enough when she wanted to. "May should be *made* to marry Hal," she informed him. "You are far too lenient with her." The dark green eyes fixed on May's flushed face. "What's the matter with you, child? Surely you don't plan to become a withered-up old spinster like Dora?"

May glanced at Dora, who had her head bent over a

gown she was smocking for Dorinda, then said, "I'd not mind being like Dora, for she seems content enough, but that's not the reason I won't marry Hal." She bit her lip, thinking: They have to know sooner or later. Plunging on, she said, "The truth of it is that I'm going to marry some-one else."

"Patrick Teipa," said Grandmaire, nodding with satis-faction.

Everybody stared at her, Dora and Juliette in disbelief, May and Stephen in bemusement. Suddenly May under-stood why she had come. Not to berate or to persuade, but to score points off the daughter-in-law she hated. She, Maire Yardley Peridot, would have the immense pleasure of breaking such unpalatable news.

"How did you know?" asked May.

Juliette said, "May, you surely don't mean—"

Dora began to laugh, a shrill, seldom heard sound.

"Quiet, Dora!" barked Grandmaire. To May she said, "So it *is* true. I thought as much."

"How did you know?" repeated May. She had hoped to break the news gradually, gently, not in this disastrous fashion. Mother was weeping, Dora's shoulders spasmed in malicious laughter, and only Father looked unworried.

Grandmaire said, "Hal told me a little. I guessed the rest. People talk, you know, and you do behave in a man-ner that stirs tongues. Understandable, I suppose, since you are your mother's daughter, and *she* always gave Auckland plenty to talk about."

Stephen was out of his chair at once, helping her up and saying, "I'll see you out, Mama." To Dora, who was still doubled over her smocking, he said, "Go upstairs and stay there until I send for you. And Tawa, come help my mother, would you, please? It's high time she was going."

"I can't believe it!" wailed Juliette as soon as the door closed. "I refuse to believe it."

"I'm sorry that the news was broken to you like that, but it is true. I love him, Mother. And I do intend to marry him."

"I won't let you do it. I *can't* permit it. You'll ruin your life."

372

"How? Mother, I'll be happy with him. He's clever, well educated, and such fun to be with. Who cares how he makes his money? Brewing is as ancient an art as baking bread. And does it matter that he's a Maori?"

"You'll have *dark children.*"

"I'd probably have dark children if I'd married Hal. Would it matter if I did have brown babies? This is New Zealand, and Maoris are part of this country more than we are."

"May, you can't do it! He's not *accepted* anywhere. He's . . . oh, it's too dreadful."

"Illegitimate? Does it really matter? Mother, I love him, and I don't care. Don't you want me to be happy? I was so afraid of marrying Hal and having a marriage like Lena's or Ellen's—"

"Ellen's marriage is perfectly happy."

"Is it? There's no joy in her face or laughter in her voice. And it made me ill to see the love shining out of poor Lena's face when everybody knew how horrid Mr. Ogstanley was to her."

"But Hal is nothing like Mr. Ogstanley. He's like Stephen. I've always thought so. That's why we hoped—"

May pulled up a footstool and sat on it, holding her mother's hands and gazing up into her face. "He *is* like Father, but only in some ways. He loves the sea and is dedicated to the Mondrich Line, but that doesn't mean that he's suitable for me."

"And this . . . creature is? Oh, dear! When Jack Bennington asked Stephen to find a good school for him I feared that Patrick would be trouble, but I had no inkling how much." When Stephen came in, she stretched her hands out to him and said, "Please make her see sense."

May said, "I do apologize for breaking the news in front of Grandmaire."

"It made her day. She loves drama. Apparently Hal is lurking at Fintona. He's been in a brawl with Barge Norrimmer, and the police have been there questioning him. It was he who blurted out Patrick's name, so she came around here to sniff out the gossip."

Juliette said, "I don't know how you can treat the subject so lightly, though no doubt *she* will be laughing all the way back to Fintona."

"Then let her," said Stephen with astonishing calm. "I think that we should worry about May first, our family second, and all the citizens of Auckland lined up in proper order of importance with my dear, malevolent Mama right at the tail end of the line." He patted May's cheek. "Perhaps you'd best tell us all about this young man before any more surprises are sprung."

Juliette looked stricken. "Aren't you going to refuse consent?"

He looked at her seriously. "Do you really want me to? After what Samuel said—that he feared May would become sour and embittered over her experience with Hal? Shall we really tell May that she can't marry this young man?"

Juliette looked at her daughter. May held her breath.

Stephen said, "If I thought she was going to become a desiccated old maid like her cousin upstairs, I'd marry her off at gunpoint to the first person who came along."

May looked into her mother's apprehensive face. "I love him, Mother. Please agree. I'll be so happy with him."

"What will people say?" said Juliette.

Stephen laughed. "They'll say it anyway now, whether she marries him or not. Now that my mother has the bit between her teeth, she'll not stop until there's a scandal raging. But I think that we can turn it into a triumph if we stand together. What do you say, Sweet Olivine? Do we trust our daughter's judgment?"

Juliette still looked unhappy, but she nodded. May cried out with joy and flung her arms about her neck. "You won't be sorry," she said. "He's wonderful, and he loves me."

"Ah, but is he worthy of you?" asked Stephen.

Tears threatened again. "Worthy? If you only knew *how* worthy," she said.

Bobby Terrill was grooming Negus in the pen beyond the stables. As May skimmed across the lawn toward him, he stopped what he was doing.

"I hope you don't mind, miss," he said anxiously. "I

374

were going to take a photograph of me da posed all proud on horseback like one of them splendid paintings at the museum. Negus is the handsomest horse in the stable. You don't mind, do you, miss?"

"If you can persuade him to keep still, you are very welcome," she assured him. "But could you please run an errand for me first. There is a gentleman staying at the cottage. Would you please ask him to come over? Tell him that he is invited to Mondrich House for dinner."

Placing the currycomb on the top rail, Bobby said, "What time shall I tell him to come, miss?"

"Time?" She laughed. "Tell him to come as soon as he's ready, of course. As soon as possible. Tell him that Mr. Samuel Peridot is waiting to open a bottle of champagne. Oh, Bobby, isn't it marvelous?"

"I don't rightly know, miss," said Bobby blankly. "I never tasted champagne meself."

"You will today," she promised him.

At Fintona, Hal's Christmas was proving to be anything but marvelous. From the time he had appeared on the doorstep with a grotesquely swollen face, Grandmaire had given him no respite except when she paused to fuss over Rupert. She had begun by playing his mother's favorite theme, Kendrick. It was his responsibility to find him, Grandmaire said. Hal should show proper consideration. It was not right that an old woman should be made to lie awake, fretting over what might have happened to him. With Hal's contacts he could find his brother in no time.

And then it was his broken nose. What a disgrace, having the constabulary call at Fintona twice about such *common* incidents—first the brawl in Captain Norrimmer's office and then about the destruction of a hotel room. No wonder poor Abigail was at the end of her tether. Young Kendrick was often in scrapes, admittedly, but only harmless mischief. *This* was trouble, odious trouble. And look at what his temper had led him into! He was almost unrecognizable. Kendrick might have had his faults, but he never once soiled his fist with barbaric pugilism.

Finally she sharpened her carving skills for May. It was then that Hal's temper exploded into an indiscreet torrent of abuse against Patrick. While he raged, Rupert cowered at Grandmaire's skirts, clutching his toy train, but she leaned forward greedily, snatching every detail, every clue, like a frog snapping at flies.

Afterward he regretted his outburst and lapsed into a morose silence. When Grandmaire prepared to go out, he slouched down to the beach, where he sat glumly on a log. He was still there when Ellen came down the path, this time without the children. She sat beside him in the bright sunshine, her face under the bonnet rim lit by reflection from the sea.

"Why do you endure her?" she asked him. "I know you can't go home, but wouldn't it be more peaceful back on board ship?"

"I can't risk staying there. Not while Norrimmer's men are looking for me. I gave him a few home truths, you might say."

"Was it they who beat you?"

Hal nodded but did not elaborate. "One expects to be ill-treated by one's enemies. When the blows come from friends or family, it is a different matter."

"Do you mean Jon? I thought I heard you quarreling earlier."

Hal squinted across the harbor. His mouth tasted of blood. "I was shocked when I discovered that he had obtained the Federated Seamen's Union position for Mr. Kine. It seemed an incredibly backhanded thing to do, considering Jon's connections with the Richmond Line. Do you know what he said when I taxed him with it? He treated it lightly, saying that with Derwent Kine as their spokesman the whole union cause was doomed to failure. Perhaps he's right, but I find his attitude very cold-blooded."

"He's cynical." She smiled briefly. "He always has been. You've not changed either. All you can talk about, even now, is the shipping business."

"There seems little point in changing."

She scraped a line along the smooth white wood with her thumbnail. "We've squandered our lives on wrong decisions, you and I. Did you realize that?"

Hal was not sure what she meant, so he said, "You don't

have to stay here forever surely? I don't know how you can put up with her and her intolerable ranting."

"If I were a servant, I could leave. And would. Miss Von Sturmer left because of her carping, and Tawa told me that no white servant has stayed more than a month. And she's showing signs of senility, which makes her company worse."

"Dora could tolerate her."

"She misses Dora," said Ellen, tilting her face to the breeze. The sun was soaking into her black gown, making her uncomfortably warm. "More than anything in the world I wish that Dora would come back," she said, then added unexpectedly, "I'm sorry things didn't work out with May."

"Are you really?"

"Yes, I am. When you were first engaged, I was envious, but then I decided that one of us might as well be happy. So I tried to be pleased for you."

"Those are generous sentiments, considering that I didn't treat you very well."

"You treated me shabbily," she said, so crisply that he half expected her to stand up and walk away.

When she stayed, he said, "I know it's too late for any kind of an apology, but—"

"Is it?" Her flat voice had a current running through it that made him glance up at her. "Is it really too late for us, Hal?"

"Of course it is."

"Take me away," she said harshly, as if he had not replied. "Take me with you when you go. We could live in England. On the far side of the world. Away from everything. Away from this place."

Without thinking he blurted, "But I couldn't do that! I could lose my job."

"Your job!"

"I didn't mean it quite like that," he amended lamely. "I meant that you are my brother's wife. It would be dishonorable to help you to run away from him."

Her profile was hard. "Your honor is no more to you than a set of heavy-weather sails is to a clipper. You take it out and put it on to help you through a stormy situation.

Honor! You were honest the first time at least. The Mondrich Line is all you really care about. I used to say that to you long ago, and it is just as true now as it was then."

In his mind's eye he could see her chaffing him good-naturedly about his obsession with work. She had been happy then, a different person altogether. Curiously he asked, "Are you really so unhappy with Jon?"

She shrugged. "What do you care?"

"I do care, Ellen. Every time I see you I feel guilty. In an odd way I feel that I'm to blame."

"Don't be. This is my own fault. I married Jon, and for that mistake I can blame nobody but myself. I did escape at the first opportunity, thinking to find refuge with my parents, but I arrived home to find—"

"I know," said Hal uncomfortably. "I know."

"As soon as the funerals were over, I went to Uncle Stephen and begged him to help. He was going to buy all my parents' property and advance me enough money to establish myself somewhere far away, overseas, so that Jon would never find me, but Grandmaire sent word to Jon the minute I arrived in Auckland. She guessed what had happened. She can read us all so easily."

"But you have always been her favorite. She treasures you."

"She *owns* me, you mean. Now I'm her prisoner companion, and Jon is her willing slave. She may have doted on me once, but she dotes on Rupert now. It hurts me to see how she is spoiling him, turning him from a loving child into a selfish wretch. Roseanne is already being coached to disobey me. I'm sorry, Hal. I didn't mean to burden you with all this." She smiled ruefully. "Once I would never have let my unhappiness show, but now I trail it around behind me like a torn petticoat. I keep telling myself that Grandmaire means well, that things will improve, but I know that's not true. All I can be sure of is that for me there is no prospect of any other life."

"Perhaps there is," he said. "Perhaps I can help you."

"Do you mean you've changed your mind?"

"No, Ellen," he said quickly. "I can't. I truly can't take on any responsibility."

"Then how am I to escape?" She laughed bitterly, and a

378

sea gull that had been stalking across the sand on its scarlet legs paused to look at her. Ellen said, "I suppose I'm going to be spirited away to a new life. No, Hal. I shall be free when I die and not a day sooner. Even when *she* dies—and I doubt that she ever will—Jon will still be here to guard me."

"Is money all you need to get away?"

Her face swung around at once. "You'd give me money for that?"

"I have about a thousand pounds to spare," he calculated. "Some of it was to be spent on a carriage. Do you recall how Kendrick gambled Mama's carriage and four grays? She has been badgering me to buy her a new coach, so I did. I ordered a new gig, but when it was delivered, she sent it back to the coachbuilders'. Nothing would do for her but a phaeton with a liveried driver." He snorted. "So it's nothing. She can do without her carriage and you can have the money. I rather think you'll take longer to spend it than it took me to earn it, and there's something comforting in that thought. But what will you do? Where will you go? Oh, don't worry, you can confide in me. I'll not say a word to anyone."

"I shall go directly to Pindleton."

"Not to funny Mrs. Rugmore?"

Ellen nodded. Her face looked softer already. "She will help me find employment. Something genteel, where I can keep the children with me."

"Employment? Ellen, you couldn't."

"And what do you think I've been doing here, Hal Bennington?" she demanded with spirit. "What would you call nursing Grandmaire and running after her all hours of the day, getting up in the night whenever her bell jangles, reading to her until my throat dries up?" She stopped and looked at him sharply. "Do you really mean it, Hal? Would you give me your savings?"

He shrugged. It would be one in the eye for all of them—his mother, Jon, and especially Grandmaire. "I don't need the money. You can have it and welcome." He took her hand and squeezed it in a comradely fashion to show he was sincere.

When she smiled, it was with such joy that for a second

he glimpsed the old Ellen again. "And to think that I had misjudged you. I imagined that you would go through life without a single backward glance at me. I never imagined such kindness would come from you. Oh, thank you, Hal."

"Think nothing of it," said Hal.

Thirty Two

🌿 "Sweet Olivine, stop worrying," said Stephen. "This wedding is going to be a triumph. We cannot possibly be snubbed. The guests have already accepted their invitations, and nobody will have made other plans. The notice in the *Herald* will announce that the wedding will go ahead as planned, but Patrick's name will be inserted instead of Hal's."

"Nobody will come!" Juliette frowned at him from across her breakfast tray. All around her on the violet counterpane were lists of things to be done.

"Of course they will. The announcement will cheat them out of the opportunity to decline, and since they can't snub us, they'll come out of curiosity. Oh, they'll make elaborate excuses to each other about why they are here, but come they will."

"Do you really think so? Patrick is such a persona non grata that I fear—"

"But why is he not 'received'? Have you ever asked yourself the reason? Other Maoris and other illegitimate people are accepted in society, and as for his business . . . well, money oils the way here as it does anywhere else. He's shunned because of your sister, with Mama backing her up, *and* the fact that Patrick has never made any attempt to insinuate himself into society. Actually, if he could be accused of a crime, that would be it." He sat on the bed, steadied the tray, and helped himself to a piece of toast. "It's been the fashion for years to gossip about him. He's been accused of everything from stealing his father's estate to being effeminate—that because he purchased a supply of the new safety razors, would you believe—and while everybody has avidly gossiped about this mysterious person, nobody has met him socially. Not until now. You'll be astonished at how many folk will turn up." He picked up a list. "Is this the wedding breakfast menu?"

"Yes. I thought we would dine à la russe. It's so elegant."

"Not dozens of courses with no more than a teaspoonful of anything on each plate?"

"You are exaggerating, Stephen."

"Not by much." He grinned at her. "By all means, have your elegance for the special marquee, but you'd best consider calling in the 'army caterers' as well—you know, the crowd that puts down the hangis for the Queen's Birthday picnics."

"But they cater for hundreds of people."

"I thought a hangi for a thousand might do. We've got the Maoris from the pa, all the workers from the Hamilton breweries plus the local fellows, Samuel's friends. There'll be mobs of people here. I speculate that it will be the biggest gathering since that great Maori feast of the forties. I tell you, Sweet Olivine, this *will* be a triumph!"

She began to be infected by his mood. "We can have music and dancing. Outside if the weather is fine. And have awnings made from sails and put up everywhere just in case it's not. The ceremony could take place right here, in the little chapel. If the doors are open wide, it will seem as if the wedding were being celebrated on the cliff top itself. May would like that. She wanted to be married there originally, but Hal wouldn't agree."

"Abigail wouldn't agree," he corrected with a smile.

"It will be fun," said Juliette. "Oh, Stephen, if only I weren't so worried about her choice."

"Listen," said Stephen, and they sat quietly. Voices bubbled in the garden outside, then laughter: May's clear tones and a deep, warm voice.

"They are happy together. There's no denying it."

Stephen said, "I wanted Hal for a son-in-law, but I can see why May is attracted to this fellow. He's a fine man. And he loves her. That's important."

Juliette sat very still. Her eyes slowly filled with tears.

"What is it?" whispered Stephen.

"I could hear an echo of your voice just then. Long, long ago, when I was a young girl at Fintona. A silly young girl infatuated with Leigh. You were trying to warn me about the shallowness of his affections." She swallowed. "You said nothing against him, just that it was very, very important that I married someone who really loved me. You were telling me that *you* loved me, weren't you? Only I didn't realize it at the time. I didn't understand until much later—almost too much later really. If you knew how much I regretted that . . ."

"I say!" he said chidingly, moving the tray and enfolding her in his arms. "In the name of Jove, don't cry now! This is a happy day for us. We're planning May's wedding. We're together, we're happy, healthy, and we still love each other. Do you have any idea what a miracle that is after all these years? And you're sobbing because we had a late start!" He chucked her affectionately under the chin and said, "If you plan any emotional tears during the wedding service, you'd best shed them in advance. Mama's newshawks will be watching you every minute, so you'll have to smile like an imbecile all day long."

"I'll do it, too. You're right again, you know. Grandmaire assumes that we're unhappy about this marriage. If we conspicuously prove her wrong, it will be quite a blow to her pride."

"I have another blow planned, too." Stephen chuckled wickedly. "Mama sets such a great store by her fireworks display that I decided to outdo Fintona's best efforts with a magnificent display of our own. I've placed an order with the Chinese merchant that will have them working day and night to fill, and all the Chinese uncles and cousins are going to set and light the display personally. I doubt that Mama will attend the wedding, but when that display begins, she and the rest of Auckland won't be able to avoid knowing that our daughter is married and that we are proud and happy about it."

"Are we? Don't you have even a few reservations?"

He kissed her brow. "I had one. After that business at the soup kitchen I worried how she might face people—strangers, crowds. Yesterday Samuel offered to take her into town, and apparently she and Patrick both went. She

383

trotted along the pavement, happily holding his arm and greeting her friends. Samuel said some of the reactions were a treat, but she wasn't in the least fazed. Explained his face by saying that he and Hal had fought over her. She has your courage, my dear. 'Why pretend?' she said. 'It's no secret. We only look silly if we lie about it.' That's what she said." He smiled at his wife's shocked face. "And she asked me what the fireworks would cost. Quite rightly she said it was a crime to spend so much money on show when there is so much hunger in the city. She made me promise to provide a wedding feast downtown for the poor, too, so that there would be no ill feelings. No, Sweet Olivine, I have no reservations at all. May will be happy because she's made up her mind to be. So let's be happy for her."

On the afternoon of the wedding day, May had just returned from the bathhouse. Swathed in a long toweling robe, she was hurrying up the back stairs when she heard, from the landing, the butler talking to the Vinton girls in the front hall.

"Send them up!" she called, and they followed her into her room, giggling nervously.

"It looks like a medieval battlefield out there," said Martha. "All those tents. And the *people!* We could hear the Maori songs for hours last night."

"Martin said that a whole flotilla of canoes was anchored out in the harbor, serenading you. He rowed out to see what was going on. Isn't it *romantic?*"

May said, "Father didn't think so. He couldn't get to sleep until after three." She embraced the girls with relief. "If only you knew how pleased I am to see you."

"We didn't know whether you still wanted us to help you dress, did we? We called in here on Thursday, but Dora was so curt with us that we didn't know what was happening."

"You'll have to excuse her," said May. "She's taken it very badly that I'm not marrying Hal. I'm afraid she won't speak to me at all." ·

"And you're marrying his brother instead?" Martha giggled and clasped her hands together. "It's so exciting. We're all *bursting* with curiosity!"

384

"Everybody is. But we'd best help you dress. Mrs. Wey and Mr. Albertson are getting in each other's way in the morning room as they set up cameras, tripods, and all the paraphernalia. They both asked how long it would be before you are ready." She giggled. "Ages and ages by the look of you."

At four o'clock, when the first heat of the sun was fading, May and Stephen emerged from the front door of Mondrich House and walked toward the chapel. Both sides of the way were lined with a dense mass of people, some smiling, some dabbling tears from their eyes, some Maori women shredding rose blooms and tossing the petals in their path. Shrouded by her scalloped veil, May fastened her gaze on the copper spire and matched her step to her father's slow tread.

When the distance was half covered, someone in the crowd struck a chord on a guitar, and a few hesitant voices sang the first words of the Twenty-third Psalm. Those first tremulous words faded, and then the song swelled anew as more voices joined in, then more until May felt as though she were being buoyed along by the music. Now she could see Patrick, standing beside Uncle Samuel, waiting for her in the chapel.

"What is it?" murmured her father, for her step had faltered.

She clutched his arm more tightly.

"It's not too late to change your mind."

"Oh, no!" He could see the curve of her smile under the veil. Her eyes were shining like sparkles of sun on the sea. "I'm so happy that my throat aches. There is so much joy inside me that I could share it with all these people here today and still have an abundance left over for Patrick and myself. Thank you for this wedding, Father. We both appreciate it so very much. If only you knew what your generosity means . . ."

He patted her hand to silence her. "You'll have *me* shedding tears if you go all sentimental, and what in the name of Jove would your Grandmaire say to that?" He cleared the lump in his throat. "Come on, lass, your bridegroom's waiting."

When the feasting began, the guests segregated into two groups, and those with the gold-edged cards went into the large marquee while the others circulated around the dozens of other tents nearby. Juliette was relieved to see that the marquee was full. She spent the first hour of the banquet moving around the linen-draped tables, greeting friends, but it was not until she had heard the hundredth assurance of goodwill that she began to relax and enjoy herself.

Instead of staying at the head table in the marquee, May and Patrick kept constantly on the move. With so many people wanting to wish them well, they had no time for leisurely dining but, instead, sampled food from all the trestle tables outside. Near the hangi tables they met old Governor Grey, who was reminiscing about how he had long ago attended Abigail's wedding at Fintona. May was surprised to see him. She hadn't realized that he had been invited.

"It's an excellent chance to catch up with old friends," he said, taking her hand. "And an opportunity to make new ones. I see that you enjoy our native food, Mrs. Bennington."

"Mrs. *Teipa*-Bennington, if you please, sir," said May. "We know it sounds clumsy, but there was nothing else to be done."

The governor closed one eye and stared at her in a gesture that had characterized him since youth. Behind him Maori women ladled peas, meat, pickled mussels, and kumara onto plates. Under the tables young children squatted with leaf fans which they waved to keep the flies away from caldrons of trifle, jelly, and fruit salad.

The governor said, "You never knew your grandfather. He would have been proud of you. He admired independent spirits and generous hearts, and he loved the Maori people. Today would have gladdened him, but your choice of name would have touched his heart."

"Thank you, sir."

"Where is Mrs. Yardley Peridot? When I called on her a week before Christmas, she could talk of nothing but the wedding. She urged me to come. Mind you"—and his gaze swung to Patrick—"things were a little different then, hey, lad?"

"It's her health," explained May, but as they walked away, she began to laugh. "If Grandmaire doesn't come— and she won't, of course—Father is going to say in his speech—" She stopped and brushed the veil back from one side of her face. "Look, that's her phaeton drawing up beside the marquee. I'm sure that's hers."

The old Maori driver was berating some young children who had come running to pat the horses and play with the brass ornaments on the harness. When he saw Patrick, he spoke to him in Maori.

May thought she had picked out the meaning. "I'll talk to her," she offered, and opened the phaeton door. "Good afternoon, Grandmaire. How lovely of you to come," she began then stopped.

Maire Yardley Peridot was sitting very erect. From her reddened eyes and the set of her mouth it was clear that she had very recently been crying, and May, who had never associated her grandmother with signs of weakness, was shocked into silence.

After an awkward pause Grandmaire said, "Fetch my son, child, and don't stand there gaping. And shut the door."

"Well," said Patrick, eyebrows raised, "that was a pretty speech of congratulation, I must say."

"What can have happened to upset her so much?" said May as she gazed around for Stephen. He had been down at the hangi pits a few minutes ago. "Where can he be?"

"He's tasting the stirabout," said Patrick, and, with a few swift words in Maori, sent a boy zigzagging through the crowd to fetch him. "When your father was talking about mixing up a canoeful of that flour-and-sugar sludge, I thought he was teasing your mother, but he meant it." Patrick laughed. "I know that the Maoris used to relish that revolting stuff in the old days, but they'll sample it today just to be polite. Ice cream and sherry trifle are more to their taste now. Come, let's go back into the tent. I think I am sufficiently prepared to meet a few more of those hawk-eyed society matrons."

"Poor Patrick. Today is quite an ordeal for you, isn't it? Everybody staring and whispering."

"Ah, but it's worthwhile." He bent to whisper in her ear, and when she smacked his hand, he laughed out loud. "You look positively radiant when you blush. I shall have to make you blush often, won't I?"

"Mr. Teipa-Bennington, you are positively wicked."

"And you, Mrs. Teipa-Bennington, are pleased that I am. Wicked people have interesting ideas. Do you know what we are going to do when we return from our honeymoon?"

"I hesitate to ask."

"We'll live at Mondrich House as your parents wish, but we shall hire someone to keep the cottage clean, tend the garden, and so on. Then we can steal away there whenever we want to be alone. In the summer we can while away the hours in the garden, and in the winter the fire could be lit to make the front room cheerful."

"We could toast cheese," said May, "and make broth with barley and carrots in it. I'm no cook, but I do know how to brew a delicious soup."

"And we could . . ." He leaned mischievously toward her again.

Trying not to laugh, she pushed him away. "You are embarrassing me, and there are people watching. *No,* Patrick. Wait until we are alone together."

"I'll try to be patient, but it's difficult," he said. "Do you realize that we have only the rest of our lives together? We must be careful not to waste any of it." And with mock gravity he took her arm for their entrance into the marquee.

Because he had not been warned, Stephen was as shocked as May had been to see his mother's ravaged face. Only once had he ever seen her cry, but on that occasion she had dried her tears as she turned from Richmond Yardley's grave and braced herself to face the prospect of rearing five children and running a shipping company in the wild town of Kororareka. Since then, through the death of her second husband and the deaths of her children—even the deep mourning for her beloved son Leigh

—he had never witnessed her tears. Stephen was apprehensive. Something truly terrible must have happened.

"It's Rupert," she said.

"Rupert, dead? In the name of Jove, how—"

"Not dead, though he might as well be." And with a flash of her old fire she snapped, "Get in and shut the door. I'll not tell all the riffraff of Auckland my troubles."

Ignoring the slight to his guests, Stephen climbed in. The carriage had a sour, musty smell.

"Well, what has happened?" He was annoyed with her for giving him a fright like that and was now on the defensive. She'd spoil today for him if she possibly could.

"Stephen, please, will you tell me where Ellen has gone?"

"So that's it. She's run away at last."

"I didn't think the news would surprise you. Tell me where she's gone, so I can fetch her back." When he shook his head, she said, "And don't tell me that you've no idea where she's taken herself off to. Someone's helped her, given her money. She's left everything at Fintona, you see. All her clothes, the children's things, Rupert's toys, all the little sailor suits I bought for him . . ."

"Mama, please don't upset yourself. Perhaps she's sulking. Staying with a friend . . ." he said, though he knew Ellen would not do that.

Thickly she said, "I've sent messages to everybody who might have helped. There's only you and Hal. But Hal sailed two days ago, and she left early this morning. Stephen, what can I do? I know she's run away, but where? I can't face that house without Rupert. He was everything to me. Every morning he came running in to bring me a flower from the garden. He sat on the bed and shared everything on my breakfast tray. Ellen didn't approve. Oh, she tried to keep him away from me, but she couldn't succeed.

She's certainly succeeding now, thought Stephen.

"Ellen always was ungrateful," continued Grandmaire. "She didn't try to be happy at Fintona. Always curt and laconic, and never patient and helpful like Dora. If only she would be guided by me, she might have enjoyed living there. I did try, Stephen." Her green eyes fixed on his face.

389

"I'm ninety-three years old, and it's not right that I should be abandoned, left to fend for myself."

At that he almost laughed aloud. Fending for herself in that house full of servants? He said, "Why don't you ask Dora to come back? It could be months before Ellen is found. In the meantime, Dora would be company for you and Jon."

"Dora? Why should I want Dora?"

"Come now, Mama. You must know that I've asked her to go. Gossip travels faster than a full-rigged ship in a gale, and this time it's true. Patrick and May will be living with us, and Dora would find that intolerable. I've given her several options, but if you ask her, I know she'd gladly come home with you." He opened the door. "But before you go up to the house, why not join the celebration for a few minutes? There are dozens of your friends here, and I know they'd like to see you."

She sniffed. "Good day, Stephen."

He said. "Governor Grey asked after you. I told him how you had been the first to hear the happy news about Patrick—"

"Governor Grey is here? At this wedding?" She looked as if he had struck her.

"Good luck with Dora," he said, reaching in to kiss her. She snapped her head away. "Judas!" she said.

Thirty Three

On June 10, 1886, Mount Tarawera in the center of the North Island exploded in a series of violent eruptions. One hundred and forty miles to the north, residents of Auckland woke after midnight to see that the sky was rippled with red and orange. As the newspaper described it next day, "The clouds were dipped in blood and hung to dry in front of a gigantic fire."

People were frightened. Some feared that a meteor was about to crash into the earth. Others recalled rumors of Russian warships and wondered if New Zealand was at war. May and Patrick lay in bed at Mondrich House and talked about the northern lights they had seen while on a tour of Europe the previous year. At Fintona, Maire Yardley Peridot clutched Dora's hand and whimpered about hell.

Then the noise began. Faraway funeral drums muttered under the beat of huge muffled drumsticks, thunder rolled like a shudder across the sky, and one after another came the booming sounds of low-key smothered explosions.

"It's a volcano," said Stephen when May and Patrick came out to join them on the balcony. "Definitely a volcano and quite some distance away, thank goodness."

Juliette was hanging onto his arm. "Ever since I first saw these hills and learned that they were extinct volcanoes, I have feared this. Oh! Did you feel that? An earthquake." She glanced at May in alarm. "You shouldn't be out here in the cold, dear. Make her go back to bed, Patrick. She needs her rest."

"I'm quite warm, thank you, and I have weeks and

391

weeks to go," said May with blithe disregard. "Isn't that sky absolutely glorious? I do wish—"

"That I could take photographs in color, finished Patrick as he gave her a teasing hug. "You've been saying that ever since you first pointed a lens at the pink and white terraces, and our honeymoon was three years ago. It's time you learned a new song, dear wife. A lullaby perhaps?"

"Perhaps." She smiled at him. "But I'm not giving my camera away."

Juliette sighed. Mondrich House bubbled over with love and warmth when that pair was in residence. Things were as lively as when the two boys had been alive. And when May and Patrick were on their jaunts abroad, she missed them so keenly that the house itself echoed with emptiness. Next year, when they were used to having a baby to consider, they might be more settled.

"Are you sure it's a volcano, Father?" asked May. "That noise sounds like gunfire."

Stephen hunched his shoulders under the greatcoat collar and shoved his hands deep into his pockets. "I don't see why the Russians would want to attack us. They may have just invaded Afghanistan, but that country lies right along one of their borders. We are thousands of miles away."

"And big only in the idea of our own importance," said Patrick. "No, pet. Your father is right. It's a volcano."

"Speculation will be rife in the city," said Juliette. "At the hospital aid meeting last week Mrs. McLendaugh told us that the soldiers at North Head have been on full alert since that sighting of the *Vestnik.*"

"The military is desperate for an excuse to justify its extravagance, if you ask me," said Stephen. He nodded toward North Head, which looked sleepily innocent, a dark smudge on the orange-lit harbor. "That place is as hollow as a mason bees' nest now and stocked with enough gunpowder to blow us all to kingdom come. Cannon poking out at all angles, caves stuffed to the roof with cannonballs." He snorted. "Supposed to make us feel secure, though I feel anything but easy with all those muzzles pointed this way."

May blew on her fingers and held them against her

cheek, saying, "Perhaps the Russians want to buy some of our frozen lamb."

Juliette said, "You're perishing in the cold. Do make her go back to bed, Patrick. She mustn't take risks, especially with the first. . . ." She paused and said in alarm, "Stephen, why are the dogs barking like that? They usually cower in their kennels when there is a thunderstorm."

"It's Dr. Nunn," said Stephen, looking over the railing. "What in the name of Jove could he be wanting at this hour?"

Dora was wearing a camel's hair robe and a surly expression. She ushered them into the parlor and was turning to go when Juliette said, "Why didn't you tell us how ill Grandmaire was? Dr. Nunn said she developed this complication three weeks ago and has been growing steadily worse. Really, Dora . . ."

Dora's face was impassive in the candlelight. Though she had once been fond of her aunt, she had never forgiven Juliette for the way she and Dorinda had been shoved out of Mondrich House. "Mrs. Yardley Peridot issues all the orders here," she said. "Jon takes care of her business affairs, and I have looked after the house since Tawa died. We keep to ourselves because that's the way Mrs. Yardley Peridot prefers it to be."

"Mrs. Yardley Peridot!" said Stephen.

May followed Dora out into the corridor, saying, "But you don't have to shut yourself away surely? I'd be so pleased if you could find the time to bring little Dorinda to see me. She must be almost six years old now, and surely she would enjoy an outing. I would like to photograph her, too—"

"*You'd* like!" The harsh candle flame etched every one of Dora's forty years onto her face. "You'd like, you'd like," she mocked. "I think my silence has made it plain that what I would like is never to have anything to do with you again."

"Dora, please don't be bitter. I'm so happy myself that it upsets me to see you miserable."

Dora flung May's hand off her sleeve. "Mama predicted that you would be nothing but a disaster for Hal, and you

393

were, weren't you? Leading him along by the nose, flaunting yourself about when he was away, and then making laughing stocks of all our family by jilting him to marry that—" She broke off as the door opened.

Juliette said, "Are you all right, dear?"

"Unfortunately, yes," said Dora, and with one last glare she shuffled away, her thin gray plait quivering against her back.

May shrugged and tried to smile. "I think she trampled all over my olive branch. I tried only for Dorinda's sake."

"You must expect hostility from her," said her mother. "Abigail has never recovered from the blow either."

"And don't waste your pity on her," said Stephen, picking up a figurine and squinting at the writing on the base. "If all of them got on with their own lives instead of wishing calamities on ours, they'd be as happy as we are." He looked at May. "Are you sure you want to come in, lass? Grandmaire might be less than pleasant."

"Yes," agreed Juliette quickly. "Perhaps you'd best wait out in the carriage with Patrick."

"No, Mother. I want to come in."

"It could be extremely upsetting."

"No doubt. But I do want to see Grandmaire again." She put an arm about her mother's shoulders and gave her a quick hug. "She can't eat us, can she?"

"She can do worse than that, as well I know," said Juliette.

Only two candles burned beside Grandmaire's draped four-poster bed, but there was no need for further illumination in the room. The curtains had been pulled right back from the bright windows, admitting all the sky's wild light. Golden reflections shimmered over the ceiling, the silent bed, and the bent figure of the nun who knelt, praying, at the bedside. The moving patterns of light played over a row of large stuffed toys on the mahogany dresser, giving them the eerie appearance of superficial life.

May glanced at the toys in surprise. Then she understood. These and the others arranged on shelves behind the bed were Rupert's toys, waiting for his return. Years ago she had heard gossip that Grandmaire would allow

394

none of his things to be touched, though all of Ellen's and Roseanne's abandoned possessions had been burned like lepers' belongings.

While Stephen went to the bedside, May hung back with her mother and studied the room with curiosity. Dozens of silver-framed photographs covered the walls. A few were of Queen Victoria at various stages of her life; she recognized one as Leigh Yardley, but all the others were of Rupert. Rupert in a Grecian setting with pillars and urn, in a pastoral arrangement surrounded by fallen leaves, Rupert leaning on a sundial, Rupert looking formal beside a globe and desk, young sailor Rupert with ribbon-trimmed hat and toy yacht. He had sailed away, all right, thought May. Sailed right out of his great-grandmother's life and taken her sunshine with him. And all of Grandmaire's ships, her men, and her money had not been able to find him and bring him back again.

Following her mother around to the other side of the bed, May tripped and almost sprawled over a protruding rocker. In the corner shadows Rupert's rocking horse began to nod, its rails scraping on the floor with a slow wheeze, its eye glinting at May as its head moved in and out of the watery light. May shivered, stroked by a sensation of malevolence.

Stephen had settled on a straight-backed chair beside the bed, and now his wife and daughter stood close behind him, all looking down at the shrunken figure whose body barely disturbed the surface of the smooth black counterpane. Grandmaire was apparently asleep, breathing silently. She wore a black nightgown, and a black lace cap was pinned over her hair. Noticing those, May thought: But Tawa died almost two years ago.

There was a heavy smell of camphor. The odor of mourning, thought Stephen. He waited until the elderly nun had finished her prayers, made the sign of the cross, and risen awkwardly to her feet.

"She is in deepest mourning for the loss of her great-grandson," the nun said quietly. "Your mother has mourned him since the day he was taken from this house."

Aware that her voice contained a reproach, Stephen said, "I didn't realize. I am not in the habit of visiting my mother's bedchamber, and you must be aware, Sister Amy, that I am invariably refused an interview whenever I call at this house."

"I refuse to grant you an interview," said his mother, her eyes still shut, "because you refuse to grant me a favor."

"Mama, you must see reason," said Stephen, unsurprised. "I have no more idea where Ellen is than I have about Kendrick. And I've made every effort to find *him.*"

"But none whatsoever to find her."

"I've assured you that I did nothing to help her leave. Isn't that sufficient?"

"I must have Rupert back. I must see Rupert before it's too late." As she spoke, Grandmaire's eyes opened, not with a blink but slowly, like blinds drawing up.

To the horror of the three gathered there, she began to scream: faint, pitiful noises like mewing. The nun bent over her with a reassuring murmur, but she cried out in terror. "I told you to make it go away! Pray for my soul, Sister Amy. Make that go away!" And she fell back onto her pillows, her hands crouched like beetles over her eyes.

As the nun resumed her kneeling posture, she said, "It's the lights, Captain Yardley. They've frightened your mother. She's convinced that she's dying and hell is opening its gates to consume her."

"Then close the curtains in the name of Jove."

"No." Sister Amy's hand stopped him.

Grandmaire said, "I must be able to see it so that I will know when it has gone away. Hell is something I shall conquer." Though she was shivering visibly, she said, "I refuse to be afraid."

Stephen said, "What you can see out there is the light from a volcano. And I doubt that you are dying just yet." He tried to look stern. "You've called me here because despite all my protestations, you still blame me for Ellen's disappearance, don't you?"

"You must know something. An unescorted lady and two small children can't walk out of this house and simply vanish. Please, son"—and she stretched out the black stick of an arm—"don't go without telling me. Tell me now, before it's too late."

396

He shook his head. "Be a good girl and rest."

She was immediately petulant. "Why are elderly people patronized like children? I'm dying, and I know I am. Hell is waiting for me, and all I want is to see Rupert before . . ." At that moment she noticed Juliette and uttered a dry cackle of laughter. Immediately distracted, she said, "*You'll* be seeing hell, too. Oh, yes, you will. You might be playing the high-and-mighty society lady now, but I know you. I know better than folks who think your mouth's too cool to melt butter, don't I?"

May glanced at her mother, expecting to see a disdainful expression; but instead, Juliette's face was white, and her eyes were nervous with apprehension.

Stephen began to say, "I warn you, Mama, that ill or not, I shall not permit—"

Grandmaire dashed his words aside with a gesture of impatience. She had finished with him. To Juliette she said, "So you came to see me die, did you? That you had to see. A dying woman, helpless in her bed."

"Mama, you are *not* dying."

Juliette licked her lips. "I came to pay my respects."

"Respects? Ha!" Another dry rasp of laughter. "What do you know of respect? You don't even bother to respect the laws of God. You disobeyed God's laws when you wantonly seduced my son and bore him a bastard child—"

"Stop it, Mama!" said Stephen.

May gaped at her mother. Stephen was leading her away, holding her by the upper arm. Her face was fixed in the same expression of blank nervousness, and her head turned so that she could keep her eyes on the figure in the bed.

Grandmaire's voice rose with her triumph. "Then you sinned by committing adultery with my other son. You are a shameless, evil woman! No wonder God has punished you! All your sons have been destroyed, just as you destroyed mine. God's curse has wreaked its vengeance on the whole family. Even Daniel is being punished by—"

"Grandmaire, stop it at once!" cried May, leaning over the end of the bed.

Grandmaire hesitated while she focused on May's face. She nodded with satisfaction. "Ah, of course. Like mother, like daughter. Playing one brother off against the other. Hal rues the day he first set eyes on you. Your mother's daughter—that's what you are!"

Forcing a light tone into her voice, May said, "What nonsense you talk, Grandmaire. We came here out of courtesy. Can't you offer us courtesy in return?"

"Your mother is an evil woman." She pointed toward the blazing sky. "That hell waits for her, too. She'll not escape. She stole my sons, and she'll burn in hell for her wantonness." The wavering finger pointed at May. "Take care, or you will follow in her footsteps."

"What rubbish," said May. "I know that you hate Mother, and I know why. You are jealous of her."

"What?" Grandmaire's nostrils flared, and she appeared to be struggling for breath. Sister Amy chafed her hand as it lay on the coverlet.

May was aware that her parents remained where they had been when she first spoke, just inside the room. She could hear her mother sobbing, and the sound flared inside May, igniting indignation into angry determination. She was about to speak again when suddenly an earth tremor shook the house, wobbling the water in the glass jug on the bedside table and chiming the crystals in the chandeliers. In a distant part of the house someone screamed. Grandmaire clutched at Sister Amy with both hands.

She really is terrified, thought May. She *is* convinced that this is hell coming to get her. For an instant she felt real pity for the old woman, but the echo of her mother's sobs nudged her to continue. "Everybody in Auckland knows why you hate Mother. You cannot abide the fact that both your sons loved her more than they ever loved you."

"How dare you?" Unable to grasp May, she shook the nun instead, venting her frustration on her.

May said, "They both loved Mother more than anything in the world. They both married her against your wishes. They both turned against you—not because of her scheming, but because of yours—and you cannot see that."

Her hands dug into the nun's shoulders. "Stop her, Sister Amy. Make her stop!"

"You are ill with jealousy, but what good has it done

you? All this hatred, Grandmaire—who has it harmed? Not us. Mother is happy at Mondrich House. Why didn't you do the wise thing and make peace with her? Is it because, like me, she will not bow to your wishes? Why must you always try to manipulate people's lives? It's so destructive, Grandmaire. It drives everybody away. Everybody leaves you, even Ellen and Rupert—"

"No!" cried Grandmaire, for Sister Amy had freed herself now and was taking May's hand, gently leading her toward the door. "Don't leave!" Grandmaire wailed. "Don't leave me alone! The gates are open for me! Don't go!" And she lapsed into muttering, her hands plucking at the counterpane, her eyes turned in terror toward the hot, bloodstained sky.

May hesitated. Sister Amy tugged at her hand, and from the doorway Juliette called to her in an undertone, urging her to come away. On an impulse May brushed the nun's fingers loose and hurried back to her grandmother's side. Leaning down, she placed a firm kiss on her brow.

Grandmaire jerked her head away, but May only smiled. "You'll not go to hell, Grandmaire. The devil himself could not endure your mischief," she said.

Outside, the road was bright and the way clear, but the horses had to be whipped every step of the way. The silent group in the carriage listened to Terrill's cursing and the fear-laden whinnying and snorting.

Patrick finally broke the silence inside. "If she's not dead, and she's not suffering pain, why is everybody so gloomy? I thought you'd all come out of there talking nonstop, but nobody's said a word all the way home."

"She was unpleasant," said May. "Everything she said was vicious and untrue."

"Aye, and best forgotten," said Stephen.

Juliette huddled quietly. May thought: I said too much. Mother must know that I've been listening to gossip about her. She wanted to reach out a reassuring hand, wanted to say, It doesn't matter. What happened long ago doesn't matter.

Stephen said, "One thing I don't understand. After all that vituperation why did you go back and kiss her?"

"I felt sorry for her," said May.

"Poor Mama, she'd have loathed that. Pity was the emotion she most despised." He sighed. "Still, I'm glad one of us kissed her. I doubt we'll see her alive again."

Thirty Four

The Mount Tarawera eruption scorched and crushed four villages, killed 153 people, and smothered hundreds of acres of land, including the beautiful pink and white terraces that May had photographed on her honeymoon. On the day following the devastation the sky was black with blankets of ash that blotted out the daylight as completely as the fire had wiped away the darkness the night before. And as the shocking news of the tragedy reached Auckland, it blotted out other news. Sometime during the day Maire Yardley Peridot died. As Stephen observed, her hell was a personal one. It was her fate to die unnoticed, while the attention of Auckland was focused elsewhere. Nobody was with her when she died.

But if her death was a simple passing, the aftermath more than compensated. Hers was the most magnificent funeral Auckland had seen since Governor Hobson died in 1842. The fence in front of Fintona blossomed a double row of crape rosettes, and a mattress of straw was spread over the road beyond so that the sounds of passing traffic could not enter the silent house. Official mourners stood outside the gates in shifts. Enough had been hired to line the funeral route to the railway station.

All morning the coffin had rested, open, in Fintona's parlor while the curious of Auckland streamed through to view her. They stood around the bier, remaining no more than a minute or two, for the parlor was as chilly as the winter's day outside. All the visitors noticed that in death Grandmaire had lost her striking resemblance to Queen Victoria. They felt cheated. In life she had

401

been a truly regal figure, and now she was simply an old dead woman.

Shortly before the undertakers were due to close the coffin, Stephen and Samuel arrived at Fintona and were shown into Jon's study, where Jon was deep in conversation with old Mr. McLeay's assistant, Vincent Opal.

"It's a family matter," said Stephen, noticing that the study, at least, was warm. "But don't go, Vincent. Your advice could be needed. Samuel thinks he's discovered news of Kendrick."

"Where?" said Jon at once, distaste at his uncle's rumpled appearance immediately giving way to interest.

"Up north, on one of my tracts of old milling land. Very close to where Daniel took us on the first searching expedition. After we'd closed the search, I posted a reward with the Maoris of the district, just to encourage them to keep looking for him. Last week that reward was claimed. One of the locals found a body high in the hole of a kauri tree."

"A body?" said Jon. "That's a blow. I suppose we'd never really given up hope . . . But how would a body come to be up in the hole of a tree? Those kauris have trunks that stretch sixty-odd feet up to the first branches, don't they?"

"This one had an eighty-five-foot drop," said Samuel. "It's easy enough to get up there if you know how. A missile—an arrow or such—and a length of rope, something to anchor it on to, and up you go. Gum diggers go up to gather Kauri gum from the holes. That's how the body was discovered."

Samuel pulled a pipe from his pocket and began to prod at the bowl with a matchstick. Apart from Jon, who disdained tobacco, the others in the room had already busied themselves lighting cigars. All suddenly felt the need to release the tension that was building in the room.

Finally Jon said, "So the poor sod starved to death? What a damned terrible way to die."

"We're not completely sure it is him, though it seems likely. I've had the body transported back to Auckland, with the idea that when Daniel comes to New Zealand in October, he can make a positive identification from what's left of the clothes. Yes, it's as sketchy as that. The question is, gentlemen, do we say anything to Abby?"

Jon paused, turning a scrimshaw paperweight over in his hands. Though nobody had ever been able to read Jon's thoughts, Stephen could guess them now. He doesn't want to have to break the news, he thought. Nor does he want to be the one to try to comfort her afterward.

"We'd best say nothing until we know for sure," said Jon. "It's been such a long time already. I'll contact Hal and ask him to come home for a spell. Can he be spared from the transatlantic run, do you think? God, but this is going to knock Mama for six. Starved to death." He dropped the paperweight. "But if it was close to the valley where Daniel and he had camped, how come Daniel didn't hear him shouting for help? Kendrick wouldn't have sat up there meekly and made no attempt to call out. This means that Daniel's story about looking for him was a total falsehood—"

"Easy, lad," said Samuel. "There were strips of cloth with the body, indicating he'd been bound and gagged. He'd have had to be knocked unconscious anyway, to be hauled up such a distance. Unless he'd fainted from loss of blood." He glanced around at the others. The tension in the study was almost tangible. "He'd been mutilated."

Jon shook his head as he listened to the details. "All I can say is that I'm surprised that he didn't jump. Kendrick would not have wanted to live after that." He stood up, indicating that the interview was over. "If you gentlemen will excuse me, I must supervise the last stages of Grandmaire's journey. Would any of you care to pay your final respects before we have the coffin closed?"

"Jon acts as if he's taken over Fintona completely," complained Samuel on the way to the train. "Did you notice how he was giving orders to Dora as if she were a servant? You'd think that the whole shooting box belonged to him now."

"Perhaps it does." Stephen wondered if it was going to rain. The clouds were a sodden gray; it seemed likely.

"But you are Grandmaire's son! And her only surviving child! Surely everything automatically goes to you?"

Stephen smiled. "I imagine she expected to outlive me, and I probably don't even feature in her will. Think on it, Samuel. You knew Mama as well as anybody. Do you think her will is going to be predictable? No, and if it is, I'll be disappointed in her. She would have spent years composing it with all the cunning of a political plot. Nothing will be bequeathed without conditions being imposed, conditions that will no doubt twist the beneficiary's life into tortured knots. Her machinations will reach as far into the future as she was able to arrange. If she's left the house to Jon, he will be made to earn it." He chuckled. "And now that I've said all that, it's not necessary to add that I hope she's bequeathed me nothing."

"What about Daniel? He's her only true grandson. And now that Rupert—"

Daniel has problems enough already, thought Stephen, switching his mind away from his brother-in-law's prattle. An empty-headed wife with what sounded like a dangerous alcoholic addiction, and four young children to worry about as well. And now this business about Kendrick was looming over them like a specter. The devilish thing was that Grandmaire had known all about Kendrick and Verona and young Benedict.

"I'm afraid for Daniel," said Stephen. "And in all honesty, Samuel, I'm praying that Mama cut him out of her will. What he doesn't need right now is a bequest from her."

Jon was wondering about the will, too. Or so Vincent Opal suspected. That had to be the reason Jon had asked him to ride along in the carriage that contained the coffin. Just the two of them—and her. Vincent felt ill at ease and would have been unamused to learn that most of the crowd on the platform assumed that he was one of the funeral directors, with his dark crow looks and dour expression. But what made Vincent most uncomfortable was the way Jon was talking. From the moment the train had jolted into motion, he had been complaining about the price of funerals, and now, as they racketed slowly across the expanse of brown fernland toward Glen Eden, he was still calculating the cost in aggrieved tones.

"And I'm helpless to stop it," he said. "She had every detail written down and the whole list in the hands of the morticians. *They* are taking pleasure in fulfilling every wish, and well they might, for they'll be paid handsomely for this needless extravagance. Such ostentation! Fifteen carriages—why, it's more appropriate for the transport of a jungle circus than a funeral cortege. And every carriage draped with hundreds of yards of crape. And these flowers! Have you any idea how much one simple wreath costs at this time of the year?"

Vincent Opal didn't know. He stared out at the waves of thin gray drizzle, trying to overcome the feeling that the old lady was lying there listening to every word. Even though he knew what a cold fish Jon was—look at how he'd behaved when Ellen ran away, you'd think he'd never been married or fathered two children for all the reaction he showed—Vincent was shocked by his carping. He sat in gloom and waited for the question he knew would come sooner or later.

"I'm sorry, Mr. Bennington; but Mrs. Yardley Peridot confided only in Mr. McLeay, and he would never discuss her affairs with anybody. We all have to wait to see what her will contains. But Mr. McLeay did mention that the reading might be on Tuesday."

Jon exhaled slowly. Tuesday. It would have been better to know at once, but he could wait until Tuesday. Until then he would carry on with full confidence.

When the Glen Eden cemetery had been first consecrated, Grandmaire had chosen the plot for her marble mausoleum and had supervised its construction herself, taking as much interest in the design and materials as if it were a new house. Seeing the tomb for the first time, Stephen understood the reason for her choice of location. Here on the hilltop the view stretched to the city in one direction and the Waitakere ranges in the other. This was a better site than the corner of a churchyard already crammed with graves. From here she could hold center stage into eternity.

Stephen gazed back along the path to where the train sighed as it waited to take the mourners back to the city. Below the crape swags at one window he could see Juliette and May, their faces blurred in the rain. In the next carriage Dora's black bonnet leaned toward a small oval face. Dorinda, who had inherited all of Abigail's beauty and Lena's marigold coloring. What sort of life would she have, shackled to a sour old maid like Dora?

My age is proving treacherous to me, thought Stephen. These legs threaten to buckle after only a short climb, and each breath I draw seems to give me only enough energy to draw the next. My mother is dead, yet I feel no emotion. Of all the Yardleys who once lived in that house overlooking the Bay of Islands, I am the only one still alive, and Daniel is my only true link to future generations. And he's settled abroad. Will descendants of my own blood ever live in New Zealand again and love this magnificent country as I do? Ah, listen to the Maoris wailing. The pallbearers must have assembled to bring the coffin to us. The Maoris will mourn Mama in proper fashion. They understand how to bid farewell to the spirit, and they loved her in their own way, just as, God knows, I loved her in mine. We all shall be the poorer for her going. She forged strength in us. We were forced to become strong in order to resist her will. Mama, I shall miss you.

In the carriage May was scanning the morning paper. An inch of black border framed the front page. "The End of an Era for the City," announced the headline. The editorial proclaimed a day of mourning and declared that Auckland had lost its oldest and most revered resident.

"At first glance anybody would think the queen herself had died," said May. "Look at this photograph! Grand-maire is sitting in her open landau, looking exactly like the queen."

"I saw it." Juliette leaned back on the green leather seat and closed her eyes. The carriage smelled of damp smoke and the peppermints May was chewing to relieve her indigestion.

Flapping the pages, May said, "But this is one of Bobby Terrill's pictures! I remember it well. He took it at the

406

spring race meeting shortly after he joined the newspaper staff. They must have filed it away, ready for Grandmaire's obituary."

"Probably."

"Are you feeling all right, Mother?"

She opened her eyes. "I'm depressed, dear. I thought that this would be a joyful day for me. I'd dance on the grave, feel victorious somehow, but though I can't pretend to be sorry she's dead, I am not happy about it either."

"*I'm* sorry she's dead. She was abominable in many ways, and I would never have trusted her, yet I admired her tremendously, and I have no idea why. Does that sound ridiculous?"

"I understand." And Juliette quoted, " 'Children judge harshly, but grandchildren applaud.' That's as true today as it ever was."

She's afraid I'll judge her, thought May. Those accusations Grandmaire made may have been true, and they may not; but I no longer care. It was wrong of me to want to pry into Mother's past. She had every right to hide things from me, just as I have a right to my own secrets. The pity of it is that I had no respect for her privacy until I came to value mine, and to try to explain would only compound the wrong I have done her.

She said, "If you feel depressed, why not think about Daniel's visit? We're going to have such fun at the Queen's Jubilee celebrations with all of them here to share it with us. Daniel, Verona, Benedict, little Stephen, and the twins. You can't be unhappy for long when you have so much to look forward to. Mondrich House is going to be in utter chaos. There will be five grandchildren by then."

"Have you given more thought to a name yet?"

"Not yet." She watched the pallbearers carry the coffin through the cemetery gateway. The coffin was covered with a kiwi feather cloak. May said, "I'm astounded by the number of people who have come. The road is jammed with carriages as far as you can see. All the men are doffing their hats, and the women bowing their heads. Oh, dear, I should have been paying attention. I've lost sight of Patrick." She was silent, searching, her brow resting against the beaded glass.

There he was, with Samuel. They were talking to an elderly gentleman. May thought it might be Governor Grey, but she could not be sure. All detail was lost in the mist of rain. May was suddenly aware of an inner flooding of perfect contentment.

"Can you see him, dear?"

"Yes, I found him. You know, I'm so glad that Patrick has never been tempted to follow the fashion and grow whiskers. A clean-shaven face is so easy to pick out in a crowd. Whenever we go to a social or a ball, all I have to do is glance around quickly and I find him at once."

Juliette said, "When I look back now, I wonder why I was so against the idea of your marrying him."

"You wanted to protect me. I always understood that." She shivered. "When I look back, it frightens me to think of how close I came to marrying Hal. If he had agreed to take me back to San Francisco, I'd have married him straightaway. Everything seemed to be going wrong here, and I blamed New Zealand for that; but once I decided to marry Patrick and I *had* to hold my head up and look everybody straight in the eye, my problems simply disappeared. Uncle Samuel was right. The problems were with me, not New Zealand."

"You are fortunate. It took me many years to learn that. I spent such a long time trying to run away from—" She stopped.

May said gently, "I'm glad I didn't go to live in San Francisco. It would have meant leaving you and Father behind. I'd have missed you."

Juliette looked into her daughter's eyes and saw nothing there but love and that luminous innocence she had retained since childhood. No matter how fearfully she searched she could see no sign of judgment or suspicion. She sighed, a tiny shuddering of breath. "I'm very happy you stayed," she said.

Outside, it had begun to rain in earnest. The hillside was now a garden of taut black umbrellas. All along the cemetery daffodils were bursting into bright trumpets, and on leafless branches above them, strings of blossoms hung like ragged gold decorations.

May said, "The kowhai trees are blooming early."

"The Maoris say that is an omen for a long, hot summer."

"Oh, I do hope so," said May. "With the Jubilee and the family gathered together, we're going to have a marvelous time, aren't we?"

Juliette leaned over and kissed her daughter's cheek.

"What was that for?" asked May.

"Just for being you," said Juliette.

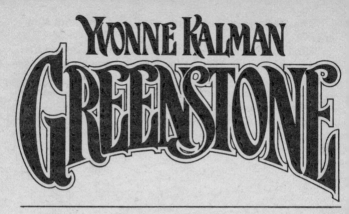

YVONNE KALMAN
GREENSTONE

Set in the beautiful savage wilderness
of New Zealand, this sweeping saga captures
the passion and courage of a spirited beauty
struggling to overcome the obstacles
life has set in her path and her ultimate
triumph in a blaze of truth and fiery passions.

"Like THE THORNBIRDS...GREENSTONE has
all the ingredients of a hit...
Guilt, grief and love in a story of
revenge, manipulation and fate."
Richmond Times Dispatch

An **AVON** Paperback   62414-1/$3.50
